About the Authors

Susan Stephens is passionate about writing books set in fabulous locations where an outstanding man comes to grips with a cool, feisty woman. Susan's hobbies include travel, reading, theatre, long walks, playing the piano, and she loves hearing from readers at her website. www.susanstephens.com

Monica Richardson writes adult romances set in Florida and the Caribbean. Under the name Monica McKayhan she writes adult and young adult fiction. She currently has nine titles in print. Her YA novel, *Indigo Summer*, was the launch title for Mills & Boon's young adult imprint, Kimani TRU. *Indigo Summer* snagged the #7 position on the Essence bestsellers list and appeared on the American Library Association (ALA)'s list of Quick Picks for Reluctant Young Adult Readers. To schedule an appearance, book signing or interview with Monica, please email publicity@monicamckayhan.com

Teresa Southwick lives with her husband in Las Vegas, the city that reinvents itself every day. An avid fan of romance novels, she is delighted to be living out her dream of writing for Mills & Boon.

A Tropical Christmas Escape

SUSAN STEPHENS

MONICA RICHARDSON

TERESA SOUTHWICK

MILLS & BOON

First Published in Great Britain 2021
by Mills & Boon, an imprint of HarperCollins*Publishers* Ltd,
1 London Bridge Street, London, SE1 9GF

www.harpercollins.co.uk

HarperCollins*Publishers*
1st Floor, Watermarque Building,
Ringsend Road, Dublin 4, Ireland

A TROPICAL CHRISTMAS ESCAPE © 2021 Harlequin Books S.A.

Back in the Brazilian's Bed © 2015 Susan Stephens
A Yuletide Affair © 2015 Monica Richardson
His by Christmas © 2017 Teresa Southwick

ISBN: 978-0-263-30253-0

MIX
Paper from
responsible sources
FSC™ C007454

This book is produced from independently certified FSC™ paper to ensure responsible forest management.

For more information visit: www.harpercollins.co.uk/green

Printed and bound in Spain
by CPI, Barcelona

BACK IN THE BRAZILIAN'S BED

SUSAN STEPHENS

For Carly. Welcome back!

CHAPTER ONE

'YOU VOLUNTEERED ME to do *what*?'

Shielding her eyes against the bright morning sun, Karina Marcelos stared at her brother in disbelief. They were standing on the balcony of Luc's eyrie on the penthouse floor of his magnificent cream marble flagship hotel with Rio de Janeiro laid out in front of them. Luc was one crazy polo player—he could be dictatorial when he was in ruling his business empire mode, but he was always considerate of her feelings.

Her brother looked at her with surprise. 'Why the fuss? You're the obvious choice. The job of events organiser for the polo cup couldn't be awarded to anyone better than my highly qualified sister.' With a shrug he left her clenching and unclenching suddenly clammy fists.

She followed him in. 'You'll have to *un*-volunteer me,' she said firmly.

Luc scowled as he sat heavily at his desk. He wasn't used to being denied anything, unless his beloved wife Emma was in the picture.

'I mean it, Luc,' Karina insisted. 'My schedule's packed. I could only give the project a couple of weeks and it's going to need a lot more time than that.'

She could make the time. She could make the event

fly, but that wasn't the reason she was shying away from this plum of a job.

'Too late,' Luc said flatly. 'The posters have gone out and your name's on them. I didn't expect you to kick up a fuss. When I put your name forward to the team, they nearly bit my hand off.'

By team, Luc meant Team Thunderbolt, the world's most infamous gaucho polo players. Luc was a mainstay of the team and so was Dante Baracca, Karina's nemesis. This year it was Dante's turn to host the Gaucho Cup.

'What's wrong now?' her brother demanded, glancing up impatiently from his paperwork.

Where to begin? She didn't want to arouse Luc's suspicions, and finding a plausible excuse not to work with Dante wouldn't be easy. Nor would handling the whisper of awareness that skittered over her skin at the thought of being close to Dante again.

'I need you to do this for me, Karina.'

'I do know what this event means to you, but there are other events organisers.'

'None as good as you,' Luc insisted. 'There's no one who understands the world we work in better than you.'

Karina's glance landed on the cabinet where Luc kept his trophies. He'd left a space for this year's prize. Right next to it, in a pointed reminder that it would be hard, if not impossible to get out of this, there was a trophy belonging to Karina. The International Association of Events Planners had awarded it to her for exceptional merit, and Luc was as proud of that trophy as he was of his own gleaming cups.

'I need you to give me an answer, Karina,' Luc pressed.

'And I need time to think,' she countered.

'What's there to think about?' Settling back in his

chair, Luc pushed his papers to one side. 'Planning the polo cup is easily the most prestigious work you've ever been asked to do, so what's your real problem, Karina?'

She loved her brother dearly, but Luc had no idea what he was asking. She had avoided face-to-face confrontations with Dante for a very good reason—the man was a hundred per cent ice-cold arrogance. She'd avoided him at polo matches, had been forced into his company when Luc and Emma had got together, but apart from that she was always careful to keep her distance from him. If she accepted this commission her avoidance tactics where Dante Baracca was concerned would be shot to hell.

'You should at least have consulted me before you went ahead with this.'

'My apologies,' Luc mocked, gesturing widely to express his frustration. 'I can't imagine why I thought you'd be thrilled. You're the go-to events organiser in Rio, Karina,' he reminded her tensely. 'Who else am I going to ask?'

Her brother was right in that arranging the fixture would be an exciting challenge. It was just the man she had to deal with that was the problem.

'Dante Baracca is an arrogant, humourless dictator,' she murmured, speaking her thoughts out loud.

'He's a powerful, successful man,' her brother argued.

'Didn't I just say that?'

Black eyes flashed as the Marcelos siblings stared each other out.

Karina didn't want to upset her brother, but Luc was equally determined that she would take the job.

'What aren't you telling me?' he demanded shrewdly.

Ice slid down her spine.

'There has to be something,' he insisted. 'We've known

Dante for years. I play on the same team. I'd know if there was a problem. I hope you don't believe his press?'

'He doesn't intimidate me, if that's what you think. And as for his reputation…' She blew out a contemptuous breath. 'Dante's the devil incarnate if you listen to the media—and much as I would love to take on the challenge of working with someone like that, I would have thought that my brother, of all people, would do me the courtesy of allowing me to refuse this job.'

Luc shook his head. 'No can do, Karina. Too much money has been invested in publicity for you to pull out now.' He gave her the look that had melted a thousand hearts. 'Do this one thing for me and I'll never ask again.'

She smiled thinly. 'Until the next time?'

'I've never known you to be so unreasonable.'

She shared a lot with him, but not everything. 'I'll sort something out,' she promised.

'There's nothing to sort out,' Luc insisted. 'We want you. Dante wants you.'

Somehow, she doubted that.

Her mind was already racing. If the posters had gone out, she would have to have a banner added, announcing her replacement. It would have to be someone good—someone who was trusted by the polo community. She might not want the job, but she would do everything she could to make sure things went well for Luc and his team. She would still be cheering for them.

'If it's Dante private life worrying you, it's none of our concern. And he won't have time to notice you in that sense as he'll have so many admirers around him.'

'Thanks for the reassurance,' she said dryly. Luc was right in that there were always polo groupies hanging round the players, and she had never been the glamorous type, let alone wanted to compete with them.

'You're my sister,' Luc pointed out now with exasperation, as if that were enough in itself to disqualify her from attracting male attention. 'Dante will only want to do business with you. I hope you've got more sense than to think anything else?'

'Of course. What do you take me for?'

'A highly successful and very beautiful woman, who could never think of Dante Baracca as anything more than a childhood friend and my teammate.'

'And a man to avoid,' she murmured beneath her breath.

'What was that?' Luc asked suspiciously.

'I don't have to like all your teammates.'

'You don't have to take an unreasonable dislike to them either. Sign the contract, Karina. I'm done waiting.'

And throw herself across Dante's path again—work with him on a daily basis?

It had been a long time since she'd been the tomboy tagging along with her brother's gang, sharing a prickly if somewhat reluctant acceptance from his friends. But she should do this for Luc. He'd done so much for her. He'd brought her up single-handed when their parents had died. There was just one fly in that ointment. Luc had done a brilliant job but had often been distracted, which had given Karina all the time she had needed to get into mischief and more.

As Luc uncapped his pen she was forced to accept the fact that her brother meant more to her than her own stubborn pride. She would just have to put the past behind her, as they had told her to do in the hospital. She would lift up her head and move forward. Dealing with

Dante Baracaa was not beyond her. And she'd put a good face on it. Luc deserved nothing less.

'I should thank you for putting my name forward,' she admitted as she stepped forward to sign the contract.

Luc laughed with relief. 'Everyone wanted you—and if I hadn't suggested you, I think you'd have cut me off at the knees.'

'Maybe.' Angling her chin, she gave her brother an affectionate grin. At least one of them was happy. And she would be a fool to turn this down. This wasn't just the most prestigious job to come her way, it was *the* job.

Luc came around the desk to give her a hug. 'All that fuss about nothing. This is going to be the best thing you've ever done.'

Dante Baracca was *not* a fuss about nothing. Hiding her concerns, she returned Luc's hug. Stepping back, she assessed one of the most striking men in polo. All the players on Team Thunderbolt were forces to be reckoned with, and her brother Luc was no exception. She made allowances for his dictatorial side. He tolerated her constant challenges. They loved each other, and of course she'd do this for him, regardless of the consequences.

'I know Dante used to provoke the hell out of you when you were young,' Luc remarked as he relaxed into his triumph. 'No one was more surprised than me when you practically made him guest of honour at your eighteenth birthday party.'

Karina flinched as she remembered and had to pin a smile to her face. 'My friends wanted him there.' She shrugged. 'And there's been a lot of water under the bridge since then.' Monumental understatement.

Unaware of the undercurrents, Luc laughed off her comment. 'If you say so. I haven't seen you anywhere near Dante since that night, so I'm guessing he said something out of turn, but whatever he did to upset you, my advice is to leave it in the past so you can see the bigger picture.'

She could see the bigger picture and it wasn't pretty.

Turning away, she walked to the window to put some distance between herself and her sharp-eyed brother.

'Dante is the lynchpin of our team,' he stressed. 'He's hosting the polo cup. We need someone to organise it. What more do you need to know?'

'Nothing,' she agreed, staring blindly out of the window.

Karina would be the first to admit she'd been a wild child. Dante had been a big part of that past, but while he'd been worldly and experienced, she'd taken longer to grow up. She'd been naïve and a bit of a dreamer, and had paid a high price for her lack of sophistication. Growing up fast had been forced on her. Putting her sensible head on had come too late. She had clipped her party wings, but it still tore her up to know that by then the damage had been done. It had been a steep learning curve ever since, and that had been something in which Dante had played no part...

'I understand this is the biggest contract you've ever handled,' Luc remarked, misreading her preoccupation. 'You're bound to have concerns, Karina, but I know you can nail this.'

'I'll do a good job for you,' she promised, turning to face him.'

'I know you will. That's why I want you and no one else to handle this contract. And, believe me,' Luc added with a smile to reassure her, 'no one finds Dante easy.'

'With the possible exception of the women in his life,' she countered dryly.

'What's that to you?' Luc said suspiciously.

'Absolutely nothing.' She held his stare steadily until he looked away.

Leaning back against the cold, smooth glass, she remembered begging Luc to let her continue her studies abroad. She'd given him the excuse that she'd had enough of Rio and being under his wing, and that it was time for her to make her own way in life. Luc hadn't guessed for a minute that all she'd really wanted was to get away from Dante. Luc had paid for her to go to catering college, which had turned out better than she had expected. She'd ended up winning a full scholarship to a prestigious Swiss training facility for event planners, where she had excelled. Equipped with an honours diploma, she had returned to Rio ready to change the world—or, at least, her brother's hotel chain—only to find a highly sceptical Luc waiting for her.

She had won her spurs by working on small assignments for him, until he'd finally allowed her to work on his bigger projects. This Gaucho Polo Cup was the biggest project to date by far. And, yes, she wanted to be part of it. And, yes, she knew she could make it a success. She had the expertise and the inside knowledge when it came to the world of polo. But she'd be working with Dante, and that was a problem. She wasn't the person she'd been in the past, but would Dante see that? According to the press he hadn't changed and the word 'wild' still defined him. She only had to open a magazine to see him dating another woman. Dante Baracca attracted glamorous females in dizzying succession, but then he discarded them twice as fast. So nothing had changed.

'Dante Baracca, the hard man of polo.' Her brother said this with amusement, quoting a phrase most often associated with his teammate. 'You'll be the envy of half the women in the world.'

'Half the women in the world don't need a wake-up call from me,' she argued. 'And, if they did, I'd tell them that their idol has feet of clay.'

Luc drew back his head to give her a look. 'That's a little harsh when you've barely spoken to the man for years.'

'For a very good reason,' she dismissed. 'Who needs trouble like Dante Baracca in their life?'

Dante could be charming when it suited him, but he could also be hard and cold. If Dante would behave professionally, she might be able to make this work. If not... Her thoughts took her back to a man with black hair, black eyes and a black heart, a man who looked like a Gypsy king with gold earrings glinting in his ears. She could still remember the night Dante had punched those gold hoops into his own earlobes because she'd challenged him to do so. They'd both been wild when he'd been fourteen and she'd been ten, back in the day when they could take risks and get away with them.

'Stop frowning, Karina. Anyone would think I'd hooked you up with a monster. Here...' Luc held out a magazine, which he obviously intended to reassure her. 'Take a look at this—Dante's riding the crest of the wave at the moment.'

Dante Baracca was on the front cover. Of course he was. Where else would the god of the game be?

'There couldn't be a better time for you two to be getting together.'

'We won't be *getting together*,' she insisted. 'I'll be working alongside him.'

'Of course you will,' Luc agreed—to placate her, she suspected.

She made herself stare at the photograph while Luc looked on with approval.

Thank goodness Luc couldn't hear her heart thundering at the sight of a man who had always affected her profoundly, both for good and for bad. The photo showed Dante seated bareback on a horse at sunset on the fringes of the surf. He was stripped to the waist with his face in profile. His powerful torso was warmed to a seductive bronze by the mellow rays of the setting sun. He was a daunting sight. The shadows pointed up the harsh angles of his face and delineated his formidable muscles. She had no doubt the photographer's intention had been to big up the legend that was Dante Baracca, and in that he had succeeded.

Dante had more tattoos than she remembered. All the members of Luc's team had a Thunderbolt inked on their torsos, but it wouldn't have surprised her to learn that these new additions to Dante's hard frame had been handcrafted by the devil.

Her mouth dried as she thought back. She would never shake the past. In many ways she didn't want to. The memories were bittersweet. The loss had been too great, the sadness too searing, and Dante would always be part of that. He was still wearing the earrings that matched her own. Dante had given them to her on her eighteenth birthday—teasing her, saying they could be twins, but the look in his eyes had not been that of a sibling, and the earrings had been pushed to the back of a drawer after the party, because they'd become too cruel a reminder of Dante and everything he stood for…too close a reminder of kindred spirits who had almost destroyed each other.

'Stop fretting, Karina,' Luc coaxed when she frowned. 'You can handle one barbarian. Why not two?'

'If Dante is prepared to do things my way, it might work,' she mused distractedly.

'That should be fun to watch,' Luc commented dryly.

'This is no joke, Lucas.'

'Clearly, as you're calling me by my Sunday name.'

'I mean it,' she said, rounding on her brother. 'My work is a serious business. You and Dante may have grown up wild on the pampas—'

'As did you,' Luc cut in, his tone turning hard. 'What's wrong with you, Karina? You never used to be like this. Just because you're about to do business with a man women lust after doesn't mean you have to wear a hair shirt. You can loosen up and make this project a success, or you can carry this ridiculous grudge you seem to have against Dante to its ultimate conclusion and wreck the match.'

'Okay,' she said, holding up her hands. 'Just so long as we get one thing clear. You can't just hire me out to your friends whenever you feel like it without my permission. No more Dante Baraccas—okay?'

Luc turned to face the door where his secretary was miming an apology for the interruption. 'Why don't you tell Dante that yourself? Come in, my friend...'

Striding forward to greet his fellow polo player, Luc added, 'Karina can't wait to tell you what she has planned.'

CHAPTER TWO

TIME HALTED AS they stared at each other. Dante's body reacted instantly as the past flooded back—a past best forgotten while her brother was in the room. He hadn't seen Karina this close since the night of her eighteenth birthday, when he'd seen her in infinitely more detail than he was seeing her now.

'Come in, my friend—come in.'

He broke eye contact with Karina as Luc drew him deeper into the room, but the aftershock of his feelings for her blanked out everything but Karina. The strength of those feelings made him wonder if his first impulse had been correct. He'd been strongly tempted to veto Luc's suggestion when Karina's name had been suggested to the team. Why resurrect the past? He didn't need that sort of trouble in his life. Karina had been wild, as had he, and though he'd heard how successful she had become, he had no proof that she'd changed.

In the end he had decided that vetoing Karina on the strength of evidence from the past was mean-minded of him, and that as the sister of a teammate he should at least give her a chance. He had already made plans to keep contact between them to a minimum while she was working on his ranch. She'd avoided him for many years, so he was confident that that was what she would want too. But now, being in the same room as Karina, he was forced to rethink. Her effect on him was profound. He understood now why no other woman had ever matched up to her. But all the old reasons for resisting Karina remained. He was a player in life as well as on the field, and as the sister of his teammate Karina Marcelos was forbidden fruit.

'Dante…'

Her voice was soft and polite—for her brother's sake, he suspected, as the expression in her eyes was at odds with that professional exterior as she crossed the room to greet him. There was no intimacy at all in her gaze. Intimacy? She was almost hostile towards him. Had that single night all those years ago taken such a toll? Apparently, it had. There was nothing to be done about it. Karina had wanted more from him than he'd been able to give. He had thrown her out of his bed for the best of reasons. He had nothing to give her in the emotional sense, and still marvelled that he had put his concern for Karina above his own selfish lust. He'd been utterly selfish back then.

He was still where women were concerned, he reflected as her cool gaze levelled on his. He still had nothing to offer. The only difference today was the fact that she wasn't interested. Worse. The light had gone from her eyes. Where was the Karina he had known? What had happened to the tomboy who would give him as good as she got?

'You look well,' he said, still searching for clues.

'Do I?'

His groin tightened at the challenge. She wasn't so dead inside after all. She had always been a good actress, and he could understand why she was cool with him. The blow to her pride must have been immense. Saving her from him had come at a heavy price. Their friendship was dead.

'You look well, Dante.'

'Thank you.'

The polite exchange over, he returned to assessing Karina. She was all woman now, not a girl to provoke and tease. Her figure had filled out and her thick black hair gleamed with good health, though since that night she had started tying it back severely. Whenever he caught a glimpse of her at a polo match, it was dragged back, and it was dragged back today—so different from the past when it had cascaded in wild tangles down her back. They had both changed. They were both very different people now. He had responsibilities, while Karina's career had obviously grounded her, and though that reassured him on a professional level, this was not the girl he had vowed to stay away from for her own good but a woman who would keep him at bay.

'Can I get you something to drink?' she asked politely.

Hemlock, her eyes suggested, which made him force back a smile. 'Just water, please.'

Her expression gave nothing away as she turned to do the honours, but when she returned and gave him the glass and their fingers brushed, her cheeks pinked up betrayingly. She could act all she liked, but she still felt the connection between them, just as he did.

His hunting instinct rose and swirled around them. Sensing this, she shot him a warning glance. She hadn't forgiven him for kicking her out of his bed. He couldn't blame her when he hadn't bothered with explanations. A prior, pressing appointment had done the job. If she'd stayed they would have destroyed each other. She'd been

too young, too innocent for him. Progressing their friendship into something more than one night had been a car
crash waiting to happen, but all Karina had seen was
his betrayal.

His eyes devoured her as she crossed the room. It
amused him to think that she was putting as much distance between them as she could, when at one time she
would have stayed to plague and tease him. No other
woman made him feel this way, as if he was risking
everything—his place on the team, his friendship with
Luc—his very sanity, just by being in the same room as
her. And then jealousy swamped him. Who had held her
since that night? Who had heard Karina scream with
pleasure? Who knew that if they stroked her from the
nape of her neck to the small of her back she would whim-
per with need and raise her hips, inviting even more intimate touches? Who had tasted her innocence since that
night?

'It's so good to have you here, Dante.'

He shot into fully alert mode as her brother spoke to
him. Luc had an easy manner with his teammates and as
he crossed the room to put an arm around Dante, it was
in complete contrast to the tension between Dante and
Luc's sister. He had to put all thoughts of Karina aside
before he could respond to his friend. 'Thank you, Luc.
It's good to be here.'

And then they were talking about the match and their
latest pony acquisitions, but all the time he was aware of
Karina. He'd ridden with her brother since they'd been
boys. Luc and he were brothers in arms, both fiercely
competitive, and he had never once discussed Karina with
her brother. A man's sister was inviolable, and though for

years he had burned to know if Karina had a lover, it had been a question he would never ask Luc.

'Karina has signed the contract!'

'Excellent.' He swung around to face her after her brother's announcement. 'There's no one I can think of who is better qualified to organise the Gaucho Cup.'

'No one understands the demands of polo players better than my sister,' Luc confirmed warmly.

Karina said nothing.

Luc, who appeared not to have noticed his sister bristling, stared at the water in Dante's glass. 'Are you sure you wouldn't like something stronger?'

'I'm certain, thank you. I want to keep a clear head.'

Karina's stare sharpened on his face.

'Shall we?' she said, glancing towards the boardroom table.

'Certainly.' He walked across the room to hold her chair for her.

Karina proved her worth within minutes, picking up points his lawyers had missed. He should have felt completely confident in her abilities, but found himself disappointed instead. Knowing Karina as he had, he had anticipated something extra, a little dose of magic that would have lifted the event above the norm. Her initial thoughts were well thought through, considering she'd only just signed the contract, and he had no doubt those plans would be executed flawlessly, but her ideas lacked oomph. They were pedestrian and he had expected more of her.

'Well, I think that's it,' she said when her thoughts were exhausted. 'I hope you have a pleasant journey home.'

He had intended to leave immediately after the meeting, but now he was determined to stay. He wanted to

get to the bottom of the changes in Karina and to make
a final decision as to whether or not she could realise the
vision he had for the polo event. From what he'd seen so
far, he had some doubts. Smiling easily, he relaxed back.
'I'm in no hurry.'

Her expression hardened. He raised a brow. Her brother,
once again, remained oblivious to the undercurrents between them. In fact, it was Luc who rescued the situation,
saying, 'You're not leaving yet, surely?'

He smiled back at Luc. 'No, of course not.'

'Karina,' Luc chastised her when she remained silent
and still. 'Are you forgetting your manners completely?
Dante can't leave yet. This calls for champagne.'

He added his support to Luc's suggestion. 'I agree
with Luc. What's the rush?'

The look Karina gave him called for more hemlock.

She clearly didn't want him to stay, which made him
wonder why she was feeling quite so defensive and angry.
Could she have held a grudge for so long? Apparently, she
could—but there was one interesting fact: she might be
looking at him as if he were the devil, but not a devil she
wanted to run from, rather a devil she wanted to stay and
fight. That was a great improvement. It fired her up—
turned her from an expressionless automaton into the
Karina he had known.

'You're the client. Whatever suits you,' she said, smiling a plastic smile.

Hard eyes. Hard mouth. Hard man. How could she ever
have imagined she could work with Dante? He couldn't
know, of course, that what they'd done had set in motion
a train of events that would have such far-reaching reper-
cussions. She had to remind herself that the past had no

part to play in these business discussions. She was proud of the career she'd built up. She'd worked hard for it, and would allow nothing and no one to take it from her—not even Dante Baracca. She'd give him no cause for complaint. If there was one thing she'd learned while working for her brother, it was that a woman had to be twice as strong as any man in the workplace, and that emotion had no part to play.

'Your sister seems preoccupied,' Dante remarked to Luc, as if she'd left the room. 'Do you think she will find it impossible to work with me?'

'I think she can handle you,' Luc said dryly.

She swung around to confront them both. 'I'm still in the room. If you expect me to run this project for you, please don't discuss me as if I'm a blotter on my brother's desk.'

Dante's wry glance look suggested she had fallen into his trap. He had meant to provoke her to draw her back into the conversation.

'Please excuse my sister,' Luc joked. 'You remember what she's like, don't you, Dante? But there's one thing I can assure you, she's very good at her job.'

'I'm sure she is,' Dante agreed, with a look that made her cheeks burn.

'Well… If you will both excuse me?'

Karina stiffened as Luc started collecting up his things.

'I've got another appointment I simple can't miss.'

You can't leave me!

Ignoring the look she gave him, her brother did just that.

Clever Luc. He'd left her with no alternative but to stay and entertain their guest.

Dante broke the silence first. 'Well, Miss Prim.' His voice was low and amused. 'Why are you so reluctant to work with me?'

She drew herself up. 'I don't know what makes you say that. I'm looking forward to this project immensely.'

'Liar,' Dante murmured.

He sucked the breath from her lungs with that single word.

'Are you still hurting after that night?'

Shock coursed through her. She couldn't believe what he'd just said. 'My *only* interest is to organise the best event the polo world has ever seen.'

'Worthy and dull?' he flashed.

Her cheeks blazed red under this attack. Was that was how she'd come across? When her brother left the room, she had been expecting a few pleasantries, and then the chance to make another appointment to see Dante to discuss her plans—and only that.

'I expected more of you, Karina.' His tone was scathing.

Completely thrown, she went into defensive mode. 'I'll give you my best. My clients have never been disappointed. My past record speaks for itself.'

'Maybe your previous clients haven't been as demanding as me.'

She couldn't believe he was being so aggressive and, unsettled, she looked away. Reaching out, he cupped her chin and brought her back so she had nowhere to look but into his eyes. 'Why so defensive, Karina?' he goaded. 'What aren't you telling me?'

'I don't know what you mean. You're a valued client, and I never break my promise to a client. That should be enough for you.'

Dante's eyes narrowed. 'You haven't answered my question.'

Nor would she. Shaking him off, she stepped back. 'If we're going to do business together—'

'You will have to lighten up,' he supplied, in a tone that spoke worryingly of Dante's growing doubt that she was up to the task.

She had to remind herself how many difficult clients she'd had in the past, and that Dante was just one more. But though she had always succeeded in winning clients over in the past, Dante was a unique case, and the way he was looking at her now, as if he wanted her to defend herself...

'If you don't like my suggestions—'

He cut her off with a laugh. 'Brava, Karina. I had begun to think there was nothing left of the wildcat I remember.'

There wasn't anything left of that reckless young woman. Was he suggesting she had learned nothing since that night?

'You accepted this assignment because you can't resist it,' he accused her, bringing his face close. 'How do I know this?' With a shrug he stood back. 'You accepted this contract because you won't let your brother down. And you won't let yourself down because you have far too much pride.'

'I have pride?' she demanded on an incredulous laugh.

'Honoured client?' Dante reminded her, easing onto one hip.

She would come to regret those words, Karina suspected as she looked away.

'My driver is waiting downstairs.'

She stared at him blankly.

'You're coming with me.'

She shook her head. 'I have work to do.'

'Yes,' Dante agreed. 'My work. My contract that you just signed.'

'Seriously, I really don't have time for this.'

'Then make time,' he said coldly, reminding her of just how harsh he could be. 'I can't do business with you while you're tense like this.'

'Tense? I'm just busy, Dante. I only wish I could leave,' she lied, softening her tone in the hope of placating him, 'But, unfortunately, I have a very busy day ahead of me.'

'With important clients?'

He knew there was no client more important than he was, and the air was electric between them. Two wills colliding and neither one of them prepared to back down. But Dante had the better of her today because he knew she wouldn't let her brother down.

'This trip?' she prompted. 'What did you have in mind?'

'Let's get out of here and then I'll tell you.' Dante held the door for her, and as she walked through he murmured, 'One thing you will discover about me, *chica*, is that I never do anything without a very good reason.'

She stopped dead right in front of him. 'Let's get one thing clear from the start. I am not your *chica*.'

Instead of taking offence, Dante stepped up close. He stood so close, looking down at her, that she could see the tiger gold in his eyes. She held his blazing gaze steadily, though her stomach was coiled in a knot.

'What are you frightened of, Karina?' he murmured in a voice she knew so well.

A quiver of awareness rippled across her shoulders even as she stood up to him. 'Not you, that's for sure. Shall we go?' she said.

'You're very confident that I won't take my business elsewhere,' he said as they walked along the corridor side by side. 'Why is that, Karina?'

'You're not a fool?' she said.

Dante's husky laugh ran a full-blown shiver of arousal down her spine. His laugh was so familiar, too familiar. Dante had always possessed an animal energy that attracted her, however hard she tried to fight it off. And he had always understood her as no one else could. He probably knew that right now every part of her was on full alert just being close to him. After that night she had wondered if she would ever be capable of feeling anything for anyone again. She had also wondered if the connection between them would fade across the years. She knew now that neither one of those suspicious was true. If anything, she was more aware of him.

She had to forget the past if she was going to do business with Dante. She would have to forget everything, just as he must accept that everything in her life had changed.

'You never married?' he queried out of the blue as they stepped into the empty elevator.

She looked at him, shocked that he could ask such a personal question, then remembered that Dante had always been known for speaking his mind.

'Neither did you,' she countered. Fixing her stare on the illuminated floor numbers as they flashed on and off, she tried not to respond when he shrugged and smiled faintly.

'I've been too busy, Karina. What's your excuse?'

'Do I need one?'

She spoke mildly, but there was the faintest of threats

in her voice. *Leave it, Dante,* came over loud and clear. He loved it when Karina came back to life. He loved to see fire flashing in her eyes as it once had. Every woman seemed pallid to him by comparison with Karina—until he had walked into her brother's office this morning and wondered if there was any of her old spirit left. There was, and there was more for him to tease out, he suspected, though she stood as far away from him as possible in the elevator. When the door slid open and she walked out ahead of him, she didn't speak a word as they headed for his limousine. Perhaps she didn't trust herself to speak.

His driver opened the door for them, and she got in. She remained silent at his side, allowing him plenty of time to weigh up the shadows in her eyes.

'You haven't told me where we're going yet,' she reminded him, conscious of his scrutiny.

'You always used to like surprises, Karina.'

'And now I don't have time for them.' She crossed her legs and sat up primly to make her point. 'I have a working life to consider,' she added, when he continued to stare at her.

'Then stop worrying, because the place I'm taking you is directly connected to the business between us.

'Relax,' he advised.

'I'm perfectly relaxed,' she snapped, staring straight ahead.

Dante's driver drove carefully through the crowded streets. It was carnival. How could she have forgotten? The city was packed with musicians and performers, and crowds

from all over the world. At one time this had been her
favourite event of the year.

'You used to love carnival,' Dante commented, as if he
had picked up on her thoughts. 'Has that changed now?'

'It hasn't changed.' She felt a charge as she turned to
look at him. His hands, his lips, his face, his body all so
familiar, were within a few scant inches of her, and her
mouth dried as she turned to look out of the window at
the exuberant crowd. Carnival was all about rhythm and
music, abandonment and lust, and here she was, old before her time, dressed in a sober business suit, feeling
like a dried-up leaf.

'I'm not dressed for this,' she murmured, uncon-
sciously voicing her inner concerns.

'I don't know what you're worried about,' Dante argued as his driver parked. 'Who cares what you're wearing? It's the spirit of carnival that counts.'

That was what worried her. She'd used to have plenty
of spirit, but life changed you.

'I can't—these heels…'

Dante glanced at her feet and laughed. 'That's the
worst excuse I ever heard.'

She shook her head in disagreement. 'We can't afford
to waste time here when we could be discussing plans
for the polo cup.'

'That's precisely why we're here,' he argued, reaching
for the door handle. 'The event will be a huge success—
if you can relax enough to organise it.'

'I can relax,' she insisted, pressing back against the
seat. 'I just don't have a lot of time. I thought you understood that.'

'I understand that you're making excuses,' he said,
opening the door and getting out.

What the hell was wrong with Karina? What had happened to her sense of humour—her sense of fun? At one time it wouldn't have been she leading him astray and distracting him from his work. In the past it hadn't been possible to keep Karina away from carnival, but now it seemed she hadn't even registered the fact that that it was carnival week in Rio. She'd be no use in this sombre mood to the event he wanted to create. He had expected the Karina he'd once known, would come up with something fabulous, something that would appeal to all ages. 'Shall we?' he invited, helping her out of the car—or rather drawing her out, as she seemed so reluctant. He was beginning to wonder if he'd made a huge mistake to allow Luc to talk him into this.

'Lead the way,' she said, with the same lack of enthusiasm, as if he hadn't touched her at all.

He intended to lead. He intended to elicit a reaction from her. When they had all been kids together the annual carnival had been the highlight of their year, and that was exactly what he wanted to re-create on his ranch for the Gaucho Cup.

'All work and no play will destroy your creative juices,' he warned, as she stared around.

'If you say so.'

Her small smile was better than nothing at all, he supposed.

'We need to get a move on, Karina,' he prompted. 'The procession will start any time now.'

'Okay.'

Wobbling on the cobbles in her high-heeled shoes, she did look out of place—as she so obviously felt. His stone heart responded just a little. Even back when Karina had been a tomboy, tormenting the life out of him, he'd cared about her in his offhand teenage way. He still cared about her, and felt compelled to get to the bottom of the changes in someone who had used to shed light, but who now cast only shadows.

CHAPTER THREE

IGNORING DANTE'S OFFER to link arms, she walked ahead. This wasn't a personal expedition, this was business.

Really?

Dante didn't need to know that just being within touching distance of him made her heart go crazy, or that she beginning to feel the excitement of carnival thaw the ice around her heart. She hadn't done this for ages—walked in the city for no better reason than to have fun. She hadn't felt this free for years. Her gaze was darting around like a hermit let out of a cave as she desperately tried to soak up all the sights and sounds and smells at once.

She felt drunk on them, elated, after the hushed silence of her brother's luxury hotel, and for a moment she was so wrapped up in events around her that she stopped walking altogether and got jostled along by the crowd. She almost lost her balance and then a steadying hand rescued her—Dante's. She sucked in a noisy breath, glad that the ruckus from the crowd drowned it out. Even that briefest of touches was a warning of how receptive she still was to Dante.

She shouldn't have come here with him, she fretted as she made for some shadows beneath the awning of a shop. Carnival in Rio was the highest-octane party in the world. No one came to carnival to discuss dry business deals or to cement business relationships. If couples talked at all, their faces were close and their eyes were locked on each other.

The music, the colour, the spectacle, the noise, the heat of the sun and the warmth of the cobbled street beneath her feet, combined with the scent of cinnamon and spices, made a riotous feast for the senses, and she had been on an austere diet. Appealing to her senses was the very last thing on her agenda for today. Logic and facts were all she needed to make the Gaucho Cup a success.

But she was here. *And* with him. *Get over it. Get out there and make the most of it.*

'Hold on,' Dante cautioned, as she followed a sudden impulse to plunge into the crowd. 'It gets wild from here.'

Like she didn't know that—though anything was wild compared to the way she'd been living. She exulted in the beat of the approaching drums as they grew louder. Maybe she wasn't so dead inside after all. She wasn't— she wasn't dead at all. In fact, she had to fight the urge to go along the crowd and lose herself in the echo of a different life.

'Karina!'

Dante's shout brought her to her senses just in time. Of course she wouldn't have followed that impulse, and of course she held back. She knew better than to let herself go these days because she knew where that led.

They had reached a small square. The crowd had moved ahead of them, leaving just the two of them on the street. Dante was leaning back against a wall, watching her with a puzzled expression on his face. His forearms were crossed over his powerful chest, and somewhere along the way he'd removed his jacket and tie. However hard she tried to look away, she couldn't, and when she tried desperately hard to blank her mind to the image of a ridiculously good-looking man, she failed there too.

Then she noticed that an elderly couple had stopped to watch them, as if they had somehow created a mini-drama to be played out in silence between them. She quickly dragged her attention from Dante, only to see the old lady wink at her. She wanted to explain that there was nothing between them, but that wouldn't have been very professional of her so she smiled instead. The elderly couple were having such a happy day—why spoil it for them? But if her feelings were so obvious to them, were they obvious to Dante?

He smiled at the old couple too. He could be charming when he wanted. And then the crowd thickened once more and the elderly couple disappeared into the throng, while Dante stood in front of her to protect her as the crowd surged past.

'I can look after myself,' she protested, when he put an arm around her to draw her close.

'Is chivalry out of fashion these days?'

His look was mocking. She responded in kind. 'Chivalry? That's not a word I readily associate with you.'

'Why not?' he demanded, looking at her keenly.

She looked away. She didn't want to get into it. They were here in the middle of carnival with nowhere else to go. She had to make the best of it, and with more than two million people milling about on the streets of Rio it was important to stay close.

The crowd pushed them together as they walked along. Her body tingled each time she touched Dante. It was a distracting client relationship tool, she told herself sternly. Cold emptiness had been her companion for so long she felt each light brush as if it were an intentional touch. And then he was distracted by one of the beautiful young samba dancers and her stomach squeezed tight as she watched them exchange kisses on both cheeks like old friends. She carefully masked her feelings when he came back to her.

'My apologies for not introducing you, Karina.'

She shrugged it off, but Dante wasn't fooled. 'Are you jealous?' he probed with amusement.

'Certainly not. Why would I be?' she demanded, as a little green imp stabbed her with its pitchfork.

Dante's smile broadened infuriatingly as he took her arm to steer her through the crowd. 'We must head for the main square where all the performers are gathering.'

More choice for him?

Whatever Dante did or didn't do with half the girls in Rio was no business of hers. Carnival was full of beautiful women. It was a showcase. *It was Dante's hunting ground.* There wasn't a samba school in the city that wasn't represented, and the samba beauties could swivel their bodies to stunning effect. All the men were transfixed by them, and all the girls played up to the most famous man of all: the infamous Dante Baracca.

She *was* jealous.

She was not!

'Karina…'

'Yes?'

As Dante turned to look at her she was determined he wouldn't see, not by so much as the flicker of an eyelash, that she was affected by him, and more than she could ever have anticipated.

'Stay close,' he advised.

That proved impossible when a gang of young girls mobbed him, and she ended up defending him. They wanted his autograph, and, by the look of it, his clothes. Elbowing her way through the scrum, she spread out her arms in front of Dante. 'Senhor Baracca has an important appointment to keep, but I noticed a television crew around the corner—' Barely were the words out of her mouth when the young girls screamed with excitement and ran off.

Dante was amused. 'When I need a bodyguard I'll know who to call.'

'It will cost you extra,' she warned him dryly, moving on.

Dante was right about things getting wild. The decorated floats had arrived and everyone was excited as they trundled into view. 'Your safety's my responsibility,' he explained, when he yanked her close.

'And you're my honoured client,' she reminded him, pulling away. 'If anyone gets protected here, it's you— and you haven't paid my fee yet,' she said dryly.

He laughed. The first honest, open laugh she'd heard from him so far.

'You're one tough lady.'

'Believe it, Dante. You became my responsibility from the moment I agreed to accompany you to the carnival, and I won't let any harm come to you.'

'And I will allow none to come to you,' he assured her with an intensity that made her blink.

Did the same rule apply these days to the women in his bed?

'I can look after myself,' she repeated, wondering if her treacherous heart could beat its way out of her lying

mouth. Having Dante this close made her doubt everything—her willpower, her powers of reasoned thought...

His husky laugh put an end to her brief moment of
panic. It coincided with some more girls recognising him
and crowding round. His black eyes mocked her when
they went on their way, and he shrugged as he excused
himself. 'They said they knew me.'

'I'm sure they do,' she agreed. 'Please, excuse me if
I'm interrupting your congregation in the act of worship.'

He laughed again—a wolf laugh, sharp and faintly
threatening. 'You *are* jealous. Why fight it, Karina?'

'May I suggest we move on?' she said coolly.

Another few yards on and a girl dancing on a float
called out to Dante. All the men were agog as they stared
at her. She was beautiful. Wearing feathers and spar-
kles and not much more, it was no wonder Dante was
so spoiled when every woman laid it on a plate for him.

Including her, Karina remembered, firming her jaw
as Dante swung his arm around her shoulders.

'Sorry,' he said again, with a smile that could melt the
stoniest of hearts.

She resisted the temptation to melt at his feet. 'Please,
don't worry about me. There are plenty of distractions
here that prevent me watching you baste your ego.'

'Ah, Karina,' he growled softly, 'have you forgotten
that I'm your honoured client?'

'I have forgotten nothing. We signed a contract,' she
reminded him crisply, 'so I've got your business.'

'So you don't need to try?' Dante suggested with an
amused look.

'Where business is concerned, I can assure you of
my full attention. Where anything else is concerned?'
She shrugged.

That was the end of that conversation as they were forced into silence by one of the samba bands marching past. The rhythm was infectious, making it impossible to remain tense. Everyone around them had started dancing. The performers and their supporters had put so much effort into the parade even she allowed herself to respond to their energy. It occurred to her as she started dancing that at one time she would have been up there on a float, dancing along with the best of them.

'This is good, Karina.'

Her glance flashed up to Dante.

'Watch and learn, because this is exactly what I want you to re-create on my ranch.'

'Carnival?' She stared up at him in surprise.

She couldn't help noticing how attractive Dante looked when his lips pressed down in wry agreement. 'I'm not asking for too much, am I?' he probed.

He was asking for the world—and he knew it. Carnival took a year to plan, and she had a matter of weeks.

'After all, I'm paying for the best.'

He shrugged again as he said this, and his tone of voice had changed from coaxing to rather more calculating as he added, 'I'm paying for the best, so I expect the best.'

'Of course,' she agreed, relaxing into this return to business, even as she wondered if it could possibly last. 'The impossible I can do.'

'Miracles might take a little longer?' he suggested. 'You will have to work fast.'

There was no leeway in that statement, and she prided herself on always doing the best job faster than anyone else. Dante had turned away to throw a roll of banknotes onto a passing float, reminding her that all the performers were collecting money for charity. People who often had very little themselves worked hard all year to raise money during the parade, which was what made carnival so special. Locating all the cash she had, she tossed it onto the float. She would never lose sight of what this city had done for her. Working here had saved her. The vitality and the energy of Rio de Janeiro had lifted her, giving her barely enough time to brood or think back.

Until now. Dante would never change, she reflected as another group of dancing girls gathered around him. They were all exquisitely dressed and very beautiful, while Dante appeared like a dark pagan god in their midst. She had never felt more like a dowdy grey sparrow as she waited for him outside the circle of girls. If only she'd taken time to change out of her formal business suit, though something told her that more than the suit would have to go if she was going to do business successfully with Dante. She would have to find some of her missing *joie de vivre*—and stand up to him at every twist and turn.

She gave a start when he turned to look at her. Angling her chin, she made as if to leave. She couldn't find it in her heart to blame the girls for loving Dante when his ridiculously handsome image appeared on every Thunderbolt poster in the city, and he looked even better in the flesh, but she was determined to get on with this research project, rather than indulge his slightest whim.

How was her determination to appear disinterested in Dante as anything other than a client going so far?

Not so well. Dante Baracca was back in her life, whether she wanted him there or not, and now it was up to her to harness the tornado and make it co-operate with her vision of how carnival could be adapted to suit the confines of a ranch.

'I'll make sure we enjoy some quality time together so we can have a proper chat about my plans,' Dante reassured her when he returned to her side.

'My plans will take a little time to formulate,' she responded mildly. Dante had a samba girl hanging from each arm. She made no comment when he shooed the girls away.

'We will discuss my plans shortly,' he said.

'I'm prepared to consider your suggestions,' she said, and emphasised, 'Unless it's your way to pay a dog and bark yourself?'

His mouth curved in a grin. 'This new business partnership should be interesting.'

'Exactly as my brother predicted,' she confirmed, turning away.

'Your brother?'

'Shall we get on? Time is short. We should head for the main square,' she reminded him.

Dante drew her into a doorway as the previous year's samba queen danced past. The noise from the accompanying drums was like thunder, and for a few seconds she was glad to lose herself in someone else's moment, but then the girl stopped to put on a special dance for Dante. A leopard never changed its spots, she mused wryly as Dante tucked a roll of notes into the waistband of the girl's thong.

'Turning into a prude, Karina?'

'Miss Prim?' she threw back at him. She shrugged and smiled as the girl with the flawless body danced on her way. 'You do what you like. It's nothing to do with me.'

'Such a shame,' Dante murmured, his dark glittering eyes staring deep into hers. 'I rather thought you might keep me in line.'

'I think you'd enjoy that too much.'

His lips pressed down. 'You never used to be such a killjoy.'

And he was the reason she'd changed, she thought.

No sooner had she dispensed with this latest salvo from Dante than a good-looking guy stopped in front of her and started dancing. Her first impulse was to smile and move on, but then it occurred to her that if Dante could flirt and tease without restriction, why couldn't she?

She was about to find out, Karina guessed. Judging by the look on Dante's face, what was good for the goose definitely wasn't good for the gander. Then another woman—who, having recognised him, began to dance in front of him—distracted Dante, and with a look in her direction he brought the woman into his arms. Retaliation was one thing, but she had no intention of cosying up to her own partner, and had to content herself with covertly watching Dante prove just how good a man could look when he had been born with the rhythm of Brazil in his veins.

This was carnival where anything was possible. Yes. Dance with the devil and you would get burned, she added silently when Dante brushed against her. She knew he was teasing her deliberately, he always had, but she refused to respond and danced on, though Dante made her partner look like a beardless boy.

CHAPTER FOUR

It was a relief when the band for that particular float moved on and their dance partners drifted away with the rest of the crowd. She had realised by that time that she couldn't play games with Dante because the stakes were just too high.

'Why so tense?' he demanded. 'I brought you here to relax and take everything in. Didn't you enjoy dancing with that boy?'

'That...*boy*?' she queried frowning.

Dante shrugged. 'I noticed you kept your distance from him.'

'Are *you* jealous now?'

His look made her shiver. She'd kept her distance from the youth for a very good reason. She didn't want his hands on her. And he had been no threat, but that didn't matter to Dante. There was still fire between them. Maybe there always would be.

More floats arrived, swamping them in noise, colour and people, and saving her from a potentially awkward moment. The happy smiles made it impossible to remain immune to the spell woven by carnival.

Drummers marched in front of each float, and they set up a sound that reverberated through her, making it

hard to keep still. In the end she didn't try, and it was
while she was swaying to the rhythm that she carelessly
backed into Dante. He grabbed her. His hands closed over
her body—over a part of her body she never looked at,
never showed to the world, kept hidden from everyone,
and especially from him. It didn't matter that her shame
was covered by layers of clothing, that awkward stumble
was all it took for her eyes to fill with tears.

Jostling through a crowd, looking out for each other,
was nothing they hadn't done a dozen times before when
they had been younger, but today everything had taken
on a deeper significance. It was time to put some distance between them. Baring her soul to Dante was the
last thing she wanted to do. She had kept her feelings to
herself for too long to break down now.

'Dance?' he suggested, at the worst possible moment.
Dance with him?

Dante's warm breath caressed her skin as he leaned
closer. 'Dance and forget everything but carnival, just
as you used to.'

Just as she used to? That wasn't possible. Having
Dante's hands on her body wasn't possible.

'If you've forgotten how to dance, maybe you have
forgotten how to inject the spirit of carnival into your
projects,' Dante suggested with narrowed eyes.

Maybe it was the music of her youth and the fact that
Dante was offering to dance with her, but more likely it
was the challenge in his eyes that pressed her into doing
something she had shrunk from for too long. She let herself go. Kicking off her high-heeled shoes, she took one
step and then another, and soon she was dancing on the
warm, dusty streets of Rio.

Raising her arms, she swayed in time to the music,

allowing the rhythm to dictate her movement. The beat was repetitive and sexy, and her hips seemed to move of their own volition. Closing her eyes, she gave herself up to the music and the sunshine. It was so easy to dance once she'd started, so easy to forget so that all she felt was the urge to live and love and laugh again, and not care about tomorrow…

Which was exactly what had got her into trouble in the first place, she remembered, sobering up fast. 'I think we should go now.' Straightening her suit jacket, she dipped down to pick up her shoes.

'We can't go. Not yet,' Dante ruled. 'This year's samba queen hasn't been crowned and it would be rude to leave before that.'

'People will notice if we're not there?' She turned to give him a sceptical look and then remembered she was talking to Dante Baracca. Dante had been spotted several times by performers on the floats, and his absence at the crowning would definitely be noted, even in a crowd this size.

'If you've got all the information you need for the event, I can call my driver and have him take you home. Or…there is another alternative.'

Her gaze flashed up. 'Which is…?'

'You could tell me what's wrong with you.'

'There's nothing wrong with me.' But her cheeks had gone red, branding her a liar.

'You're starting to worry me, Karina.'

'Why?'

'Because you seem lost in the past.'

'Are you surprised?' she challenged, as her night with Dante came flooding back to her.

'You're holding out on me.' Catching hold of her shoulders, he made her gasp. 'What aren't you telling me, Karina?'

She wielded her willpower like never before. 'You're right, you should stay on for the crowning of the samba queen,' she said calmly. 'That's gives me the chance to go back to the hotel so I can start putting my thoughts down on paper.'

'You can stay with me and do that later.'

He was making it impossible for her to leave without causing a scene. There was a part of her that didn't want to leave—that wanted to make up for every moment they'd been apart. And she knew how dangerous that was. 'I need some thinking time alone. I'd like to be organised when we meet to discuss the event.'

'As I would expect,' Dante agreed. 'There will be plenty of time for you to do that on my ranch.'

Her mouth dried at the thought of going to Dante's ranch. 'I need to work while my ideas are fresh,' she argued. 'You want carnival as your theme, and I'll give you carnival, but I must make my notes before all the detail of today escapes me.'

'You have all the answers, don't you?' Dante stared down at her. 'Except for the one answer I want.'

She ignored that, but not before she saw the flash of anger in his eyes. Dante liked to control everything. When she started work on his ranch she would have to make sure that Dante and his people didn't take over. This was her contract, her reputation at stake. He played on a team. Dante should be able to work with her. But would he work on her team? Her best guess was no. She maintained a diplomatic silence as they walked on side by side to the crowning.

The piazza where the celebration was to take place

was packed. Towering walls kept in the sound and the heat, creating a dizzying counterpoint to her jangling thoughts. She had always known when she had agreed to take on this project that her biggest challenge would be Dante. They were both strong characters with set ideas of their own, but he would have to learn to compromise, just as she would have to learn to keep her thoughts confined to the job.

'I'll take you back,' Dante insisted, when he saw her glance at a taxi rank.

'I can walk.'

'I won't let you. Do you think I'm going to abandon you in the middle of the city?'

She almost laughed. Feeling abandoned by Dante was hardly a new sensation for her.

The crowd was thickening as people gathered to watch the ceremony, but Dante guided her safely through with his hand in a safe place in the small of her back. It was incredible that such a light touch could have such a profound effect on her body. Why could she remember his touch so clearly? Why did those hands directing her pleasure have to spring to mind now?

Dante seemed totally at ease. He bought them both a bottle of water and a pair of flip-flops for her from a market stall so she could take off her high-heeled shoes. She groaned with pleasure as she replaced them with the simple footwear.

'Please, stop,' she begged, when he added a shawl that was billowing above them like a sail. 'You don't have to do this.'

'But I want to,' he argued, as he draped the soft jade-green fabric around her shoulders. When he drew it tighter over *that* part of her body and she flinched, he gave her a questioning stare.

'I'll need this,' she said, gazing about to distract him. 'The wind is cool at night.'

Dante stared at her for a moment, and then relaxed. 'It just reminded me of that dress you wore on your eighteenth birthday.'

Why wouldn't he remember? He had enjoyed sliding it off her.

'Your party was themed. Arabian Nights, wasn't it?'

'That's right. And as for that dress,' she added with relief, glad that he'd turned from suspicion to thinking back, 'I could hardly expect my guests to turn up in costume while I wore a suit.'

He huffed a laugh as he scanned her office outfit. 'I doubt you had one in your wardrobe. You didn't dress like an undertaker back then.'

She stroked the shawl as she remembered the soft folds of chiffon of her birthday dress beneath her hands. The outfit she had chosen to wear at her party had been floating and insubstantial…and very easy to remove.

Time to change the theme of their conversation to a safer track. 'I love the shawl. Thank you.' An involuntary quiver crossed her shoulders as his hands brushed the back of her neck. He was only lifting the shawl a little higher to protect her against the wind, but it was close enough to the danger area to make tremors of an unpleasant kind run through her. And then, thankfully, a group of people recognised him and crowded around, letting her off the hook.

'You're a complex man,' she said, when he'd signed the last autograph.

He frowned. 'I'm complex because I talk to people?'

'You're so generous with your time, and that's not the image you give out with the team.'

'Ah, the team.' His dark eyes turned black with amusement. 'The brooding and unapproachable barbarians.' He laughed. 'Do you think we would attract the same crowds if our publicist worked the image of clean-shaven, pipe-and-slippers men?'

Against her better judgement, he made her laugh. 'There's no danger of that.'

Their gazes lingered a little longer on each other's faces than perhaps they should have done, and then Dante turned serious. 'These people are my audience, Karina. Of course I respect them. I'll always make time for them. Without them I'm nothing.'

'I think you're more than you know,' she murmured to herself.

She wondered again about the years they'd been apart and Dante's meteoric rise to fame and fortune after a childhood that had been less than perfect. His father had squandered the family fortune, by all accounts, and Dante had been proud but poor. Proud, but poor and determined, she amended. There had never been anyone like him, the rumour mill said. Dante was a natural horseman, and with his looks he had soon been inundated with requests from sponsors to become the face of first this big brand and then the next. She doubted he'd had to buy a car or a watch for years, and apart from those smaller perks the money that went with the huge deals had made him an extremely wealthy man. If Dante's father could see him now...

Baracca senior had been a cold, self-serving man who could always be depended upon for one thing, and that was to be dismissive and scathing about his son. He had never been interested in what the world had thought of Dante's emerging talent because all he'd cared about had been recounting the times when he had done so much more.

'Wool-gathering again?' Dante suggested, staring keenly at her.

'I was thinking about your father.'

His expression instantly closed off, but then, to her surprise, he admitted, 'My father was an unhappy man, who was always locked in the past.'

Always trying to belittle him, she thought as Dante fell silent. She couldn't bring herself to feel charitable towards a man who had been so relentlessly critical of his own son.

CHAPTER FIVE

'IS THERE SOMETHING WRONG?' Dante asked her, when they were sitting in the car.

'I was just thinking about the logistics of accommodating thousands of people on your ranch.'

'No need to worry,' he said, cutting off her thoughts. 'My ranch is big enough to accommodate however many people want to come—and I have the funds to support them and give them the time of their lives.'

She knew a lot of wealthy people, but Dante's wealth nowadays was on a different scale. Were even those even huge contracts from sponsors enough to supply an apparently bottomless pit of money?

'So now I've reassured you, how about you open up to me?' he pressed. 'We haven't had chance to talk for years. I'd like to know what makes you tick these days, Karina.'

Her heart clenched tight. 'My work,' she said.

'There has to be more to you than that.'

'Does there?' She shrugged. 'I work—I sleep—I eat. That's it.'

He frowned. 'We used to be friends. You used to trust me.'

She bristled. She couldn't help herself. She was re-

membering that night. 'That was a long time ago, Dante.'
She turned her head to stare out of the window.

'Butt out?' he suggested wryly.

'Something like that,' she agreed. She had buried the
heartache deep where it was safe from anyone's scrutiny.
At the time Dante was talking about she had thought she
knew it all.

And she couldn't have been more mistaken.

They spent the rest of the journey in silence. When
they arrived back at the hotel and Dante stepped out of
the vehicle he was immediately surrounded by admirers. And why not, when his face was on every billboard
in Rio? He had wealth beyond imagining, plus he was a
notorious player in the game of life as well as on the polo
field. Every woman with breath in her body wanted him.

With one notable exception, Karina told herself firmly
as she got out of the car.

She stood back until Dante was on his own again,
when she thanked him formally for a lovely day and for
coming up with the perfect theme for the event.

'I hope today has proved productive.' He stared deep
into her eyes until she had to look away. 'Are you sure
you know what I want now?'

Was he still talking about the cup?

'I'm sure,' she said tightly.

'After you,' he said politely, as he waved the doorman
away so he could open the door for her himself.

Following his gaze once they were inside the lobby,
she stopped dead and refused to move another inch.
'Oh, no—I can't. I'm sorry.'

'You can't? Not even for an honoured client?' Smiling faintly, he lifted a brow. 'You're far too busy?' he
suggested dryly.

For dancing with Dante? Yes. She should have remembered that every year after the parade her brother kept the party going by hiring one of the best samba bands in the city to entertain his guests. 'I really don't have time for dancing,' she excused herself, pinning an expression of regret to her face.

'Why not?' he asked. 'One dance with me can't hurt you, surely?'

One dance with Dante could do more damage than he knew.

'We've had a lovely day, a useful day, but now I've got so much to do.'

Her breath seemed to have taken on a life of its own as she stared at the dancers, closely packed...couples entwined...hands reaching, seeking, touching, stroking. Her chest was tight with panic and her breath was short at the thought of being pressed up hard against Dante. That was one risk she couldn't afford to take.

But Dante was determined. Taking her hand in a firm grip, he steered her onto the dance floor.

Her heart was going crazy as all the potential consequences of a simple dance swept over her. The last time she had danced with Dante had been at her eighteenth birthday party and that had led to catastrophic consequences. A harmless dance, her friends had called it, while she had laughed. She hadn't a care in the world at that time, and hadn't needed much persuasion to get up and drag Dante onto the dance floor.

She'd been up for anything then. And had fallen down a slippery slope faster than she would have ever believed possible. She stiffened now as he drew her close, and then relaxed a little because his hands were in a safe place. So long as he kept them there... She let out a tense breath when he showed no sign of moving them. He towered over her, and there was a faintly mocking and, oh, so confident expression on his face, and however hard she tried to resist him his familiar scent and strong, hard body worked its magic on her and she was lost. Dante was a rock against which her soft frame yielded all too easily.

'The perfect end to the perfect day,' he murmured in a whisper that brushed her ear. 'Now I just need you to relax.'

That was never going to happen. She came to her senses just in time, but turning to give him some smart retort she found herself staring into those mocking black eyes, and their faces were close, so close their lips were almost touching...

And then he brushed her lips with his.

Jerking her head back, she broke contact.

'For goodness' sake, Karina, what's a kiss between friends?'

Friends?

'I don't want Luc to see us,' she told him frostily.

'Luc? You care what your brother thinks?' Dante's black eyes blazed with disbelief.

'I don't think it would be very professional for him to see me kissing a client in the lobby of his hotel. It would be hard to pass that off as a business discussion, don't you think?'

Dante's massive shoulders eased in an accepting shrug, but suspicion had returned to his eyes. As well it might. There had been something so natural about their two bodies coming together. The way they moved as one would make anyone suspicious. Her body responded to Dante whether she wanted it to or not, making a dance with him more like a prelude to sex than a series of technical moves to music.

'You dance well, Karina,' he said, when the band fell silent. 'I should have remembered just how well.' She looked away from those mocking eyes. 'No, you don't,' he said, tightening his hold on her when she tried to pull away.

'I'm sure if I leave you, you won't be short of partners.'

'There's only one partner I want, and that's you.'

Dante's expression had hardened, making that a command.

'This has to stop,' she cautioned softly.

'Or we can't work together?' he suggested, with an edge of warning in his voice.

'Is that a threat?'

His answer was to dip his head and rasp his stubble against her neck, making her shudder out a gasp of indignation.

'You're shameless!'

'I'm curious,' he argued. 'Curious about you, Karina, and why you're so tense.'

She couldn't retaliate as they had attracted quite a crowd. When the national hero danced with the hotel owner's sister it was hot news and cameras on phones were flashing. There was no escape for her. She had to see this through. This was carnival season when people expected excitement and passion and, yes, hot news.

A small cry escaped her throat when Dante rubbed against her. He *was* shameless. This wasn't a quiet, safe man. He never had been. Dante's expression was knowing and mocking as he led her in the dance. He could prove so easily how much she still wanted him, just allowing her to feel the hard proof of his desire. And then the band struck up a sexy samba. She should go...

'You can't pretend you don't know the steps,' Dante insisted, murmuring the words against her ear. 'There are only three.'

There was too much laughter in his eyes for her to ignore his insistence that they have this one last dance, and willing his hands to stay where they were, and for her body to behave, she kept on dancing. Her body did the rest, with Dante's lightest, safest touch egging her on. He felt so good as they danced that she even began to relax. He felt so hard and sure, while she was so yielding and soft...

But not in the head, hopefully, she concluded, pulling away.

With a laugh Dante caught her back again. 'You're not so prim on the dance floor, are you, Senhorita Marcelos?'

'I'm doing this as a courtesy to a client and nothing more,' she said, living up to her prim tag.

'Of course you are,' Dante agreed dryly.

'And now I really do have to go,' she insisted, peeling herself away from him when the number ended.

He looked at her from beneath his brow. 'And our discussions?'

'Will be continued.' If there had been even a hint of business in his eyes she would have made an appointment with him there and then. But as it was... 'I'll get my secretary to call yours.'

He laughed at this. 'How about you call me?'

Not a chance. She had almost slipped from the straight and narrow and had no intention of risking it again. She was going to keep things formal between them from now on. 'Someone will call you,' she confirmed.

'It had better be you,' Dante warned.

She shivered involuntarily at the tone of his voice, and then gasped when he caught hold of her arm, but he was only delaying her so he could shrug off his jacket to put it around her shoulders.

'You don't need to do that—I've got my shawl.' She was wearing the shawl he'd bought her like a scarf, and had tossed it around her neck when they'd begun to dance.

'You can give the jacket back to me when you see me next,' Dante told her with a smile. Drawing it close around her, he enfolded her in his heat. 'Take your time with those notes. I want you up and running when we arrive at my *fazenda*.'

His ranch. His kingdom. His power to wield and enforce...

'You're shivering again, Karina.'

Stop fretting, or you'll make him more suspicious that ever. You can do this, she added to that instruction as she lifted her chin to stare Dante in the eyes. Deciding that making light of it was her best defence, she curved a smile. 'You've already given me your jacket. Shall I take your shirt next?'

She didn't stay to watch as Dante teased her with a wicked grin as his fingers toyed with the buttons on the front of his shirt.

She remembered those hands... She remembered those fingers...

She cursed silently, remembering what lay beneath that shirt.

It was time to forget all that and concentrate on business.

Turning on her heel, she walked away, and was more

than relieved when she reached the bank of elevators and one opened for her right on cue. Once inside she hit the button for her floor with a sigh of relief.

Dante was frustrated and pacing his bedroom with Karina on his mind. What a day it had been. Seeing her again *was* a thunderbolt. He could never have anticipated the way she made him feel. He had thought the attraction between them would have faded by now, but instead it had grown.

Yet she had catapulted away from the most innocent of kisses.

Why?

Admittedly, the kiss hadn't been all that innocent—it had been a trial, a test, an exploratory mission with motive behind it. She was hot. He was hungry. A kiss had seemed inevitable to him. He should have remembered that women harboured memories like sacred vows, while he, like most men, responded to the moment.

That insight couldn't help him now. Other woman shrank into insignificance by comparison with Karina. And she was a woman now, not a teenage siren who didn't know her own mind. She was a very beautiful woman and he wanted her. Her feelings towards him were tantalisingly ambiguous. There was the same heat between them, but there was a new reserve in her manner that he couldn't see his way past.

That wouldn't stop him trying, he accepted with a wry grin as he stopped to stretch in an attempt to ease his cramped muscles. The inactivity of city life was killing him. He longed for the freedom of the pampas. He was keen to get Karina to the ranch to see if she would relax in the setting where they'd both grown up. Luc said she hadn't visited the pampas for years, preferring life in the city. He wondered if that was true, or if she was hiding in a crowd. If that was the case, what was she running away from?

And why was he taking time out to ponder questions like that when he should be concentrating on the job she had been hired to do?

He turned as his laptop chirped and smiled thoughtfully when he saw the name at the top of the email. So she was up too. He hesitated before opening it. Karina's initial suggestions had been lacklustre. They'd been adequate, but no more than that. He hoped the trip he'd taken her on had infected her with the magic of carnival. People changed as they grew up, but he needed the old Karina's fairy dust for his event. Her flawless reputation in the events industry wasn't enough.

He had agreed to her handling the project because the Karina he'd known and grown up with could bring more than meticulous planning and attention to detail, she could bring flair and originality, but so far he'd seen little sign of that. He could only hope that fairy dust hadn't vanished in a gale of righteous living and rigid structure.

Making the decision to leave her email until a pint of coffee had fired up his brain cells, he headed for the shower. As he stepped beneath the icy water it seemed to him that in trying to protect her he had he hurt her more than he had intended. He had certainly ruined their friendship.

Karina had had the worst night's sleep ever. If she was honest, she hadn't slept at all. But she'd made good use of the hours up to dawn, spending most of them at her desk, working on an outline plan for the event. Hitting 'send', she'd sent her preliminary thoughts through to Dante. There was no point going into too much detail, because everything would need tweaking and adapting, depending on what she found at his ranch.

Her stomach plummeted at the thought. There was no getting out of it. She had to go to his ranch. Evaluating the existing facilities at the site of any new project was her first rule.

Taking herself off to shower and dress, she put on her business face along with her suit. She would meet Dante at Luc's office. Neutral territory was best. Checking her appearance one last time, she straightened her jacket and smoothed her hair. Dante was paying for her business expertise, nothing more.

How would she explain the black circles beneath her eyes?

She didn't need to explain them. Foraging in her tote, she found the concealer pen in her make-up pouch and carefully painted on some wide-awake crescents. It had shaken her, seeing him again, no question.

Shaken her? It had rocked her foundations to the core, but today would be different because today she knew what to expect and today would be all about business.

'Who put those worry lines on your face?' her brother demanded helpfully the moment she entered his office.

'I'm working. I'm preoccupied. That's *all*,' she insisted when Luc shot her a sceptical look. Flashing him an impatient glance, she began to pace his office.

'Let me guess,' he said. 'The frown has something to do with Dante?'

She turned her head and gave him her dead stare. 'Really.'

'Just don't tell me yesterday didn't go well. I heard rumours you went to carnival. Big mistake, Karina. This is business. Carnival is the wrong place to do business.'

'Says you, who spends a fortune on carnival and takes clients there. You even have a special stand erected for hotel guests, not to mention the samba band in the hotel lobby—'

'That's different,' Luc insisted.

'How is it different?'

'*I'm* different,' her brother informed her with a shrug.

'How are you different? Oh, I remember. You pee standing up.'

'Karina—'

'We had a good day, as it happens,' she said, deflecting his mocking look.

'I'm pleased to hear it. I always knew you could handle Dante.'

'I can handle him,' she confirmed. 'Shall we get started?' She glanced at her watch. 'He's late.'

'Don't you think you should wait for your client?'

'We don't know how long he's going to be.' She shrugged. 'For all we know, Dante's got something more important to do.'

Luc looked at her shrewdly. 'He has got under your skin.'

'Can we make a start, please?'

'Whatever you say.' Luc grinned with the anticipation of fun as he sat down at his desk.

'Apologies for my late arrival.'

She nearly jumped out of her skin when the door flew open. Dante's blazing stare found hers immediately.

'You're not late. We're early,' Luc pacified, smiling as he stood.

She watched the two men punch fists and hug. She

felt like an outsider when once she had been an honorary member of their gang.

That had been years ago.

She turned back to business—and tensed when Dante pulled his chair up close to hers. 'Those notes you emailed over…in the middle of the night?' His amused eyes scanned her face. 'I've taken a look at them. You get some good ideas at three o'clock in the morning. I hope I wasn't keeping you awake?'

'You weren't,' she said coolly, conscious that every part of her body was responding eagerly in spite of the fact that that was the last thing she needed. It was interesting to know Dante had been awake too, she conceded as he pushed his response notes in front of her.

'We made a good choice in your sister,' he said to Luc.

'I agree. I think Karina will do a very good job for us.'

'Excuse me—I'm sure I've mentioned this before, but I'm still here.'

'Of course you are,' Dante said warmly. 'My apologies, Senhorita Marcelos. Why don't you add to your notes a suggestion for classes so that gaucho polo players can learn better manners?'

'Good idea,' she murmured, as she studied his comments.

'I've written some notes on the back of that,' he said, leaning towards her to turn over the document she was studying.

Like an idiot, she bent her head to read, 'Dinner Cellini's. Eight o'clock.'

'Seriously?' She glanced up. 'I don't think we need to consider this, do you?'

'On the contrary *senhorita*,' Dante argued with a perfectly straight face. 'I think I've raised a very important point that should be considered right now.'

A point she was forced to award to Dante. 'Your notes are certainly comprehensive,' she agreed with a rise of her brow.

'Exactly as I intended. And your answer?'

'I'll give it some thought.' She smiled to reassure her brother, who was watching this exchange closely. She hoped Luc was oblivious to the undercurrents, though she doubted it when he asked to take a look at the page she was clutching to her chest.

'Maybe I can help clear up Dante's meaning so you can decide what to do?' he offered.

'That won't be necessary. It's perfectly clear to me.' Moving the papers out of her brother's reach, she stowed them away safely in her briefcase.

'Then can you please stop frowning so we can get on with the meeting?' Luc suggested. 'I can't tell if this is going well or not.'

And long may that last!

'Karina and I are going to work together just fine,' Dante assured Luc.

'If you say so.'

Luc looked less than convinced. And he'd better not be smiling, she thought as her brother covered his mouth with his hand. If bringing her together with Dante was his idea of a joke—

'How soon will you be going out to the *fazenda*?' Luc asked, directing his question to Dante.

It would have to be soon, Karina thought, frowning as she weighed up the hectic schedule ahead of her. There were several big projects pending—not as prestigious as this one but, then, what was? And whatever the job, she prided herself on giving it her best. But the clock was ticking.

'Tomorrow morning?' Dante suggested, turning to her to seek her approval. 'I'll have my driver pick you up.'

So soon? Her heart lurched at the thought. But that was exactly what she needed to happen, she reminded herself—not that that made the thought of going with Dante tomorrow sit any easier in her mind.

'Unless that's too soon for you, Karina?' Luc probed, seeing her frown.

'No. The sooner I can get started, the better it is for me. I have other commitments not too far down the line.'

'None that are going to interfere with this project, I trust?' Dante asked with a raised brow.

'Of course not.' Her heartbeat spiked as he continued to stare at her.

'You can't put a deputy in your place for an event like this, Karina,' he made clear.

'I know that. And it won't happen,' she assured him.

They stared at each other for a few moments longer until Luc shifted in his seat.

'I'm sorry to break this up, but I've got somewhere else to be,' her brother informed them. 'Copy me in on your reports, Karina, but wait until you've assessed the facilities at Dante's ranch before you finalise anything.'

'Of course.'

'I'll leave you two to it, then.' Luc came around the desk to shake Dante by the hand. 'I know you'll take good care of my sister.'

Karina clenched her jaw. She was as close to her brother as it was possible for siblings to be, but where Dante Baracca was concerned Luc didn't have a clue.

For the sake of maintaining a good client relationship, she called Dante to formally refuse his invitation to supper. She decided it would be better to slip it casually into the conversation with the excuse that she had to pack for the trip tomorrow. The main thrust of the call would be to ask what time she should be ready for his driver to pick her up.

'Senhor Baracca isn't taking calls, Senhorita Marcelos,' the receptionist told her, when she rang Dante at the office.

Whose bed was he in now?

Stop being ridiculous! she told herself firmly, adjusting her grip on the phone, noting that her fingers had turned white with the pressure she was applying.

'If he's not in the office, may I leave a message, please?'

'Of course. Oh—wait a minute. My apologies for not seeing this right away, *senhorita*. Senhor Baracca has left a handwritten note on my desk. He is having supper at Cellini's tonight, and expects to see you there. If you can't make it, I can try and get a message to him?'

'That won't be necessary, but thank you. I was just calling to confirm our arrangements.' She cut the line. Why shouldn't she meet up with him? Did she want Dante to think she was too affected by him to meet him out of the office? Theirs had to be a relationship of equals if she was going to work alongside him to make the polo cup the best it could be.

Dante had invited Karina to supper because he had to be sure she shared his vision for the event. He'd read her notes and was still worried she was playing it safe.

In life and in business, he mused as he drove to the restaurant, wondering why that should be so. Tonight was an opportunity for her to taste the energy and passion that brought people together and gave them the will to create carnival. He was certain the Karina he'd once known was still in there somewhere, and it was up to him to strip her barriers away. He smiled at the thought. Then he frowned. Up to now she had done everything he'd asked, when at one time she would have challenged every word he said. But without conflict there was no story, and he didn't want the event he was hosting to be a bland affair. He wanted it to be remembered for all the right reasons, for Karina's magic, the magic he was sure she could still bring.

The doorman took her coat and then the maître d' escorted her into the main body of the upscale restaurant— where she stopped dead. Dante was certainly hosting a supper, but it wasn't the intimate get-together she'd anticipated. Far from it. It seemed that every member of the samba group who'd appeared at the hotel was seated at his table, along with their mothers…and grandmothers— and probably their aunts and cousins too, by the look of things. And they were all dressed in their finest clothes. She fingered the collar of her tailored office suit self-consciously. Champagne was flowing, while the chef's finest dishes were being carried aloft.

He'd seen her.

Dante threw a sharp glance her way. Then his face mellowed into a look of confident amusement. She'd been set up. He'd known what she'd think when she saw that note. He'd put out the bait and had let her imagination to do the rest. The look on her face must have pleased him. It would have told him more about how she felt about him than anything else could.

She'd make the best of it, she determined as she wove

her way through the tables. She wanted her life back, and hiding in the shadows behind her business was no way to do that.

'Karina.' Dante stood when she reached the table. 'What a pleasure,' he added. 'I'm so glad you could join us. I wasn't sure you would come.'

'I wouldn't miss this for the world,' she said, smiling at everyone.

Turning his back briefly on his guests, Dante raised an amused brow. 'I'm really pleased you're here.'

'You've already said that.'

'But I want you to know I mean it.'

As Dante stared into her eyes, her heart thundered a warning. Instead of being here and feeling the old magic washing over her, she would have been safer staying at home and banging her head against the wall in the hope of knocking some sense into it.

She had recognised some of the people around the table, and they were quick to bring her into their midst. An older lady pulled out a chair for her between herself and Dante. 'It wouldn't be complete without you here, Karina,' she said, a comment that caused Dante to swing around and stare at her with a frown.

'Thank you.' She dipped her head to hide her burning cheeks as Dante continued to scan her face with interest. What she did in her private time was none of his business.

'What did she mean?' he asked her with a frown the moment he got a chance.

'I'm an asset to any gathering?' she suggested dryly.

'That won't cut it,' he assured her, sitting back so he didn't exclude their guests.

Tough. She'd told him all she was going to.

Dante had arranged cabs to take everyone home. Before the girls and their relatives left, Karina offered the use of the hotel spa free. The older women protested that this was too much, but she insisted, and all the girls begged their relatives to relent.

'It's the least I can do,' she said. 'You all work so hard to bring pleasure to visitors from around the world.'

'And increase the business at your hotel,' Dante murmured dryly, so that only she could hear.

Ignoring him, she added, 'Just give my name at the desk and I'll make sure that you're expected.' As Dante helped her on with her jacket, she told him, 'I can see you now for half an hour to discuss flight details and any other business you might have.'

'How very good of you.' His mouth slanted in a mocking smile as he shook his head in disagreement. 'We'll talk at the ranch. I'll have my man collect you at seven prompt tomorrow morning. Don't be late.'

If looks could kill, she had just murdered the most popular man in Brazil.

CHAPTER SIX

A SECOND NIGHT without sleep was not the best of starts for a research trip. Lack of sleep made her cranky, made her vulnerable, made her brain tick slowly, and she needed her wits about her more than ever this morning. On top of sleep deprivation, being with Dante again last night had rattled her. Instead of checking that she'd got everything she needed for the trip, she was pacing up and down, waiting for dawn, fretting whether it was actually going to be possible to work alongside Dante without telling him everything.

Could she get away without telling him all of the truth? He was already suspicious about what had happened while they'd been apart, but he had no proof and no way of getting any. She wasn't such a coward that she couldn't bring herself to tell him, but was there any point in opening Pandora's box when the past couldn't be changed?

Pausing by the window, she stared down at the hotel gardens, so calm and beautiful in the moonlight. The gardens had been designed to soothe—an impossibility where she was concerned, because she was flying out of her world and into Dante's world soon, and that was a raw, unforgiving world where the secrets she was harbouring could eat her up inside.

Sitting on the edge of the bed, she put her head in her hands, thinking back to a time when they had both been wilful and unpredictable and had got away with it. They had enjoyed adventures on the pampas that made her toes curl now she thought back. The bigger the risk, the more likely they had been to take it. Then they'd grown up and life had become complicated, with innocence gone for good.

Seeing Dante again now had upended her feelings for him like a tube of sweets, shaking them out and forcing her to confront all the things she couldn't change. All the sadness she'd kept safely bottled up. She had never told anyone about losing her baby. Who could she tell? Luc? Dante? The medical team had said she was 'lucky' because she had lost her child in the relatively early stages of pregnancy. She hadn't felt lucky. She'd felt devastated. When she'd left the hospital and even the kind attention of the medical professionals had been taken away, she had felt alone, grief-stricken, with no consolation to be found anywhere. It had been a very long and slow road back to recovery, and she wasn't even sure she'd reached her destination yet.

Maybe she never would. Closing her arms over her head as if that could block out the nightmare, she tensed as the scene played out in her head. She had asked the lady operating the scanner if her baby was dead, as if by some miracle the little light she had cherished for so short a time could still find a way to shine. There was no reason for it, the doctor had told her. Nature could be cruel. And once was enough to get pregnant, he had added disapprovingly when she had least needed to hear that.

Once with Dante.

She'd been too young, too inexperienced to handle something like that on her own, the same medical team had advised. But she'd had to handle it. Her mother was dead. She couldn't say a word to her brother and risk breaking his heart. It would have destroyed the team, set him against Dante. Worse, it would have destroyed her brother's trust in her, and how could she do that after everything Luc had done for her when their parents had died? She loved her brother too much to put him through that. He would never know.

Why hadn't she told Dante?

Lifting her head, she gave a sad smile. Practising the art of making babies was Dante's specialty. Dealing with the aftermath? Not so much.

But this wasn't all on Dante. According to what she'd overheard when they'd been younger, he'd had a life as a child that no one could envy. It was no wonder that he'd cast about, trying to find love. She was no better. At age eighteen she was supposed to know it all. She had certainly thought she did, and that was the impression she'd given Dante at the party. And he'd used protection. What more was he supposed to do when she had been an all-too-willing partner?

It had been bravado in front of her friends that night. She had wanted to take the bond, the friendship she'd had with Dante and move it on to the next level—preferably before one of her girlfriends landed him. She'd taken the initiative, and she had led him to her room where hot, hungry nature had taken its course.

She should have told him she was a virgin, but she could hardly do that after putting on such an air of experience. She was lucky he had prepared her so well that all she remembered was pleasure. And it had been more than once. They had made love throughout the night. Well, she had. Dante had had sex with her. Maybe he wasn't capable of anything more…maybe his ruined childhood had numbed him to feelings.

It certainly hadn't affected his stamina. That had been inexhaustible. He had been inventive and had known how to use every surface in the room. She had never expected anything like it, and knew for a fact she would never experience anything like it again.

What a klutz. What an eighteen-year-old klutz. She should have known that every action had a consequence. She might have anticipated Dante would throw her out of his bed. What else was he going to do? Marry her? Marry a girl on the threshold of life, who'd been his friend and who had taken that friendship and mangled it?

And now she was going to leave the security of her job in the city, with a brother who cherished and cared for her, for the wilds of the pampas with a man she hardly knew these days.

What were her options? Back down and throw away the chance of a lifetime because she was too scared to face the past? Appoint someone else in her place to handle the job? Dante had ruled that out from the start. And she could never live with herself if she did that. Should she live out her life in the shadows from now on, never admitting what she wanted, which was to be judged on her own merits—merits that felt thin and few right now?

It all came back to Dante. When she had discovered she was pregnant, she'd hung on, trying to find the right time to approach him and tell him, but he'd become elusive, moving in such sophisticated company she'd rarely seen him, except from a distance at a match. When she'd lost the baby, nothing else had mattered, and she'd been too bruised to face the rigmarole of trying to convince Dante that he was the father of her child—the child she'd lost. What was the point when there was no child? And so she'd kept her secret all these years.

And then she'd embarked on her fightback, going to college abroad, where she had got her head down and learned what had been expected of her in the hotel trade, which had been to be impeccably groomed at all times, and to have the type of quiet manners that reassured people.

How would Dante react if she told him all that now?

He'd be furious and rightly so, and she couldn't risk alienating him so close to the polo cup, though with his suspicions already roused she might be forced to tell him. He could always read her. She couldn't use the argument that many youthful friendships didn't survive the changes in people, and that they'd moved away and apart, and there'd never been chance to tell him about the baby—she couldn't do it, because that tiny light still shone too brightly in her mind, and the bond between her and Dante was still so strong.

Once they were isolated on his *fazenda* could she lie to him? Or would she tell him the truth and face the consequences?

As Dante's sleek executive jet descended to a smooth landing on the narrow airstrip, Karina was both apprehensive and excited, as well as interested in what she'd find at his home. How would the world-famous barbarian live? She knew so little about him these days. Her brother didn't dabble in gossip of any kind. Bottom line. She really didn't know anything about him. He might as well be a stranger she was visiting. And she shouldn't be remotely interested. Staring out at the endless swathes of emerald green and gold pampas, she reassured herself that it wasn't necessary to understand the ins and outs of a client's private life in order to do business with them.

'We are here, *senhorita*...'

She glanced up into the smiling eyes of the cabin attendant. Gathering her belongings, she unfastened her seat belt and got ready to disembark.

She must stop thinking about Dante, she warned herself as the jet engine died to a petulant whine. Her glance had flashed instantly to the cockpit door. She would see him soon enough. They'd be working together, remember?

'Senhorita?'

She followed the flight attendant to the exit door. And blinked as she inhaled her first lungful of warm, herby air. Even laced with aviation fuel, it was familiar and intoxicating. She'd been away too long. But now she was home. Closing her eyes, she lifted her face to the sun. If it was possible to be changed in a moment, she was changed. But not so changed that she had forgotten why she was here. She ran through a quick mental checklist of everything she'd brought with her. She was still a professional, even if the lure of the pampas was strong in her blood. And she was still determined to handle Dante a lot better than she had at eighteen.

'Senhorita?'

'Sorry.' She smiled as the flight attendant indicated that she might like to exit the aircraft—preferably some time this year, Karina guessed with a rueful grin.

Reality hit as she walked down the steps. She smoothed an imaginary crease in her jeans with damp palms as she took in the fact that this wasn't her land, this was Dante's land. He lived his unknown life here. She wished she'd dressed up a bit more, to add to her confidence and to reinforce her professional image. She had chosen to dress casually for the flight, as it wouldn't have been a surprise to find that Dante had two wild horses waiting to transport them bareback to his ranch. She'd got that badly wrong. There was no sign of Dante, but there were two top-of-the-range off-road vehicles waiting on the tarmac. The one closest to the aircraft had a young gaucho standing by the passenger door, who nodded to her as she hesitated.

'Welcome to Fazenda Baracca, Senhorita Marcelos.'

'Karina, please,' she replied with a smile.

'Gabe. Ranch manager.'

Gabe's handshake was brisk and firm, and he was about a foot taller than she was, though not as tall as Dante.

'Senhor Baracca sends his apologies, but he may not join you today.'

From this she assumed Dante meant to keep her on tenterhooks. Good luck with that, she thought, firming her chin. She was here to work, not to idle her time away, waiting for him.

'He has his usual checks to carry out,' Gabe explained, seeing her expression change. 'He asks that you make plans to tour the ranch tomorrow, and meanwhile he asks that you make yourself at home and get to work on your plans for the cup.'

Was that a rain check or a reprieve?

Thanking Gabe, she settled into the passenger seat and he closed the door. She stared around with interest. Dante's land radiated order and care. From the pristine fencing around the paddocks stretching away towards the horizon to the impeccable airstrip, where his private jet sat like a gleaming white bird, it was obvious that no expense had been spared. This was gaucho polo in a diamond-studded frame. She was already excited at the thought of organising an event here. She'd known Dante was rich—all the polo guys were wealthy—but this was money on a vast scale.

Inevitably, she began to brood. Where had the money come from? Dante's parents had lived beyond their means, as far as she could remember. Her parents' ranch had enjoyed much better facilities, which was why Dante and all the other young polo hopefuls had come there to train. Dante held several valuable franchises now he was so successful, but was that enough for a private jet, this ranch and his glittering lifestyle?

She jolted alert, as Gabe called out through his open window. Dante was just climbing behind the wheel of the second off-road vehicle. His eyes were hidden behind dark glasses, but he raised a hand when he saw her looking. Then he started the engine and drove away. His interest in her was as fleeting as it got, as if it was enough for him to check her transfer from jet to ranch was going smoothly.

That suited her fine, she told herself firmly. Settling back in her seat, she turned her mind to the project. Everything she saw and experienced from this moment on might be crucial to the polo cup. Nothing must escape her notice. She had to be like a sponge and soak it all up. She had no idea what to expect. She had only visited the Baracca ranch a couple of times as a child, and had never been invited into the main house. She remembered it as being dark and forbidding. Money had been tight for the

Baraccas, her mother had explained, because of the high life Dante's father made sure he enjoyed.

Gabe drove cross-country for around ten minutes before they reached some imposing gates. These marked the formal entrance to the main ranch house complex, he explained. The entrance had been pulled back considerably since the last time she had visited. Opening the window, she leaned out to stare around with interest. The barns and buildings had been developed and improved to the point where the run up to the ranch house was more like a drive through a well-ordered village set in a beautiful emerald-green frame than a potholed track flanked by the rotting buildings she remembered.

Mellow stone and burnished wood combined beneath a sultry sun to turn Dante's large ranch house a soft, shimmering bronze, while a frame of trees added shade and coolness to the entrance. She was impressed. More importantly, for the purposes of the polo cup, visitors would be impressed.

Her excitement for the project was building. There wasn't a thing out of place. The vivid floral displays in the formal grounds around the house were breathtaking. The image visitors would carry away would be that of a perfect ranch, with perfect grounds and perfect animals happily grazing. She could see the flyers and the brochures she'd have printed now, showing warm wood, sun-kissed stone and white paintwork, flanked by brilliantly coloured flowers and emerald-green paddocks stretching away into the distance, with choice groupings of well cared-for animals. This year's polo cup was shaping up to be the easiest event she'd ever been asked to promote.

She had to organise it first, Karina reminded herself as the familiar excitement rose inside her. It was tinged with a slight attack of nerves as she considered the enormity of the task ahead of her, but she put those aside for now to smile at Gabe as he drew up outside the open front door, where a beaming housekeeper was waiting to welcome them.

'I can't believe the changes here since the last time I visited.'

'That must have been some time ago,' he commented. 'Dante has renovated everything, and the main house has been added to substantially since he's been in charge.'

'Have you worked here long?'

'For the past few years—since Dante's other interests started taking up more of his time.'

His other interests?

'I've got my own spread,' Gabe explained. 'This is a temporary placement—a favour for Dante. He's done a lot to help me build up my own breeding programme and so I said I'd help him out. He assures me that he's going to settle down here one day,' Gabe added with a wry look. 'But so far no sign of that.'

So he hadn't settled down. Her heart thundered and her brain was clicking. What other interests could Dante possibly have? Surely the ranch and his polo took up all his time? A glance at Gabe's face suggested he would be no more forthcoming than Dante.

'Did you know his father?'

Gabe stared at her for a few long seconds before volunteering in a lazy drawl, 'I've heard about him.'

It wouldn't be anything complimentary, she guessed. Apart from instinctively not liking Dante's father, she remembered her mother saying Dante had *saved* his mother from his bullying father. She'd been too young to remember the detail. It still sent a shiver down her spine. His mother's suffering had been bad enough, and the thought of the things Dante must have seen and endured as a child made her feel sad for him.

'I didn't really know Senhor Baracca senior that well myself. Strange really when you consider that Dante, my brother and I spent endless days on this ranch as kids. It was an amazing setting for any child. Though I don't suppose there are any children on the ranch now?' she queried curiously.

Gabe exploded with laughter. 'No children?' he echoed. 'I hope you're not allergic to the little brutes, because you're going to find hordes of them here.'

'Hordes?' she questioned, but Gabe wasn't giving anything away.

'What about you, Karina?' he pressed. 'Family?'

'No.' Her voice sounded strained, but she found a smile to reassure Gabe.

'You must love your job to make it everything,' he said, staring at her keenly.

'Yes, I do.' It helped her to live with the memories by taking up so much of her time, and she was looking forward to escaping the safety net Luc had always provided for her. She wanted to taste life, to try and learn to live with the past, and where better to do that than here on the pampas she had almost forgotten she loved so much?

'Hey, Dante!'

Her heart leapt into her mouth as she swung around to follow Gabe's greeting. She was just in time to see Dante vault a fence as he went to check on some horses in the paddock.

His virility shocked her. How could she have forgotten?

She hadn't forgotten, but in this setting it seemed more

pronounced than ever. Dante was brutally masculine, so strong and hard-muscled—and yet so gentle and affectionate towards the horse, she noticed. Animals loved him, and she loved watching his interaction with them. There was nothing left of the polished businessman here, or even the startlingly good-looking playboy featured in so many magazines. Dante was a gaucho through and through, and here on his *fazenda* he was at home, back in control of his land.

She tensed as he raised a hand to acknowledge Gabe, noticing how Dante's black stare remained fixed on her.

CHAPTER SEVEN

KARINA WAS REALLY HERE. Forget the checks he usually made on his return to the ranch. Gabe could handle them. Dante felt alive—more alive than ever before. His senses were on full alert, with every instinct he possessed honed to the sharpest point. Having Karina on his ranch and under his roof was like warm honey singing through his veins. They'd been apart too long. And here there could only be truth between them. The pampas was too vast, too beautiful, too unforgiving to allow for human shortcomings. It revealed and exposed. It was harsh and true. It brought out the best in people…and the worst.

Seeing Karina here took him back to the past, a place he usually avoided. It was never easy to remember the way his father had treated his mother, not even troubling to hide his countless infidelities. His father had seen these as proof of his virility, rather than a tragedy that had broken his mother's heart. He glanced at the ranch house his mother had called home, and which he had renovated in her memory, knowing the housekeeper would be settling Karina in, and she would be meeting up with the happy chaos that characterised his lifestyle. He smiled to himself as he wondered what she'd make of it.

* * *

The housekeeper welcomed Karina into a vaulted hall-way where the noise levels were off the scale. Gabe was right. There were hordes of children. Which was the last thing she had expected of Dante.

'*Descuplas!* My apologies!' the housekeeper, who had introduced herself as Maria, exclaimed with an indulgent laugh as she took hold of Karina's arm to steer her out of the way of a makeshift raft on wheels manned by several youngsters. 'Today is a very special day. The master is home and everyone is excited.'

Dante, the master of all he surveyed? Karina smiled, admitting to herself that she felt completely at home here in the chaos. Riding tack and footballs, along with dis-carded toys and a number of junior bicycles piled up in a heap competed for space with sturdy antique furniture, polished to within an inch of its life.

'So?' She jumped at the sound of the deep male voice. 'What do you think of my home, Karina? Do you ap-prove?'

'Dante!' She spun on her heel. 'I didn't expect to see you here today.'

'Why?' He shrugged. 'This is my home.'

'Gabe said—' She bit her tongue and let it go. Dante was entitled to change his mind.

'Do you like what I've done with the house?' he prompted, giving her a look that made her stomach clench with pleasure rather than alarm.

He was talking about the mess, which she didn't care about at all. It was a happy home. She could feel that right away. And that was all that mattered.

'As it happens, I like it a lot,' she said.

'Good.'

Dante's deep, husky voice shivered through her like a hot knife through melting meringue. His wicked smile was something she hadn't seen enough of, though he was making it increasingly hard for her to confine her thoughts to business. It didn't help that he was as tall and as dark and as devastatingly handsome as he'd ever been—but not quite so menacing now that he had a group of children clinging to his legs.

Even as she took all this in, she felt her frantic city life drop away and the pampas claim her. She felt different. Even Dante looked different here, and the longing to ride free and wild with him was suddenly overwhelming.

'I'm going to the kitchen to grab some food with these urchins,' he said. 'Join me when you've settled in, and then we'll discuss my agenda.'

Dante had changed? Maybe not that much! She held back on a salute. 'I trust you'll be equally open to discussing my agenda?'

'That all depends on what your agenda is...'

He held her stare a beat too long, his mouth slanted in a challenging smile and his eyes glowing with an emotion she couldn't read. She still hadn't figured out where the children fitted into his lifestyle, and was halfway up the stairs when a female voice called out, 'Karina?'

Her stomach contracted as she turned around. The girl was very beautiful.

'Honestly, they're impossible,' the mystery girl exclaimed, shaking a play fist at the children. 'You're very brave to come here.'

Karina got over her initial reaction fast. She liked the girl on sight. 'It looks like fun to me.' She smiled down.

'I'm Nichola, but everyone calls me Nicky. Sorry!

Can't shake your hand. I'm covered in finger-paint.'
Nicky brandished both hands palms up as proof.

'You're in charge of the children?'

'In charge?' Nicky's laughter pealed out as she thought
about that. 'That's one way of putting it! I love them, but
I'm always glad to hand them back to their parents. But
what about you? Apparently, you're amazing—according
to Dante,' she explained, when Karina looked surprised.
'The children from the families of those who work on the
ranch treat this as their second home,' Nicky explained,
'and Dante brings more in from the city to experience life
on a ranch. He says he loves the place to be used, and I'm
usually around, a bit like an adoptive auntie, I suppose,
which in a way I am, being Dante's sister...'

'Sister?' Karina queried, thinking back. She couldn't
remember Dante having a sister.

'You were away, I expect, when I moved in, or you'd
have heard all about me. I'm Dante's father's love child,'
Nicky explained, with the same openness that had drawn
Karina to her. 'Not that there was much love involved,
from what I can understand.'

Were there any similarities between father and son?
A knot snagged in Karina's stomach.

'Dante's mother brought me here to live with them
when my own mother died,' Nicky explained. 'Things
weren't easy for Dante's mother, but I suppose you know
that—it was common knowledge. That didn't stop her
taking me in. You probably remember, that was the sort
of woman she was.'

'A saint,' Karina agreed, as pieces of the jigsaw that
made up the life of Dante Baracca flew together at break-
neck speed. 'I'm only sorry I didn't get the chance to
know Dante's mother better. I only met her a few times

when I was a child, but my mother used to talk about how good she was.'

Nicky shared her grimace as they thought back. 'Dante's father liked to keep her out of the way—kitchen sink or his bed were her only permitted zones, from what I can understand.'

Karina guessed they both felt the same shiver run down their spines, but Nicky soon lightened the mood with her smile. 'Sorry. I'm keeping you from settling in. Let Maria show you to your room—I have to pack anyway, as I'm leaving soon.'

'You're leaving?' Karina was disappointed, having found someone she believed could be a friend.

'Yes.' Nicky heaved a mock sigh. 'Dante will have to fend for himself, though my best guess is that his adoring staff will do the fending for him, leaving Dante free to bring in more waifs and strays.'

'Waifs and strays?' Karina was beginning to feel like a parrot, but this was so much information in the space of a couple of minutes she couldn't get things straight in her head.

'Dante has a plan for the future,' Nicky revealed enigmatically.

There was only one certainty, Karina concluded when Nicky headed off across the hall. Every preconceived notion she'd had about Dante Baracca had been turned upside down.

'I'd make the most of having the day to yourself today if I were you,' Nicky shouted back to her. 'Knowing Dante, he'll be knocking on your door at cockcrow in the morning. Just remember the fun starts tomorrow, so make the most of the peace and quiet today.'

Karina's head was spinning, but it was hard not to be

optimistic when Maria ushered her into the most beautiful guest room. Light and bright, it was beautifully decorated in shades of ice blue and coral. If it hadn't been for Dante and the history they shared, she would have been more thrilled than ever to be back on the pampas she loved, especially when Maria threw back the drapes to reveal a wide, deep balcony overlooking fields full of foals and their mothers. What more could she possibly want than this?

Answers?

Her life was what she'd made it, though it was impossible not to think about Dante and try to piece together the nuggets of information Nicky had shared. Did Dante take after his cold, self-serving father or after his mother, a woman who had cared enough to bring the orphaned child of her husband's mistress into her home?

That was a question for another day, Karina concluded as Maria suggested that Nicky's idea was a good one, and that tonight Karina might like to take supper in her room later.

'I would. Thank you.' She'd spend the rest of the day working on her laptop, then a hot, foamy bath beckoned, before food and bed. Something told her she would need her sleep, and that tomorrow would be soon enough to start piecing together the puzzle that was Dante Baracca.

She had barely finished her shower the next morning when she heard the clatter of hooves outside her open window. Grabbing a couple of towels, she covered herself and padded barefoot to the window. And shot back, seeing Dante on horseback. Her heart was racing, arguing with all the sensible plans she had made to be detached where he was concerned, and above all sensible. It didn't matter that they had both grown up and moved on in ten years, or that Dante was now a client whose sole intention was to show her the facilities on his ranch. It was enough that he was out there, looking as sexy as sin, for her heart to pound ten to the dozen.

'Hey, Karina!'

Firming her jaw, she stared out as if she saw a man who looked as rugged and sexy as Dante every day of the week. The impatient look he was giving her suggested that by sheer willpower alone he believed he could draw her down from the window and onto the saddle of the horse at his side. Let him stare. She'd just got out of the shower. Dante might have the turnaround capabilities of a holiday jet, but that didn't mean she had to rush about. She would behave calmly and act professionally, as she always did.

'Good morning. Can I help you?' she asked politely.

'I want you down here now.'

She flashed five fingers, indicating more time was required.

'And I don't have all day to waste,' Dante growled threateningly.

His expression made her think one finger would have been enough.

Taking the full five minutes, she tied her hair back, and changed into breeches and shirt. She was neat, she was organised. She was ready.

For anything.

Which was probably just as well, as Dante had undergone the full gaucho transformation. His wild black hair was held back by a blood-red bandana and his gold earrings glinted in the sun. He was wearing well-worn, snug-fitting jeans beneath the battered leather chaps all

the gauchos wore, and a tight-fitting black top emphasised his bunched and banded muscles. Could she blank
her mind to that?

She could blank her mind, but her body had a will
of its own, and her nipples rose to salute him when she
joined Dante in the yard.

'So you're ready at last?' Looking her up and down
with a lazy smile, he handed over the reins of her horse.

She knew that look and gave him one back that said
clearly, *You're wasting your time.* She didn't sleep with
clients, however 'honoured' they might be. She never
had. She didn't sleep with anyone, come to that. How
could she? Dante might be the most tempting piece of
forbidden fruit around, but she had to think of him as
the spoiled fruit the wasp had got to first. If she did that
she'd be fine. It was that, or risk getting her heart broken all over again.

'I take it you can still remember how?'

She looked at him as she checked her horse's girth, and
that look said it all. They both knew horses could hold
air in their lungs when the strap beneath their belly was
fastened, and then they let it out again once the rider was
mounted, causing the saddle to slip dangerously. Guessing the type of ride she was about to have with Dante,
she was going to take every safety precaution necessary.
Springing into the saddle, she gave him a look. 'I think
I'll keep up.'

Closing her eyes for a moment as she sucked in a lungful of sweet, clean air, she promised herself that nothing
was going to spoil this for her. This was her first ride
on the pampas for too long, and she was going to enjoy
it to the full. She would learn everything she needed to

about his ranch, and then she'd go home to plan the event, happy, single and sane.

Dante led off at a canter, issuing information and instructions as he rode. His facilities were world-class. She had a rough idea of what a set-up like this must have cost. Her brother maintained a vast and well-equipped stud, but Dante's equestrian centre was on another level again. He had built a full-sized polo club that would have sat proudly in any country, and there was the best accommodation possible for visiting horses, riders and grooms. She already knew about the veterinary hospital and exercise pools, because Gabe had pointed them out to her, but now she discovered there was an Olympic-size swimming pool for their human guests.

'You live in some style,' she commented wryly when they finally reined in.

'Don't you approve?'

'It's not up to me to judge you.'

'But you do judge me, don't you, Karina?'

Before she could reply, Dante turned his horse and was soon lost in the distance, a silhouette against the vast blue sky. He was like a dark angel, brooding and powerful, and for now she was left in pursuit. Urging her horse forward, she caught up with him.

'Where are we going?' she asked, riding alongside him.

Turning to slant an amused look at her, he chose to ignore the question. 'You still ride well, Karina.'

'I always could keep up with you,' she commented dryly.

'But you never used to be so suspicious.'

'And neither did you,' she pointed out. 'But that was a long time ago, Dante.'

When neither of them had cause to be suspicious of each other, she thought as his black stare levelled on her face.

Relaxing in the saddle with just one hand on the reins, he shifted his weight almost imperceptibly and his big black horse took off again.

Leaning low over her horse's neck, she gave him his head. At least riding was as good as she remembered. Her anxieties and suspicions remained, as did the ghosts from the past, but gradually she was relaxing in a way she had never found possible in the city. Maybe the pampas was where she had to be in order to lay those ghosts.

'There you are,' he murmured, when she trotted up.

'You have a bigger horse,' she pointed out logically, finding the pride of her youth, where competing with Dante was concerned, was still one hundred per cent intact.

He shrugged. 'Change horses and I'll still ride faster than you.'

She weighed up his stallion. 'Would you care to put that to the test?'

They dismounted.

The stallion's acceleration was phenomenal. It was like sitting on a rocket...*or on Dante*. Her laughter was carried away on the breeze. She hadn't felt like this for years. She was soon well in front, with confidence thrilling through her. How could she have forgotten how good riding with Dante felt?

'*What?*'

She gasped with outrage when he suddenly appeared in front of her. 'How did you do that?'

There was no chance he could hear her. He was half a mile ahead. Whispering in the stallion's ear, she left the big horse in no doubt as to what he had to do. She hadn't raced like this with Dante since they had been kids riding wild on the range, and she'd have to brush up her skills, as well as the tricks they used to play on each other, if she was going to stand a chance of keeping up. Doggedly, she turned his big stallion in Dante's direction, and when she finally caught up they exchanged horses without a word.

'There must be a lot of things you want to ask me,' he commented as they left their reins loose and allowed the horses to choose the way for a while. 'Well?' he prompted. 'Or are you concerned I might do the same to you?'

His stare on her face was level and hard, and she realised how tense she could so quickly become under his scrutiny. Having picked up the reins and shortened them as if for flight, she was gripping them as if her life depended on it. She wanted to say something, make some excuse, but words wouldn't come, and with a last cold and knowing look into her eyes Dante gathered up his reins and rode away.

CHAPTER EIGHT

KARINA WAS HOLDING out on him, and trust was essential if they were going to work together successfully. He'd replayed the night they'd slept together over and over in his head, and he was more confident than ever that he'd done the right thing. He could maybe have dressed things up a bit better, but he'd been younger then, and impulsive.

'Dante?'

Karina was looking at him with concern.

'Is something wrong?' she pressed, glancing away as if she knew very well that he expected her to be more open with him.

'Time is short, and we've got a lot of ground to cover,' he said curtly. His questions would have to wait. They had too much to do to waste time on conversation outside the event they were planning. He led the way through a group of trees planted to screen some groundwork and then reined in.

'What's this?' Karina asked, as she stared down at the ugly gash in the land.

It was the only blemish on his otherwise flawless ranch, but it was one that paid for his lifestyle and for everything that visitors to the polo cup would enjoy. 'It's an emerald mine.'

'Are you serious?' Karina's shocked gaze flashed to his.

'Perfectly.'

She frowned and he could almost see her thinking that this answered a lot of her questions about the source of his immense wealth. 'Is it yours?'

'I have a major stake in it,' he confirmed.

'At least it explains your Midas touch.' She relaxed as she smiled—with relief, he guessed.

'So now you know my secret.'

'One of them.' She stared at him steadily. 'Nicky said you had plans for the future. Plans involving the young-sters who come to the ranch?'

He stonewalled her question with a question of his own. 'No secrets of your own to share?'

'No,' she said flatly, clearly irritated that he wouldn't share the smallest detail with her. 'My life would bore you, and even if that weren't the case, I don't see how it's relevant to our business discussions.'

'One ride across the pampas is hardly going to restore the friendship of our youth.'

'I hope you can trust me in business?'

He raised a brow. 'So do I.'

'So,' she said, clearly keen to change the subject, 'can we have tours here on the days of the tournament, or would security be an issue for you?'

'We can have tours,' he confirmed.

'Good,' she said stiffly. 'I'll add them to my list.'

'Shall we move on?' he suggested.

She was holding out on him. Each time he looked at Karina her eyes darkened and her lips plumped up, as every female hormone she possessed danced with his machismo. She'd pulled back in Rio rather than risk kissing him, and she was still reluctant to share the smallest personal detail with him. *Why?*

'You look thunderous,' she commented, as they cantered along side by side. 'Has some detail of my planning annoyed you? If you'd rather leave the tour to the emerald mine out…'

A muscle flexed in his jaw as he stared straight ahead. She'd seen his home. She was living under the same roof as him, *pelo amor de Deus!* And now she'd seen the emerald mine. He was running out of surprises to try and jolt Karina into sharing whatever it was that was eating away at her. What was so bad she couldn't tell him?

'Why don't you tell me more about the mine, Dante?' she said in an attempt to restore normality. It made his hackles rise even more. She'd pick any topic to stop him questioning her, but for the sake of their *working relationship* he'd go along with it—for now.

'Mining isn't my specialty, though there have always been old workings here,' he explained. 'The old-timers talked constantly about the green ice they used to find here—that's what they call emeralds—so I decided to investigate. I sold the exploration rights and brought in experts. I used the same consortium that revived the Skavanga diamond mine in northern Europe. The deal was that I got to keep a share in whatever they found. It turned out to be one of the richest seams of emeralds in the world.'

She laughed—with relief at the relaxation in the tension between them, or with genuine pleasure at this discovery of unsuspected riches, he couldn't tell.

'I'm not really surprised now I've got over the shock of you owning an emerald mine,' she confessed, smiling at him. 'I can't imagine you doing anything on a small scale.'

'Not if I can help it,' he agreed, tight-lipped. Urging his horse forward, he put some much-needed thinking space between them.

She allowed her horse to pick its own way down the slope as she considered the tension in Dante. His back was like an unbreachable wall. Suspicion was riding him, and so far she'd told him very little, but she wouldn't be rushed into anything. She'd choose her time.

When?

Soon.

To break the tension between them, she decided on a change of subject when she caught up with him. 'I met your half-sister, Nicky. She's lovely.'

'She's great,' Dante agreed tersely.

'Who takes care of the children when she's not here on the ranch?'

'Why? Are you volunteering, Karina?'

'No.' She huffed a wry laugh. 'I've got my own job to do.'

'Relieved?' Dante suggested.

She shrugged. 'No, but those kids are quite something.' She paused, hoping Dante would tell her more, but he wasn't so easy to unravel.

'The staff will take over.' He shrugged.

Dante took off again at speed, preventing her asking him any more questions. Hooves were soon thundering beneath them, making any form of conversation impossible, but she guessed Dante would want more answers when they got back to the ranch. She slowed her horse, allowing him to ride ahead of her, just to drink him in.

There was no law against glutting herself on powerful shoulders and hard-muscled arms. She had always loved watching Dante ride. He appeared so casual and yet he was fully in control, with one hand on the reins and the other relaxed at his side. He rode smoothly and efficiently, employing minimum effort for maximum result.

Much as he'd ridden her.

Air shot from her lungs at the rogue thought entered her head. She had to shake herself round fast, and then she realised that Dante had turned his horse and was coming back for her.

'What are you waiting for?' he demanded. 'Reminiscing?'

'No. Thinking forward,' she argued firmly.

'About?'

'About the work we have to do, and the short time we have to complete it in.'

'*You* have to complete it in,' he stressed with a look. 'If you're having second thoughts about your ability to handle a project as big as this one, you'd better let me know right away.'

'I'm not having second thoughts.' She met his demanding stare head on. 'I'll get this job done in good time, and it will be something we can both be proud of.'

'It isn't enough for me that you get it done. I expect more from you than that. And as for me being proud?' He frowned. 'It's more important to me that I feel passion coming from you where this job is concerned. I want you to inspire the people who visit my ranch. That's the only way you'll make something memorable out of this.'

'It will be memorable.' She matched him with all her old fire.

'That's all I need to hear,' Dante confirmed, turning away.

She watched him ride off, marvelling that she had ever been so young and naïve as to believe they would stay together just because they'd slept together. Anything had seemed possible on that magical night. Consequences hadn't even crossed her mind. Dante had made her feel so safe.

Had he?

Wasn't it more likely that she had embroidered the facts to fit her fantasy version of a relationship with Dante? Everything about that night had been reckless—from the flimsy dress she had chosen to wear, to her dancing and then their lovemaking. An eighteenth birthday was supposed to mark the transition from childhood to adulthood, but she'd had to take everything to the edge. The validation of everything she'd been, and everything she'd hoped to be, had seemed to lie in the hands of one man—until Dante had thrown her out. Which she now understood had probably been a good thing, though it hadn't seemed so at the time.

Good, because everything since that moment had made her face up to the fact that it was up to her to make her own fate, search out her own opportunities and her own path through life. Before the party she had still believed in fairy tales, and had saved herself for Dante. She had taken what had been a childhood friendship and changed it in her mind into true love, believing she'd touched him somewhere deep.

It had been a real slap in the face to discover that she hadn't touched Dante anywhere. He had a deadline to keep, he had told her that night as he'd stared pointedly at the floor where her clothes lay scattered. He'd told her to pick them up and get out. She could still remember her shock as she'd stared at him numbly, trying to work out what she'd done wrong. 'Take a shower and get out,' he'd barked as she'd scooped up her clothes as if he couldn't wait to get rid of her. She remembered holding them against her body, feeling suddenly ashamed of her nakedness.

'Why are you frowning?' Dante demanded, jerking her out of her recollections.

If love were a fairy tale, Dante had got the frog and prince thing completely wrong!

'Are you going to dismount and let your horse drink?' he prompted.

She sprang down to the ground before he could help her out of the saddle. She didn't want to risk him touching her.

'I'd like your opinion on this living accommodation...'

She refocused rapidly to take in the block of luxury apartments in front of them, and then realised they had ridden down a pathway flanked by the most beautiful gardens.

'This is spectacular,' she gasped, as she stared around. 'It's like an oasis in the desert. It's ideal for what we need. Can we go inside and take a closer look?'

'This is where we'll house the VIPs during the cup,' he called back as he led the way.

It was hard to believe they had ever lain in bed together, or that they had known each other as intimately as any couple could. His broad, muscular back was turned against her, making him seem like a stranger.

The building was so striking, it took her mind off her troubled thoughts for a while. The block of apartments curved in a horseshoe around the banks of a glittering manmade lake. When she stepped inside she was silenced as she stared around the light-filled space.

'There's a hot spa and a small heated outdoor pool for each apartment, as well as a butler service on call,' Dante explained.

'Butlers on horseback?'

'In helicopters. It's faster.'

'Of course.' Somehow she managed to keep a straight face. She had a lot of wealthy clients who had all sorts of unimaginable luxuries they took for granted, but in all her experience she had never heard of anything to compare with this.

'Take your time to look around. I'm going to leave you to it, while I inspect the rest of the units to make sure they're all up to the standard I requested.'

He filled every inch of her world with heat and machismo, and he made her ache with wistfulness for everything they'd lost; a loss he didn't even know about. She quickly busied herself making notes, as he paused and turned to face her.

'There's just one thing you need to keep in mind,' he said. 'The Goucho Cup means everything to me. The game is my passion, and it's a passion I want to share with the world. I'm determined to prove that it isn't a game for a privileged few but an exciting spectator sport. I'm going to need your help to make that dream a reality. Are you in?'

'You know I am.' How could she not be infected by his enthusiasm, or by Dante's dark, compelling stare?

Those few moments of intensity between them left her reeling, and it was almost a relief to move on to discussing food outlets and supply chains, though there was a moment later in the day when he turned to her to demand, 'Who would have thought fate would throw us together again like this?' But then he shook his head and snapped, 'Forget it.'

That was one thing she couldn't do. Fate had always meant them to be together—just not in the way she had expected.

CHAPTER NINE

When they returned to the ranch house she made the excuse that she needed a chance to compile her notes. Dante was way too distracting, and she was glad of some space. She ate alone and went straight to bed, but she couldn't sleep.

Getting up, she worked through the night. There was a point in the cold dark hours when she wondered if frustration could actually cause a physical ache. The pain when she thought about Dante seemed real enough. She set up a calendar to mark off the days to the Gaucho Cup, and from that to her next job, but that only made the black hole without Dante yawn in front of her like an unbridgeable chasm.

She managed a few hours of sleep before dawn. The scent of blossom was heavy in the air when she opened the window. Leaning out, she dragged in some greedy breaths—then shot back, seeing Dante in the yard. Even cloaked in shadows he was a stunning sight. She watched him prowl into the stable block and wondered why he was up so early. The urge to follow him, to find out where he was going proved to be one old habit that time hadn't dimmed.

Remembering the thrill of riding out with him at dawn

the day before, she tugged on her breeches as fast as she could, pulled her hair into a ponytail and dragged on a top and riding boots—then stilled, hearing the sound of hooves on cobbles. She smiled at the sound of Dante's husky whisper as he coaxed his horse to leave the prospect of an early feed in favour of the wide open spaces of the pampas. She'd catch him up—stalk him on horseback, as she had years ago.

She hurried downstairs and crossed the yard, heading for the stable block. Tacking up the same horse as yesterday, she led him out. Dante had a head's start but the sun was rising, showing her the way. She was confident she'd find him. She'd trust her instincts and those of a horse seeking out his stablemate.

She trailed him at a distance. Dante was riding at a steady pace, making it easy to keep him in sight. She had a small setback when the early morning sun went behind a cloud, and when it cleared again there was no sign of Dante. She looked about, searching for him, and then shrieked with alarm as strong arms scooped her from her horse.

'Now we talk,' he snarled as he lowered her to her feet in front of him.

'We're in the middle of nowhere!' She was still shocked, and angry that he had got the better of her.

'Exactly,' he agreed. 'No distractions.'

'You set this up?' She was trembling with fury—and something else she didn't care to analyse.

'I set you up,' he confirmed with a look.

Angling his stubble-shaded chin, he stared at her with all the old arrogance. She couldn't believe she'd fallen for it, but she had always been gullible where Dante was concerned.

It was as if the two of them were alone on a massive stage, with the strengthening sun dazzling her like a spot-light. All the early birdsong fell away as Dante's black stare drilled into hers.

His grip tightened on her arms. 'You've successfully avoided talking to me face to face for almost ten years. My best guess?' His black stare speared into her eyes. 'If you hadn't been forced into my company, you'd still be avoiding me. I'm giving you one last chance to tell me what you're hiding from me. And be warned, I won't ask again. I'll appoint investigators to find out the truth for me instead.'

She felt sick and faint. It had never occurred to her that Dante would go to those lengths. Dragging in a breath, she tried to remain calm, but the steel in his eyes and in his voice had thrown her.

'Why are you here, Karina? Why did you follow me?'

'I was curious,' she said with a shrug, in an attempt to make light of it. She had followed him because she had wanted to be close to him, she added silently.

'You're curious?' With a laugh, he shook his head. 'How do you think I feel about you?'

Dante's laughter was as cold as his stare. She should have listened to the gossip that said no one could reach out and touch Dante Baracca. Many had tried, but they had all given up. Only she was stubborn enough to be-lieve that the man she had spent her teenage years dream-ing about still existed.

'It's about that night, isn't it, Karina? It's something to do with that night.'

'Don't be silly,' she said defensively, desperate to change the subject.

'Tell me, Karina. Tell me every detail of what's happened to you between that night and this.'

'Why should I?' she stormed, lashing herself inwardly as she tried to skirt the truth.

'Because the woman standing in front of me is not the Karina Marcelos I used to know, and I demand to know why.'

'You demand?' she interrupted, laughing at the bitter irony of them both searching for something that didn't exist any more. 'The Karina Marcelos you mean no longer exists. She was a stupid—naïve—girl...'

Dante pulled his head back. 'What are you trying to say, Karina?'

She tried to breathe and could only suck in air in great gasps.

'Karina!' Dante all but shouted. 'Tell me what is wrong.'

Holding out her hand as if to fend him off, she somehow formed the words. 'You left me pregnant.'

Her voice sounded too loud, and the impact of her words shocked even Dante into silence. They stood together without moving, without breathing, without reacting at all, until he ground out, 'Why didn't you tell me this before?'

Her wounded gaze flashed to his. 'Because I'm not the person I was then.'

'You held this information from me?' He looked at her incredulously with eyes that had turned to steel—whether with fierce empathy or with fury, she couldn't tell. She could understand his shock and something of what he must be feeling, but she had no words to reach him.

'Don't you have anything to say to me?' His voice was harsh with frustration. 'Don't you think you at least owe me an explanation for your long silence?'

Her glance flashed to his hand on her arm and he let her go.

'What happened to our child, Karina?' he said. 'What happened to my baby?'

'There is no child.' Her voice sounded faint and far away. She was shaking so much she didn't recognise herself. She had imagined this scene so many times, and had even planned how she would phrase the words Dante must hear, but there were no words, she discovered now.

'Karina.'

She looked up to see Dante's expression had changed. Bringing her in front of him, he asked in a far gentler tone, 'Can you tell me what happened?'

'I lost the baby.'

She pressed her lips together as if that could stop it being true as silence swept over them again, holding them tight in its unfeeling grasp.

He wasn't sure how long they remained standing together, frozen and barely breathing as they stared at each other. 'You were pregnant,' he managed at last. All his anger and impatience with Karina had gone, leaving him feeling completely numb.

Her eyes searched his. 'I couldn't tell you, because you were away, and because—' Her mouth snapped closed again, and she shook her head as if it was too painful to go on. After a few moments had passed she drew a deep, shaking breath and continued. 'There were many reasons why I didn't get in touch with you, and by the time I saw you again it was over, and there didn't seem much point.'

'Much point?' he echoed softly, still trying to come to terms with what she'd told him.

'No point in upsetting you,' she explained.

He relaxed his grip on her arms and stood back. 'You

should have told me. You can't keep something like that to yourself. Who was there to help you?'

The answer was in her eyes.

'You told no one? Not even Luc? I would have been there for you if I'd known. I would have cancelled anything to be there for you.' It was a fight for him to keep rock solid as her eyes filled with tears. 'Yes, this has been a shock,' he admitted, 'and it would have been a shock then. I was younger. I was wild. But I was never uncaring. You should never have had to go through that alone.'

Actions had consequences, his conscience told him. This he knew, but what Karina had just told him was worse than anything he had imagined. How young she'd been—just eighteen. He'd been twenty-two—and reckless. But Karina had been alone with no one to confide in. Not that she would have done so anyway, he guessed grimly. She would hardly have told Luc, and if he had been around, *would* she have told him? Karina had always prided herself on standing on her own two feet, and she would have viewed explanations as a plea for help.

'I don't know what I could have done to help you,' he admitted. 'I was different back then—selfish and wild— and I know how independent you've always been, but I still can't believe you had to go through this on your own.'

She looked away and he knew he'd lost her.

'This was a mistake,' she said, confirming his fears. 'I shouldn't have told you. What's the point?'

'You're wrong,' he argued firmly. 'There's every point. What happened was my responsibility as much as yours.'

'No.' Her eyes blazed briefly. 'I don't need your counsel, Dante. I don't want you to feel sorry for me. I've told you everything you need to know. Now, please...don't mention it again.'

But had she told him everything? The look on her face, the flicker in her eyes told him she hadn't. 'Karina?'

'No,' she flared, pushing his hand away. 'I miscarried, something that happens to many women, the doctors told me.'

'Don't,' he warned quietly as her face turned grim and still. 'Don't try to dismiss this as if it means nothing to you, when I can see that it's breaking your heart.'

'I don't know what you're waiting for me to say,' she blazed.

The thought that there was more than this—more that she wouldn't tell him—tore him up inside. They'd been friends. They'd shared everything. And now, just when she needed someone, whether she knew it or not, Karina was turning her back on him.

'I know you,' he said quietly. 'I know that even at eighteen, if things had worked out and you'd had the child, you would have coped. As it was, you handled the tragedy and came through it alone.'

'Leave it, Dante,' she cried out. 'What's the point in this? I can't change anything—and neither can you!' she exclaimed with frustration. 'We just have to accept, you and I, that everything turned out for the best.'

'For the best?' he echoed over her. Now he knew something was badly wrong. 'I can't believe you just said that. This isn't the Karina I knew talking, and I refuse to believe you mean it.'

Sucking in a shuddering breath, she turned away. 'Can we please get back to business? We're wasting precious time talking about something neither of us can change.'

Her eyes were shuttered when she turned back to face

him. The subject was closed as far as Karina was concerned. But not for him.

'Back in Rio, you said my business acumen was all you wanted from me,' she reminded him. 'I hope that's still true.'

'You carried my child, Karina. That changes everything.'

She looked at him in silence for a few moments and then, returning to her horse without another word, she mounted up and rode away without a backward glance.

He needed to ride. He needed time to think so he could take in everything Karina had told him. She'd been pregnant and had kept that from him. He couldn't get his head around it. She'd lost the baby and had suffered that loss on her own. His guilt was like a living thing riding heavily on his back. The pampas had always been his outlet, a non-judgemental channel for his thoughts, but he doubted that even riding across the land he loved could bring him solace today.

He could never repair the past—never make up for not being with her when she'd lost a baby, their child, and had soldiered on unsupported. That was so typical of Karina—stubborn, dogged, brave and strong. She was like a cork, in that whatever life threw at her she always bobbed up. Luc had supplied all the necessities of life when she'd been growing up, including his unconditional love, but Luc had been too busy trying to find his own way to keep watch constantly over Karina. She wouldn't have listened to her older brother anyway.

He rode faster, as if that would give him the answer. When they had been kids, trust had been a simple matter of asking a question and receiving an honest answer.

They'd had no reason to lie to each other or to keep the truth from each other. Too much had happened for them to pick up the ease of those early days, but he had to do something because he knew for certain that there was more Karina wasn't telling him—and if that was as bad as what she had already told him...

His mood darkened as he considered the possibilities.

If he hadn't broken with her that night...

He'd had to break up with her. They had both been too young, too passionate, too unformed when it came to knowing who they were and what they wanted out of life. Sex had been an outlet for their energy and frustration, an impulse they had recklessly followed. Animal instinct had taken him over, as it must have gripped his father so many times. The break-up afterwards had been driven by his dread that one day he would become his father, and so he had pushed Karina away.

As the years had passed and he had matured and changed, he'd known for certain that he wasn't and never would be his father. That was why he'd opened up his home, and why he intended to do more of it, welcoming people of all ages to experience life on a working ranch. His childhood home would no longer be a place of fear and shadow but a home filled with happiness, purpose and light. He wanted Karina to experience the same redemption, but to do that she had to trust him first.

Karina was riding fast and hard in an attempt to forget that she had opened Pandora's box—to forget the past, to forget the present, to forget she'd told Dante about the baby—wishing with all her heart that she hadn't opened up, and yet glad that she had, and so glad that she'd retained the sliver of reason required to hold the rest of her secrets in. They were nothing to do with Dante. Why burden him?

For a while the concentration she required to ride at speed worked for her, but deep down the truth was burning, and Dante wouldn't let up now he suspected there was more.

Easing back in the saddle, she slowed her horse to give them both a much-needed break. Riding the pampas had always been healing, but what she'd been doing had been needlessly reckless. Her only excuse was that it had been too long since she'd ridden with the wind in her hair, and with the past driving her she'd gone all out.

Her horse responded happily to the change of pace with a high-stepping trot. It gave her the chance to look around and appreciate the countryside. The scent of herbs and grass beneath his hooves made her smile through her sadness. When had been the last time she'd taken the time to notice her surroundings? This dawn ride was such an evocative reminder of her childhood, when she had used to ride out with Dante, and it let a little optimism into her thinking.

She could see him in the strengthening light, riding in the distance, riding fast. They still had a lot of ground to cover. She understood that he had needed space after her revelations. He was doing what she had tried to do, which was to ride the sorrow out. Reining in, she watched him cut a path through the flatlands in a cloud of dust and thunder. At full stretch on horseback, Dante was a stunning sight. It was an image she'd always keep etched on her mind.

With a wistful smile, she sucked in a breath. This was Dante's home. At one time it had been her home too, but nothing stayed the same, and now her horse was chafing at the bit, impatient to be free. She knew how that felt.

'Okay,' she whispered, leaning low to reach his ears. 'Go get him!'

Her mount responded eagerly with a surge of speed that thrilled her as he set off after his stablemate.

Dante had reined in and he turned in the saddle when she trotted up alongside him. His expression was unreadable, and she tensed immediately, wondering what he was thinking now. She concluded the only thing she could do was break the ice.

'I'd forgotten how much I love it here.'

'The city didn't fulfil your expectations?' Dante queried, searching her eyes keenly.

'I thought it had until I came back here,' she admitted honestly. It was a struggle to keep everything except an open smile off her face. She gestured around to give herself a moment. 'The city could never compete with this.'

She was putting on the act of her life. When Karina looked into his eyes he could see her pain, however hard she tried to hide it. He responded with a swell of emotion he had thought he was dead to. Underneath her bravado and her professional veneer Karina was the same girl he had known all those years ago, but she was wounded now.

'Is there any of the ranch left to see after our tour yesterday?' she asked him brightly.

Some people might have expected more grief from her after the dreadful news she'd shared, but he knew Karina. He knew her strength, and now he knew her weakness. She had been keeping secrets for so long she didn't know how to share them. 'There's plenty left to see,' he told her truthfully. 'We'd better get on.'

He had to do something to help her, but there wasn't

time to do more than watch over her now. Her work had saved her, he guessed, just as Team Thunderbolt had saved him. The team had become his family, giving him a safe outlet for his youthful aggression.

The team had also given him back his sense of pride after his father had stripped it away, and a satisfaction in his work that his father had always denied him. Team members prided themselves on their loyalty to one another. If one of them hurt, they all hurt. If one of their loved ones hurt, there wasn't a team member who would stand by and do nothing. And this was Karina. How much more did he want to help her to reclaim the *joie de vivre* she had once enjoyed and spread around? But he could do nothing for her while she was keeping secrets. And no one knew better than he that Karina Marcelos had the strength to keep those secrets for the rest of her life if she chose to do so.

'Don't scowl, Dante.' She flashed him a look of concern. 'Life is full of twists and turns, and we just have to stay on our feet.' Closing her eyes, she demonstrated her intention to carry on with the job as if she wasn't breaking up inside. Throwing back her head, she murmured, 'It's such a beautiful day.'

He nodded curtly when she opened her eyes and turned to look at him. He was capable of nothing more in the face of her strength, because that was the same strength that was destroying her. Clicking his tongue, he led the way forward, hoping Karina would find some outlet for her trapped emotions in the beauty of the pampas so she could turn her back for good on shadow and doubt.

CHAPTER TEN

THEIR NEXT STOP was a group of buildings that could best be described as rustic rather than ritzy.

'This is the accommodation for visiting children, teachers and guardians,' Dante explained.

Now they were getting to it. She remembered Nicky's remark about Dante's plan, but why hadn't he been more forthcoming? If he needed long-term plans for the children it was going to be a much bigger job than she had bargained for—and in the time available he was stretching her to the limit.

'I think you'd better explain,' she said. 'Is this more than just about the Gaucho Cup? Because, if it is, I need to work out how I'm going to splice in your plans for an ongoing programme with my plans for the polo cup.'

'If you can't—'

'This isn't about my capabilities,' she interrupted. 'This is about you being frank with me, so I know what I have to do.'

'Me being frank with you?' he queried with a sceptical look.

'Yes.' She firmed her jaw. 'Either you want me to do this job or you don't.'

She held her ground as Dante stared at her. She guessed

no one, with the possible exception of his team members, stood up to Dante these days.

The standoff lasted a good few seconds, and then he grated out, 'Your job will be to enthuse the young people, draw them into the life of a working ranch. I'll give you all the plans I've drawn up so far.'

'Thank you. Gauchos,' she murmured, quickly summoning up in her mind the type of help she would need in the short a space of time available.

'Good idea,' Dante conceded, as she outlined her instinctive initial thoughts.

'Where to now?' she asked him briskly before he had chance to change his mind.

'To our last stop for today.'

She'd leave her questions about his long-term project for now. When time was squeezed it paid to be organised.

The last stop turned out to be the first ugly building she'd seen on his ranch.

'Vaults aren't meant to be pretty,' he said when she frowned. 'You might change your mind when you see the jewels inside this fortified cell.'

'Green ice,' she murmured, feeling a thrill of anticipation as Dante punched in a code and the outer door swung open. Lights flashed on automatically, illuminating the steps leading down into the ground. Another door, another code, and they were in.

The large underground room took her breath away. Glass cabinets, lit discreetly, lined the walls. It was a billionaire's showroom, alight with fabulous jewels. Diamonds and emeralds flashed fire on every side. She guessed the diamonds would be from the Skavanga mines Dante had talked about, and the combination of ice and fire was extraordinary. 'I'm lost for words,' she admitted, when Dante looked for a reaction from her.

'Well, that's inconvenient,' he said, locking the door behind them, 'because you're here to talk.'

She tensed as he leaned back against the wall.

Karina was smart. She knew why she was here, and it wasn't just to look at his priceless collection of jewels. She had never leaned on anyone in her life, not even her wealthy brother. She had no history of confiding in anyone, but he had a plan.

Unlocking one of the display cases, he reached for a rough diamond. 'This is me...' He placed the lump of unpromising-looking stone in her hand. 'And this is you.' He selected what looked like another pebble. 'Both these lumps of rock hold secrets at their core.'

'And you have to know how to release the secrets?' She gave him a jaundiced look. 'First you have to know what you're looking for,' she pointed out.

Never underestimate Karina, he reflected, slanting a smile as he replaced the stones in the cabinet. He explained the stages the stones went through before they were ready to be set in precious metal, but she knew what he was really saying. He had never brought anyone this close. He had never allowed himself the indulgence of a personal life. He didn't confide in anyone.

'Would it be possible to arrange tours here, as well as to the mine?' she asked on a practical note. 'Or would security be a headache for you? I wasn't just thinking about the VIPs who might place an order, but the young people for whom this could open up a whole new range of possibilities—careers,' she explained.

His eyes lit at the thought that she had engaged with his project. He'd barely told her anything, just a hint, but she'd taken that hint and had obviously been thinking about it. 'Your brother told me that you pay for a young girl to go to school.'

She was instantly defensive. 'Out of my own money—and Luc shouldn't have said anything.'

'It's nothing to be ashamed of.'

'No, but Jada wouldn't like anyone to know—that's the girl I help,' she explained awkwardly.

'How long have you been doing charity work?'

'Since I—' Her mouth snapped shut.

Since she'd lost the baby, he guessed, and had needed something to focus on and set her life back on track.

'It's not reaching out on your scale or my brother's,' she said after a few tense moments. 'I just do what I can afford. When I can do more, I will.'

Shaking his head, he disagreed. 'What you do is personal. I don't know the names of half the people helped by my foundation.'

She mulled that over for a moment, and then she said, 'So can I add tours here to the youth programme?'

'Over to you,' he agreed with a shrug.

It was a great idea. Opening young minds to careers connected to gemstones was original and pure Karina. It was maybe the first step to finding that fairy dust of hers. He held out a chair, leaving her in no doubt that he wasn't so distracted by her brainwave that he had forgotten why he'd brought her here. Her gaze darted to the door. He folded his arms and leaned back against the wall. Seeing there was no escape, she perched on the edge of the chair in fight or flight mode.

'Dante—'

Chair legs scraping across the floor silenced her. He

pulled up another seat and sat so their knees were almost touching.

Tension soared between them.

He let the silence hang until she said, 'Okay. What more do you want to know?'

'Everything,' he suggested. 'And, as you pointed out, the clock is ticking, and there's a lot of work to do to get this cup organised.'

'It isn't that easy,' she admitted. 'Some things can't be said quickly.'

'What can't you tell me? I can't believe there's anything worse than you've already told me.' Leaning close, he took hold of her hands.

She drew them back and balled them tightly in her lap. 'I can't. You chose your path. I chose mine—'

'That's not enough.' He stood.

She stood too, facing him defiantly. Anything was preferable, as far as he was concerned, to Karina in shutdown mode. 'Tell me,' he insisted fiercely.

The flash of pain behind her eyes said he was delving too deep, too fast, into places even she didn't go, but he couldn't let her go back into her shell now.

Emotion burned starkly in her white face. She knew there was nowhere to hide. She also knew he was the biggest client she'd ever have, and that her brother, not to mention the rest of the team, was depending on her to get this event right. She'd clawed her way to success, which was why people trusted her. He had to believe she wouldn't let that trust go now.

'Will you, please, let me out of here?'

He sensed she was holding herself tightly in check. 'You can leave at any time.' He recited the code for the door.

She sucked in a few tense breaths, and then she made

the decision he had fully expected. 'I'm not going anywhere, Dante, because you're right, that would be far too easy for me—for both of us.'

If this were the time she finally unburdened herself, he'd take anything she had to throw at him. His pride, his concerns, his life counted for nothing while Karina was in torment. And she was in torment. When she lifted her chin he could see the pain in her eyes and he felt it as his own. He had to tamp down the urge to drag her close and tell her that everything would be all right, and that he would make it so, because that would be a lie. This was something Karina had to do for herself.

He clenched his hands into fists as she drew in a long shaking breath. The urge to reach out was overwhelming him. But he mustn't touch her. He mustn't speak. If he did anything to distract her, this moment would be lost, and then she would be lost.

Closing her eyes tightly shut in a failed attempt to hold back her tears, she said, 'You do know if there'd been a child I would have told you?'

'Of course I do.'

'I was fine,' she lied, hurrying to reassure him. 'Life doesn't grind to a halt when a tragedy happens, and it's amazing how we find ways to cope.'

He clamped his lips shut as he raged against his inability to say anything that could make the slightest difference, and he felt even worse when she touched his arm as if it were he who needed comfort and reassurance.

'I'm sorry, Dante. I've had longer to adjust than you have.'

But she hadn't moved forward.

'I promise you this won't affect my work. I'll give

you everything I've got to make this the best polo cup there's ever been.'

His brain was racing as he searched for a way to shake her back on track. He needed something that would shock her into leaving the business between them to one side for now. She was hiding something bad, and this was his best—maybe his only—chance to help her. He barely heard the rest, and there was no way he could dress this up. A shock was needed, and a shock was what he'd give her.

'Did you take a lover after you lost the baby?'

Dante's question was like a slap in the face. Her mind blanked for a moment. She was still taking tiny steps. They had warned her in the hospital that it would take a long time to recover fully, and that in the meantime she would find coping strategies, but that no stage of her recovery could be rushed.

She had rushed. She would have done anything to ease the pain. At the time her actions had seemed to be the one thing that might help her to forget Dante. It had turned out to be her worst mistake, and had left her feeling more of a failure than ever.

'Well?' Dante pressed now, staring fiercely into her eyes. 'Are you going to answer my question?'

Desperate to close down this line of questioning, she shook her head. 'You can't ask me that.'

'I am asking,' he insisted grimly. 'I've listened carefully to everything you've said. I haven't missed a single nuance or hesitation in your speech, which is why I know there's more, and if it's something you can't talk about after what you've told me—if someone's hurt you physically, mentally, I want to know. And if you expect me to accept some lame excuse, you're dealing with the wrong man.'

'I've told you everything,' she insisted in a shaking voice. 'You can't hold yourself responsible for everything in my life. And you don't have a hold on me, so let me go.'

Breath gushed from her lungs as Dante dragged her close. 'If I live ten lives and devote them all to you, I will never make up for what happened to you, so if you think I'm going to let you go, let *this* go, you're mistaken.'

Guilt was careering through her when he dragged her close. She was shocked by his passion and should have remembered Dante had always channelled his emotion into action. A few blank seconds passed and then, like a dam breaking, her emotions flooded in as he drove his mouth down on hers. His kiss was like oxygen to her starved senses. The reassurance of his arms was like water in the desert to a dying man. It was too precious to squander, too welcome to ignore. For everything that had gone before and couldn't be changed, Dante was so instantly familiar. All fear of kissing him, of becoming close to him again seemed irrelevant suddenly. She was close to him. She had always been close to him—always would be close to him.

Lifting his head, he stared down. His black eyes were ablaze with inner torment as he grated out, 'I should have been there for you.'

Lifting herself up on her toes, she laced her fingers through his hair, and then she cupped his face, loving the scratch of his sharp black stubble against her palms. She wasn't a teenage temptress without a care in the world now, but a woman who knew her own mind. 'You're here now,' she whispered.

Dante's kisses changed and became lighter and more

reassuring, and then he did something that only he could. He started whispering things that no one else knew about them—small things, confidences they'd shared when they'd been younger, personal moments of triumph and defeat, times that hadn't been so good, and those that had been better, and times when a look between them had been enough to share the burden of what they had both been experiencing at home.

What he was trying to tell her was that nothing had changed between them, not really. He was reminding her of what they'd shared in the past, and reminding her that she'd never had cause to doubt him before that night when passion had run so high between them that neither of them had been thinking clearly.

She smiled into his eyes. She loved everything about him. She loved the way he made her feel, and the way he made her remember. She loved the way he soothed her, and the way he reminded her that they had faced tough times before and had always come through them. She loved the way he could make her smile when her heart was breaking, and she loved knowing that there was no-where else on earth she wanted to be than here, with him.

The need to be closer still overwhelmed her and, tug-ging his top from his jeans, she exclaimed with pleasure when her hands found his hot skin. Dante had started work on the buttons of her shirt, but he soon lost patience and ripped it off her, scattering buttons everywhere.

'What is this?'

Dante frowned as he stared at the scar on her shoulder.

'It's nothing.' Her head had cleared immediately as she shrugged it off.

Dante wasn't convinced. 'You didn't have a scar on

your shoulder when you were eighteen. I would have re-membered something like that.'

She shook her head and laughed, hoping to give the impression that he was making too much of it. 'If you must know, some insect bit me.' She huffed another laugh in the hope that he'd forget.

Dante didn't forget anything, and his frown deepened as he traced the scar with the pad of one finger.

'This is it, isn't it?' he said, lifting his head to stare into her eyes. 'This is your problem. Did someone do this to you? No,' he murmured after she had been silent for a while. 'It's worse than that, isn't it? Has someone intimidated you into silence, Karina?'

She wasn't looking for his pity. Everything she'd done in her life she'd done with her eyes wide open. 'Who's going to hurt me?' she scoffed. 'Have you forgotten I'm armour-plated?' She hastily pulled the remnants of her shirt back over her shoulders and crossed her arms over her chest to hold the two halves together.

Letting her go, Dante stood back as if he was disap-pointed. 'You will tell me eventually. But for now it's time we returned to our work.'

She wouldn't be so sure of that, Karina thought as he opened the door for her. She'd buried her secrets deep where not even Dante could find them.

CHAPTER ELEVEN

When they got back to the ranch Dante dismounted and handed the reins of his horse to a waiting groom. She did the same. Unbuckling his leather chaps, Dante handed those over too. Down to snug-fitting jeans and a tight black top that moulded to his powerful body perfectly, he was a riveting sight, but he had become distant with her. She guessed her inability to confide in him had set their tenuous personal relationship back, and it was crucial now to restore communication between them.

She quickened her step to follow him across the perfectly manicured lawn. Everything inside the house was plain and good. There was no flash, no show. And no children, she discovered when they stepped inside. No staff either, by the look of things. Just the scent of freshly cut flowers and beeswax, contained with a heavy, but not oppressive silence.

'I've given everyone the day off,' Dante explained.

So they were alone. Had he planned this? She was instantly tense, imagining the interrogation she might face at any minute. 'What fabulous flower arrangements,' she commented, for want of something to say.

'It's the first thing I do each morning,' he said, turning to give her a look. 'Right after I muck out the horses.'

She relaxed into a laugh. Dante had always known how to reach out and touch her when no one else could.

'Coffee?' he said, heading for the kitchen. They had missed breakfast for the second day in a row.

They walked past the foot of the grand staircase, an elegant sweep of highly polished mahogany with a scarlet runner down the centre held by gleaming brass rods. There was a grand piano tucked neatly beneath the curve of it.

'You play?' she asked with surprise. The lid was up and there was music on the stand. 'Before you arrange the flowers, I'm guessing?'

Dante's tension also eased into a smile. 'I play whenever I get the chance,' he admitted. 'I just don't broadcast it.'

'The team would mock?' she suggested.

'They'd only do that once,' he commented dryly. 'My mother insisted I learn,' he explained in a rare moment of openness. 'She said it would relax me.'

'And does it?' She ran her fingers across the keys.

'It helps,' he said tersely, as the bell-like sounds faded into silence.

'You're full of surprises.'

'And you're not?' he challenged, flashing her a sharp look.

Her cheeks blazed red as the man who looked like a barbarian but who now turned out to have all the sensibilities of an aesthete continued to stare at her. Would the surprises never end where this new Dante Baracca was concerned? She was certainly getting to know him all over again.

'Before breakfast I have another idea, Karina.'

Thrown off balance, she hesitated. 'What idea?'

'I need to unwind,' Dante admitted as he rolled his powerful shoulders. 'You do too.'

Unwind how? She followed him across the hall and down a corridor into an impressive leisure facility where there were marble floors and glittering fountains, and beyond the fountains an enormous swimming pool. 'You want to have a swim?' she queried. The time issue made her frown as she asked the question, along with a far more personal concern.

'I thought we'd both have a swim,' Dante said, as he stared at her keenly.

And reveal her body? She froze with horror at the thought.

'You don't find it cold in here, do you?' he asked with surprise.

'I hope the water's warm,' she said, to excuse her involuntary shiver.

Dante frowned. 'You never used to care. You swim too well to feel the cold.'

She never used to have scars to worry about at the time he was talking about. Her body hadn't just failed her when it had come to carrying Dante's baby, it had failed her as a woman, and she had paid a heavy price for that. Seeking comfort in someone else's arms had seemed a solution, the means of forgetting Dante. Looking back, she realised her behaviour had been so out of character she must have had a breakdown. The doctors had been right. She should have sought professional help, rather than trying to go it alone. They'd warned her that her hormones would be raging for quite some time, but they hadn't explained how that would affect her. She blamed herself for losing the baby, and blamed herself again for everything that had happened afterwards.

'Take a shower,' Dante suggested, thankfully oblivious to these thoughts, 'and then join me in the pool.'

'I can't swim in jeans and a top.' She smiled back at him as she shrugged an apology.

'No problem. I keep a stock of swimsuits for my guests.'

'Maybe it isn't such a good idea.' Her alarm rose to fever pitch. 'I've got so much work to do—'

'And a swim first will allow you to clear your head.'

'I'd rather not.'

'Give yourself a break, Karina,' Dante insisted. 'Work is important to both of us, but we also need to take some downtime.'

She stared at him in silence for a moment, knowing there was no getting out of this.

From the selection of brand-new costumes still in their packets, which had obviously been chosen for women with far more style than she had, she selected a sports costume that covered up a lot more of her body than the flimsy bikinis on offer. There had been a time when she had raced Dante across the lake in freezing water, and had never cared about fashion, so he wouldn't be surprised to see her in such a modest costume. She might just get away with this if she was lucky.

Dante was slicing through the water by the time she came out of the changing room. His powerful body, so bronzed and muscular, was fully extended, and for a moment it was enough to stand and watch him swim. He had such an easy grace he barely made a ripple in the water. Her heart speeded up when, sensing her arrival, he stopped swimming and looked up. She stepped to the water's edge, in a hurry to dive in. The sooner her body was fully submerged, the sooner she could relax.

He felt rather than saw Karina enter the pool area.

Her choice of costume surprised him when there were
so many more attractive options to choose from, but he
shrugged it off. He stopped at the far end of the pool and
turned to see her framed in light. It was as if the rays of
the sun were attracted to her and had fired blue sparks
into her ebony hair.

It reminded him of the dozens of times when they'd
gone swimming in the lake, when he'd thought her wild
black hair looked like a thundercloud with lightning running through it. But then she set about taming it with re-
morseless resolve. He wanted to tell her not to tie it back,
but to let it cascade around her shoulders like a water
nymph. She should also take off that regulation costume
so she was completely naked. He doubted water nymphs
wore anything.

Feeling his stare, she stepped back into the shadows,
but not before he had seen the flush of awareness on her
cheeks. His body responded instantly. He wanted the
wild Karina he had made love to, the Karina who would
have chosen the most outrageous bikini in the brightest colour, and would have flaunted it to taunt him. Instead, a wounded woman was hiding in the shadows,
having picked out what she had obviously decided was
the drabbest choice of costume and the one least likely
to entice him.

He raised a hand in greeting, only for her to pull her
hair into an even tighter knot on top of her head. As sub-
liminal messages went, that one was clear enough. He
could look, but this water nymph wasn't for touching.

He swam towards her underwater. He wasn't a saint,
and the sight of Karina in a tight-fitting swimsuit, even
one as severe she had chosen, made full immersion of his
aroused body a practical necessity. The costume showed

off her voluptuous figure to perfection. He would have to be unconscious not to notice how good she looked.

He surfaced halfway down the pool to find her still fiddling with her hair. He didn't need any reminders of how glorious that hair had felt beneath his hands when he'd laced his fingers through its silky thickness. It pleased him to see that, in spite of her best efforts to achieve a severe look, soft tendrils were still escaping. He dipped his head beneath the water so she couldn't see him smile, and when he surfaced he was in time to watch her perform a perfect swallow dive. She swam to reach him, and it was a relief to see her face was almost free from tension by the time she reached him.

'Oh, that feels good!' she exclaimed.

He was tempted to catch her close, but he wanted to be sure she'd loosened up and was ready for that first.

'Race?' she challenged, to his surprise.

'Why not?' he agreed. 'Want a head start?'

She huffed with mock contempt and took off without him.

Catching up easily, he swam alongside her until the last couple of yards when he pulled ahead.

'You are so unfair,' she complained. 'You always do that.'

'And you always fall for it.'

She lifted herself clear of the water in a cloud of silver bubbles, and then, scooping water, she splashed it in his face.

'Like that, is it?' he threatened.

She laughed. Dipping her arm into the pool again, she thrashed it across the water, dousing him completely. He couldn't let a challenge like that go unopposed, and launching himself across the pool he brought her down beneath the surface with him.

She escaped like a seal, wriggling free from his arms with no difficulty at all—but not before he had felt a tantalising brush of her breasts against his arm and her heat all over him.

'You'll pay for that,' she threatened as they faced each other.

'I'd like to see you try!'

Diving down beneath the surface, she grabbed hold of his legs and tried to bring him under. He resisted her easily, and diving down with her he brought her to the surface, struggling furiously in his arms. If there was a more erotic experience than having a hot, wet Karina fighting him off, he had yet to experience it. When he finally subdued her, she was laughing. 'You have to let me go,' she protested.

'Why, when this is much more fun?'

'For you.'

'For both of us.'

She saw the change in his expression and grew still. Winding his fist through her hair, he drew her head back slowly and then, taking his time so he could savour every moment of it, he brought his lips down on hers.

Hot and cold, wet and warm, the dark secrets of her body were yielding themselves up to him. He plundered her mouth with his tongue, mimicking the sex act he craved—the act that had gone on all night the first time. He could never forget how wild she'd been, how responsive, how abandoned. He could still remember her screams of pleasure and the way she had called out his name at the moment of release.

Karina had been insatiable and so had he. Bringing a premature end to that glorious encounter had been torture for both of them. They had discovered a capacity for pleasure he guessed neither of them had previously suspected. She was sucking his tongue now as she had sucked him that night…and now she was biting his bottom lip, just as she had teased and tormented him. She'd rubbed her warm breasts against him in open invitation as she'd wrapped her limbs around his, making him her captive, as he had gladly been that night—until he'd turned her beneath him to show her the meaning of deep, thrusting, rhythmical pleasure. She had responded by pressing her legs as far apart as far as she could, in order to isolate that most sensitive place for his attention. She'd cried and groaned and panted out her need, and as he pressed his erection into her now, he could feel the soft swollen warmth of her core yielding against him, just as it had that night. Her lips were wet, her mouth was hot, and he was as sure as he had ever been that Karina in her confining swimsuit was ready for him to take, to pleasure, to satisfy—

'No!'

She reeled away from him in the water as he began to ease her swimsuit down and quickly backpedalled in the water as if her life depended on putting distance between them.

'You stay in,' she insisted, reaching for a towel before she had even climbed out of the pool.

He sprang out to join her, shocked by her sudden change of mood—perplexed as she backed away, as if he were a threat in some way.

'What now?' she asked him warily, still backing away.

He shrugged in an attempt to ease the rigid tension between them.

'Now we get a massage,' he said casually, looping a towel around his waist.

She gave a nervous laugh, clearly unsure of his motive. 'You have masseurs on tap?'

'I have a phone. I'll take a shower and meet you by the massage tables.'

Her eyes widened. 'You have massage tables?'

'I have a gym with tables at the far end,' he said a trifle wearily, but she'd become so tense and serious he had to try and lighten things up. 'What type of place do you think I run here?'

'I... I don't know. If I believed your press—'

'Don't believe my press,' he warned.

'Y-you seem to forget I've got a b-brother,' she stammered.

'And?'

'And until Luc got married I wouldn't have put anything past him.'

He huffed a dry laugh. 'Getting married certainly slows a man down.'

She took a moment and then visibly recovered. Drawing herself up, she said, 'I don't expect that's anything you have to worry about.'

He shrugged, 'Your brother's a greatly changed man—and for the better, in my opinion.'

She had to agree with that. Luc had made a good choice of wife, and Emma had no trouble putting up with him, by all accounts.

'I've never seen my brother so happy,' Karina confirmed. 'Emma's been good for him, but the two of you are so similar I don't know how she puts up with him.'

'I don't know what you mean.'

'Use your imagination,' she suggested.

That was a very dangerous idea where Karina was concerned.

CHAPTER TWELVE

KARINA WAS SHOWERING, feeling tense, tracing her scars as she thought about Dante naked in the shower stall next to her. Every part of her was tingling and aware, but her emotions were in turmoil. She couldn't let him touch her again. It had raised the ghosts of the past and stirred them up into a shrieking frenzy. She should never have agreed to this.

What made it even more poignant, more painful was that on the night of her eighteenth birthday it hadn't been all about sex. There had been quiet times when they had lain naked on the bed, staring into each other's eyes, when she had believed they had never been closer. She'd been so naïve, imagining that making love with Dante meant they'd stay together for ever, and now here she was, blundering into another emotion-fuelled mistake.

She stilled as he turned off the shower.

'I'll be waiting for you outside, Karina.'

'Okay.'

Turning off the water, she reached for a towel. Confident he'd left the changing room, she stepped out of her own shower stall to find Dante just a few feet away. In the split second it took her to realise that he had his back turned and couldn't see her scars, ice shot through her.

Her heart lurched a second time. There weren't many men with a back view as good as their front, but Dante was one of them. He had a towel slung around his waist and was dripping water everywhere as he eased his powerful shoulder muscles in a gesture she was all too familiar with.

She stiffened as he turned to look at her.

Without losing eye contact, she reached blindly for another towel. He frowned as she wrapped it tightly around her. 'No need for that, Karina. The masseur's waiting for you.'

No point?

She made a disappointed face. 'I'm afraid I really have to take a rain check—not that I don't appreciate the offer of a massage, but by the time I dry my hair—'

'You're coming with me,' he said firmly.

Dante took hold of her arm to guide her out of the changing rooms, but she pulled back.

'What are you frightened of, Karina?'

'Nothing.'

He stared at her for a moment. 'Five more minutes to dry your hair and then I'm coming back for you.'

When he'd gone she stared in the mirror at her rabbit-in-the-headlights face. She couldn't keep running like this for ever.

'Where do I go for this massage?' she asked, when she came out of the changing room.

Barefoot, but dressed in jeans and a black top that emphasised his powerful physique, Dante led the way to the far end of the gym, where a luxurious sunken area had been designed to induce peace and relaxation. There were comfortable sofas and massage beds arranged around a decorative fountain; the scent of essential oils fragranced the air.

'Shall I lie down here and wait? You don't need to stay with me...'

Her voice was shaking and she realised she had backed up against one of the comfortable beds. The frame was jabbing into her lower back.

'What are you doing?' she exclaimed as Dante tried to take one of her towels away.

'You can't have a massage while you're wrapped up like a mummy,' he pointed out.

'I'm sure the masseur will tell me when to lose them,' she protested, taking a step to one side.

She frowned as she watched Dante pick out a bottle of massage oil from the selection on the shelf. 'Shouldn't we wait for the masseur to do that?'

And then the penny dropped. Dante had no intention of calling a masseur.

Bolts of alarm stabbed at her chest. She couldn't do this. She had gone along with it up to now to allay his suspicions, but this was as far as she could go. It had to stop.

'Get on the couch, Karina.'

Her mind was racing as she tried to find a way out of her predicament.

'Okay,' she agreed finally. 'But we do this my way.'

Dante's stare was dark and amused. That was how she planned for it to stay.

'This starts with you,' she said firmly.

His brow creased as he looked at her, and then his lips pressed down with amusement. 'I have absolutely no objection to being dominated.'

'Good,' she said lightly. 'Now we've got that settled, would you like to undress and lie down?'

All that was left was for her to instruct her heart to continue beating and breath to enter her lungs.

Dante had absolutely no worries about exposing his body to her and Karina hid her blush as he deftly stripped off his shirt and jeans. Turning towards the robes she'd noticed hanging nearby, she grabbed one and put it on over her towels before dropping them to the floor. Dumping them in a wicker basket marked 'Laundry', she belted her robe and an oil to use on Dante, choosing sandalwood—sultry, spicy and perfect for him. Warming it between her palms, she tried not to let her gaze linger on his powerful body, which was now stretched face down on the couch, awaiting her attention.

He shifted position impatiently. 'When you're ready...'

'I thought this was supposed to be our chance to relax? What's your hurry?'

'We've both got work to do,' he growled.

'Thank you for reminding me,' she said dryly, and with a deep breath she began, but not before she'd draped a towel over his taut buttocks. If she couldn't see them she would be able to resist feeling them beneath her hands!

Dante tensed the moment her hands touched him. She hadn't expected that. She hadn't expected the muscle memory in her fingers to hold such an acute recollection of the play of muscle beneath his skin. Her breathing quickened when he groaned with pleasure. She was obviously doing something right. Applying more pressure, she allowed herself to enjoy his silky heat. His body was hard and muscular, and there were sinister ink whorls on his powerful back and on his biceps. The staggering width and strength in his shoulders, tapering to a lean waist, reminded her how she'd felt when he'd loomed over her.

He was built to scale, she remembered, her mind going

back to that night. Thinking about such things was easy
and safe, but actually *doing* anything like that again was
another story; a story that was lost in the darkest part of
her mind...

'Giving up already?' he demanded.

She swallowed convulsively, caught in the act of an
extremely erotic thought. 'Of course not.'

She grew in confidence and Dante relaxed. Leaning
over him, she threw all her weight into the massage,
kneading his knotted muscles until they softened. She
had plenty of time to think about the man she was getting to know all over again. Before she'd come to his
ranch she'd had a vague idea that he would live in soli-
tary splendour with an army of servants to do his bid-
ding, when now she knew that nothing could be further
from the truth—

'Is that it?'

She was startled to find Dante sitting up and staring
her in the face.

He shrugged and swung off the couch when she didn't
reply, tucking the towel she'd covered him with around
his waist. 'Your turn now,' he said.

She flinched back as he stripped away the linen sheet
he'd been lying on and replaced it with a clean one.
'Well?' he prompted. 'What are you waiting for?'

She couldn't move. She was filled with dread, but if
she made him wait he would become more suspicious
than ever. If she did as he asked, he'd see what she had
been trying to hide from him.

She'd gone too far to get out of it, she decided, and her
back was a safe zone. Unbelting her robe and slipping
it down her shoulders she climbed up on the table and
made sure she was lying on her stomach. Nervously, she

waited—and tensed when Dante moved the robe down further but still covering her buttocks.

She relaxed as much as she could—which wasn't much at all—and remained on full alert when he moved away. She couldn't see what he was doing and the anticipation was killing her. The first touch of his hands nearly sent her into orbit. It delivered shockwaves to every part of her body. Her nipples pebbled, her breath quickened, and her body moistened, though she had contracted like a sea urchin flinching from a touch.

Sensing she was super-wired, he soothed her with long, firm strokes. Dante had always been the master of pleasure, and he knew just which muscles to work. He began at her shoulders and worked his way down her body with wicked skill. She was annoyed with herself for responding so eagerly, but all it took was a few short minutes and it was as if his hands had lifted the tension out of her, allowing her body to respond and soften, allowing her troubled mind to forget. Turning her face into the sun-bleached sheet, she inhaled deeply as she allowed herself to enjoy the experience of having Dante work her body. It was impossible not to progress her thoughts to that other night, and that deeper pleasure when she'd been in heaven, or somewhere very close.

When he stopped she almost cried out with disappointment, and only relaxed when he drizzled more oil on her back. The oil was warm and Dante's touch was soothing, and very soon the last of her tension had seeped away. Turning her head, she risked a glance at him, and saw the warmth and humour in his eyes.

Humour had always been her undoing where Dante was concerned. It was his most lethal weapon. She turned her face back into the sheet again, smiling. Humour was

personal between them. It brought them close, and had
done since they'd been young. She thought again about
the night of the party, when Dante and her brother's
friends had teased her as a matter of course. She'd given
back as good as she'd got, accusing them of being more
use to a horse than a woman and then not much use at all.
They had laughed and drifted away…all except Dante.

'Don't you trust me, Karina?'

'Sorry?' She was confused for a moment as the past
and the present clashed.

'I asked you to turn over,' he repeated.

'Onto my back?' The consequences of doing so destroyed her relaxation at a stroke.

'Unless there's another side of you I don't know
about?' Dante murmured to himself.

Grabbing for the towel he presented her with, she covered herself and sat up. 'That was great. Thanks. But I'm
done.' She was already swinging off the table. 'I need
another shower,' she explained. 'I'm covered in oil—'

Breath rushed out of her as Dante scooped her off
the couch.

'Where are you taking me?'

'Where I should have taken you from the start.'

He was striding down the gym. Panic overwhelmed
her and she stiffened like a board. A surprised breath shot
out of her when he set her down outside the door. Ball-
ing his hands into fists, he slammed them into the wall
on either side of her face.

'What's wrong with you, Karina?' he gritted out.

Apart from her longing for shadows to hide in, or a
door to slip through, did he mean? All out of options, she
turned her face away from his.

'Don't hide from me,' Dante ground out, and cupping her chin he forced her to look at him.

'What's wrong with *you*, Dante? Do you find it so hard to believe that there's a woman in this world who can resist you?'

'You know that this has nothing to do with sex.'

'Do I?'

'And if it were, is that so terrible? I've seen the way you look at me. Either you're lying to yourself or you have a problem, Karina. Which is it?'

Firming her lips, she refused to speak.

Letting her go with a frustrated sigh, he stood back. 'I give up. Get dressed.'

Pulling away from him, she stalked angrily back to the changing room, where she found her clothes and tugged them on. She didn't care about her appearance or her hair. She just wanted to get away—away from Dante and his scrutiny, and his questions.

But he was waiting for her on the other side of the door. Slouched on one hip with his hands dug into his pockets, he leaned back against the wall. 'Before this project forced you out of the shadows, you were hiding away in your brother's hotel.'

'Hardly hiding,' she argued. 'I was working for my living.'

'Living life vicariously,' he continued, as if she hadn't said a word. 'Arranging other people's big occasions. Making other people happy, and making a name for yourself into the bargain. I think that was a side benefit you hadn't expected.'

'Any more words of wisdom or can I go?' Drawing herself up, she looked past him.

'You do a good job, I don't deny it,' Dante continued

unperturbed, 'but the fact that you were *so* good brought you to everyone's attention, which I imagine was the last thing you had in mind—especially when it brought you to *my* attention.'

'You are one arrogant—'

'You have a gift for organisation,' he said, talking over her in a low, intense voice. 'You cast your fairy dust on every party or event, but then your carefully constructed house of cards came crashing down when I walked back into your life. You couldn't ignore your secrets then, could you, Karina? For years you've done everything you could to avoid me, but now I'm back. The one person you should have confided in is back, and you won't get away with silence now.'

Huffing out a frustrated breath, she shook her head firmly. 'I have nothing to tell you.'

'You're a liar.' He pushed his face into hers. 'You never used to be a liar, Karina. So, what's happened to change you?'

'You,' she said icily. Her passion had soared way past the danger level, and caution had gone out of the window as they confronted each other unblinking. 'You think you know so much about me—but did you also know that I was a virgin that night?'

'Deus!'

She had the satisfaction of seeing Dante's look of horror, but little else. She was ashamed of herself for telling him that way. She had never meant to use it as a weapon, and on her birthday night she hadn't wanted to stop him. She had wanted to go the whole way with Dante, and had set out to do just that. Dante hadn't taken advantage of her. She had taken advantage of him.

'If this is this the truth, Karina, why didn't you tell me?'

'Why didn't you ask?'

'You—' Dante broke off to rake his hair in the familiar gesture that made her feel guiltier than ever, for springing something else on him that he couldn't possibly have known. 'Why, Karina?' His eyes were black with emotion.

'I thought you'd laugh at me if I told you.'

'Laugh at you?' he demanded incredulously.

'We didn't have that type of relationship. We were friends. I was a tomboy—one of the gang. You were always bragging about your conquests, all of you.'

He gave a short laugh. 'I didn't make love to you because you were one of the gang.'

'We were both wild that night—reckless.' Her mouth dried as she remembered. 'That's how we were—how you expected me to be. I didn't want you to think I was…soft.'

'It isn't soft to be a virgin. It's a life choice, and one some people stick to because it suits them.'

Shaking her head, she disagreed. 'Don't make me out to be some sort of saint when I was stupid and naïve. I wanted you. I wanted a magical end to my birthday. I didn't think any further than that. And it was special— for me at least. It was everything I'd ever dreamed of and so much more. But then you sent me from your bed and I was devastated. How do you think I can trust you now?'

'I made a mistake,' Dante admitted. 'You were savvy and smart, and we moved with the same wild group. You seemed to know it all. You were so beautiful that night and I wanted you. There seemed no point in waiting once you made it clear that you felt the same.'

'If you'd known I was a virgin, would it have made a difference?'

'Honestly?' His lips pressed down as he thought about

it. 'No, not if that was what you had wanted. But I would have been more careful with you.'

He groaned as he thought back to a night of hot, hungry passion when a go-slow had never been on the cards. 'I wanted you for all the wrong reasons. You were like a flame, drawing every man at the party towards your heat, and I had to have you. I had to claim you to show everyone you were mine.'

'And then you had to discard me?'

'And then I came to my senses,' he argued. 'I tried to save you from myself—a man who was nowhere near ready to settle down. I know you were trying to pretend you were someone else that night, and you're doing it again. You won't tell me what's hurt you, because you think you can tough it out on your own. How's that been going for you so far, Karina?'

'Let it go, Dante. Our lives have moved on.'

He shook his head. 'You carried my child. You're my friend—or you used to be. You're Luc's sister. Choose any reason you like, but that makes you my concern whether you want to be or not. You can't hold this poison inside you for ever or it will rot you from the inside out.'

'Let the past be!' she exclaimed. 'I don't need anyone to rescue me, especially not you. I've done okay and I'll do even better in the future. Yes, I was wild and, yes, I got pregnant, but when I lost my baby I knew my wild days were over for good, and there was only one way back, which was to have a purpose in life. Only then could I find my way forward again. You're wrong about me hiding away in Luc's hotel. I went after a career with the same single-minded determination that I went after you that night.' She dashed her tears away impatiently.

'And if our baby had lived, I would have done everything I could to be a good mother.'

'You don't have to convince me. I know that's true. But we're talking about then, and this is now, Karina. Let me help you. It's not a sign of weakness to reach out, and if you're in trouble, please, trust me enough to help you make it right.'

'You can't,' she said flatly, withdrawing like a wounded animal into her burrow.

'*Deus*, Karina! How are we going to work together if we can't communicate on any level?'

'This conversation has nothing to do with my work, and my personal life has nothing to do with you.'

'It has everything to do with me,' Dante argued fiercely. 'If someone I care about hurts, I won't turn my back on them.'

She shook her head and stubbornly refused to change her mind. 'In my case you'll have to make an exception.'

CHAPTER THIRTEEN

SHE GLANCED LONGINGLY towards the ranch house.

'Yes, you should go,' Dante agreed. 'Why don't you just give up and go home? I'm sure you can find a replacement to organise the polo cup.' He shook his head with annoyance.

Karina was annoyed with herself. Luc had taught her not to be a victim. Her brother had instilled in her the necessity for a spine of steel. Was walking out now the way to repay him?

'I'm not going anywhere until I've finished this job,' she said firmly.

Dante shook his head. 'It's not that easy, Karina. That decision is no longer yours to make. Either you tell me what you're hiding or you can leave.'

'You're threatening me?'

Dante remained silent.

'I have one week left. In that time I'll draw up my initial plans. The rest I can do from Rio. I'll tell you everything you want to know—'

'When will that be?' Dante asked harshly. 'Will you tell me to my face? Or will you text me on your way home? Perhaps you'll remember to send me an email when you get back to the safety of Rio. Why should I believe anything you say, when you stun me with the news that you were a virgin that night—horrify me with the fact that you lost our baby, and then hold back on this? You're not a woman I recognise, Karina. You've become a stranger to me.'

Stung and shocked by Dante's coldness, she fired back at him, 'And you're a man without a heart—a man who pushes everyone away except strangers, because they never get too close, do they, Dante? You bring people to your ranch and do so much good work on the projects, but by your own admission you don't know the name of a single person you help. You're more damaged than I am. You were hurt as a child and you still bear the scars of your father's contempt. You shy away from relationships. You're frightened of love. You're frightened to lay yourself open to hurt again.'

'I'm not frightened of anything!' His laughter was cruel as if he meant to hurt her.

'Prove it!' she challenged.

Driving his mouth down on hers, he did exactly that, kissing every rational thought from her head. Numb with shock for a moment, she felt his need as her own and kissed him back. Matching his passion, she fuelled it, knowing she had driven him to this. They had driven each other to the extremes of what it was possible for either of them to withstand.

And Dante's wasn't gentle with her, or playful, as he had been in the swimming pool. His kiss was the kiss of a man on the edge. She might have secrets but he had a whole world of hurt and bitter confusion inside him. Deep in his emotional core Dante Baracca, the hero of so many, was still trying to make sense of what he could have done to make his father hate him.

She knew the answer. He'd done nothing wrong. Dante thought no one knew, but people talked, and as a child she'd heard how he'd saved his mother from his father's violence, which had been the noblest, bravest thing a son could do. Dante had surpassed his father in every way, and that was his only fault. He'd had rebuilt his life as well as the family ranch where so many people came to explore new possibilities. She ached for him and cried for him, and for everything they'd lost.

He tasted salt on her lips and knew without doubt that for all her complex, stubborn ways there was no other woman on earth like Karina. She infuriated him, she frustrated him beyond measure but, then, she always had. There was only one Karina, only one woman who knew what made him tick. She knew his strengths and the weakness he never showed the world. She knew everything about him. He didn't have to explain his past.

There had been times when a sympathetic glance, or a brush of the hand, had been all that had been needed for two young people to acknowledge what had been going on at home, and it had helped them to know they hadn't been alone, and now it was enough to be together. Being with Karina was so natural it was like *coming* home, and even better when the pace of his kisses slowed and gentled and she softened in his arms.

There had been times when she had doubted they could ever recapture the closeness they had known, but now... She gasped with pleasure as Dante feathered kisses down her neck, and moaned softly when he rasped his stubble against her skin. The sensation transferred to every part of her, making her yearn, making her moist, and making her thrill with excitement, knowing she could feel normal again. With Dante it seemed that anything was possible.

'We've got all the time in the world,' he murmured as she tightened her hold on him. 'There's no rush, Karina.'

But she was in a rush to prove there was nothing wrong with her, and pressing against him she shivered with desire as his mouth brushed her ear, her cheek, her lips…

'Are you cold?' he asked, when she shivered.

She laughed softly. 'Anything but.'

He smiled into her eyes. 'And you trust me?'

He kept on kissing her as he led her back into the house, and in between those kisses he whispered outrageous suggestions that made her laugh, that made her lust, that made her believe they could pick up where they'd left off. He told her she made him happy. He made her smile. The closeness she had once taken for granted, and which had proved so elusive as they'd grown up, seemed to have returned.

They were still laughing when they reached the foot of the staircase—faces close, arms entwined, gazes locked on each other. She had never felt closer to another human in her life than she felt to Dante. And now he began to remind her of all the tricks she had used to play on him—innocent times before life and all its difficulties had caught up with them. The warmth they'd known had returned full force, she thought as he took her up the stairs. She was so lost in laughter and good memories she barely noticed crossing the threshold into his room.

'Don't pull back now,' he joked, not realising she was serious.

Her gaze darted about, taking in her masculine surroundings. An enormous bed filled her vision. She was transfixed by it as Dante took hold of her hand.

'Is there a problem?' he murmured, smiling down into her eyes.

'No. Of course not,' she said tensely. She flashed a smile meant to reassure him, and then he kissed her again and she wondered what she had been worried about.

'I'm going to make love to you—really make love to you,' he promised, as he steered her across the room. 'I want to make up for lost time.'

Dante was happy—confident—confident in her and her response, but she was already tense at the thought that he wouldn't want her when he knew.

'I'm sorry—'

Pulling back his head, he stared down at her in surprise. 'What do you have to be sorry about?'

So much she didn't know where to begin.

Lifting her into his arms, he carried her to the bed and she stared into the face she had loved since she was a child. This was right, this was good, she told herself firmly. She was a healthy female, and every part of her body was responding to Dante as it should. Nothing could go wrong this time.

When he lowered her to the floor at the side of the bed she reached out to free his top from the waistband of his jeans. Hooking his thumb into the back of the neck, he brought the top over his head, displaying the beautiful torso the cameras loved almost as much as she did. She would never get used to the sight of Dante naked. He was breathtaking. His stare on her face was dark and certain. He didn't need to tell her that he wanted her when she could see it in his eyes, and knew he would see the same in her own.

But would her body allow this?

'Karina?'

Sensing her abstraction, Dante clasped her shoulders to bring her back into the moment. She smiled up at him, though not before an involuntary swallow on a dry throat had gripped her. She could do this, she told herself again. She kept her gaze steady on his face to prove that she could—to him and to her.

'If you have any doubts…'

'I don't,' she insisted. This was Dante, and nothing was going to spoil it for her. Dante and Karina. Karina and Dante. Fate had always meant them to be together.

Tracing the broad sweep of his shoulders with her hands, she leaned forward to kiss his chest. Dragging greedily on his familiar clean, musky scent, she kissed him again. She wanted him to know how committed she was to this. She wanted him to know that this was quite different from the last time when her virginity had been hidden from him. Turning her face up to his, she stared him in the eyes and saw everything she'd hoped to see. Even the fact that Dante was so obviously holding back made her want him all the more. Her body was hungry for him and in no mood to wait. Moving restlessly against him, she closed her eyes, shutting out the last of her doubts.

She stiffened a little when he took off her bra, and then reminded herself that she was hidden in the dark. And then he touched her and the pleasure was extreme. When he cupped her breasts she groaned with pleasure and forgot everything but Dante's touch. It sent sensation streaming through her, and, more than physical, the way he touched her plumbed her emotions, making tears spring to her eyes. They were together, and that was all that mattered. They could never make up for what they'd lost, but they could start again.

Lowering her onto the bed, he lay down beside her. She was his, body and soul. Stretching out his length against hers, he smiled into her eyes. His face was inches away and in shadow, but she could sense the warmth in his face and hear his certainty in his steady breathing. He could seduce her just by being close, she mused wryly.

Reaching down, she found his belt buckle and freed it, and then she lowered the zip, her hand brushing the hard proof of his desire. Far from being intimidating, she longed to have him inside her.

No fear at all? How long would that last?

It would be all right. She would make it right. They were discovering each other all over again, only now they were old enough to commit on a deeper level. There wasn't a part of her that didn't crave Dante's touch, a part of her that didn't crave his love. He would never hurt her. Nothing could hurt her now.

He was devoted to Karina and to her pleasure. Whatever else he had expected today, it hadn't been this complete and welcome reversal into the girl he remembered, the girl who had used to be such a big part of his life. There was only one Karina. Even when she had avoided him, his hungry gaze had sought her out at every match. He'd got into the habit of scanning the crowd at polo matches, knowing he wouldn't play his best unless Karina was watching. He had never had the chance to tell her that she was his lodestone, his totem, and that when he had needed a reality check only Karina could challenge him and bring him down to earth. He'd missed that. He'd missed her. He'd missed the woman who could push her own concerns aside so she could help everyone else.

He'd been determined to have her the night of her party—determined to keep her, until things had gone so badly wrong. His callous behaviour had split them apart like a thunderbolt, forging a chasm between them and leading to tragic consequences.

Consequences Karina had been forced to go through alone.

'Dante?'

She had brought the sheet up to her chin, and was clinging to it like a comfort blanket. He eased down the bed to reassure her. He kissed and caressed her until she relaxed. He didn't need to test her to know that she was ready, but he wasn't taking a single chance this time. She cried out with pleasure at his intimate touch when he plundered her lush folds. She was soft and moist and swollen, and so ready for him that when he traced a finger lightly over her, she clung to him, gasping with need.

He protected them both. His aim was simple. He wanted to make up for that night. He wanted to hear her sigh with pleasure in his arms, and he wanted to take his time getting her to that place. But Karina didn't want to wait. It was almost as if she had something to prove—to him, to herself, he wasn't sure which. He only knew that she was responding with such fierce need it was sending him crazy with desire for her. But still he made himself wait. After everything she'd been through, caring for Karina was his only concern. It was his test, his trial by fire, and he would come through for her.

'I want you, Dante.'

'I know you do.'

She was still clinging to the sheet, but he understood

her modesty. She was even more beautiful than he remembered, and he found her vulnerability endearing.

She writhed with pleasure on the cool, crisp sheets, while Dante's hands worked their magic on her body. She was gaining in confidence every moment as he intensified her pleasure. There were no doubts left. She was as normal as any other woman. Dante had led her to a place of exquisite pleasure, and everything he did proved his care for her.

Throwing back her arms in an attitude of absolute trust, she held his stare as he moved over her. She sucked in one sharp breath when he teased her with the tip or his arousal, but then he did no more than draw it back and forth, which felt so incredible. She wanted him so badly she was aching for him and, acting on instinct, she arched up to claim him, but the instant he dipped inside her she pulled back.

'Karina?'

'I can't! Stop! Please... *Stop!*'

Tears of shame and failure sprang to her eyes as she pressed her hands against his chest in an attempt to push him away.

CHAPTER FOURTEEN

IT WAS A reflex action. She couldn't have stopped herself pushing Dante away if she'd tried. She had thought she was cured, that Dante had cured her, but her fear of love-making was instinctive. She had failed. She was broken. There was no cure.

She wasn't sure what she had expected from him, but it wasn't this. Dante had caught her tightly in his arms and he was holding her as if he had pulled her back from an abyss. Softening his grip, he brought her close and held her like a baby, but when he spoke his voice was firm. 'No more lies, Karina. I know I haven't done this to you, so who has?'

There was no going back now. Even if the truth drove him away, she had no option but to tell him. Sucking in a shuddering breath, she picked through her mangled thoughts in an attempt to make sense of the incomprehensible. Her fear was real, but irrational, and she had never spoken of it out loud before. 'After I lost—'

'I know that part,' Dante whispered, as he stroked her hair. 'Take your time.'

She did as he said and took longer to pull herself together. 'I had to rebuild my life,' she said then. 'A life I believed you were no longer part of.'

'And with good reason,' he agreed.

'While I was recovering, I knew I could do one of two things. I could retreat from the world or I could get back in the saddle and take another tilt at it.'

'And you decided to get back in the saddle.'

'Yes, I did. But then I discovered that moving too fast is not a good thing when your life is in turmoil. My judgement was off. Going away to college was the right thing to do. I made some good friends, and I found something I had a flair for. If I'd left it there and come home after my course, everything would have been okay, but I was too needy—'

'You were vulnerable,' Dante argued.

'Don't make excuses for me.' She pulled the sheet tight. 'I stayed on, and then there were complications...' She stopped and frowned.

'Go on,' Dante prompted.

'There was a man—one of my college tutors.'

'Older than you?'

'Much older,' she confirmed. 'But I was mature enough to know what I was doing.'

'You'd lost a baby. You were alone.'

'My head was all over the place, but because things had gone so well with the course and my friends it was easy to persuade myself I was ready for everything else—a new relationship, for example... Someone to help me get over you.'

'You were looking for reassurance, which is hardly surprising,' Dante agreed.

'Don't try to make me feel better. Everything that happened was my fault.'

He shrugged. 'I can't comment. You haven't told me what happened yet.'

'I'm not going to pretend to you. I was like a ship without an anchor and for a short time this man made me feel safe.'

Now she saw the expression she had expected to see on Dante's face: the face from the posters, a face turned grim; a man no one crossed, unless they had a death wish.

'He made you feel safe because you had no one else to confide in, and he took advantage of that fact. This happened, not because of something you did.' Dante's face blackened. 'It happened because I wasn't there for you when you lost the baby.'

'No.' She shook her head decisively. 'I was weak. And it ended badly,' she added. 'And you don't need to hear the rest.'

'You can't stop now, Karina.'

As Dante's black eyes blazed into hers she knew he was right. Inhaling raggedly, she told him the rest of it. 'I thought I could forget you if I was with someone else. I thought I could forget that night and start over. I thought it would dull the pain of…'

This time he didn't try to rush her. He waited until she was ready to start again, and she had never appreciated his calm strength more.

'I knew it wouldn't be exciting, but…' she stopped again and pulled a face as she thought back '…it would definitely be calmer,' she said at last, staring into the distance as she put herself back in the past. 'I pictured myself contented—settled down—an academic's wife even. Perhaps it wasn't the life I'd dreamed about but, then, my fantasies had always let me down.'

'So you slept with him?'

Dante's face was rigid. 'If I'm going to tell you, please let me finish.'

He nodded.

'He wasn't you, but you were no longer part of my life. Someone as different from you as possible seemed the logical answer at the time. It all came to a head one night when he'd taken me out for a meal. I'd had too much to drink. He took me back to his place. I'd seen this coming for a while, which was probably why I drank too much in a failed attempt to numb myself. That's why he's not wholly to blame,' she insisted. 'It's not like I was an innocent, walking into this with my eyes shut. I used him to get over you.'

'Losing a baby would affect you in all sorts of ways,' Dante growled. 'Did he know what you'd been through?'

'Yes, of course. He was my tutor. We were supposed to confide things like that so the tutors could reach out to help us.'

Dante's expression turned grim. 'So you told him everything and he took advantage of your fragile mental state.'

'I allowed him to do it,' she argued stubbornly. 'After losing the baby I felt like a failure. I didn't know if I would ever be anything but—'

'*Deus*, Karina! So, he made it his mission to prove you wrong?' He stared into her face intently. 'How could you put yourself in such a vulnerable position?' And then he slumped back. 'You were already in a vulnerable position,' he groaned softly, answering his own question.

'I had this idea that sex and I were enemies,' she went on over Dante's pain. 'I had to confront my enemy and conquer my fears. If necessary, I was prepared to face the alternative—a life without sex. Lots of people live perfectly happy lives without sex,' she insisted, when Dante stared at her.

'Not in my world,' he ground out.

'Your world's different from most other people's,' she said wryly. 'There's a popular conception that you only have to be young and healthy to be at it like rabbits, but I broke that mould, because I don't like sex.'

Dante's scowl broke into an incredulous laugh. 'And you say that because of your professor?' And then his face darkened again. 'Or are you saying it because of what happened with me?'

She shook her head and thought back. 'He took me to supper and then to bed. I told myself it would be all right. I had put myself on the Pill—belatedly, I know. I just couldn't face another loss. And I had squirrelled away a tube of lubrication, so I can hardly claim to be the innocent party here.' She ignored Dante's look and went on, 'I thought to myself, What can possibly go wrong? He'd do it. I'd be over you, and I would have proved myself normal.'

'So what went wrong with this master plan?' Dante was practically snarling.

'I couldn't do it. When it came to it, I just couldn't do it.' Raising her head, she blazed a look into his eyes. 'Why can't you men accept that some women just don't like sex?'

'Don't speak of me in the same breath as that man,' he warned softly. He let a few moments pass, and then prompted gently, 'Are you ready to tell me the rest?'

She drew a steadying breath. 'I did everything he asked, but then he couldn't do it.' Ignoring Dante's facial expression, she tried to explain. 'He said it was my fault because I wouldn't relax. He said I was too tight for him. I tried to help him but I couldn't, and then he was angry with me, and that's when he fell into a rage—'

'The insect that bit you?' Dante's tone was incredulous.

Lowering the sheet, she took hold of his hand and moved his fingertips slowly over the rest of her scars. 'I ran into a swarm of insects.'

He hissed through his teeth, but let her continue.

'He beat me so much that eventually I fell out of bed, but not before he broke my nose.' Touching it, she huffed a humourless laugh, remembering. 'It wouldn't stop bleeding so I had to go to the emergency room.'

'Did he take you there?'

'No. Of course not. I took myself. He said he was glad to be rid of me, and that I was a pathetic excuse for a woman. Narrow escape, huh?' She tried to smile, but it didn't come off. 'While I was in the emergency room a nurse gave me a full exam. She said it was usual when there was so much bruising. It wasn't just my nose,' she added, quickly staring down to avoid Dante's molten magma stare.

'I told the nurse everything—how he'd tried with his hand, and even with a sex toy he'd bought. It was all a waste of time. I'd...closed up completely. I couldn't understand what had happened to me, until the nurse explained that it's a recognised medical condition. It can be due to physical causes, she told me, though in my case she thought it was more of a psychological reaction to losing the baby and then the violence of that night. She said it wasn't something I could control, and that it would take time and therapy. She fixed me up with a therapist who told me I was lucky I hadn't been raped.' She glanced up. 'That was the end of the therapist. I didn't feel lucky. I felt dirty and ashamed.'

'And now?' Dante's voice was gentle.

'And now I shouldn't be here,' she said, changing her tone to bright and cheerful.

'Because?'

'Because now we both know that there's something wrong with me—and that it could get in the way of our work here.'

'There's nothing wrong with you, Karina.' Dante stated that with such certainty that she didn't even try to resist when he drew her into his arms. 'You've had one trauma after another, and have never given yourself a chance to recover. You're too hard on yourself,' he said, as he pulled back to stare into her face. 'Sometimes it's not possible to bounce back just because we decide it's time. Sometimes we have to ask for help—even you, Karina.' Holding her arms lightly, he brought her in front of him. 'Do you want me to find some professional help for you?'

'No!' She recoiled at the thought.

'You only have to say the word and I'll arrange it with someone who knows what they're doing.'

'Sorry.' Shuddering, she drew in a breath. 'I don't mean to sound ungrateful. It's just that I've tried therapy and I know it doesn't work for me. I honestly think it would set me back.' She said nothing for a long time and then she looked at him. 'Could you help me?'

'I'm going to help you,' Dante confirmed, as if there could be any doubt. 'And I'll do it by starting from scratch.'

'What does that mean?'

'We both know the clock is ticking as far as this event is concerned, so neither of us has the time to concentrate properly on anything else until it's over.'

'What are you saying Dante?'

Easing back, he lifted his shoulders in an easy shrug.

'Whatever happens next will happen naturally, or it won't happen at all.'

Fear of losing him swamped her as he left the bed. She watched him scoop up his jeans and tug them on, feeling she'd already lost him.

'I'm going to leave you to sleep now.' His face was set. His eyes were cool. 'I'll take one of the guest rooms. Tomorrow work on your report. When you're finished, I'll read it. Then we'll have a meeting and decide where to go from here.'

He might even fire her, she thought. Her lips felt wooden as she commented lightly, 'That sounds a bit cold-blooded.'

Dante's stare steadied on her face. 'It is.'

She had to tell herself that what he had suggested made perfect sense, but that didn't stop a chill of apprehension rushing through her. Where would they go from here? Anywhere?

She would concentrate on the event to the exclusion of everything else, she told herself firmly. She would make it the best it could be. She would forget her worthy ideas and go full out for carnival at the Gaucho Cup. She got out of bed, making sure to wrap the sheet tightly around her as she swung her legs over the side. She gasped when Dante snatched the sheet away, leaving her completely naked.

'This is your last day of being a victim, Karina. You're moving forward from now on. You took a wrong turning and that's all.' He shrugged. 'We all make mistakes, as I should know. And here's something else...' He brought his face close. 'You've got me. Understood?'

Did he mean that? Whether he did or not, Dante was right. She would fight back. One day at a time. If she took small steps, instead of trying to leap across chasms, they might even make it together one day, but she couldn't put her life on hold until then. The next time she met Dante it would be on an equal footing, or not at all.

They worked non-stop for the next week, with no time to pause for discussions about anything other than the event, but that didn't mean she stopped feeling. In fact, the cooler Dante became, the more she yearned for his personal attention, but he was clever. He knew her too well. They'd paused for coffee in the yard on her last day on his ranch. Maria had brought it out for them on a tray.

She slanted a glance at him as he issued orders, drank coffee, tapped notes into his phone, and answered questions—anything but mention what had happened between them. Somehow that made his big, powerful body a source of fascination. Had she really shrunk from that? It seemed impossible in theory. Looking at him now, she wanted nothing more than to rub every inch of her against his hard frame. She wanted to taste that bronze skin and, yes, she wanted to remind herself that the straining bulge in his jeans really was that big.

'You look happy,' he commented, sliding her a look.

'Do I?' She glanced around, hoping he hadn't noticed her interest in the manifold attractions of his body. What was wrong with her? She could lust like any normal woman—could yearn for a man's arms around her. She could think the most erotic thoughts, but when it came down to it—

'We'd better get on,' he said, heading off.

Working alongside Dante was a revelation. He was brilliant. Fast thinking and decisive, he was the perfect partner. She had never worked with an associate before. Certainly not one as hot as Dante, she reflected as she walked behind him with the sole purpose of admiring his impressive iron-hard butt. She didn't know anyone else who worked the hours she did, and who barely slept when there was a project to nail down—though the work ethic was a good thing. It kept her sane when frustration of the very real and sexual kind was nagging at her constantly.

If only she could be normal. But if she were there was no time to indulge herself—not at this pace of work. Although, if Dante would care to toss another bucket of icy well water over his head, as he had done this morning in the yard, she was quite happy to take some down time to admire his naked torso—

'Karina?'

'Just thinking through things—making sure I haven't missed anything.' Maintaining an expression of wide-eyed innocence was getting harder by the hour.

'Time to stop thinking and get doing.'

Was he smiling when he turned away? Those black eyes of his were so expressive. And he knew just how to play her. Dante was the master of torment, the maestro of seduction—and he knew it, she thought as he walked away. There was a swagger in his stride and a confidence she suspected had nothing to do with the polo cup.

She braced herself to go and see him before she left the ranch. Half a dozen people were in his study, but he sent them out when she arrived. They both knew she only had a few minutes as a pilot was waiting on the airstrip to take her back to Rio. Final arrangements for the match had reached fever pitch.

'Got everything you need?' he asked.

Not nearly, she thought, taking him in. 'Everything. Thank you.' With his fists braced on the desk as he leaned over it, Dante was like a pent-up volcano just waiting to erupt. It was no surprise to her that he had held the meeting standing up. All that energy…

'I've got something for you.'

'For me?' Her heart stopped.

'A keepsake.' Straightening up, he dug into the back pocket of his jeans and brought out a stone. 'Here—take it.'

She knew what it was and looked at him in surprise. 'Are you sure?' She knew enough about them to know that uncut emeralds were worth a fortune.

'It's just a rough, hard rock.' He said this wryly and she got the message. 'It improves once it's polished up.'

'Some things are fine as they are,' she said, taking it from him.

The corner of his mouth lifted. 'I knew you'd appreciate it.'

She smiled. 'I do. Thank you,' she said quietly, tucking it away in her pocket.

The silence changed and suddenly she felt awkward. Should they kiss on the cheek or shake hands—or neither of the above? She decided to maintain the honoured client routine and shook his hand briefly. That seemed to amuse him, though he overruled the smile and turned his expression to neutral.

She had her hand on the handle on the door when he said, 'You're okay, Karina. You can do this. You don't need anyone now.'

She turned to flash him a quick smile, and tried to pretend that what he'd said was okay. In many ways it was, but it left her uncertain where Dante's feelings for her were concerned.

Maybe that was a good thing?

No, it wasn't.

She drew herself up to tell him, 'I'll be back for the match.'

'Of course.'

'Are you sure I can keep this?' She felt for the stone in her pocket.

'That's what keepsake means,' he said. 'Take it as a reminder of your time here, and all the things we've done together.'

Together. She'd take that word and seal it in her heart.

CHAPTER FIFTEEN

KARINA WAS SO busy when she got back to Rio that her head was spinning. That didn't stop her feelings for Dante keeping her awake at night. They'd put in so much good work on his ranch that everything was falling into place. They worked well together, she reflected as she glanced at his incoming email. She longed to find something personal in them and never did. She still read his new email avidly, as if she were a code-breaker, searching for clues.

After-match party: You know what I expect. Make it the best. Budget no object. D

Elephants? Dancing girls?

She smiled as she shook her head. Dante didn't waste words. Fortunately, she knew what exactly he wanted—carnival, big and brash and bold. And because the honoured client always got what he asked for, carnival was exactly what he was going to get.

The big day of the cup had finally arrived. Dante had hardly had chance to draw breath since Karina had left him at the ranch. His pulse banged as he thought of seeing her again, blood rushing to a part of him that thought about her constantly—inconvenient when he was on a horse. He shifted in the saddle and shouldered his mallet. Nothing had ever mattered to him more than polo. The team had been his family for as long as he could remember. It was his source of warmth and friendship, but now there was another vital element missing in his life—so where the hell was she?

Karina was glad of her VIP pass and doubted she'd make it through the crowds in time without it. Dante's vision was a reality. Carnival in Rio had been transferred to his ranch, and the world was going crazy for it. He was well on track to fulfilling his wish that polo became a popular sport, rather than an elitist game for the fortunate few. She had done everything she could think of to make that possible.

Outside the stadium there were high-quality food outlets, sideshows and a fairground boasting a big wheel, among other rides. There were samba dancers clothed in feathers and sequins performing on the stage, where popular bands were due to take over in the evening. Some of the best musicians in Brazil had offered to give a free concert to raise money for the charities the teams supported, and there was an information pavilion showing all that was best about Brazil.

Everywhere she went people seemed to be dancing and smiling, confirming her impression that the project was a success. Dante was having some quiet time, she'd been told. He'd been away with the team at a secret location, preparing for the match. No one could tell her where he was as the minutes ticked away towards the start, but she had an idea where he might be.

* * *

The ranch house door was on the latch, so she let herself in and quietly closed it behind her. 'Don't stop playing,' she whispered, as he paused in mid-phrase.

Dipping his head in concentration, he started playing again. It drew her across the hall towards him like a magnet. She stopped and smiled. He was such an incongruous sight. Dressed for the match in breeches and a snug-fitting top in his team colours, she doubted there had ever been such a brutal display of muscle and power, and yet the sensitivity in his fingers allowed him to create the most beautiful music. It soothed her like a balm, while he excited her beyond reason.

When the last chord echoed around the hall she stilled, waiting to see what he would do. She had turned away from him to look at a painting as he'd played, and when he walked up behind her she didn't turned around. She remained staring at the same image of the ranch painted just as it had been when he had taken it over. It was a stark reminder of how far he'd come. She had chosen that same image for the back of today's programme, with the most recent image on the front.

'You're back,' he murmured.

Leaning her head towards him, she sought contact, sought warmth, and thrilled all over when his hands gripped her upper arms. She didn't resist him when he lifted them above her head and pinned her against the wall with his weight. Her whole body responded—aching, melting, needing. Arching her back, she thrust her buttocks towards him, responding to those feelings instinctively.

'Keep that thought,' he murmured, dropping a kiss on the back of her neck.

It took a moment of complete stillness before she was capable of turning to watch him stride across the hall in the direction of the front door. Pausing only to grab his helmet and mallet, he headed out for the match.

By the time Dante arrived Team Thunderbolt had assembled. Each man was silent with his own thoughts. This wasn't the time to ask Luc where his sister would be sitting in the crowd. He couldn't believe he'd forgotten to ask Karina where she would be when he had seen her—but he'd had other things on his mind. He had to clear his thoughts now. His colleagues had one thing in mind, and that was obliterating the opposition.

Would he spot Karina in the crowd?

Mounting up, he exchanged a few terse words with his friends. His confidence had never been in doubt where the outcome of this match was concerned, unlike the chance of spotting Karina.

As they rode out to acknowledge the cheers of the crowd, he knew he would entrust his life to the team. They were solid. Their ponies were in top-class condition. They had never been better prepared for a match. He scanned the faceless mass of people. Where was she? He knew she'd be busy with last-minute checks and ground his teeth with frustration as he turned his concentration back to the team.

It was always going to be a close match when the opposing team was captained by the formidable Argentinian Nero Caracas. It all came down to the last chukka. Team Thunderbolt needed one more goal to secure the match...

Nero tried to ride him off, and he was almost unseated, but his pony waited that necessary split second until he was ready, and then she set off again.

He was at full gallop with the goal in his sight when he spotted Karina in the crowd. She wasn't in the stand where he had expected she might sit, but practically on the field, with her body pressed up hard against the barrier. Her face was ashen as she watched Nero chase him down. He could hear the thunder of hooves behind him, but he'd seen Karina, so anything was possible.

And he hadn't just seen her—he'd seen the gold earrings she was wearing—the same gold hoops he'd given to her on her eighteenth birthday.

Raising his mallet, he drove the ball home.

By popular choice, Karina was elected to award the prize. She was waiting at the rostrum for him. 'Congratulations, Dante, and to your team. I always had every confidence in you.'

'As I did in you,' he murmured, as they exchanged chaste kisses of congratulation on each cheek.

'You can let go of my hand now,' she prompted.

As she smiled into his eyes he realised that his teammates were backed up behind him, with the opposing team members also waiting to receive their medals. He smiled and stepped back.

When all the presentations had been made, he lifted the trophy in the air to rapturous cheers from the crowd, but for once in his life all he could think about was being somewhere else—preferably in a nice firm bed with Karina.

Karina was very relieved that Thunderbolt had won, but she was even more relieved that Dante was safe. She felt alert and alive, excited and light-headed as Dante looked at her over the heads of his teammates. They were separated by convention and not much more. They had to see the presentation ceremony through to the end, but the tension between them was like a high wire stretched taut.

She told herself to be patient. It would be some time before they could be alone.

At last the podium cleared and Dante left with the other players to check on the horses. She found him in the stables, where he was rewarding each animal in turn with affection and treats. The ponies' ears were pricked, and they seemed as proud as Dante was of their victory. Somewhere in the distance she could hear a band starting up. They were alone. Everyone else had left to go to the party, which would be an all-nighter.

'Hey…congratulations,' she said, leaning over the half-door of the stall.

'To you too,' Dante said, without looking up as he checked this pony's legs. 'You made one hell of an event here today, Karina.'

'I didn't do it on my own.'

Dante hummed.

For a moment she couldn't think straight. Just looking at him was enough, though his strength went a lot further than power and muscle. He was a good man. He was an exciting man. He was a gaucho. He was a working man, who was entirely the opposite from the glamorous playboy the press liked to portray.

'You wore my earrings,' he said, viewing her through narrowed eyes as he straightened up.

'For you… For good luck.'

Leaving the stall, he bolted the door and turned to face her.

'And I brought you this.' She tossed the stone he'd

given her and with whip-fast reflexes Dante caught it in his fist as it spun through the air.

'Now what?' he murmured, staring at her darkly as he tightened his big hand around it.

'Now you kiss me.'

They came together like a force of nature. This was where she wanted to be. She belonged in Dante's arms. He laughed deep down in his chest, as if the same feeling had hit him in the same moment, and then he backed her steadily towards a bed of hay.

'At last,' he ground out. 'Though this wasn't quite the setting I had in mind.'

'Where better than here?' she argued, breathlessly stripping off his clothes.

It was like a race to remove the last barrier between them, and Dante devoured her mouth as he lowered her onto the hay. There was no need to say anything. A look conveyed all they needed to know. This was the man she knew and remembered. This was her friend, the man she had always trusted, always loved. This was redemption. This was the end of a very long journey. This was coming home. Stroking her hair, Dante brought her close to drop a kiss on her collarbone and then her neck. He laughed softly when she whimpered with pleasure.

Karina was the only woman who could tame him. She was his equal in every way. She was the only woman he could think of spending his life with. There was only one question remaining now. 'I love you,' he whispered.

She stared into his eyes as if she needed to be absolutely sure, but then she smiled. 'I love you too.'

He brought her into his arms to promise her that he would give her babies, and instead of flinching from him in doubt and fear she looked into his eyes with trust and laughter. 'Right now?' she asked him, smiling into his eyes.

'Why not now? Whatever fate and Dante Baracca dictates,' he teased her gently, and then, kissing her, he soothed her as he led her at his pace into an erotic world.

He was determined that everything would be perfect for Karina. She deserved nothing less. She'd known violence and grief, and had no reason to trust a man. It was up to him to prove that he was different. There was still a glimmer of fear in her eyes. Until she tried it, she didn't know how it would work out. He understood her concerns, and was going to prove that she was normal in every way. Even now, when passion had never run higher between them, he was going to give her all the time she needed to discover that he was right. She tensed a little when he moved over her, and again when his hand found her. She was ready in every sense, and that was all he needed to know.

She flinched when Dante eased her legs over his shoulders. She felt so exposed, so vulnerable, and was worried that she might still disappoint him, but he was endlessly patient, and so sexy that she couldn't overlook the fact that her body was entirely on his side. Positioning her, he cupped her buttocks and when he dipped his head it was to give her pleasure on a scale that didn't allow for rational thought. She could only feel—wave after wave of incredible sensation.

Lifting his head, he said wryly, 'Why are you waiting?'

'I've got no idea,' she admitted, realising she was clutching handfuls of hay in her fists, as if that could stop her falling off the edge.

'Then don't,' he advised.

Dante didn't give her a chance to argue, and she cried out with shock at the intensity of feeling. He had to hold her firmly. She was wild with pleasure. She was exultant. She was free. She was also breathless and moaning out her approval of everything he did, as Dante made sure she enjoyed every last second of release. But it was more than that, she reasoned as he brushed kisses over her face and neck to soothe her down. They were well on the way to rebuilding everything they'd lost.

She made no pretence of holding back a second time. Dante had taught her something else about her body today. The deeper he led her into his sensual world, the more she wanted him, and the more sensitive she became. Lowering her legs from his shoulders, he drew her into his arms and lay with her in silence for a while, but the instant his hand found her, she closed her thighs around it to increase the pressure and the pleasure, as she worked with him, moving rhythmically and steadily towards her goal.

She'd almost reached it when Dante slid one lean finger deep inside her. Her body was so slick and welcoming there was no tension, no pain, only pleasure. She trusted him completely. He knew how far to go, and he didn't try to rush her or move too fast. Far from shrinking from him, she rolled her hips to catch more pleasure, working her tender bud against the heel of his hand. Soon the pressure began building again, and almost immediately she found herself teetering on the edge.

He'd said don't wait...

Dante held her as she fell and shrieked his name. The pleasure was indescribable and now she realised that it had increased with his penetration. She worked her body hard against his hand as the violent pleasure waves went on and on, and when he suggested more, she warned him not to stop.

'You're smiling?' he growled, bringing her beneath him.

'Because I can do this.'

'Of course you can do this.' Shaking his head with amused exasperation, he dropped kisses on her swollen mouth and brought a second finger into play, and soon even that wasn't enough for her, and reaching down she found him.

'Don't,' he warned.

'Are you saying you'd lose control?'

'I'm saying that holding back is torture enough already.'

He groaned as she caressed him. She loved the feel of him beneath her hands, the heightened sense of anticipation that a promise of commitment was waiting to be sealed between them.

'You have the perfect body,' Dante murmured, working some magic of his own. 'If I had my way you'd never get dressed.'

'If you had your way, nothing would ever get done.'

'You'd get done,' he whispered.

Brushing back her hair, he stared into her face. 'I love you more than life itself, Karina. I've always loved you. You were mine from the first moment I saw you.'

'Do you mean the day you sauntered into my father's stables while I was sitting on a hay bale, eating my lunch?'

'Why?'

'The lunch you stole from me and fed to the dogs?'

Dante eased his powerful shoulders in a lazy shrug. 'What clearer sign can a boy give a girl that he's interested?'

She moved over him to lean on his chest. 'You owe me lunch.'

He laughed. 'I'll have to do something about that. Lunch in kind?'

'I am now officially insatiable,' she agreed.

'And perfect.'

'And I love you.'

'I know you do,' Dante agreed with a wicked smile.

'You're such an arrogant…'

'Barbarian?' he suggested. Smiling seductively, she moved down the hay. She tasted him and then drew him deep into her mouth.

'What did I warn you about torturing me?' he demanded in a strangled tone.

'I just like to hear you gasp,' she admitted huskily as Dante drew her up to him. Turning her beneath him, he repeated the stroking motion until it was her turn to beg. 'Please…'

'Your wish is my command,' he murmured, and slowly sinking deep he filled her completely. Pausing until she had totally relaxed and temporarily stopped gasping with pleasure, he stared into her eyes and began to move. He only managed a few firm thrusts before she fell helpless and screaming into a deep black pit of ecstasy. And when he started moving once more, rhythmically and firmly, she fell a second time, even harder than the first.

'More?' he suggested wryly when she quieted.

'If you ever stop…'

'I've no intention of stopping, but I do think we should take this to the ranch house so there are no interruptions in the morning.'

With that kind of promise she made no complaint. Withdrawing slowly and carefully, Dante helped her to her feet, and wordlessly they grabbed their clothes and pulled them on, then he grabbed her hand and walked with her out of the stable block. By the time they exited they were running. They ran across the yard, barged into the house, slammed the door behind them and raced up the stairs. They crashed into his bedroom and fell on the bed, where they ripped off each other's clothes in a frenzy of hunger and need. There was no foreplay this time, none necessary. Dante spun her beneath him and entered her in one deep, firm stroke.

They were wild with excitement, and breathless with the energy required to make love furiously and hard. All her fears had left her and had been replaced with a desire to be one with Dante. And once definitely wasn't enough—not for either of them. They had to endorse the mating of their souls, their trust in each other, and their love, over and over again. And still he left her whimpering with urgent need.

'More,' she whispered, stroking his powerful chest.

'Oh, must I?' Dante teased her, sinking deep with an exquisite lack of haste.

Rotating his hips to a lazy rhythm, he kept on until she couldn't control herself, and moving convulsively, she fell into yet another delicious climax. Her cries rang out as her body bucked uncontrollably. She was glad of his big hands on her buttocks, holding her firmly, guiding her movements, ensuring that she benefited from every single pleasure pulse until they faded.

'Good?' he murmured, when she quietened.

'But not good for you—not fair,' she protested.

She was greedy for her next release and, reading her, Dante smiled. Bracing himself on his forearms, he stared down into her face. 'I'd say you were being more than good to me.' And to prove it, he thrust deep.

Holding him with her inner muscles, she moved with him, and this time when she fell he fell too, finally claiming his own savage release, and when they finally fell back exhausted, she knew the ghosts of the past had been banished for good, and she drifted off into a contented slumber. And when she woke they were still entwined in each other's arms.

'Do you think there's the smallest chance we'll ever get enough of each other?' she asked, her lips touching his as she murmured this.

'Hopefully not,' Dante said, smiling, 'though I think I should put that to the test on a regular basis, don't you?'

'Why not now?' she agreed, as he moved behind her.

Thrusting his hand into the small of her back he lifted her buttocks, exposing her even more to him. Seconds later he was sheathed to the hilt. Arching her back, she pressed back hard against him. 'You're right,' she managed breathlessly before giving herself over completely to pleasure. 'Who could ever get enough of this?'

It was dark and the night was full of stars and romance by the time they left the ranch house. Parties for all age groups were in full swing and music rose around them on every side. Samba rhythms added to the heat of the night as they walked together arm in arm. It was only when they smelled the scent of food grilling on countless barbeques that they realised they couldn't remember the last time they'd had something to eat. They stopped to grab some sticky ribs, and that was where Luc found them.

'There you are!' he exclaimed. 'Where on earth have you been?'

Karina was careful to keep her innocent face on. She

adored her brother, but once again Luc had proved that when it came to his sister he was incapable of registering the possibility of romance.

'We've been checking the horses,' Dante said, carefully not looking at Karina. 'I didn't realise you needed us.'

'Of course you're needed,' Luc said, as he swung an arm around Dante's shoulder. 'In case you've forgotten, you scored the winning goal, and my sister organised the event. There's a huge crowd waiting to thank you.'

Karina glanced at Dante and laughed. As she finger-combed her hair, she realised there was still some hay sticking in it, and her hands were covered with sticky sauce. Luc still didn't have a clue.

'Here,' he said, whipping off his bandana. 'Wipe your hands. And for goodness' sake, do something about your hair—' He stopped suddenly, and stared at her intently. 'Oh,' he said, and then he spun on his heel.

Fireworks lit up the sky as they mounted the stage. The applause was deafening, and in spite of his recent epiphany Luc had recovered sufficiently to give them both a more than generous introduction. 'For my team-mate and friend, Dante Baracca...' Covering the mike with his hand, Luc murmured to Dante, 'You'd better do the honourable thing or I'll rip your head off.' Turning, he smiled for the benefit of the crowd.

'Trust me. I intend to,' Dante growled, as he brought Karina close.

'And for my sister, who arranged this whole event,' Luc continued, once the cheers had died down, 'I couldn't be happier for you both,' he admitted gruffly, as glittering confetti cascaded down from the nets suspended about their heads and the crowd went wild.

'Nothing—not even this trophy—means as much to me as you do,' Dante told Karina, as they stood together to take the applause. And then he provided them all with the surprise of the day. Handing the trophy to Luc, he got down on one knee. To the delight of the crowd, he asked, 'Could you marry a barbarian?'

'Now I've tamed him?' She pretended to think about it as the crowd waited in a breathless hush. 'Yes,' she said softly, 'I can definitely marry the man I love.' And then she covered the mike with her hand. 'I always knew barbarians could be romantic, but aren't you afraid of spoiling your image?'

She laughed as Dante sprang up.

'I don't care about my image,' he said, as he swung her into his arms and carried her away into the night.

CHAPTER SIXTEEN

How things had changed, Karina mused as she hosted the two men she loved best in the world in her new and much larger office. The Gaucho Cup held on Dante's *fazenda* had been such a success that the team had voted for it to be held each year at Fazenda Baracca, with Karina arranging the event.

'You can't get out of it now that you and Dante are to be married,' her brother remarked as he stared with pride at the gleaming replica trophy that had barely left his hands since Karina had awarded it to him. The team had decided the original cup should stay with one man, and that man was Dante.

'Are you threatening my fiancée?' Dante growled, as the two men locked stares.

'Yeah,' Luc agreed happily. 'I can't think of two people who deserve each other more.'

'So this was all your idea?' Karina smiled at her brother, who refused to meet her eyes, making her instantly suspicious that he'd set her up—though, on this one occasion, she was prepared to forgive him as she stared at Dante and then at the beautiful emerald ring he'd given her—the same rough stone, her keepsake, now polished to its full eye-catching glory.

'I always knew you'd make a good team,' Luc murmured distractedly, as he paced the room to admire the trophy, which he had placed temporarily on her desk, from several different angles.

'Is that why you volunteered me for the job?'

'Could be,' Luc admitted, 'though I got some persuasion from a certain direction.' He glanced at Dante.

'That's enough, Luc,' Dante warned, as he gathered Karina into his arms. 'And now you'll have to excuse us as Karina and I have another appointment...' Walking to the door, he held it open. 'See you at the engagement party tonight.'

'I'll be there,' Luc promised, fielding Karina's accusatory look with an unapologetic grin. 'I wouldn't miss it for the world,' he assured them, flashing Dante an amused glance as he snatched up his precious trophy.

'We've got another appointment?' Karina queried once the door had closed behind her brother.

'You're a very busy woman,' Dante murmured, as he turned the key in the lock.

'Dante, we can't.'

'Who makes the rules around here?'

'Well, I do, but...'

Dante raised a brow and then raised her hands above her head as he pressed her back against the wall.

'Keep that thought?' she suggested, her pulse shooting up as Dante stared into her eyes.

'Not for long,' he assured her. Lifting her skirt, he dispensed with her underwear and let it drift to the floor.

'Please,' she gasped, all out of reasons why they shouldn't as she locked her legs around his waist.

'It would be my absolute pleasure,' Dante assured her, sinking to the hilt with his first firm thrust.

Losing control almost immediately, she had to bury her face in his shoulder to muffle her cries of pleasure as he rammed her repeatedly against the wall.

'Again?' he suggested dryly, when she quieted, knowing what her answer would be.

'Do you need to ask?'

He chuckled softy as he tightened his hold on her buttocks. 'I have to take advantage of you while I can,' he murmured against her mouth.

Dante was referring to her workload, which had increased considerably since the Gaucho Cup. News of her success had spread rapidly, and her diary was crammed to the point where Dante had asked her in all seriousness if she would have time to get married. 'On the hoof,' she had told him dryly. 'In between arranging the sheikh's wedding, and the naming of the Greek's ship.'

Dante, of course, came up with the perfect solution. They'd get engaged on one day and married the next, and then spend the rest of their life enjoying a series of honeymoons.

'You are a very bad man,' she told him much, *much* later when they were on their way out of the building.

'What are elevators for?' he demanded, when she made a half-hearted attempt to stop him with her hands pressed flat against his chest.

'They're for going up and down,' she said, frowning at his question.

'Exactly my point,' he agreed.

Their engagement party was being held at a café in the projects, and Karina's face was wreathed in smiles when she saw how many people had turned out to wish them well. Several samba bands had come along and the drums were thundering as they walked into the square. Everyone was in their best costume, with feathers in rainbow hues and enough sequins to sink a small ship. Swinging her into his arms, Dante held her close as they moved to the samba rhythms. 'They love you almost as much as I do,' he said, dropping kisses on her neck.

'I'm just so glad everyone can celebrate with us, but you did say it would just be a few of friends, along with Jada, the girl I sponsor, and her mother, and some people from the café.'

'Don't you prefer this?'

'You know I do, but I can't believe how many people are here.'

'What?' Dante asked with concern when her expression changed to a frown.

'Do you think that elevator has been reported out of order?'

'Let Luc worry about that,' Dante soothed. 'This is your night off, remember?'

He laughed as she pulled a face and the next moment they were in the thick of it, with everyone surrounding them. Dante's teammates and their wives were waiting for them too, but it was more like a gathering of a happy clan than a group of rampaging barbarians.

Which was the truth of the matter after all, and just the way it should be, Karina reflected happily as Dante led her into the café, with all their guests crowding in behind them. What use was a rampaging barbarian without a strong woman to channel all that energy?

She wouldn't change Dante in any way. They had both been isolated and mistrustful. Dante because of a father who had derided everything he'd done, while she had hidden from the world after losing the baby until it had become a habit she couldn't break. But they were stronger together than they had ever been apart. She'd heard that the professor who had abused her had recently lost his job, and was being held by the police for attacking several other women.

When she had asked Dante how his cruelty had first come to light, all she got was a shrug, but not before she'd seen the flash of warrior fire in his eyes.

'Happy?' he murmured, pulling her into his hard body.

'As I've ever been,' she said honestly.

'Well, that's lucky, because you, soon-to-be Senhora Baracca, are vital to my existence.'

'As you are to mine,' she said. 'What?' she asked, instantly suspicious, when she saw a particular look flash in Dante's eyes.

His lips pressed down as he gave her a wicked look. 'No one will notice if we slip away.'

'Of course they will—it's our engagement party.'

'We'll say we're making arrangements for the wedding.'

'But our wedding's tomorrow,' she said, as he guided her through the crowd. 'And all the arrangements have been made. I made them myself, so I should know.'

'Karina,' Dante murmured, as he pulled her into the shadows. 'There's no law against rehearsing for our wedding night, is there?'

'If there were such a law, you'd surely break it.'

'That's my duty as a barbarian,' Dante insisted, as he steered her ahead of him.

'So you just want me for sex?'

'I definitely want you for sex. And for the baby we're going to make. I can't do it without you,' he pointed out.

'How have we managed to leave the party without anyone noticing?' she marvelled.

'A tribute to your good planning,' Dante insisted, as he edged her deeper into the shadows. 'Everyone is enjoying themselves so much they haven't noticed that the guests of honour have left.' Kissing her, he frowned as he rested his hand on her stomach. 'And I really do need to make a start on your most important project for this year.'

'A start?' she queried. 'I thought we'd already done that several times over.'

'There's nothing wrong with perfecting our technique.'

'Dante...'

Suddenly scared at the thought of a baby, she clung to him, but Dante's confidence remained rock solid. 'I'll be with you every step of the way,' he said quietly and intently. 'And you're strong, Karina, never forget that.'

'*We're* strong,' she agreed.

'Together we're stronger,' Dante confirmed. Dragging her against his hot, hard body, his lips tugged in the familiar smile that could always melt her, as her barbarian lover kissed the woman he adored.

EPILOGUE

CHRISTMAS WAS ALWAYS a special time of year, but this year there was an extra miracle in the Baracca household as Dante showed off their son to the world. Reporters had come from every part of the globe to witness the transformation of yet another rampaging barbarian into a happily married family man.

'He looks just like me,' Dante proudly told the waiting press.

'Like a barbarian?' Karina murmured beneath her breath. 'He's far more beautiful than that.'

'At the moment,' Dante agreed with a frown as he studied his son's face. 'But he'll no doubt grow rugged and tough like his father in time.'

'I don't care what he grows into, so long as he's happy,' Karina argued, once they were alone.

'You know I feel the same,' Dante reassured her. They had returned to the fabulous penthouse apartment in Rio that Dante had bought for his wife as a wedding present.

'But I bet you've already picked out his first pony,' Karina guessed.

'Of course I have,' Dante said, as if anything else were unthinkable. 'My son will be the most famous polo player in the world.'

'Of course he will.' Karina smiled at her own, personal barbarian. 'And I'm glad we're both thinking along the same lines because, as it happens, I've already picked out his wife.'

'You have?' Dante's gaze turned suddenly fierce as it clashed with hers.

'No, of course I haven't,' she said with a groan of amusement. 'We've both agreed that our children will choose their own paths through life. Our son may not even like horses.'

'Unthinkable!' Dante exclaimed, dismissing this preposterous idea immediately.

'Whatever he decides to do, I know we'll back him to the hilt.'

Dante grunted and frowned, but as he passed his infant son over to the woman he loved more than anything else in the world, he knew Karina was right. Their children would have two loving parents to encourage them in everything they did.

'Do you think that having a wife and an infant son with reflect badly on the image of the team?' Karina asked later, when they were standing on their balcony in Rio, watching the fireworks go off to herald the advent of Christmas Day.

'It changes nothing about the team,' Dante assured her. 'If anything, it adds a new dimension, a new mystique.'

'Giving hope to women everywhere that a rampaging barbarian can be tamed?' she suggested wryly.

'With the right woman—someone strong and stubborn like you,' Dante agreed.

'I must be a glutton for punishment,' she said, snuggling close.

'Talking of which,' Dante murmured, 'you did say a glutton for pleasure?'

'That too,' Karina admitted wryly as she steered Dante back into the bedroom.

* * * * *

A YULETIDE AFFAIR

MONICA RICHARDSON

For my Granny, Rosa A. Heggie

(November 1927–2008)

She was special in so many ways, and the
strongest woman I knew. My life is rich
because of her.

Chapter 1

Alyson Talbot hadn't planned on spending so much time in the Eleuthera Islands, Bahamas. She loved her family and her childhood home, but it was no place she had intentions of ever living again. In fact, she'd made a perfect home in Miami by purchasing a beautiful condo that overlooked the Miami River. Florida was where she needed to be—it was where she was building her clientele. After leaving a booming real estate company, she'd recently decided to branch out on her own, make a name for herself. Alyson Talbot and Associates wasn't quite where she wanted it to be, but the business was well on its way to making a statement in the industry. Just last year, she'd earned a decent salary, one that supported her comfortable lifestyle. But she was looking for more than just comfort, and her goal was to double those earnings in the coming year. She was certainly on a good track, and well on her way to accomplishing just that. She vowed to never move back to the islands nor help to run her family's B and B on Harbour Island.

Each of her siblings had vowed the same thing—that they would not be moving back to the Bahamas. Her oldest brother, Edward, was too busy working his political career and had ties to the mayor's office in Florida. Her brother Nate, who lived in Atlanta, was an artist and had no desire to run a B and B. And conversation around him moving back to the islands had always been a sore spot for him. Problems with a former girlfriend had limited his visits to their childhood home. Whitney was busy teaching small children at her Dallas elementary school and had claimed that she would return long-term, but hadn't. Their youngest brother, Denny, had already begun his tour of duty in the Bahamian military. He was the family's rebel, had opted out of attending college. Jasmine had been the only one to sacrifice and move back to the island. She had been instrumental in the Grove's renovation. But now that the family business was up and running, she needed help. Which was why she had turned to her older sister, Alyson. However, for Alyson, moving home was definitely not in the cards.

What *was* in the cards was helping to plan her sister's elaborate Christmas wedding. Without her contribution, Jasmine's wedding might not be as elegant as it could be. After all, she had connections, and people owed her favors. Not to mention, the Talbots weren't just an ordinary family anymore. They were more than just a two-parent family with six adult children scattered about the world. As owners of the Grove, the newest and fastest growing beachfront property on the island, the Talbots had quickly been placed in a league of their own. She knew that when the first member of the Talbot clan got married at the Grove, it had to be an event to remember. And it was up to her to make sure that happened—thus, causing her to spend way more time on the islands than she'd ever dreamed she would.

"Turn around and let me see the back," she told Jasmine, who modeled her seventh ivory dress.

It was a Vera Wang, and her sister looked like a model in it. She truly hoped Jasmine liked this one, because she was quickly running out of patience. She'd tentatively scheduled a meeting with an important client—a meeting that had already been postponed twice. She was committed to the wedding, but also had business in Miami.

"It's okay, but I don't get that warm fuzzy feeling about it. Mother said that I would know which dress was the right one. She said it would speak to me."

"It's a Vera Wang. What else would you like for it to say, honey?" Alyson asked. "Not only that, but our mother got married at the justice of the peace some thirty-plus years ago. What does she know about picking the perfect wedding dress?"

"That's just rude," said Jasmine.

"It's the truth, Jazzy!"

"Our mother may not have had the wedding of her dreams, but she definitely married the man of her dreams."

"I can't argue that."

Their father, Paul John Talbot, was a man whom both women cherished. Any man that walked into their lives had large shoes to fill.

"I want the dress to feel special," Jasmine insisted.

Her sister could wear almost any dress she wanted to, yet she made the task of finding a dress almost impossible. Jasmine had the perfect figure. Alyson wasn't nearly as fit as her sister, who worked out on a daily basis. She had to work hard just to maintain her ample figure. And as much as her patience was running thin, she had to keep reminding herself that this was not her wedding. In fact, she had no intentions of ever getting married. Marriage was overrated, and she hadn't had one single prospect anyway. She'd had her share of trysts and a few relationships that had lasted a month or two, but nothing serious. Her life was just fine the way it was, though.

"As much as I'd like to spend the day picking out bridal gowns, I think your husband-to-be is expecting us at the Grove pretty soon," Alyson reminded her sister with a quick glance at her watch. "He wants your input on the Caribbean band that's auditioning for the reception. I think we should head over there."

"Okay, just let me get out of this dress." Jasmine glanced at herself quickly in the mirror one more time and then grabbed hold of the silk train before stepping down from the platform.

"No love between you and that gown, huh?" Alyson asked again.

"Very little." She grinned and then disappeared into the dressing room.

Dress shopping with her younger sister was like watching paint dry.

Although it was still early November and Thanksgiving was forthcoming, Christmas had been the focal point at the Grove with Jasmine's impending wedding. The Clydesdale had already been decorated with gold, red and green lights streamed throughout. In the Grand Room, a huge, fifteen-foot Christmas tree stood tall in the corner of the room, garnished with garland, lights and unique ornaments. It was reminiscent of Alyson's childhood home in Governor's Harbour—a place where Christmases were an important part of her life. But more important than Christmas Day was the day after—Boxing Day. Boxing Day was when Junkanoo took place.

The festive street parade with music, dance and unique costumes was what dinner conversations were made of. Inspired by a different theme every year, it was the focal point of the Christmas holidays and the New Year, and it was the highlight of the year in the Bahamas. It took months to prepare for Junkanoo. There were costumes that needed to be made and feasts that needed to be prepared. When Alyson and her siblings were young, their father would take them to Nassau, where the largest Junkanoo parade took place. Although the Junkanoo parade in the Eleuthera was festive, nothing could compare to the one in Nassau. Now with the anticipation of a Christmas wedding, coupled with Junkanoo, the Talbot family were beside themselves with excitement.

The Caribbean band had set up their instruments in the center of the Grand Room and was playing an old Bob Marley tune. With locks that hung down to the center of his back, the band's lead singer danced around the room. Jackson, Alyson's brother-in-law-to-be, was so into the performance, he didn't even see them walk in. When he spotted them, a wide grin covered his handsome golden face as he bobbed his head to the music. He raised a glass of cognac in the air and motioned for Alyson and Jasmine to join him.

"You're just in time," Jackson said. "They're just getting started."

"They sound good," Jasmine said.

Samson, Jackson's friend, walked up and the two men shook hands. Alyson inconspicuously observed Samson as he chatted with Jackson. Didn't want him to notice that she was checking him out. She'd labeled him as the mystery man that had shown up on the island, with no real reason for being there. He was renting a room at their family's B and B for an extended period of time, and he'd been introduced as Jackson's buddy from college, but her knowledge of him was very limited. The lack of information intrigued her.

"Why don't you play something?" Jackson asked Samson, and then told everyone in the room, "He's an accomplished guitarist."

"I'm an amateur at best," Samson insisted.

"He's being modest," Jackson countered. "Get on up there and give us a little something."

Reluctantly, Samson joined the band at the center of the room. The band's guitarist handed over his instrument, and Samson began to play. Alyson tried desperately to peel her eyes from his sexy face, and she'd never intended to focus so intently on the way his lips curved when he was in his zone. She certainly didn't mean to stare at his muscular arms, or the way the sleeveless shirt hugged his chest. With his tattooed arms and unshaven face, he was definitely not her type. She preferred her men refined and sophisticated. But she couldn't help but be impressed by the way he played the guitar and how he meshed perfectly with the other members of the band.

Get yourself together, girl, her inner voice whispered. *What in the hell is wrong with you?*

She didn't have time to watch this man play a guitar! He wasn't even in the band—he was a wannabe. And what was he doing in the Bahamas, anyway? The nuptials weren't taking place for weeks, and he wasn't even an attendant in the wedding.

"I don't need to see anymore. I think this is our band for the reception," announced Jackson. He then turned to Jasmine. "What do you think, babe?"

"Bravo!" Jasmine clapped her hands as each member of the band took a bow. "I agree."

At least she agreed on something, Alyson thought as she raised an eyebrow at her indecisive sister. "How about deciding on a wedding dress, boo?" She'd said it aloud before realizing the words had actually come out of her mouth.

"Don't start, Alyson." Jasmine pointed a finger at her sister.

"No luck finding a dress today?" Jackson asked Jasmine.

"She's going to be wearing that tablecloth if she doesn't choose a dress soon," Alyson teased.

"I really don't care what my bride-to-be is wearing on that day, just as long as she meets me at the altar and becomes my wife like she promised." Jackson grabbed Jasmine from behind and gave her a tight squeeze.

The two moved to the sound of the Caribbean music. Although Alyson rolled her eyes, secretly they gave her hope that love actually was attainable. She was happy for her sister and wished her a lifetime of bliss with the man of her dreams. The two sisters had only recently hashed out their differences and gotten over old wounds, and Alyson was grateful that they were able to put the past behind them. And she was happy to be an integral part of her sister's life and wedding plans.

"What's the story on your friend over there?" Alyson asked the question that had plagued her since the day Mystery Man had shown up in the Bahamas.

"He's my college buddy," Jackson said.

"Old information. I gathered that days ago," she told him. "I mean, what's his story?"

Jackson placed an arm around Alyson's shoulder. "What exactly would you like to know about him?"

She pulled away and exclaimed, "I'm not interested in

him, if that's what you're insinuating! I'm just curious as to why he's here. Normal people have careers and families that prevent them from relocating to a tropical island for an extended period of time."

"He's just here for a little while. Needed to get away."

Get away from what? she thought as she gave Samson another quick glance.

"What happened in Chicago?" she asked.

"Maybe you should ask him yourself," Jackson said as Samson finished the set and walked up.

Samson gave Alyson a dazzling grin and nearly pierced her with those seductive light brown eyes. He gave her a nod of hello.

"You're far from a novice, boy. You're a professional." Jackson grinned and gave Samson a strong handshake. Then he turned to Alyson. "I'd like for you to meet my future sister-in-law, Alyson Talbot. Alyson, this is Samson. I don't think I've had the chance to formally introduce you two."

"Pleased to meet you, Samson." She offered her hand.

He took it and gently kissed the back of it. "The pleasure is all mine."

She quickly retrieved her hand from the man who'd instantly caused her to feel things—*strange things*—that she shouldn't feel when meeting someone for the first time. Samson smiled, apparently completely aware of his effect on her. She rolled her eyes. He was trying too hard, and she wanted him to know that he didn't stand a chance with her. Maybe if she were a twenty-two-year-old groupie, his charms would work. But she wasn't twenty-two, nor was she one of those desperate women who threw themselves at the feet of charming men, and he needed to know that. She'd always been one to sift through the smoke screen and get to the heart of the matter.

"Talbot women certainly are beautiful," said Samson.

She noticed the word *Toni* etched across his left biceps, and asked herself, *Who has the names of their ex- or current girlfriends etched into their skin*?

"Alyson is a real estate broker," Jackson offered. "Her company is quickly becoming the go-to for real estate on the island and abroad. You mentioned taking a look at some beach homes while you're here. Maybe she can show you around."

Alyson gave Jackson the evil eye and then looked at Samson. "I generally don't dabble in the competitive market. But I have a lot of connections and would be happy to pair you with one of my associates who could show you around."

"I think she just told me that I can't afford any of the properties in her portfolio but she'd pawn me off on someone who can show me some cheaper ones." Samson smiled, and the entire room seemed to illuminate.

"I think she did," Jackson agreed.

"What is it that you do for a living, Mister..."

"Steel."

"You steal for a living?" she asked.

He and Jackson both laughed a hearty laugh.

"My name is Steel. Samson Steel," he said.

"Oh." She felt silly, but offered a gentle smile. "The most modest home in my portfolio, Mr. Steel, appraised at half a million dollars last week. We're asking much more than that."

"Great! I'd like to see it."

He was wasting her time! Between helping to plan a wedding and juggling appointments with clients in Miami and the islands, she didn't have time to play games with Samson Steel. She pulled a business card from her purse and handed it to him. "My website is on there. Why don't you peruse the homes on my site and see if there's anything that you're interested in? Save us both a lot of time and effort."

He studied the card. Flipped it over. "So I can reach you at this number?"

"If necessary," she said.

"Is it your personal cell, or will this take me to voice mail?"

"I don't do voice mail, Mr. Steel. My clientele is way too important for that. I have a personal assistant who handles all of my calls."

"Ah, I see," he said thoughtfully. "I'll give you a call in the morning. Maybe you can fit me in tomorrow afternoon."

"Can't tomorrow. Early afternoon, I have an appointment with a client. And then right after that, I'm scheduled to taste wedding cake with my sister."

"Um, Alyson... I meant to tell you that we'd rescheduled that appointment for Friday," Jasmine chimed in. "The bakery called this morning."

"When exactly were you going to tell me?" she attempted to whisper.

"I called Jules and had her check your schedule, and she penciled you in for the tasting on Friday. So it looks like you're free tomorrow afternoon...to show Samson some properties..." she caught Alyson's wicked glance "...*or not.*"

"Call my office tomorrow, and I'll try to fit you in." There was no way out of this one.

"I appreciate that, Alyson Talbot." He smiled widely again. "I'm looking forward to you fitting me in."

He shouldn't get it twisted, she thought. This would be strictly business.

Chapter 2

No doubt, he was enigmatic—it kept people at arm's length. It allowed him to share only what he wanted others to know. He'd come to the Bahamas where the only person he knew was Jackson Conner, his buddy from college. They'd met at Harvard and had kept in touch over the years. Though they hadn't spoken every day, he considered Jackson to be a good friend. And he was shocked to learn that Jackson had abandoned his hometown of Key West, fallen in love with a Bahamian girl and taken up residence in the Caribbean. His friend had always been a city fellow. A contractor, Jackson had owned a successful business in Florida and had built some of the finest properties that Samson had ever seen. That is, until meeting Jasmine Talbot.

It was Jackson whom Samson called on the phone that day when life seemed unbearable.

"I never thought you'd leave Florida. And I'm surprised

that some woman has snagged you and taken you toward the altar!" Samson had told Jackson.

"I never thought I would, either," said Jackson, "but love has a way of rearranging your entire life."

"I wouldn't know. I'm an eternal bachelor."

"Yep, I thought I was, too," said Jackson. "You just need to bump into that woman who will turn your world upside down."

"I've had plenty of women turn my world upside down, for a good twenty, maybe thirty minutes." Samson laughed. "And then I'd roll over and fall asleep."

"I'm talking about for life, not just in the bedroom," Jackson said. "You should come over here for a visit, man! It's the best place to clear your head after everything that's happened. Besides, I'd really like for you to be here for the wedding."

"Jackson Conner's getting married," said Samson. "Wow!"

"It's not that far-fetched," Jackson said. "Now you, on the other hand, you're afraid of marriage."

"I'm not afraid of marriage. I just don't think it's necessary. There are too many beautiful women out there to settle down with just one." Samson sighed. "But that's just the world according to Samson. Obviously you have a different opinion about it, bro."

"I absolutely do. And you will, too, someday. Some little honey is going to snatch your ass up one day, have you making her an omelet wearing nothing more than an apron and your birthday suit."

They both laughed. It had been months since Samson had joked like that. There hadn't been much to laugh about.

"I can't live without her. I had to make her my wife." Jackson was more serious then. "She changed my life."

"I'm truly happy for you, Jax man. I wish you the best."

"What about you? What's your next move?"

"Don't know."

"Come over here for a few weeks," Jackson had insisted. "Relax a bit. Get a new perspective."

"I don't know, man."

"I'll have Jasmine hook you up with a room at the Grove," Jackson said emphatically.

The Grove was a trio of old homes that had been transformed by Jackson's construction company into beautiful beachfront properties. Each home had its own distinct personality, theme and name. Ironically, Samson had chosen to stay in the home that happened to share his name, Samson Place. It was tranquil and bold, much like him. Decorated in Caribbean colors—pink, blue and yellow—Samson soon found his temporary home there. After settling in at the Grove, he'd resolved to only return to Chicago when his head was clear, and not a day before.

When he'd first laid eyes on Alyson Talbot, he thought she was beautiful. Her hard exterior was a dead giveaway. She was able to fool everybody else, but he had her figured out from the beginning. She was insecure. He flirted because…hell…he was a flirt. Samson was charismatic and loved women—and they loved him. He knew he'd never settle down with any of them for any significant length of time anyway. So he had fun—enjoyed life. Not because he had a fear of commitment, but because he knew he'd never find everything he wanted in one woman. It was impossible.

As beautiful as Alyson Talbot was, she wasn't his type. In his opinion, she was snooty and judgmental—two qualities that he wouldn't tolerate. He'd already read her, and had met a million other women just like her in his lifetime. And concluded that she'd been hurt by someone in her past, which was why she'd decided to take it out on every man alive. And that, he didn't have time for. He was too busy healing his own wounds, which was why he was in the Bahamas to begin with.

He sat on a stool, the acoustic guitar resting on his leg, his fingertips fretting the strings. He closed his eyes for a moment. Listened as the music resonated through the room. It was a beautiful love song, and the band's lead singer sang the Caribbean ballad with confidence. When Samson opened his eyes, he caught Alyson eyeballing him from across the room. Her eyes were focused on him, and his on her. For a brief moment he thought she was feeling him. That is, until she seemed to realize she'd stared too long, and looked away. She began toying with her phone.

She was dressed in business attire, and he doubted that she even owned a pair of sweatpants or jeans. She probably didn't dress down very often. Always on guard, always prepared, regimented. A pair of black slacks hugged her ample hips. A gray jacket barely contained her generous bosom. He thought she was sexy as hell, with long flowing hair, high cheekbones and a gorgeous, fleeting smile.

He wasn't interested in settling in the Bahamas, but he was interested in getting in between Alyson Talbot's thighs. If spending time with her meant he had to look at beautiful properties along the island's coast, then he'd entertain it. Contrary to what she believed, he could own just about any property he wanted on the islands. He'd invested his money well and had built quite the nest egg. He had money and could afford any of Alyson's properties, but it wasn't real estate that he was interested in at all. Besides, he was sure that the island life wasn't for him. After all, he was a big-city man with big-city hopes and dreams. And the thought of living on an island seemed too constricting.

Chicago had been his home all of his life. He grew up in Hyde Park. His grandfather Conrad Steel had served for many years as a Chicago police officer before retiring. His father, Cecil, had followed in his footsteps, and joined the force at a young age. Becoming a police officer had never been Samson's dream, and even with the pressure of preserving the family's tradition, he chose law instead. He'd attended the University of Chicago on a music scholarship, with hopes of becoming an accomplished guitarist. However, an undergraduate law class had changed all of that. Becoming a lawyer was inevitable at that point.

He hopped down from the stool and handed the acoustic guitar back to its rightful owner. Shook hands with every member of Onyx, the band that had welcomed him like an old friend. He talked music for a few minutes with the band members and exchanged phone numbers. He laughed with them as they all promised to get together again.

"I'm thinking you should play with us at the wedding," said Justice, the band's guitarist. "I have an extra guitar."

"I think that would be great," the lead singer, Kosmo, agreed.

"I brought my own guitar with me. It's in my room." He rarely traveled anywhere without his cherished instrument, affectionately known as Bailey. "But I don't think I'm quite ready to play at the wedding."

"Why not?" asked Kosmo. "You're no amateur."

He looked across the room at the spot where Alyson had stood playing with her phone. She was gone.

"You were absolutely wonderful," said Bijou. Her gentle hands caressed his back, as if it was the most natural thing in the world for her to do. The Caribbean beauty had been a beast on the drums. With copper-colored eyes, a petite frame and a head filled with curly tresses, Bijou was drop-dead gorgeous.

"Thank you. You're quite the musician yourself. How long have you played?"

"All my life," she said, and then changed the subject. "How long will you be on the island?"

"I haven't decided yet." It was an honest answer.

"Maybe I could take you on a tour of the island. Show you around a bit."

"So you live here?" He disregarded her invitation. Needed time to absorb it.

"I'm here in the Eleuthera temporarily. I'm from Cat Island. Are you staying here—at the Grove?"

"Yes, I am."

"Good! I can pick you up tomorrow evening. I'll show you some of the best beaches on the island." She wasn't shy at all. "Wear your trunks."

He was intrigued by her wickedly sexy smile. A cropped top revealed toned abs; a silver ring pierced her navel. Tight denim shorts hugged her hips, and revealed a set of smooth, cappuccino-colored legs. A heart-shaped tattoo played peekaboo on the inside of her right thigh. Samson couldn't wait to kiss his way from that heart all the way up to her sweet spot.

"I'll wear my trunks," he flirted. "Will you be wearing yours?"

She moved closer in, brought her lips to his earlobe and whispered, "I usually don't wear anything at all when I swim."

She walked away, moving her hips from side to side. He watched her, admiring her round ass. She must've known he was watching because she turned around and gave him a grin and a wink. He exhaled.

"Damn," he whispered to himself.

"I'm only going to have a small window of time tomorrow." Alyson startled him as she walked up from behind. "I'll meet you at the water ferry at three. Not a minute after. Not three fifteen. Not three twenty-five. I don't like being late, and I will not wait for you to arrive. You have my business card—call if you need to cancel. My time is valuable. Please don't waste it."

She was walking away before he had an opportunity to respond. Her round hips moved to their own music. He thought that watching Bijou walk away was nice, but watching Alyson walk away was downright delightful.

for Samson to arrive. She pulled a small compact

Chapter 3

Alyson thought Samson was a musician and a drifter, and couldn't afford the guesthouse of some of the properties in her portfolio. However, she'd managed to find a few condos and a villa that she thought might be in his price range and fit his tastes. She arrived at the water ferry a few minutes early, stood on the dock and answered a couple emails on her phone.

Butterflies stirred in her stomach as she waited for him to arrive. She pulled a small compact from her purse and checked her hair and makeup, *again*. She'd spent too much time preparing for this encounter. Way too much time. And she didn't like what she was feeling. She was nervous, and for no good reason. As strong and as independent as she was, her knees still felt somewhat weak when she was in the presence of Samson Steel.

Well, that was yesterday. Today would be better. She'd exhibit more strength. He wouldn't make her feel vulnerable again. She wasn't his type anyway. She saw the way he gawked at that young girl in the band—the drummer with the small waistline, skinny legs, exposed flat stomach. He looked all goo-goo eyed. If he liked slight girls, then Bijou was more his type, not her.

She sent a text message to the owner of one of her listings, Jennifer Madison: I have a strong buyer for Madison House. All cash. Full price offer. Quick closing.

Jennifer replied after a few moments: Great. Send over the contract and I'll take a look at it.

I'm also showing it this afternoon.

The Madisons weren't any ordinary family. Jennifer Madison's father had built a successful real estate development company. They were a prominent family that owned homes on Miami's Palm and Fisher Islands, as well as properties along the coast in the Bahamas. But of all the houses that they owned, the Madison home was Alyson's baby. It was her first listing that even came close to a million dollars. Her firm had listed plenty of homes on the islands, but she'd personally nurtured this one. It was by far her most expensive listing yet, and was sure to net her a substantial commission—one that would change the financial face of Alyson Talbot and Associates. A sale of that magnitude would earn her the business of every one of Jennifer Madison's rich friends and associates. She desperately needed it.

The pant legs of her linen Armani suit blew in the wind. Her recently pedicured toes peeked through her shoes, and she'd worn a professional-looking blouse but made sure she showed just a little cleavage—just to tease Samson a bit, show him what he couldn't have.

He stepped out of a taxi wearing denim shorts, brown leather sandals, a snug gray T-shirt and a gray plaid newsboy cap on his head. He was clearly dressed down, but he even made dress-down look sexy. His perfectly manicured beard caused him to have a strong resemblance to Omari Hardwick. Alyson found it difficult to peel her eyes from his muscular, tattooed arms. She thought it ridiculous for any human being to defile their body in such a way, but there was something tantalizing about Samson's body art. She looked away. Didn't want him to catch her staring. He didn't deserve the satisfaction of knowing that she thought he was one of the sexiest men she'd met.

He paid the driver and then headed her way.

"You made it on time," she said.

"Better than that. I'm five minutes early," he boasted.

She looked at her watch, and then up at him. His arms were folded across his chest, and a smirk danced in the corner of his mouth.

"That you are." She avoided eye contact.

"Good seeing you again, Alyson. I appreciate you fitting me into your busy schedule."

She ignored his greeting and instead ran down their plans for the day. "We're going to take the water taxi over to Governor's Harbour. There are a few houses I can show you over there. They aren't as elaborate, but I'm sure they would fit into your price range."

"You don't even know what my price range is. You haven't asked."

"You're a musician. And not a professional one. I admit I'm being a bit presumptive, but—"

"I'd say you're being extremely presumptive," he said. "Is this how you handle all of your clients, or just the ones you devalue?"

"Are you telling me that you can afford a property that costs more than two hundred thousand dollars?"

"I'm telling you that you never gave me the courtesy

of asking what my price range was. You assumed that I couldn't afford the properties in your *portfolio*," he mocked her. "Isn't there a process to this? Shouldn't there be standard questions that you ask a potential client?"

"I do have a few questions, Mr. Steel. Like, what are you doing in the Bahamas for an extended period of time? What are you running from? Do you have a woman or a baby mama in the States who's chasing you for child support?"

"Those are really inappropriate questions," he said.

"I apologize. I think we got off on the wrong foot." She handed him a sheet of paper from her briefcase. "Here's a list of properties that I thought you might be interested in. If this is not your price range, we can adjust."

He took the list and gave it a quick review. Handed it back to her. "Actually, I brought my own list."

He reached into the back pocket of his shorts, pulled out a folded piece of paper and handed it to her. She opened it. Gave it a quick scan.

"These properties are close to a million dollars!"

"Your point?"

She ignored his question. "And besides, the Madison property already has a buyer."

"That's the one that I'm most interested in. I saw it on your website this morning. It was the only one that had a video. You should do that with all of your properties, by the way…add a video. Excellent selling point. And your website didn't indicate that that property was sold, by the way."

"I just spoke with the owner this morning, and she's waiting for me to send over the contract right now." Why was she explaining this to him? "I already have a solid offer on it."

"But you haven't accepted that offer yet, right?"

"Well…"

"I would like to see the place."

"Why would I show you a property that's not for sale? And if I thought for one second that you could afford it, I couldn't show it to you today anyway. It's on Abaco— over a hundred miles from here. It would take us too long to get there by boat."

"I don't have anything but time."

"It would be a complete waste of time."

"It's not the only property on Abaco that I'm interested in. There are others in the same general vicinity."

"We don't have transportation."

"Actually, we do. Jasmine told me that your cousin Stephen owns a boat, and he often transports you between the islands. She even gave him a buzz, and asked if he was available today. He was more than happy to oblige. So what's your excuse now?"

He was right. Their cousin Stephen was very accommodating whenever she needed use of his boat. Often if his schedule permitted, he'd drive Alyson between islands to meet with clients and show properties. But she didn't need her sister planning her day for her, or telling Samson Steel all of her business. She'd address that with Jasmine the next time she saw her.

Sooner than she would have liked, Stephen pulled the boat to shore and tied it to the dock. He waved for them to come along. Alyson gathered herself and walked toward the boat. Samson followed closely behind.

She wasn't sure what the day would bring, but so far she wasn't pleased with its start.

Chapter 4

On *Sophia*, Stephen's powerboat, they traveled at a fast pace across the Atlantic Ocean. Stephen steered the boat through the clear turquoise waters. Alyson reclined on the leather seat on the port side of the boat, behind Stephen, while Samson relaxed in its bow. His back was to her, so she had an opportunity to check him out without his knowledge.

Samson and Stephen chatted about everything under the sun—whatever it was that men chatted about. Occasionally she'd tune in to the conversation, which didn't really amount to anything more than a conversation about the ocean, deep-sea diving and the Islands of the Bahamas. Stephen was a diver, and boasted about it every chance he got. He'd go diving for fish and lobsters. Stephen told Samson about his and Alyson's upbringing. As first cousins, they spent a great deal of time together as children and even as teens and adults. The Talbots were a close-knit clan.

When they arrived on Abaco, Stephen tied a rope from the cleat of the boat to the dock. He helped Alyson climb out of the boat first, and then helped Samson.

"I have a couple that I'm taking on a sightseeing tour," Stephen said. "Shouldn't take me more than an hour, Chicken."

Chicken was a nickname that she'd never outgrown. It was a name that clearly didn't describe her, as she was not afraid of anything. However, some of her family members saw fit to give it to her anyway, and she hated it.

"An hour? Are you kidding me?" she asked. "Why didn't you tell me you had business on Abaco before you brought me here?"

"Alyson, this is my livelihood. I always schedule other business when we come here. You know that. I have to take advantage of every opportunity to make money."

Stephen was definitely an entrepreneur. He owned a rental shop along the beach on the Eleuthera, where he rented jet skis and surfboards by the hour. He used his powerboat to transport tourists between the islands. Though Alyson often complained, she appreciated him allowing her to tag along on his moneymaking trips. But because he was her younger cousin, she felt obligated to give him a hard time—each and every time. It was a habit that she hadn't quite grown out of. She didn't care about Stephen leaving her for an hour, but spending time alone with Samson was what she feared most.

"Hurry back." She kissed her cousin's cheek. "I need to get back to the Eleuthera before nightfall. I have an early meeting that I need to prepare for."

"Good luck with her," Stephen told Samson. "She's impossible to deal with."

"I'm not impossible! I'm just a woman who knows what she wants."

Stephen shook his head, and then stood on the deck. Lit a cigarette. "I'll call you when I'm on my way back."

Madison House was one of the most alluring properties in the Abacos. Positioned at sixty-eight feet above sea level and overlooking the Sea of Abaco, the magnificent beauty boasted six bedrooms and a great room all connected by massive breezeways. Each bedroom had its own private balcony. The vaulted ceilings, Brazilian wood flooring and the glass walls were by far the main attractions. The view of the beach from the great room was stunning.

"There are no words to describe this property," said Samson. "I don't think I've ever seen anything more beautiful."

"You like, huh?" she asked.

"It's breathtaking."

Samson followed her across the mahogany floors and into the kitchen with its upscale stainless-steel appliances and a dumbwaiter. French doors off the kitchen led to a porch that wrapped all the way around the property. She stepped outside and felt the tropical air against her face— breathed it in.

"I could live here." Samson said it softly.

"Unfortunately it's not for sale. But since you insisted on seeing it, here it is," she told him.

"Here it is, indeed."

They stepped back inside and took the winding staircase to the second level and to the master suite. Huge glass French doors led to an enormous private balcony with a view of the ocean.

"This is unreal," said Samson.

It took them more than thirty minutes to finish the tour. When they were done, she set the alarm and secured the property.

"We can use the golf cart from this house, and I'll drive

you over to a nearby property. Of course it's a little more quaint, but still very beautiful."

"I'll follow your lead," he said.

They drove the golf cart along the road to a smaller three-bedroom house on Marsh Harbour. Tall palm trees greeted them in front of the well-manicured yard.

"This one seems a little more practical," Samson said as they entered the home. "I like the kitchen. It's much bigger than the other house."

"Why would you care about a kitchen?"

"I cook. And very well, as a matter of fact."

"And what is it that you cook?" she asked with a bit of skepticism in her voice.

"A little of everything, but mostly soul food. Collard greens and the best fried chicken you've ever tasted," he boasted. "I make a mean sweet potato pie, too."

She looked at him. "You make sweet potato pie?"

"A mean one," he insisted.

"That's my favorite pie. I can eat a whole one all by myself."

"Well, maybe I'll make you one someday," said Samson. "Do you cook?"

"All my life. Mostly Bahamian dishes. Our mother made sure we all learned how to cook. Said the quickest way to a man's heart is through his stomach." She laughed. "Not that I care about getting to a man's heart. But it's nice to know how to cook, nonetheless. At least I'll never go hungry, right?"

"Why aren't you interested in getting to a man's heart? Aren't you interested in men?"

"Of course I'm interested in men." She set her purse down on the kitchen counter. "But I'm just not interested in the whole drama of a relationship right now. Don't have the time or the energy. My life is fine just the way it is."

"Relationships don't always have to bring drama. Maybe you're unhappy by your own choosing."

"I never said I was unhappy! I'm quite happy, in fact." She was convincing herself more than him. "But I'm just not interested in the whole drama of a relationship right now. Don't have the time or the energy. My life is fine just the way it is."

"Relationships don't always have to bring drama. Maybe you're unhappy by your own choosing."

"I never said I was unhappy! I'm quite happy, in fact." She was convincing herself more than him. "But what about you? You have a wife, girlfriend or baby's mother back in…wherever it is you came from?"

"Chicago. And none of the above. I'm a happy bachelor."

"So you live in Chicago?"

"Southside."

"What part?"

"In a historical, black neighborhood. A lot of culture there."

"Isn't there also a lot of crime?"

"Not any more than anyplace else. And where do you live, on Miami's Fisher Island somewhere?"

"Downtown."

"Should've known."

"What do you mean, 'should've known'? I'll have you know that downtown Miami is very cultural. A lot of history there, as well," she explained. "And why do you live in Southside Chicago, anyway?"

"It's my home. I was born and raised there. It's where I grew up. I'm proud of my home. I envy your upbringing. Must've been nice, growing up in the Bahamas."

"It was restricting. I outgrew this place. Quickly!"

It had been years since she'd lived on the islands. A native of the Bahamas, she'd gone away to college and vowed never to return to the islands permanently. And even after the completion of her family's bed-and-breakfast, the Grove, she still had no desire to return. However, visiting properties with Samson caused her to remember why she loved the Bahamas so much. It was still her home, where her family lived, and still one of the most beautiful places in the world.

Her father was a retired physician, and he was the best example of what she wanted in a man. Genuine and caring and very intuitive, he was part of the reason she'd never settled down with anyone. No one could ever compare to him. That and the fact that her mother's voice was forever in her head about everything. Her mother's little anecdotes and lessons lived in her mind. She didn't know why she listened to her mother, though. Beverly Talbot had done the opposite of what she constantly encouraged her daughters to do. She told them to follow their dreams, when she'd abandoned her own dreams only to follow their father's.

"Sometimes in life, we make sacrifices, Alyson." That had been her mother's excuse. "I wanted a better life for you guys. That's why I didn't follow my dreams."

Alyson and her siblings had certainly benefited from their mother's sacrifices. Their parents had somehow managed to put every one of them through college. Everyone except for Alyson's youngest brother, Denny, who'd chosen the military instead. He was currently away completing officer's training in the United States. The rebellious one with a mind and style of his own, he'd certainly been the exception to the Talbot family rule.

Somehow he'd also managed to weasel his way out of working for their family's business. The Grove was their inheritance—passed down to them from their grandfather Clyde Talbot. They each had a stake in the business. Jasmine had been the first to move back to the islands to oversee the construction of the family's B and B. She'd written the business and marketing plan. And after the renovation had been completed by her fiancé, she'd been instrumental in hiring staff and overseeing the day-to-day operations.

But Jasmine was becoming overwhelmed. Their youngest sister, Whitney, a schoolteacher in Texas, had made promises that she would move back home after the school year ended, but so far that hadn't happened, and Jasmine needed help. Planning a wedding and running the Grove was certainly taking its toll on her. As a result, Alyson found herself on the islands more often than she wanted to be. It had been weeks since she'd been to her home in Miami.

"If we're done looking around, I should lock up."

"I'm done," said Samson.

Her phone buzzed, and she pulled it out of her pocket. It was a text message from Stephen.

Taking a bit longer than expected. Might be another hour...maybe two. Sorry ☺

"Really, Stephen!" she said aloud.

"What?" Samson asked.

"He said he might be an hour or two longer," she explained. "I apologize."

"Don't," said Samson. "Let's just make the best of it."

"How?"

"There's a beautiful beach a few steps from here. I say we take advantage of it."

"I say we don't. I'm not even dressed for the beach."

"When was the last time you just let your hair down?"

"I can't remember. I don't have time to let my hair down."

"Well, today you will." Samson grabbed her hand and ushered her out of the kitchen and through the living room, straight to the front door.

"Just let me lock up."

* * *

Samson didn't waste any time removing his hat and laying it atop a huge rock. He pulled his T-shirt over his head, and all Alyson took in were golden brown abs and strong arms and the beautiful sunshine beaming against smooth skin. He removed the leather sandals from his feet and headed for the water. He didn't even bother to remove his trousers before jumping in for a swim.

"The water's warm!" he yelled.

"That's nice."

"Why don't you take your clothes off and come in?"

"Imagine that," she said, and then decided to remove her leather pumps.

The last thing she needed was to ruin a perfectly good pair of Manolo Blahnik shoes. Never mind that she'd caught them on clearance at a Saks end-of-season sale. Still, they weren't cheap! And she would not be removing her clothes in front of a man that she barely knew. She was appalled that he would even suggest it.

She rolled up the legs of her pants, tiptoed through the sand and moved closer to the water. Samson was doing a backstroke in the water. He was moving farther away from the shore, and she feared that he was being careless.

"Hey!" she called. "You shouldn't swim so far out."

He smiled and waved and continued to swim farther out. Soon he disappeared, and she couldn't see his head. Her heart pounded as she moved closer, and soon she was standing in the water.

"Samson!" she called again.

No response and no sight of him. She pulled her cell phone out of her pocket. She quickly tried to dial 911, but her fingers were shaking.

Samson had swam farther out into the deep part of the ocean. She was breathless when she didn't see him anymore.

A Jet Ski zoomed past, and she tried flagging it down. They waved as if she was saying hello, and kept moving. She crept farther into the water. As she pressed the numbers on her cell phone, it slipped from her grasp and fell into the water.

"Shit!" she exclaimed and crouched down to pick it up.

She missed seeing the wave that suddenly crashed against the shore *and* the side of her face. It soaked her hair and clothing with one splash. She inhaled deeply and attempted to catch her breath. Then she tried turning her cell phone on.

"Looking for someone?" Samson popped up out of the water, startling her.

"Are you crazy?" She swung at him, but he grabbed her hands. Restrained her.

"What is wrong with you?"

"I thought you drowned!"

"Well, I didn't." He grinned. "I'm glad to know that you cared, though. You were willing to save my life?"

"Let go of me! You are so twisted! And this is definitely not funny!" she yelled. "You're an asshole! My phone probably doesn't work anymore, and my hair is wet and my clothes are soaked!"

"I'm sorry. I didn't know that you thought I was drowning. I was fine. I'm a swimmer."

She rushed angrily to shore. Samson followed, attempting to express his sorrow. Her clothes and her hair were ruined, and she was livid. Stephen couldn't return to the island soon enough, she thought. Samson Steel had certainly burned his bridge with her, and there was no recovering from this.

Chapter 5

The weather in the Bahamas was beautiful—warm and tropical—but it was as cold as ice on the boat ride back to Harbour Island. Samson glanced back at Alyson, who was seated on the port side of the boat. She'd managed to pull her wet hair back into a ponytail. Her clothes were wrinkled and drenched. A pair of overpriced shoes rested next to her on the seat, and a set of earbuds was inside her ears. He wondered what she was listening to, but dared not ask. He was just grateful that her phone still worked.

"She'll be okay." Stephen caught him checking her out.

"I didn't know she thought I was drowning. I went out a little deeper than I probably should have," Samson tried to explain. "And she should've seen me swimming back to shore."

"She said she wasn't looking…too busy trying to get her phone to work. But I tell you what… I wished I'd have seen her rushing out into the water like that. I bet that was a sight to see." Stephen laughed.

"Why doesn't she date?" Samson asked.

"Oh, she dates," said Stephen. "She just doesn't commit. She's afraid of letting someone in. Whenever someone gets too close, she runs them away."

"Dealing with her seems like so much work."

"Alyson Talbot *is* a lot of work. But I believe when the right guy comes along, she'll let him in."

Samson glanced at Alyson one last time. Her eyes were closed this time.

The trio reached Harbour Island by nightfall. Samson helped Stephen guide the boat to the deck and secure it with a rope. Stephen helped Alyson climb out, and then he helped Samson. She never looked his way, just stomped toward a bench and sat down, folding her arms across her chest.

"Give me a minute and I'll drive you both to the Grove," Stephen said.

"Don't worry about it. I'll take a cab!" Alyson snapped.

Samson Place was decorated in tropical colors—pink and turquoise. It was tranquil and oozed with romance. It was the sort of place where lovers retreated for long weekends. He watched as Alyson spoke briefly with the young woman at the front desk. The woman handed her a key, and she breezed right past Samson, walking briskly toward the wooden stairwell.

"I'm sorry, Alyson." It was his last attempt at penance.

"Don't worry about it," she said and kept walking.

With a long sigh, he pulled his room key out of his pocket and headed for his room, as well.

"Where have you been?" Samson recognized the voice immediately. Bijou wore a bikini top and a pair of cutoff jeans. Flat stomach, silky smooth legs and leather flip-flops. Her toes were painted in a hot-pink nail polish that matched her bikini top. "I've been looking everywhere for you! Did you forget?"

"Forget what?" he asked.

"That we had a date, silly." Her breasts were perfectly round and buoyant. "Remember, I was going to show you around the island?"

He didn't think they'd actually set a date. In fact, he thought they were just making flirtatious small talk. "Was that today?" he asked.

"You did forget." She pouted.

"I can't today, Bijou. I'm sorry."

"Oh, no, mister!" She grabbed his arm. "I'm not letting you renege."

He couldn't believe he'd actually agreed to the rendezvous. And there was little he could do to get out of it, so he followed Bijou to an old pickup truck parked in front of Samson Place. Bijou jumped into the driver's seat and slammed the door shut. Samson reluctantly walked around to the other side of the truck, hopped into the passenger's seat and slammed his door shut. She started the engine, and although the rusty Chevy was in desperate need of a paint job, the engine hummed like it was brand-new. He held on to the door handle as Bijou peeled away from the curb. She tuned the radio to a Caribbean party station and turned up the volume as loud as it would go. He held his breath as she sped through the streets of Harbour Island. He barely heard as she pointed out some of the island's landmarks. His mind was elsewhere—on Alyson and the anticipation of making amends with her.

"Let's go for a swim!" Bijou pulled up at the beach without warning.

"Let's not," he told her. "I didn't bring any trunks."

He didn't need trunks, but had no desire to take a swim

with Bijou. He'd had his fill of swimming in the ocean for one day, and it hadn't gone well at all.

"Don't you want to go skinny-dipping?"

What man wouldn't want to skinny-dip with a beautiful woman like Bijou? He'd be crazy not to.

"Maybe another time," he said. "You think you could drive me back to the Grove now?"

"You're putting me off." She poked her lip out.

He didn't have an answer, and couldn't believe he was turning down an opportunity to skinny-dip with a beautiful woman. His buddies back home would be giving him the side-eye, wondering if he'd grown soft.

He managed a smile. "Rain check?"

Bijou wasn't giving up without a fight. She untied the strings of her bikini halter top and dropped it. Her breasts sprung to life. He noted that they were a beautiful shade of brown with perky nipples. Her fingertips reached for his face, caressed his temples. She grabbed his hand and slipped his index finger into her mouth. "Still want to go back to the Grove?"

"Those…are…very beautiful." He breathed in deeply. There was no denying he was aroused, but he stood his ground.

He didn't know when it happened, but Alyson had become his new endeavor, and getting her attention had suddenly become his focus.

"Glad you like them." She smiled seductively.

"Please put your top back on."

"Was it something I said?" she asked. "I was too forward."

"It's not you. It's me." He sounded like a cliché, but he didn't care. He had no desire to impress Bijou. "It's just that I need to get back and speak with someone."

"With that woman—Jasmine's sister. The stuffy one," she said matter-of-factly. "It's too bad she has such a bad attitude."

"She's beautiful, though," Samson rebutted.

"She's a bit overweight."

Samson laughed at Bijou's cattiness. He thought her jealousy was cute. Alyson was far from overweight, in his opinion. She had curves in all the right places. He thought she was sexy as hell, and couldn't seem to get her out of his head. Bijou lifted her bikini top back up and tied it around her neck again. She started the truck, put it in Reverse and peeled out of the sand at full speed. He wasn't sure she was able to drive at a normal pace, or even move at a normal pace, for that matter. A man usually had to work hard for what she was willing to give so freely. *Fast* was definitely her middle name. A week ago, he'd have appreciated Bijou's audacity. Women had always been his weakness. He couldn't think of anything better than a beautiful woman's body pressed against his. But his priorities were suddenly beginning to change.

In an attempt to drown the uncomfortable silence in the truck, Bijou turned up the stereo as loud as it would go. He gazed out the window to keep from looking her way. He wanted to apologize to her, but couldn't find the words. He just needed to be back at the Grove, and it seemed he couldn't get there soon enough.

He found Alyson in the common area at Samson Place. She was reclined on the tangerine-colored antique sofa, pecking ferociously on the keyboard of her laptop. Instead of approaching her immediately, he found his way to the kitchen. Raquel, one of the Grove's Bahamian cooks, stood in front of the stove with an apron tied around her generous hips.

"Can I get two cups of tea, please?" he asked.

Raquel stopped stirring something in a huge pot, just long enough to look at him. "She likes green tea, with a splash of lemon and just a drizzle of honey," she said in her sweet Bahamian accent.

"You mean Alyson?"

"Yes, Miss Talbot is very specific about her tea, amongst other things," she said as she placed a fire beneath the tea-kettle and grabbed two large mugs from the mahogany cabinet. "And how do you like your tea, Mr. Steel?"

He wondered how she knew his name. It seemed that everyone around the island had become fully acquainted with him.

"I'll have mine the same way as hers, I guess."

"She's mad. You know that, right?" Raquel asked. "You messed up royally."

"You heard her mention it?"

"The whole house did." Raquel shook her head. "Came in here ranting and raving about her time being valuable, and her clothes and hair being ruined."

"Wow," he said.

"Just be yourself, and apologize profusely."

"You think that'll work?"

"I've known the Talbots for a long time, and it wasn't that long ago that I changed Alyson's diapers." Raquel smiled. "She has a hard exterior, but the truth is, she's a real softy on the inside...if you can manage to get in there."

"I don't see anything soft about Alyson Talbot, except maybe..." He caught himself, realized that he'd said too much. "Never mind."

"Now, see, that's what's wrong, Mister Steel. You got your priorities all mixed up. Thinking with the wrong head. You're out gallivanting about town with Bijou, doing

God only knows what, and now you want to make amends with Miss Talbot. Such a man!"

"I didn't… I mean, Bijou and I didn't…"

"I don't want to hear any of the details, honey. You just need to make up your mind as to what it is that you want."

"You know a lot about things, Miss Raquel."

"I know about everything that goes on around here," she told Samson.

Samson laughed. Where he was from, there was a name for people like Miss Raquel—*nosy*. Once the teakettle whistled, Raquel made green tea with splashes of lemon and drizzles of honey and then sent him on his way.

"Now go. Be persistent. No woman wants a mouse of a man."

"I'm not a mouse, Miss Raquel. I'm far from that."

"Well, good! Because she's strong and needs someone to take charge. And don't take no for an answer." She didn't smile, but gave him a nod. "Now, go on, child."

"Thank you."

He cautiously stepped out of the kitchen and headed toward the area where Alyson was engrossed in her computer. He placed the mug on the rustic coffee table in front of her. "Just the way you like it," he said.

She stopped pecking on her keyboard for a second, looked up at him and then at the cup. "And how do you know how I like it?"

"I have my sources."

"Raquel has a big mouth." She began typing again.

"I need you to accept my apology. What I did was juvenile and thoughtless." He plopped down in the chair opposite the sofa.

"Already forgotten." She grabbed the cup and took a sip. A look of satisfaction briefly appeared on her face.

"Could've fooled me. You keep giving me these looks of disgust—scowling at me."

"Maybe it's your own imagination. Don't give yourself so much credit," she said.

"So you're not scowling at me?"

"Nope," she lied, and then changed the subject. "Did you enjoy your evening?"

"You mean my tour of the island? I did indeed."

"And I'm sure you enjoyed your beautiful tour guide, as well."

"Bijou is a nice girl."

"I agree. Hopefully she doesn't get taken advantage of by the likes of you."

"What's that supposed to mean—'the likes of me'?"

"Playboy, philanderer. You choose the term."

"I love women. That's not something I can argue. In some circles I might be considered a playboy, if you will." He wasn't helping his case very much. "But right now I have my sights on one woman—and one woman only."

"And who might that be?"

"The one who's giving me the hardest time, who won't let things go."

"I don't dwell on things, Mr. Steel."

"Then have dinner with me tomorrow evening. Give me a chance to redeem myself."

"I can't."

"Of course you can. You have to eat. Rock House at seven. I'm not taking no for an answer. Be there at seven. And don't be late." He stood and headed for the stairwell before she had an opportunity to run down a hundred excuses why she couldn't make it. He took Raquel's advice and stood his ground.

Raquel was peeking out from the kitchen and gave him

a wink as he passed. He gave her a wide grin and then headed up to his room. Didn't even turn to see the expression on Alyson's face. He was sure she was astounded.

Chapter 6

Friday morning, and she'd almost forgotten that she'd committed to tasting wedding cakes with her sister.

"I don't know who he thought he was, barking orders at me as if…" Alyson stuffed a fork filled with red velvet cake into her mouth "…oh, my God, that's good!"

"I'm partial to the white Amaretto. And oh, Lord, the chocolate Bavarian crème is simply delightful." Jasmine took a forkful of her sister's red velvet and tasted it. "But oh, this red velvet."

"I'm telling you right now, Jazzy, I am not at all interested in that man!" Alyson eyeballed the baker who sat across the table from them. She tried to lower her voice to a whisper. "He's so…so…egotistical."

"He seems very nice and genuine to me," Jasmine countered. "And you have to admit he's gorgeous. Isn't he?"

"He's a womanizer. Already running about town with that young woman from the band."

"Bijou? Oh, she's much too young for him. And not at all his type."

"Could've fooled me. And what would you know about his type? Do you even know this man?" Alyson asked her. "Does Jackson even know him? I know they claim to be friends, but how long has it been since he's seen him last?"

"They've been friends for years. And Jackson knows him very well. He's a great guy, Alyson," Jasmine said. "You should give him a chance."

"I don't trust him." Alyson licked cream cheese frosting from the side of her finger. "What does he even do for a living?"

"Well, as I understand it, he was an assistant district attorney for years. But recently he decided to run for mayor, and there were some issues that surfaced with his campaign. I don't know all the details, but I understand there was a little scandal of some sort. There were rumors that he'd accepted some bribes. Somebody had it in for him."

"See, that's exactly what I'm talking about! Scandalous."

"None of it was true," said Jasmine. "But he was so devastated, he decided to come over here to clear his head and regroup."

"You mean run away from his troubles."

"That's not what I said, Alyson. And I think you should stop being so judgmental. Give the man a break. Go to dinner! Find out who he is for yourself."

"Not interested," said Alyson. "And I'll let him know that no one gives me orders. No one!"

Alyson pulled out her cell phone to check the text message that had just come through. Jennifer Madison wanted to know why the full-price offer on Madison Place had fallen through. She didn't have the nerve to tell her that the buyer had changed his mind—found another home that suited him better. She needed the property to sell, and she needed it to happen soon. She had bills looming over her head.

"Thank you for filling in for Jackson today, sis. He hates that he's not able to participate in all the little details of the wedding." Jasmine grabbed Alyson's hand. "But I'm so glad you're here."

"Me, too." Alyson smiled. "But don't get used to me being here all the time, Jazzy, and I mean it. My life is in Miami. And I have a business there, too."

"I know. I know. But I'm just glad you're here now."

"I'm leaving on Monday. Have an early flight out," said Alyson. "You should come with me. Maybe we can visit a few bridal boutiques, look at some dresses. Maybe you'll finally fall in love with one."

"I might take you up on that. Jackson won't be back until next Friday."

"We'll leave on the first flight out in the morning," Alyson said. "I'll have Jules check rates for you."

"We'll be back by the week's end, right? We're having our family dinner next Saturday. Did you forget?"

She hadn't forgotten. Family dinners at the Talbots' home weren't an option. You were expected to be there when you lived as close as Florida. Their siblings who lived in Atlanta and Texas were given a pass. And their youngest brother, Denny, who was training in the Royal Bahamas, would also be absent. But Jasmine, Alyson and their brother Edward, who also lived in Florida, were expected to show up.

"I didn't forget," Alyson said. "How could I when Mother has reminded me every single day this week that I'm preparing the macaroni and cheese."

"Macaroni and cheese? You got off easy," said Jasmine. "I'm doing the conch salad and conch fritters."

"It's because you still live at home. You get all the grunt work." Alyson laughed. "Maybe once you move into your own home, you'll get some relief."

"It's so hard living with them sometimes. Always keeping tabs on me as if I'm still a kid. But with Jackson working and traveling so much, I prefer to be there with them. It's better than being alone in some empty house."

"You'll be a married woman soon. And maybe your husband will quit working so much and spend more time at home, so you don't have to spend so much time with the old people." Alyson laughed. "Sitting on the porch listening to Daddy's stories of the old days."

"I love Daddy's stories." Jasmine giggled.

"I bet you don't have an ounce of privacy. And how many nights do they sip on sky juice and play George Symonette albums?"

Both women laughed. While they enjoyed contemporary Caribbean artists, they knew that their parents still preferred old-school calypso and goombay music styles. It was what they knew and loved, and what the Talbot children grew up listening to.

"Every Saturday night I'm listening to George Symonette while Mother dances around the room, a high-ball in her hand. Daddy has to pry the glass from her and put her to bed," said Jasmine. "She's sipping on the sky juice more often these days."

"She's worried about Denny," Alyson said. "He should've gone to college like the rest of us."

Beverly Talbot hadn't been the least bit happy with her son's choice for his future. She'd particularly made a fuss when she learned that her baby boy would be shipped away to the US to be trained with the navy SEALs.

"He followed his heart," Jasmine defended Denny. She'd

had many conversations with him about his choice. He'd been brave, in her opinion.

"The rest of us didn't have the luxury of following our hearts," said Alyson, "except maybe you, when you went tramping off to California looking for the next acting and modeling gig."

"I try to forget about that. That was before the Grove," said Jasmine. "The Grove changed my life."

"I have to admit that you have grown up quite a bit since the Grove. You've done a fantastic job with the place," said Alyson. "I'll be honest with you, Jazzy. I didn't think you could pull it off."

"I'm sure you weren't the only hater." Jasmine laughed and threw a napkin at her sister.

Alyson threw it back. "I'm not a hater."

"You are," Jasmine exclaimed. "That's why you won't give Samson a chance."

"What is it with you and this fellow?" Alyson groaned. "He wants me to go to dinner with him tonight and give him another opportunity to mess things up."

Jasmine shook her head and took another bite of white Amaretto. "Stop being a stick-in-the-mud! Love is a wonderful thing."

"Who said anything about love? I'm talking about dinner, which I won't be attending."

"I think you should open your heart and be prepared for whatever comes your way."

"Not this time. An open heart is an open door for pain."

"Not always."

It had been in Alyson's life. Every man that she'd ever opened her heart to had left it broken. And she wasn't up for taking the risk. She loved herself, and that was love enough.

Alyson changed the subject. "I like the red velvet. It's super moist. Melts in your mouth!"

"I love the red velvet, too. It's delicious, and also festive. Perfect for a Christmas wedding," said Jasmine. "I think it's a winner."

"Good, then we're done here." Alyson stood. "I really need to get going. I have phone calls to make…paperwork to complete."

"You can run along while I finish up here." Jasmine stood and gave her sister a strong embrace. "Thanks for coming."

"My pleasure, Jazzy," Alyson said. "I'll have Jules book you on my flight in the morning."

"I'll be packed and ready to go."

"Good. I'll see you tomorrow."

"Let Samson know that you're accepting his dinner invitation."

"I can't. I have too much going on."

"Open your heart for romance."

"Goodbye, Jazzy." Alyson waved her sister's comment away as she exited the bakery.

Chapter 7

The condo was a bit stuffy, having been closed up for several days. Alyson opened the kitchen window and breathed in the Miami air, then opened the refrigerator and pulled out a bottle of water. She had roughly an hour to shower, dress and meet her clients at the title company in Fort Lauderdale. Their flight from the islands had been delayed, causing her entire schedule to be pushed back.

Jasmine relaxed on the sofa, the remote control in her hand as she flipped between channels.

"You're welcome to tag along, but you'll be bored out of your wits," Alyson said.

"I think I'll stay here and relax a bit." Jasmine curled her feet beneath her bottom.

"I'll bring lunch," Alyson said before disappearing into the bedroom.

After dressing in a fashionable suit, she rushed to her convertible BMW, slapped her briefcase against the leather seats and affixed her Michael Kors sunglasses onto her face. She looked at her reflection in the rearview mirror, dabbed lipstick on and smacked her lips together to work it all in. She snapped her seat belt on and slid a CD into the console. The Caribbean rhythm filled the car. The convertible top eased its way down as she slowly pulled out of the parking garage. She hated being late, but could probably make up some time once she made it to the interstate, provided she could navigate through rush hour traffic.

Traffic on I-95 inched along slowly, and she leaned her head against the back of the seat. She found herself daydreaming about a certain wannabe musician, with a gorgeous smile and tattooed arms that had become surprisingly enticing to her, even though she denied her attraction to him, dismissed any possibility of spending time with him. She had shunned him and his dinner invitation. Had she gone, she would have relinquished her control. And she needed to be in control of her own destiny. It had been a while since she'd given any man the time of day.

Carl had been the last straw. He was almost her father's age, but she'd tried not to notice the age difference. They'd shared the same interests—the theater, museums and exotic restaurants, something that most men her age weren't at all interested in. Men her age were still partying at the South Beach clubs. Carl was different. He was laid-back and conservative. And just when she'd started to develop feelings for him, she discovered that he was still married to the mother of his grown children. His very angry wife of twenty-two years had shown up at the restaurant where they were enjoying a candlelit dinner, and accused Alyson of being a home wrecker.

It was the last time she'd let anyone into her space. There was no time or room for a relationship. Her life was overloaded with shaping a new business, all the while trying to maintain a certain lifestyle. If she didn't grow her portfolio soon, she'd be forced to sell her beloved condo and downsize to a cheaper place. Selling the Madison property on Abaco would help her stay above water. Her real goal was to connect with Jennifer Madison's father, who was a commercial developer. There was a larger profit in commercial properties, and she wanted a piece of it. Jennifer had promised Alyson an introduction, but an introduction didn't guarantee a business deal. It would be left up to her to sell herself to the real estate mogul.

Her phone rang through the speakers in her car. She picked up with the click of a button on the car's dashboard.

"It's Alyson."

"If you're en route to the title company, don't bother," her assistant said. "The buyers can't close."

"What do you mean?"

"Changed their minds last minute."

"They can't do that!"

"They did, honey. Just got off the phone with their Realtor," said Jules. "They don't care about losing their escrow. They've decided to move to New Jersey to be closer to their grandchildren."

Alyson sighed. "Didn't they know they had grandchildren in Jersey before putting a contract on a home in Florida?"

"Apparently so, Alyson. But they didn't know they wanted to live closer to them."

"Or that they were wasting our time!" Alyson exclaimed. "Get on the phone with the sellers and schedule a time for me to meet with them. We've got to get this property back on the market right away. We're losing money every moment it's off the market. Try to schedule it as soon as possible because I'm heading back to the islands by week's end."

"Your afternoon is free, so I'll try to set it up for today."

"Thanks, Jules." She disconnected the call.

She got off at the next exit and headed back toward Miami. She drove down Calle Ocho to Versailles, a Cuban eatery in the heart of Little Havana, to grab a café cubano and a couple of empanada pies with spinach and cheese inside. She passed on the pancakes and syrup that normally accompanied her empanadas. Watching her weight had its sacrifices. Her hips were nicely shaped, but a few too many pancakes might take them to the next level—a level that she really didn't want to go to.

She loved Miami's Cuban community. Little Havana reminded her of home. It was her way of having a little bit of Caribbean without actually having to return to her childhood home permanently. It was home to some of her favorite indulgences—the little eatery that sold the best Cuban sandwiches, the Latin theaters and Domino Park, where she would occasionally stop and gawk at the old men as they competed against each other in a game of dominoes. She grabbed a copy of the *Miami Herald* and headed back to her downtown condo.

"I brought breakfast instead of lunch," she told Jasmine.

"What happened?" Jasmine followed her sister into the kitchen.

"My clients canceled," she said. "I brought coffee and empanadas."

"They look and smell delightful," said Jasmine, who didn't hesitate to dig in.

"Enjoy!" Alyson said as she exited the kitchen.

"You're not having any?"

"I'm watching my weight."

"Since when?" Jasmine yelled.

"Since now!"

Lately she'd become more cognizant that her clothes were fitting a bit more snug than she wanted them to, and something needed to change. She stepped into the extra bedroom that had been transformed into a minigym, dusted off the treadmill and stepped onto it. She found an upbeat playlist on her phone and turned up the volume as loud as it would go. She took long strides, with her spandex exercise pants hugging her hips. Her mind unintentionally drifted to Samson, and how fit he was. She wasn't sure why thoughts of him were suddenly crowding her small space, but there he was, creeping his way into her thoughts *again*. Although she hated to admit it, she admired his confidence.

What she exhibited to the world was poise and self-assurance, but underneath she was all but. She was afraid that she wasn't good enough, smart enough. That she might fail at building Alyson Talbot and Associates into a successful business. She feared that she might spend the rest of her life alone because she was too rigid, too judgmental, too independent, and if she wasn't careful, too damn fat for a man to give her a second look. She needed to feel good about herself again. She wasn't overweight, but didn't feel good about her body. She wanted to be fit, like her sister who worked out on a daily basis. And like Bijou, the woman whose body she secretly envied.

The Beyoncé track was interrupted by a call from Jules. She placed it on speakerphone.

"I've scheduled for you to meet with the Tuckers tomorrow afternoon. It's the only time they were available."

"That's fine. Thanks, Jules."

"Why are you breathing like that?" asked Jules. "You okay?"

"I'm on the treadmill."

"You mean the one that's been collecting dust since you bought it last year?"

"I don't need the judgment."

"No judgment. Do your thing, girl." Jules chuckled.

"Whenever you're done, let me know," said Alyson.

"I'm done," said a much more composed Jules.

"Good. I need you to book my sister and me a flight back to the islands tomorrow afternoon—sometime after my meeting."

"Going back so soon? I thought you weren't going back until the weekend."

"Change of plans."

"You and Jazzy going shopping for dresses?"

"Yes, sometime this afternoon. And she better find one today because I'm headed back to the Bahamas tomorrow!"

"Why the urgency? Your family dinner isn't until Saturday."

"I just… I need to go back," Alyson said. "Something's come up."

"Fine." Alyson could tell Jules wanted to pry, but didn't. She knew Alyson very well. They'd been friends long enough to know when something was different. She would find out what it was soon enough. "I'll take care of it."

"Keep it within the budget. We're watching every dollar."

"I know," said Jules. "We'll get there, sweetie. Pretty soon, Alyson Talbot and Associates will be a household name."

"Damn right it will! And you'll get your old salary back."

"I'm not worried about that. I'm living with Mama right now, so my expenses are a lot less these days. My stress level is through the roof, though. That woman is hard to live with. But at least I'm saving money."

"I appreciate you hanging in there with me."

"Don't mention it. I wouldn't be anywhere else. I'm invested."

"You're the best."

"I know!" Jules said with a giggle. "Now go finish pretending to exercise."

"I *am* exercising. I've got another mile on this thing."

"Knock yourself out."

Jules believed in Alyson, and knew that it was just a matter of time before she was on top again. Alyson loved Jules like family. They'd met in college. A native of Miami, Jules was the first person to embrace the young girl from the Caribbean, who was away from home for the first time and knew nothing about the United States. They became instant friends. After college, Alyson landed a job at a large real estate company. Jules was an accounting major, but struggled to find work. Alyson hired her as a part-time personal assistant, just until something came along. Jules had been with her ever since.

After a few miles, Alyson hopped down from the treadmill. She took a long hot shower and slipped into her favorite pair of designer jeans—the ones that boosted her self-esteem because they hugged her in all the right places. She needed all the boosting she could get.

Later that afternoon at a local bridal shop, Jasmine stared at her own reflection in the mirror as Alyson sipped a glass of red wine. She had prepared herself for a long day of dress shopping with her indecisive sister. Her heart skipped a beat when she saw Jasmine step up onto the platform wearing the soft white strapless organza gown with dramatic ruffling at the bottom. The pewter-colored ribbon hugged her sister's small waist. She was speechless for a moment.

"What do you think, Jazzy?" Alyson finally asked.

Jasmine took her time about turning around, but finally faced her sister. She had tears in her eyes. "This is it," she whispered softly.

"Are you sure?" asked Alyson.

"I'm sure," said Jasmine. "This is it."

"You look absolutely beautiful!" Alyson gave her sister a warm smile. She stepped up onto the platform and adjusted the ribbon on Jasmine's dress. Took a quick glance at the price tag. "Damn, sixteen hundred dollars. I hope Daddy's sitting down when you call him."

"I thought you would make the call, Maid of Honor."

"That was before you exceeded your budget by four hundred dollars," said Alyson, "and that's not really a maid of honor duty."

"You know this is the gown, Alyson. It's so beautiful!" Jasmine gushed.

"It *is* beautiful, but I'm not doing your dirty work." Alyson pulled out her cell phone, dialed her father's number and pushed the phone into Jasmine's hand. "Daddy's on the phone."

Jasmine rolled her eyes and took the phone, rushing into the dressing room. Alyson knew their father wouldn't put up a fuss. He would do just about anything for his children, and especially his daughters. If this was the wedding dress that Jasmine desired, she knew that it would give him great joy to buy it for her. The dress had been worth the wait, and Alyson was relieved that her sister hadn't settled. Though she was grateful that the long search was now over.

Jasmine rushed from the dressing room, still wearing the gown. "Alyson, we have to get back to the islands. Daddy had a heart attack!"

Chapter 8

Samson knew CPR, but had only administered it one other time. When a client went into cardiac arrest right there at the courthouse, he had revived her and called for emergency help. He thought he'd have to do the same thing for Paul John Talbot. The senior member of the Talbot clan had been visiting the Grove, looking for his daughter Jasmine. Samson was having tea in the living area at Samson Place when Paul John approached him and introduced himself.

"You must be the friend of Jackson's that I've heard so much about." Paul John held out his hand.

"Yes, sir. I am."

"Good to meet you. Have you seen either of my two daughters around here?"

"If I'm not mistaken, I believe they took a flight to Miami this morning," said Samson.

"Miami, huh?" He laughed a little.

Samson remembered thinking that Mr. Talbot didn't look well. He looked fatigued.

"Are you okay, sir?" he asked.

"Yes, just a little tired," said Paul John. "I wish these girls would tell us when they're leaving for the States. It's good information to know. If something happened to them, my wife and I wouldn't know anything. Jasmine packed a bag, but I thought she was staying here at the Grove for a few days. Didn't know she was leaving the country."

"Anything I can do to help?"

"Just let them know I was here, looking for them."

As soon as Paul John turned to leave, he grasped his chest and bent over. He grabbed the arm of a chair for balance. Samson rushed to his side and helped him to sit down. Paul John held on to his chest and seemed to experience light-headedness and shortness of breath. Samson attempted to hide the fact that he was panicking. He pulled his phone out, but wasn't quite certain how to call for an emergency on the island.

"I'll call the police station," yelled Raquel, who stood nearby. "They will dispatch an ambulance."

After making the call, Raquel rushed back to the living area. She handed Paul John two baby aspirin. "Here, take these, Mr. Talbot…chew them. It'll help."

He took the aspirin, stuffed them into his mouth and began to chew. Samson felt as if he was losing control, wasn't sure what to do. He was grateful to hear the roar of the ambulance's engine as it pulled up in front of the Grove. The emergency volunteers emerged from the vehicle, rushed inside and began medical treatment.

"We're going to take him in. Would you like to ride?" one of the volunteers asked Samson.

He didn't know what to say, but nodded.

"I'll call Mrs. Talbot!" said Raquel.

Samson climbed into the back of the ambulance and took a seat right next to Paul John. As the vehicle zoomed through the streets of Harbour Island and the sirens wailed, Samson began to pray. The ride seemed long and agonizing. It felt as if they wouldn't make it to their destination in time, and he'd witness something he wasn't quite prepared for.

Finally the ambulance pulled up in front of the Harbour Island Ministry of Health, and the volunteers rushed Paul John inside. Samson stayed in the lobby, pacing the floor. Praying for a miracle. He pulled out his phone and dialed Jackson's number. No answer. He left a detailed message, and then plopped down into an old chair. Dropped his face into his hands. He felt helpless and hated feeling that way. His stomach churned, and his heart began to beat a fast pace. He checked his watch, and then checked it again.

When the older woman walked in, he knew that she was Alyson Talbot's mother because she looked like an older version of her. With a flawless brown face and long, graying hair, she was a spitting image of the woman he thought of more often than he should. She rushed in to see her husband. And later, when she returned to the lobby where Samson paced the floor, he barely knew she was there.

"What's your name, baby?" she asked.

He turned to greet her. "I'm Samson."

"I'm Beverly Talbot," she said. "I understand you've been right here with my husband all morning. And you're responsible for getting him here."

"Yes, ma'am."

She hugged him. "You are a godsend."

"I'm glad I was able to help. How is he?"

"He's going to be just fine. He's resting now," she said. "Paul John has a hard head. I struggle to get him to watch his cholesterol. And he's a physician, too. He should know better."

"I'm glad I could help, Mrs. Talbot."

"You're Jackson's friend from the States?"

"Yes, ma'am."

"So nice to meet you," said Beverly. "Would you please join us for dinner at our house on Saturday?"

"I would be honored," said Samson.

"Good. Five o'clock." She smiled. "And bring your appetite. My daughters and I are preparing a Bahamian feast."

"Thank you."

She placed the palm of her hand against his face and gave him a warm, motherly smile. She reminded him of his own mother, and how he missed her. When she rushed back to be with her husband, Samson pulled his phone out of his pocket and dialed his mother's phone number.

"Ma, it's me."

"Samson, why are you calling me? You know these international rates are outrageous. You should've sent me an email, or a message on that Faceplace thing."

"It's Facebook, Ma, and you don't even visit your page. And I wanted to hear your voice," he said. "How did it go today?"

"I nailed it!" She giggled. "That damn parallel parking almost messed it up for me, though. But I did it. I got my license."

"I'm so proud of you."

"You should've seen me, Sammy, adjusting my mirrors and carrying on. And your daddy let me use the Chrysler. Can you believe it?"

"I can't believe it. He's anal about that car."

"Damn right he is! And you know how bullheaded he can be. Not wanting me to get my driver's license. It might've taken me thirty years, but I was determined. And I did it."

"I love you, Ma."

"I love you back," she said. "What do I hear in your voice? What's going on?"

"Nothing," he lied. "Just missing my favorite girl."

"Oh, shoot, I'm fine. Now tell me about the Bahamas. Are they anything like the pictures I've seen on television?"

"Better. It's absolutely gorgeous over here."

"Are you staying out of trouble?" she asked. "You've got to stop playing the field, Sammy. Find a nice girl and settle down."

"I will, Ma. One day." He knew that he needed to end the conversation before she went into her spiel. "You need some money?"

"You know I don't need your money, son. I'm doing just fine."

He'd saved his money and invested in the stock market. He'd done well. A single man with no children, Samson had more expendable funds than he knew what to do with. Early in his career, he made sure he took care of his aging parents. He knew they would never consider leaving their two-story brick home where he grew up. No, that was not an option. So instead, he'd renovated it for them— had beautiful hardwoods installed, fresh paint throughout, and all new appliances to replace old run-down ones. He'd set up a bank account for them—a place where he would deposit cash for them on a regular basis. That was before the scandal.

After the scandal, his father insisted that he shut the bank account down. "We don't need your dirty money."

It was a punch to Samson's gut, but he pretended not to be bothered. For so long, he'd lived for the approval of his father, whose footsteps he hadn't followed. And his father often reminded him that he wouldn't be in the predicament that he was in had he not followed his own path.

Samson was from a long generation of cops. His grandfather had been a police officer for over thirty years, and his father's career had been nearly as long, with twenty-nine years on the force. His older brother, Jessie, and his younger brother, Calvin, were both officers. Samson was the only one who'd taken a different route. He'd gone to the University of Chicago and then to Harvard Law School. He had no desire to chase criminals through Chicago neighborhoods. Instead, he preferred to try their cases before a court of law. He'd landed a job in the DA's office shortly after graduation.

When he decided to run for mayor, his mother had been his strongest supporter. She'd worked diligently on his campaign, putting in long hours, raising money and answering phones. She was proud of her baby, and didn't care one bit that he hadn't become a police officer. The job was way too dangerous for her taste anyway. She worried herself sick about her other two sons who spent their days patrolling the streets of Chicago, and didn't mind one bit that one of her sons had chosen a different path.

Samson was her hero, but in his mind she was one of the bravest people he knew. She'd endured chemotherapy, and the cancer had been in remission for the past two years. Yet she never missed a beat. Even when the treatments left her exhausted and sick, she kept fighting, always caring more about the next person than her own faltering health. He was so proud of her that he'd had her name etched across his biceps in bold letters, *Toni*. It was a reminder that when things got tough, her bravery was his strength.

"If you need anything, you let me know," he told his mother.

"I need a new daughter-in-law, is what I need. And some grandchildren."

"You have a daughter-in-law. Jessie's wife. And they have a kid," Samson teased. "And Calvin has a kid. Last time I checked, you had two grandchildren."

"You know what I mean, boy," Toni said. "I want you to settle down."

"Something's going on with my phone. I think we have a bad connection. Hello. Hello."

"Okay, bad connection, Sammy Steel," she said. "You just remember that time doesn't wait for anyone."

"I love you, Ma."

"Yeah, I love you, too," she said. "I'm going to have Calvin scan my driver's license so I can send you a copy by email."

"That would be nice."

"Are you coming home for Christmas?"

"I don't think so. Jackson is getting married on Christmas Day, and I want to be here," said Samson. "I've unofficially joined the band that was hired for the reception."

"Unofficially, huh?" His mother chuckled. "You got your guitar with you?"

"Of course."

"That's always been your first love. I'm glad to see you're staying true to it."

"Always."

"Send pictures of the wedding."

"I will."

"And, Samson." She hesitated. "Take care, baby."

"You do the same, Ma. I'll call you again soon."

He hung up, but held the phone against his chin. He missed her more than he realized. He missed her almost as much as he missed seeing Alyson Talbot's face around the Grove. She'd only been gone for a short time, and he already missed her presence. No doubt, she was under his skin. Which was odd, because he didn't allow women to get under his skin—he was always in control. Women chased him, not the other way around. He couldn't remember the last time he had been the chaser.

But he was chasing this time, and she was running. And he intended to figure out why. His original intent was to get her in bed, but something had happened along the way. She intrigued him, and he wanted to know everything there was to know about her.

Chapter 9

Samson was quite fond of Bailey, his acoustic guitar made of Sitka spruce with its rosewood fingerboard. He rarely went anywhere without it. He rested it on his leg, and his fingertips quickly began to fret the strings as he joined Onyx while they performed their Caribbean Christmas medley. He'd never heard Nat King Cole's "The Christmas Song" played quite like that. He felt nervous as a crowd gathered in the Grand Room to listen to the band play. They sipped wine and other cocktails and danced to the music. Some of them sang along, while others nibbled on hors d'oeuvres. Soon the crowd had grown bigger than he expected. It seemed that every guest staying at the Grove was in one room.

He was surprised to see Alyson's face in the midst of the crowd. Dressed in a business suit, with her arms folded across her chest, her lips curved into a slight smile. He gave her a wide grin and a wink. She blushed, unfolded her arms and began to move to the music a bit, trying to ignore him. After the news of her father's heart attack, he'd expected her to return from Miami soon. And he was pleased to see her. Couldn't wait to finish the set and work his way over to her.

"Look up," he whispered in her ear as he held the mistletoe above her head.

She looked up, and he kissed her cheek.

"How dare you kiss me in front of all these people?" she whispered. "And it's not even Christmas yet."

"Close enough. And you didn't seem to mind." His smile was intoxicating.

"Are you always this full of yourself?"

"Always," he said.

"I'm glad you're here." Suddenly they seemed like old friends. "I wanted to thank you for what you did for my father. You saved his life, and I am eternally grateful."

"I didn't do anything I wouldn't have done for my own father. I just went with him to the clinic."

"It was a big deal to my family," she said. "And to me."

"Maybe you can repay me with dinner."

"Maybe I can," she resolved.

"How about tonight?"

"The Rock House, I suppose," she said with a smile.

"Yes."

"I'll meet you there."

"Good." He said it casually, but could hardly contain his excitement.

He decided to walk away, leave before she changed her mind or came up with an excuse. He walked back toward the band and prepped for the next song. The anticipation of getting to know Alyson Talbot beyond her business suit and professional disposition caused him anxiety, but music always calmed his fears. He was enjoying himself in the islands, and was grateful for the recess from his life in Chicago. He wanted to forget about it, at least for now.

It had been a while since the trial, and he should've been proud of how he'd single-handedly won convictions against mayor-elect Conrad Phelps and William Blue, owner of Blue Island Properties, who had paid Phelps thousands of dollars to get their bids approved. Blue Island had funded Conrad Phelps's campaign, in exchange for him getting all of their development plans approved once he was in office. And Mayor Phelps had kept his promise.

They'd been suspected of wrongdoings for years, but the corruption continued. Finally the FBI conducted a real estate sting that brought the racket to its demise, and ultimately Mayor Phelps, several city employees, William Blue and several of Blue Island's employees were arrested. Samson, as assistant district attorney, was successful at bringing charges against them all. However, he wasn't aware of the consequences involved in solving an agelong case. For years, evidence had been *overlooked* because the mayor and Blue Island had ties that were much bigger than the FBI. It wasn't long before Samson realized just how deep those ties ran.

After the convictions, Samson had become somewhat of a hometown hero, and running for mayor quickly went from a fleeting idea to an attainable goal. He had plenty of supporters and soon left the DA's office to begin raising funds for his campaign. However, in the midst of his campaign, all hell broke loose. Suddenly, he'd been accused of accepting bribes—the same crime that his predecessor, Conrad Phelps, had been accused and convicted of. In fact, there was speculation that the reason Samson had worked so diligently to put Conrad Phelps behind bars was because he had intentions of running for office himself. It was no secret that someone was determined to bring him down.

He quickly discovered that the criminals he'd placed behind bars a few years prior had accomplices on the outside who were intent on seeking revenge. They worked diligently to destroy him—and so far, they had been successful. Although the allegations were completely unfounded, supporters began to pull their funds. And although Samson had been cleared of all misgivings, his name and reputation had already been tarnished. And all hopes of becoming mayor were gone.

He wasn't sure that returning to his old job was what he really wanted. What he really needed was to get away. Before he knew it, he'd found himself on a nonstop flight to the Eleuthera Islands. He would only return to Chicago when his head was clear, and not a day before—*if at all*.

And now, as he looked over at Alyson, who clapped her hands to the music, he wondered just how long he'd find himself in the Bahamas.

Chapter 10

She'd spent a great deal of time searching for the perfect outfit, and she'd fussed with her hair way too long for a man that she had no interest in. She ruled out her professional garb and chose a pair of cropped white pants and a simple melon-colored blouse instead. After slipping into a pair of white leather sandals, she dabbed perfume behind each ear and in between her ample breasts.

Alyson's stomach churned as she stepped onto the beautiful terrace of the Rock House. She'd never been nervous around anyone in her life, but Samson Steel caused her anxiety for some reason. She spotted him as he took a sip of his martini. *The nerve of him, starting without me*, she thought. He stood when he saw her, greeted her and then pulled her chair out. *At least he's a gentleman*. She was startled when he kissed her cheek, but smiled a little when she caught a slight whiff of his cologne. She took a seat, and her back reclined against the wooden chair. Her gaze veered toward the beautiful sunset that was now descending upon the bay.

A candle danced in the center of their table, and Alyson tried with all her might to peel her eyes from Samson. He looked dapper in his tan, slim-fit Levi's and white T-shirt that hugged his core and revealed muscular tattooed arms. A straw Panama fedora hat rested upon his head. He had his own style, and she appreciated it.

"Very nice to see you." He smiled.

"Likewise," she said.

"I was afraid you might not show up." Samson chuckled.

"I considered it." She picked up the menu to distract herself from staring at him. "But I thought it rude to leave you sitting here alone."

"You mean like you did the other day?" he asked. "That was very noble of you."

"Why the insistence that I join you, anyway?"

"I think you're beautiful and smart. And I'd like to get to know you better. What's wrong with that?"

"There are plenty of beautiful and smart women on this island. Why me?"

"Why not you?"

"I'm not looking for a man right now."

"I never said I wanted to be your man. I just said that I want to get to know you better. A huge difference." He grinned a breathtaking grin.

She scowled at him. "What is your story? Why are you even here in the Bahamas? I've heard rumors, but I'd really like to hear from you."

She'd actually Googled him and read all about the scandal on the internet, but wanted to hear the story from the horse's mouth.

"What have you heard?" He set his drink down and peered into Alyson's eyes.

"That you were doing some shady stuff in Chicago, and now you're on the run."

"Is that so?"

"I heard that while campaigning for mayor, you accepted some bribes. It was a huge scandal, and you fled to the islands for refuge."

Samson laughed heartily, and then gave Alyson a sideways glance. "I did run for mayor. That part is true. Turns out I had some enemies in high places, and they didn't want me in office. So they fabricated a story that I was accepting bribes. There was no truth to it."

"Why would someone accuse you of doing something like that?"

"I was responsible for bringing down the former mayor, who was, in fact, engaged in bribery." Samson took a sip of his martini, and then opened his menu. "Unfortunately for me, he retaliated by having someone slander me."

"You know that running away from things is never the answer," Alyson stated. "You should always face your fears head-on."

"Facing your fears is not always that easy." Samson closed his menu and laid it on the table. "I'm having the lobster tail. What about you?"

"I can't seem to find anything on the menu that appeals to me. I never really liked this place. Maybe I'll just have a salad. I'm watching my figure anyway."

"Why don't you leave the figure-watching to me and order something worthwhile," he told her. "How about a nice steak?"

"I don't eat red meat."

"Why don't you like this place? It's upscale, and bourgeoisie—"

"Bourgeoisie like me, huh?"

"I didn't say that."

"You didn't have to." She gave a slight wave to get the server's attention. "For your information, this is not my type of place at all. When I'm on the islands, I prefer an old-fashioned Caribbean meal at my parents' house, one accompanied by conch fritters and collard greens. Not lobster tails and fancy steaks."

"Yes, ma'am?" The Caribbean waitress interrupted her rant. "Are we ready to order?"

"I'd like to start with a key lime cosmopolitan, with just a touch of cranberry and a little extra lime juice," said Alyson.

"Yes, ma'am." The woman disappeared.

"I think we have more in common than you think. Although I'm not all that familiar with Caribbean food, I do prefer an old-fashioned meal myself." Samson laughed. "Maybe I missed the mark a little with this place."

"I would think that a ladies' man such as yourself would be a bit more perceptive when it came to women."

"I was trying to impress you with a nice meal and a gorgeous view."

Alyson gave an appreciative smile, but turned her head toward the bay. "You were dead-on with the gorgeous view."

"Breathtaking, isn't it?" he said softly, relaxed in his seat. She could feel his eyes settle on her.

The server placed the cosmopolitan in front of her.

"I think I'll have the Chilean sea bass," she said, and then handed her menu to the server. Took a long swig of her cocktail.

She'd decided against the salad long before. Since he'd taken the time to try to impress her, the least she could do was eat. And she did just that, and enjoyed the simple conversation. Samson was easier to talk to than she'd ever suspected, and she found that she enjoyed his company.

"Would you like dessert?" he asked.

"Let's not push it," she said. "I really am watching my figure."

"What is this obsession with your weight?"

"There's no obsession. I'm just cautious."

"I think your body is perfect."

She did everything in her power not to blush, but she couldn't help it. She looked away to disrupt the uncomfortable moment. "It's a beautiful night."

"We should go for a walk along the beach after dinner. What d'you say?"

"Maybe another time," she said. "I have work waiting for me at the Grove."

"I understand."

She ordered another cosmopolitan, and before long she was feeling mildly tipsy. The more she talked to Samson, the less she wanted the night to end. She almost rethought his invitation to walk along the beach, but wasn't about to bring the subject up again. She was too stubborn. However, she vowed that if he asked again, she'd take him up on it. But he didn't ask. Instead, he motioned for the server to bring the check.

Fifteen minutes later, Samson delivered Alyson to the door of her suite at the Grove.

"So this is good night," he said.

"I had a lovely time." She was sincere when she said it.

She leaned her back against her door, and Samson drew closer. "Can I see you again?"

She breathed in his scent. She hoped he would kiss her; she wanted him to. He leaned in, and she rested her head against the door. She decided not to close her eyes. She wanted to be fully aware of him. His nose brushed against hers.

"Well, there you are," came an intrusive voice.

Bijou appeared out of nowhere, and Alyson rolled her eyes at the interruption.

"Hello, Bijou." Samson spoke to her.

"I've been looking all over for you. The band is setting up for rehearsal. Are you coming?"

"Of course."

Bijou stood there, as if waiting for him.

"Did you need something else?" he asked what Alyson wanted to ask.

"No. I'll be downstairs," she said, and turned to walk away. "Good evening, Miss Talbot."

"Good evening, Bijou," Alyson mumbled.

Samson turned back toward Alyson and attempted to pick up where he'd left off. Alyson placed a finger in the air and blocked his lips from finding hers again.

"Good night, Mr. Steel. Thank you for a lovely dinner." Alyson turned to unlock her door. "I need to call and check on my father."

"When will I see you again?"

"I don't know. I'll be tied up this weekend," she said as she turned to face him again. "My parents are planning a family dinner on Saturday, and I'm expected to be there."

"Oh, you mean the family dinner that I've been invited to attend?" He grinned. "Your mother invited me to break bread with your family."

"Oh, she did, did she?"

"She did indeed. And I'm glad now. I have an excuse to see you again."

She felt a sense of warmth in her heart—something she hadn't felt in some time. But just as sure as she felt it, she dismissed it. She didn't have any time or room for Samson Steel in her life. She was too busy for romance, and too focused to become attached to someone like him. She reminded herself that Jasmine's wedding was the only reason she frequented the islands, and that wouldn't change.

Even if Samson's almost-kiss did have her loins burning on the inside.

Chapter 11

The house smelled of Bahamian macaroni and cheese, garlic chicken and fresh collard greens. Freshly baked johnnycakes rested on the kitchen table right next to her mother's famous rum cake. The conch had been chopped into small pieces and was ready to be tossed in a salad. Bahamian music played on her father's stereo in the living room, while her mother cooked and danced around the kitchen.

"Alyson, check the pigeon peas and rice for me," her mother instructed after taking a sip of her sky juice. "Jazzy, the conch is ready for you to make that conch salad. I've already fried up the fritters. We are on the ball."

"Yes, we are, Mother." Jasmine kissed her mother's cheek.

Alyson stirred the mixture with a large spoon. Of all the family dinners at the Talbot home, this one was causing her the most anxiety. The anticipation of seeing Samson again had her giddy.

"Why are you glowing?" asked Beverly Talbot. She brushed her daughter's hair with her fingertips.

"I'm not," Alyson denied, and pulled away from her mother's touch.

"You're wearing makeup." Beverly smiled. "Is that eye shadow?"

Alyson rarely wore more than an occasional lip gloss, and perhaps a little eyeliner to heighten her eyes.

"I always wear eye shadow," she lied.

Talbot women didn't need makeup. Their skin was flawless.

"I've never seen you wear it," said an instigating Jasmine, who stood nearby with a knowing grin.

"If you two don't stop…! I'm going to set the table." Alyson left the kitchen in a huff.

The sight of Edward walking through the front door gave Alyson a sense of normalcy. Took a bit of her anxiety away.

"Little sister." Edward greeted Alyson with a strong hug and a kiss to the cheek.

"It's about time you got here," she said. "I thought you were coming in yesterday."

"I spent too much time at the courthouse yesterday. I'm going for full custody of Chloe," said Edward.

"What? Why?" Alyson asked.

"Because she belongs with me."

"You can't get full custody!"

"Why not?"

"Because, number one, you don't have time to raise a kid. Which is the reason you're divorced in the first place," said Alyson. "And what makes you think a court would give you full custody instead of Savannah?"

"Whose side are you on, anyway?"

"I'm always on your side, but I know that courts typically rule in favor of the biological mother unless she's a lousy parent. Which you and I both know she's not. Savannah is a wonderful mother. And you two have the perfect coparenting relationship," Alyson said as she set embroidered place mats on the table. "What's really going on?"

"She's seeing some dude."

"So? You've dated women, too, since the divorce."

"But I don't bring anyone around Chloe. That's not a part of the deal. Not to mention I found out that he might be living in my house."

"Your house?"

"The one I still make mortgage payments on."

"Are you jealous?"

"Of course not!" Edward denied the obvious. "I'm concerned about my daughter. That's it. And Savannah broke our agreement. No one spends time with our daughter until the other party meets that person, checks him or her out and decides that it's okay."

"In what world does that happen?"

"In my damn world!" said Edward.

"Maybe you should have a conversation with Savannah about it."

"You don't think I've tried that? She told me that whomever she dates is none of my business. She got all self-righteous. Pissed me off! So I'm taking her to court. We'll see whose business it is when I sell the house and take Chloe."

Edward hadn't been divorced that long. She still remembered when his ex-wife had become fed up with his impossible schedule. He'd been too focused on his career, and not focused enough on his family. Savannah had begged him for more time and attention to his home life, and he'd refused. He hadn't anticipated that she would leave him and take his daughter away, but she'd followed through.

And when she filed for divorce, he was devastated. By the time he'd tried to change her mind, she was gone. Alyson suspected that he still loved her, yet he'd never admit it.

"You would do that to her?" Alyson asked.

"In a heartbeat."

"You're ruthless," Alyson teased.

"I'm not ruthless," Edward countered. "And enough about me. Why are you spending so much time on the island these days?"

"Well, in case you've forgotten, our sister is getting married in a few weeks. I'm helping with the wedding plans, *and* I'm the maid of honor."

"It's good you and Jazzy are spending so much time together. I'm happy about that." Edward smiled. "Where is my little sister, anyway?"

"She's in the kitchen with your mother..." Alyson raised an eyebrow. "Your very tipsy mother, I might add."

"She's been hitting the sky juice?" Edward laughed.

"Way too often lately," said Alyson.

Edward disappeared into the kitchen. Alyson continued to set the table, and when she looked up, she was staring into a pair of handsome eyes. Samson had arrived, wearing her favorite color. A red button-down shirt tightly clung to his chest, and a matching red-and-black-plaid fedora rested on his head. Following her father into the dining room, he removed the fedora and gave Alyson a wide grin.

"Sweetheart, have you met our dinner guest, Samson Steel?" her father asked.

"Yes, Daddy. We've met. He's staying at the Grove."

"She took me on a house-hunting trip recently," Samson added. "In the Abaco Islands."

"In Abaco? I see," her father said thoughtfully.

"I've been trying to get her to have dinner with me ever since, sir."

"I'm a busy person. With work and Jazzy's wedding, I have a lot going on."

"Maybe you should consider his offer, sweetheart. Even busy people need to eat." Her father took a drink from his bottle of water. "I'll grab you a beer from the kitchen, son. And let my wife know that you're here."

"I can get it myself, sir. You should probably rest."

"I've been resting all week! A man can't find a moment's peace with a houseful of women. I'm fine, really," said Paul John. "Make yourself at home."

Samson grabbed the stack of plates and began to help Alyson set the table.

"You should be ashamed of yourself. Lying to my father like that."

"You should listen to him and have dinner with me again."

"You should stay out of family business."

"Are you always this difficult with everyone or just me?" he asked thoughtfully.

"Just you." She couldn't help but smile.

Jackson walked in, a bottle of Merlot in his hand. "Well, hello, good people!"

"Jackson, my man." Samson was the first to give his friend a strong handshake.

"I see you found your way to the Talbot household. Glad you could make it." Jackson gave Samson a pat on the back, and then kissed Alyson on the cheek. "Good to see you, sis."

"Likewise," said Alyson.

"And where can I find my woman?" asked Jackson.

"Slaving in the kitchen," Alyson said, and then lit the candle in the center of the table.

Paul John returned from the kitchen with a bottle of Bahamian beer for Samson. He shook hands with Jackson. "Well, if it isn't my son-in-law-to-be. Good to see you, son."

"Good to see you doing well, sir," said Jackson. "I heard about your little…thing. You gave us all quite a scare."

"It was a small thing. Nothing to even discuss," Paul John said.

Alyson frowned at her father and gave him the evil eye. "A small thing," she mumbled.

Paul John changed the subject. "Did you finish that big renovation in Palm Beach?"

"All done. We put the finishing touches on the hardwood floors yesterday and installed new appliances and fixtures this morning…just in time for me to catch a flight here for dinner," said Jackson with pride. "I'm home for a while."

"Jazzy will be very happy to hear that," Paul John said as he handed Samson the beer.

"Happy to hear what?" asked Jasmine as she entered the room.

"That your man's home for a while," Jackson said, then grabbed Jasmine in his arms and gave her a strong squeeze. Kissed her lips as if he'd missed every single moment that he'd been apart from them.

"Let's retire to the living room, son," Paul John told Samson. "I'm sure there's a game of some sort on the telly."

Alyson felt awkward, standing there as the lovebirds continued to engage in a kiss. "Get a room," she said with a huff, and then went into the kitchen.

Beverly pulled a dish of garlic chicken out of the oven and placed it on top of the stove. "Let's get this food on the table, Alyson. Go ahead and take the johnnycakes and conch fritters out there."

Alyson grabbed the warm dishes with oven mitts and took them into the dining room.

"Let me help you with that," said Edward, who grabbed a warm dish and followed Alyson.

"Are you two still kissing? Jesus!" she exclaimed when she entered the dining room.

"Alyson, chill out," Jasmine said. "I haven't seen him in weeks."

"Jackson Conner." Edward reached for a handshake from Jackson.

Jackson stopped kissing Jasmine long enough to shake hands with his good friend and future brother-in-law. "Edward, how's it going, man?"

"Not bad, bro. Good to see you home."

"Glad to be here."

"Try to exercise some restraint," Alyson said to Jasmine. "Can't have you preggers before the wedding. It took us too long to find that dress!"

"Oh, sweetheart, you found a dress?" Jackson was surprised.

"Yes," said Jasmine. "I didn't get a chance to tell you with all that went on with Daddy the other day."

Alyson interrupted. "Yep, she found a dress—with a price tag that sent my father into cardiac arrest."

"Stop it, Alyson! I didn't even have a chance to tell him about the dress before I learned about his heart attack."

"I can't wait to see it." Jackson smiled.

"Not before the wedding, Romeo," said Alyson, while grabbing her sister by the arm. "Now come on, Jazzy. We need to get this food on the table."

The dinner conversation was light and jovial. The Talbot children were happy to have the patriarch of their family alive and doing well. His mild heart attack could've been much worse. They were also eternally grateful that Samson had been there and had selflessly spent the day at the clinic with their father.

"So I understand you attended Harvard, Samson," said Edward.

"I did."

"Strange our paths never crossed. Although your face looks familiar."

"As does yours."

"Jackson and I spent a great deal of time talking shit to one another during our days at Harvard." Edward laughed. "I'm proud to say that he's one of my best friends."

Jackson raised his beer in agreement. "Which is why he's my best man at the wedding. Did you get fitted for your tux, by the way?"

"It's on my calendar."

"Oh, my God, Edward! You haven't gone to get fitted?" Alyson interrupted. "Are you going to wait until the day before? What if alterations are needed?"

"Get off my back, woman. The bride only recently found a dress." Edward laughed, and caused the other men in the room to join him in laughter.

"What does the bride's dress have to do with you getting fitted?" asked Alyson. "We are getting down to the wire."

"I'm on it! I promise," Edward said.

Alyson shook her head at her brother.

"I've been so tied up with the wedding that I haven't had a chance to even think about Junkanoo." Jasmine tried to change the subject, lighten the mood.

"What's Junkanoo?" Samson asked.

"It's the highlight of the Christmas season!" declared Jasmine. "It's a huge street parade, with costumes, music and dancing."

"It's what dinner conversations are usually made of," added Edward.

"Only our dinner conversations have been about a wedding instead, this year," said Alyson.

"Junkanoo takes place the day after Christmas," Jasmine explained. "On Boxing Day."

"If you weren't getting married, I would be traveling to Nassau," said Alyson. "Junkanoo in Nassau is so much better. Folks all up and down Bay Street. There's really nothing like it."

"There's nothing wrong with being on the Eleuthera for Junkanoo," said Beverly. "It's just as nice."

"Mother, really? It's not the same," Alyson rebutted. "It's why Daddy used to take us to Nassau every year, for the bigger parade."

"It's certainly a sight to see," Paul John said to Samson. "And if you haven't experienced it, you certainly should… at least once."

"I can't wait to experience it." Samson took a sip of beer.

"What are Christmases like in Chicago?" Alyson asked.

"Christmas trees, music and family. And food, of course."

"Of course," Beverly agreed. "Your parents still alive and well, son?"

"Yes, ma'am. My father's a retired police officer. My mother was a housewife for many years. My father didn't want her to work outside the home. He wanted her to devote her life to raising us."

"I stayed home and raised my children, too," said Beverly. "Such a blessing to be able to do that."

"My wife will stay home and raise our children, too." Jackson grabbed Jasmine's hand and gave her a huge smile.

"Is there something we should know?" Alyson asked.

"No, Alyson. I'm just saying…when we decide to have children, I want Jasmine at home with them. Teaching them and loving them while I'm away working."

"Jasmine has a career. She has a bed-and-breakfast to run," Alyson said. "Right, Jasmine?"

"Well…I am sort of committed to the Grove. A lot needs to be done there," said Jasmine.

"But you said that you were going to scale back, and we were going to start a family right away," Jackson attempted to whisper.

"I know, baby, but I'm needed there more than ever now. And with Whitney deciding to stay in her teaching position for a little longer, it leaves me to handle things."

He lowered his voice. "But that's not what we talked about. You were going to talk to Alyson about moving back to the islands to help out for a while."

"That's not going to happen," said Alyson. "I'm already spending more time than necessary in the Bahamas, and I have no plans of moving back here anytime soon. And furthermore, what's wrong with Jasmine having a career? She loves the Grove."

"There's nothing wrong with it," said Jackson. "It's just that we talked about something different."

"Women are more than just baby makers. This is the twenty-first century. Things aren't like they were back in the day, when our mother literally sacrificed her entire life for our father."

"What are you saying, Alyson?" Beverly chimed in.

"I'm just saying that women don't have to push their own goals and careers aside for some man. Kumbaya. We've overcome."

"I think you should stop while you're ahead, young lady." Beverly Talbot pointed a fork at her daughter. "Before you say something that you don't mean."

"I'm just saying, Mother. Are you really happy with how your life turned out? Sacrificing your career as an educator to bear Daddy's children? And for what?" Alyson pushed the envelope. "Don't you ever wonder what your life would've been like had you followed your own dreams?"

"Yes. And you wouldn't be here today had I followed my own dreams, Alyson Talbot. Now let's change the subject," said Beverly. "Before we were distracted, Samson was telling us about his family."

"My mother is a fighter," Samson said. "She was diagnosed with cancer five years ago."

"I'm so sorry to hear it," said Beverly.

"It's in remission now, and she's faring very well. Her hair has grown back, and she isn't sick as much anymore." Samson smiled. "My brothers and I have started a fund in her honor. Each summer, we host a benefit concert, and the proceeds go toward research and education. It's held at one of the biggest parks in Chicago, and last year we made almost five hundred thousand dollars."

"That's wonderful!" said Beverly. "What's your mother's name, son?"

"Antionette Steel," Samson replied. "Everyone just calls her Toni."

Alyson dropped her fork. She remembered the tattoo on his arm. She felt a sense of relief that Toni was his mother and not some woman that he still had baggage with.

"On Christmas Eve, when we gather to sing Christmas carols, we will light a candle for Toni here in the Caribbean," said Beverly. "And all the other cancer survivors in the world."

Samson offered a warm smile. "Thank you. She would be so honored."

"Let's have a toast," added Edward, raising his glass of red wine. Everyone followed his lead. "To Miss Toni!"

"To Miss Toni," everyone chanted.

Alyson found herself staring at Samson for the remainder of the evening. She was impressed by his love for his mother—the commitment he had for her. She thought it must've been hard for him, with his mother being ill. She didn't know what she would do if her mother had cancer. For the second time in one week, Samson Steel had managed to impress her, and she was certainly seeing him in a different light.

He caught her staring and gave her a wink. She looked away, pretended not to see it. She wasn't sure what to do with the energy that she suddenly felt in her heart.

Chapter 12

Bailey rested on his leg as Samson played the music. He waited for Jackson to sing the first verse of "I Want to Come Home for Christmas." The two bounced off each other as if dancing in step. Marvin Gaye would've been proud at how they brought the song to life. Beverly Talbot smiled and raised her glass in the air. The song was bittersweet and reminded her of Denny, her brave son who wasn't afraid of anything. She hoped he would make it home in time for Christmas and for Jasmine's wedding. It was the one gift that she wanted more than anything else.

Edward stuffed key lime pie into his mouth and washed it down with a glass of Port wine. The entire house was quiet and they listened as Jackson sang the words to the Christmas love song. Alyson was in awe at how precise Samson played his guitar.

Her opinion of him had changed without notice. She'd moved beyond attraction for him. Now he was tugging at her heart—a heart that had grown cold over the years. A heart that very few men had tampered with. A heart that very few people were allowed to enter. Over the years, she had become indifferent, unemotional. Emotions took too much energy, she thought. And she didn't have any energy to spare. She'd come to believe that if she hardened her heart, life would certainly be less complicated. But suddenly her heart was softening.

Moving to Miami had been the quickest way for her to alienate herself from a family that required her to love. The Talbots were family-oriented and loving. But she'd convinced herself that she wanted the opposite—that she was somehow undeserving of love. And she was doing a great job of staying away and burying herself in her work. Her career with the real estate firm had kept her extremely busy, and it seemed that her plan was working like a charm. But then the Grove was born, causing her to spend time on the islands again.

In the past, her relationship with Jasmine had been rocky. And even after they'd inherited the Grove, she told herself that she would only devote some time to getting the family's business off the ground, but she wouldn't make amends with her sister Jasmine. Their relationship had been strained for too long. Unexpectedly, though, life had again thrown her a curveball. Jasmine had somehow worked her way back into her heart, causing her to feel again. And now she was spending more time on the island than she'd expected. But even still, she'd promised herself that she would only devote herself to the details of the wedding. Just like with the Grove, planning her sister's wedding would be a job and nothing more. And as soon as Jasmine and Jackson said their vows, she'd go back to life as she knew it—busy and detached, and in Miami.

"Beautiful." Beverly clapped her hands. "Give us something else."

Jackson began to sing the words to "Silver Bells." Samson fretted the strings of his guitar, and the family sang the chorus along with Jackson—mostly off-key. Though reluctant at first, Alyson joined in with her family's Saturday evening caroling. By the time they sang the words to "This Christmas," she'd had more fun than she would ever admit to having. Edward wrapped his arms around Alyson's shoulders and gave her a kiss on the cheek. The two moved in unison to the music.

At the end of the night, Alyson found herself sharing a taxi with Samson to the water ferry. As they arrived at the Grove, there was a sense of *what do we do next* in the air, and *I'm not ready for this night to end*.

"How about that walk along the beach that you promised?" Samson suggested.

"This late?"

"The night is still young."

"Fine."

She followed him along the trail at the back of Samson Place, and down to the ocean. Samson reached for her hand, and held it tightly as they strolled along the moonlit beach. Waves crashed against the shore and played a harmonic tune. Soft Caribbean music played in the distance from the cabana. Samson moved to the music and encouraged Alyson to do the same.

"I don't dance," she said.

"Since when? I just saw you dancing at your parents' house."

Reluctantly, she swayed her hips under the sound of Beres Hammond's gentle voice. Watching her caused things to stir in Samson. He pulled her into his chest and they continued to dance. No words. He wrapped his strong arms around her waist, held her close. Soon she wrapped her arms tightly around his neck.

"The last time we were at the beach, things didn't go so well," she reminded him.

"Well, I'm hoping that this time will be different." He decided to go in for a kiss, and was glad that she didn't resist.

His lips touched hers gently, and the kiss was much sweeter than he'd imagined. His tongue found its way into her peppermint-flavored mouth. Her French-manicured fingertips danced their way across his face, caressed it. He held on to her waist. The strength of his arms made her feel safe. Wanted. Sexy. All the things she hadn't felt in a long time. Things she'd been too busy to feel.

Without a single word, he grabbed her hand and led the way back to the cabana. They stopped at the bar and Samson ordered drinks for them.

"I'll have a Kalik beer and a cosmopolitan for the lady."

She loved that he ordered for her. Though she was an independent woman, she loved that he took charge. He didn't care much about her independence. And he disregarded her attitude. Something about that turned her on. The bartender handed Samson the beer and the drink, and he carried them both inside. Alyson followed, which was something she rarely did—*follow.*

Once inside the Grove, he led the way to his room and unlocked the door, and she followed him inside. He handed her the cosmopolitan, and she took a good look around at his meticulous room, everything tucked neatly in its place. She reveled in the fact that he was clean and organized, just like her. She stepped out onto the balcony and watched as the waves from the ocean bounced against the shore.

"This room has the best view." She came back in and took a seat on the edge of his bed.

"Yes, it does. Your sister suggested it."

"Smart girl," she said. "She has more going for herself than I ever imagined. She's done wonders with this place in a very short time."

"It's a beautiful property," he agreed. "I understand that she needs help running the place. Why won't you move back here to help?"

"I made it clear to my family from the beginning. When we first learned that we'd inherited the Grove, I told them that I would not be moving back here. I have a business of my own in Miami."

"Right." He smiled. He seemed so cool and calm. "The real estate company."

"I know it doesn't seem like much right now, but I have a nice portfolio and it's growing."

"I believe you."

"The right connections would transform my company in a short time."

"And what are the right connections?"

"Commercial real estate," she said matter-of-factly. "I have a client whose father is a developer. I'd like to handle a few of his properties, or his whole portfolio if he allows me. If I can just get a meeting with him."

"Why not stick to residential properties? Seems that would be an easier market."

"It's easier and faster money, but commercial properties net more income."

"Why not just go work for a real estate firm that sells commercial properties?"

"I just walked away from one of the largest firms to start my own company," she said. "It was time. I have a degree in commercial development and finance. And I have my broker's license. I don't want to split my commissions. I know the game well enough that I should be able to do this on my own, and do it well."

"As with any new business, it takes time to build," said Samson.

"Absolutely."

"You're not afraid of much, are you, Alyson?" He sat across from her in the Georgian-style wing chair in the corner of the room.

She wanted to tell him that she was afraid of many things. Particularly him. He caused her the most anxiety.

"I'm afraid of more than you know," she said.

He stood, grabbed her hands and pulled her up from the bed. Held her tightly in his arms. "What are you afraid of, Alyson Talbot?"

You, she wanted to say, but resisted the urge.

"I'm afraid of failing at something that I've worked so hard for." It was partly the truth.

"Sometimes failing is not completely bad. Especially if you learn something from it."

"What have you learned from failing?" she asked.

"I've learned that you can always reinvent yourself. I was shamed by the scandal that went on in Chicago with the campaign. But here I am in the Bahamas, and no one knows anything about what I've endured in my past. And nobody cares."

"So you're planning on hiding out in the Bahamas forever?"

"I'm not hiding out, but I'm planning to stay here until I get my head together, figure out my next move."

"Will you run for a political office again?"

"I doubt it. But I would go back to the DA's office. That is an option. Or maybe I'll stay around here for a while."

"Why aren't you married with children?"

"You sound just like my mother. She's always asking me that."

"It's a valid question. Especially for a man who's not getting any younger," she said. "What are you afraid of?"

"Marrying someone I don't love. And besides, I haven't had one single prospect in my entire life."

"Maybe it's because you love yourself too much."

He gave her a sideways glance. "I'm just confident. I have my flaws."

Thoughts of him had interrupted her sleep since the night after their almost-kiss and invaded her mind the entire next day. As much as she wanted to find something wrong with him or his flaws, as he put it, she couldn't think of a single thing. The truth was, she admired his confidence and his heart, and she wanted to be near him.

He removed his shirt, climbed into the bed and invited her to join him. She didn't know why she obliged, but found herself climbing into bed with him. He wrapped his arms tightly around her. His lips touched hers, and his tongue danced inside her mouth. His fingertips danced against her tender breasts.

He raised himself up on one elbow and looked at her. "You're beautiful."

"You're beautiful," she said back.

His head relaxed against the pillow, and hers hit the pillow next to his. They both stared at the ceiling. He grabbed her hand, intertwined his fingers with hers. Kissed her fingertips. He grabbed his cell phone from his pocket, searching for something.

"I don't have anything Caribbean on my playlist," he said.

"Let's hear what you have."

The music permeated the small room.

"Who is it?"

"Her name is Amel Larrieux."

Alyson grabbed his phone and looked at the photo of the female artist whose voice bounced against the walls. "Is she French?"

"She's from Philly." Samson laughed. "But I think she might have some French roots. I call her my modern-day Ella Fitzgerald."

A puzzled look on her face, Alyson asked, "Ella Fitzgerald?"

"Never mind," Samson said with a laugh.

"She has a beautiful voice," said Alyson as she moved her head to rest on Samson's chest. She breathed in his scent, closed her eyes and couldn't think of a single place she'd rather have been. "You know a lot about music."

"It's my first love."

"Not law or politics?"

"Nope. They play second fiddle to my music."

"You're a wonderful guitarist," she said. "Why haven't you pursued a real career?"

"I don't want to be a starving artist. Gotta pay the bills," said Samson. "Besides, I don't think my father would appreciate me squandering my education to pursue a music career. He already has a problem with the career that I chose."

"You spent the evening with my family," she said. "Tell me about yours."

"I'm from a family of cops. My father, grandfather, my brothers."

"So you were the rebellious one."

"I've always been one to dance to a different beat. Needless to say, my father didn't appreciate that. I was supposed to be a cop, in his opinion," said Samson. "He's a rigid man. It's his way, or he doesn't endorse it."

"What about your mother?"

"She's a saint." He laughed. "But only if you don't piss her off. Then she's hell on wheels. She's strong, a fighter. She's a lot like you. She doesn't take much shit. She would like you."

"You think so?" Alyson was flattered.

"I think so." He raised himself up onto his elbow again. "Even as difficult as you are."

"I'm not difficult!"

"You are, and you know it," said Samson, "but it's who you are, so I don't mind it. You amuse me."

"Well, I'm glad that you find me so amusing."

"Not in a negative way." Samson smiled. "I love that you're true to yourself. No guessing about where you stand."

"I guess not," Alyson admitted.

As neo soul music serenaded the couple, Alyson's eyes became heavy. Before long she'd succumbed to a peaceful sleep.

Samson kissed her forehead, turned off the lamp on the nightstand and closed his eyes, as well.

Chapter 13

The sunlight crept across Alyson's sleeping face. She squinted when she opened her eyes and tried to remember where she was. She was startled to find Samson lying next to her, light snores escaping from his mouth as he slept. She took in the beauty of his gentle face and muscular chest. He slept peacefully, and she wondered what his dreams were made of. She slipped from the bed and found her shoes, grabbed them. She eased the door open and crept out of it, pulling it shut as quietly as she could.

"Good morning, Miss Talbot."

She locked eyes with Bijou, who was carrying a plate filled with fresh fruit and a cup of steaming hot coffee.

"Good morning," said Alyson.

"Did you rest well?" Bijou asked, a questioning look on her face.

"I did indeed." Alyson took the opportunity to grin slyly, and then sashayed down the hallway to her own room.

* * *

Church was a requirement for any member of the Talbot family who found themselves on the island on any given Sunday morning. Alyson didn't argue with tradition, even though she hated attending her family's small church. She preferred her megachurch in Miami, where the air-conditioning blew heavily and the wooden floors didn't creak when you tried to tiptoe in late. Luckily she was a prompt person and didn't have to worry about the entire church turning to see when she walked in.

She slid into the pew next to her mother.

"I tried calling your room last night," said Beverly. "And your cell phone."

"I was so exhausted. Went straight to sleep," Alyson said, and then quickly changed the subject. "Where's Jazzy and Jackson?"

"En route. You know they're always late," said Beverly. "Pastor Johnson wants to have a word with them after church. About the wedding ceremony."

"Of course. I need to have a word with *him*, actually. I want to make sure he knows when and where he should be on that day."

"I'm sure that Pastor Johnson has performed many marriage ceremonies. He doesn't need you to give him instructions."

"Actually, he does, Mother. I want this day to go as smoothly as possible, from the time they walk down the aisle to the moment they dance at the reception. This family will not be embarrassed."

Beverly Talbot shook her head.

"What are you yapping about?" Edward asked as he slid in next to Alyson.

"Your sister's wedding that I've put a great deal of time

and effort into. I've spent way too much time in the Bahamas putting this thing together."

"Maybe you can go home this week. I spoke with Whitney this morning, and she'll be here tomorrow. Her school is on Thanksgiving break, and she's coming in on an evening flight."

"Whitney's coming?" Their mother smiled. "I miss her."

Alyson always thought that Whitney was their mother's favorite. Their mother always wanted to be a teacher, and Whitney was living her dream.

"So maybe you can fly back to Florida with me on Tuesday," said Edward.

"Maybe so," Alyson agreed.

The truth was, she hadn't contemplated leaving so soon.

When the choir began their rendition of "Jesus Be a Fence," their discussions ceased. She could hear the loud stamping of feet on the old hardwoods, and everyone clapped to the music, while Alyson tried to catch some air by fanning herself with her program. When her cell phone rang loudly, she frantically searched for it in her purse. Her mother frowned. She silenced it and then checked the screen to see who was calling. Samson. Alyson smiled inside. She felt guilty about basking in the thought of his strong arms wrapped around her for the entire night. She wanted to feel them again.

Jackson and Jasmine finally slid into the pew behind them, and started clapping as if they'd been there all along.

"You're late," Alyson whispered.

"We know."

Alyson had every intention of speaking with Pastor Johnson after the service, but she was distracted by the sudden need to return to the Grove. She kissed the cheeks of her mother and sister and thought of an excuse to get away.

"Aren't you coming for dinner?" her mother asked.

"I've got to get back to the Grove. Need to make some phone calls and reply to some emails."

"Are you flying out with me on Tuesday?" Edward asked. "You want me to have my assistant book you a ticket?"

"No, I'll have Jules book me a flight," she said. "I might stay until Wednesday. I'm meeting a client on Tuesday."

Edward gave her a sideways glance. He and Alyson had been two peas in a pod since the cradle. She was closer to him than any of her siblings. They swapped secrets for as long as she could remember, and he knew her better than anyone.

"Okay, whatever," he said, but gave her a look that said "something's up."

"I'll catch up with y'all later. I'll try to make it back to Governor's Harbor later this evening. Save me some mac and cheese."

She slipped into the backseat of a taxi before anyone could ask another question. At the Grove, she found Samson on the back patio, sipping on a Kalik beer and watching a Bahamas football game on the television above the bar. She slipped onto a bar stool next to him and ordered a glass of white wine.

He glanced her way. "You left without saying goodbye this morning."

"You were sleeping and I didn't want to wake you."

"Where did you go?"

"Church." She smiled. "Why? Did you want to go?"

"I might have. I could use a little prayer, too, you know."

"I prayed for you," she said. *And thought about you all through service.*

"I enjoyed spending time with you last night. You think we can do something like that again?" he asked.

"What did you have in mind?"

"Maybe dinner and a romantic stroll along the beach, and anything else your heart desires."

"Dinner would be nice. I haven't eaten," she said. "I'll have Raquel put something together."

She was glad that she'd passed on Sunday dinner with her family, because sharing conch fritters and fried fish on the beach with Samson was much more fun. She stretched her legs along the beach towel and fed Samson the last bite of her fish. Her finger lingered in his mouth as he savored the taste of it.

"That was the best piece of fish I've ever eaten."

"Don't say I never gave you anything," she flirted.

"I won't."

In her room, she shut the blinds and lit a few candles. Searched for a Caribbean playlist on her phone. Tarrus Riley serenaded them as she rested in Samson's arms—those arms that she couldn't seem to get out of her mind the entire day. His lips found hers and kissed them with passion.

He reached beneath her silk blouse and loosened the hooks of her bra, pulled the blouse over her head. Her breasts sprang free, and he gently stroked them. She carefully unbuttoned his shirt and stared at his brown, muscular chest. His lips found their way to her breasts, nibbling on each one. Soon his mouth consumed one entire breast, and Alyson moaned and closed her eyes.

He led her to the bed. She lay on her back and waited for him to finish what he'd started. He removed his trousers, and tight boxers hugged his groin and strong legs. He hovered over her and slowly found her lips again. When he lowered his body onto hers, she could feel the hardness of him against her stomach.

Before unbuttoning her pants, Samson looked at her for approval. "You okay?" he whispered.

Her nod affirmed that she was enjoying him. He removed her pants swiftly, and she felt a gentle breeze rush across her bare legs. His fingertips danced between her thighs and caused her to moan. He removed her panties and then kissed her inner thighs, one after the other. A trail of kisses led to her sweet spot where his tongue began to dance. She moved her hips to his rhythm. She was captivated by him.

He moved to the area just above her waist and planted kisses there. His tongue lingered around her navel and then worked its way back up to her breasts, and again to her wanting mouth. She touched his hardness, caressed him there.

"I want you," he whispered.

She couldn't remember the last time someone *wanted* her, but it felt good. When he removed his boxers, her breathing changed. It was all so surreal, but she found herself wanting him, too. She hoped he wouldn't be disappointed.

"You're so damn sexy." The words were wet against her earlobe. He quieted her fears with his affirmation.

She needed to be esteemed. When he produced a condom and then entered her, she moaned. Hugged him tighter. They moved to the rhythm of the music, made sweet love beneath the candlelight.

After he collapsed on top of her, she stroked his bearded face—planted little kisses across his forehead and nose. He rolled over onto his back, pulled her close. She rested her head against his chest as he gently caressed her shoulder and arm.

Chapter 14

Alyson was officially distracted by Samson. She had completely forgotten to have Jules book her a flight back to Miami. In fact, Miami was the last place she wanted to be. She was perfectly content being on the island. She held on to Bailey. The base of the guitar rested on her thigh, and the neck was facing up. Samson's hands held on to hers, making sure they were in the right place.

"Now balance the neck between your thumb and forefinger," he said. "Back straight, love."

"Like this?" She stiffened her back and sat straight up.

"Relax a little."

She began to strum the strings of the guitar, in no particular rhythm. "I should probably just leave this to the professional."

"No, you can do this."

He showed her the basics. She began playing the major chords. Soon she was playing "Sweet Home Alabama" and singing along. Samson joined in on the verse, and the two made a spectacle of themselves as a crowd gathered in the Grand Room.

She stood and handed the guitar to him, and applause filled the room.

"Please stop." She laughed.

"She's being modest," Samson said as he took a seat on the stool.

"Bravo!" Kosmo clapped his hands with a grin.

Samson grabbed Alyson's hand.

"Stand right here," he said. "The guys in the band taught me this one."

She stood close as he began to strum the guitar and sing the words to Jah Cure's "Only You." It was a song that Alyson had heard a million times, but she had never expected anyone to sing the words to her, describing her as an offer that couldn't be declined, and sunshine in the rain. Though she tried to mask it, she was choking with emotion.

Samson wasn't the best vocalist, but Alyson found his performance admirable and sweet. She swayed her hips to the music. When he was done, the guests applauded.

Jasmine worked her way through the crowd and found her sister. "Okay, what was that about?"

"What?" Alyson could barely contain her smile.

Jasmine grabbed her sister by the arm and pulled her aside. "Oh. My. God."

"Jazzy, what is your problem?"

"You like him!"

"He's okay," Alyson stated, but was barely convincing. "I appreciate how he took care of Daddy. That's all."

"No, it's more. You're all giddy and he's singing love songs."

"He was singing for the crowd!"

"He was singing to you!"

"Okay, he was singing to me. So what?"

"Nothing." Jasmine smiled. "I just think it's sweet."

"Let's go, babe." Samson interrupted the rendezvous between the sisters, grabbed Alyson's hand in his. "Sorry to interrupt, Jasmine. But we have a sunset to catch."

"Babe?" asked Jasmine.

"I'll talk to you later, Jazzy." Alyson followed Samson toward the cabana at the back of the house.

"We're not done, missy! Your sister Whitney is here on the island. Her flight got in last night. She's been looking for you. You should come by the house and at least say hello. After all, she's your sister…" Jasmine stretched out the word *sister*, as if it were the last word of a song. "And what happened to your flight back to Miami this morning?"

"I missed it!" Alyson yelled.

Alyson followed Samson along the trail on the backside of the Clydesdale until they reached the ocean. Samson took a seat in the sand and invited her to join him on the ground.

"I'll get my pants dirty," she said.

"This isn't the time for prim and proper."

"These are Armani pants," she complained. "End of season last year, but Armani nonetheless."

"I'll pay for your dry cleaning."

"That's beside the point," said Alyson.

"Remind me to buy you a pair of trousers from Walmart. They don't have a Walmart on the island, huh?"

Alyson shook her head as she cautiously took a seat next to Samson in the sand.

"Do you even know what Walmart is?"

"Of course I do. They have them all over Miami." Alyson laughed.

"Good. The next time we're in Miami, we'll visit one."

"The next time *we're* in Miami?" Alyson asked.

"You need to go home soon, right? Don't you have appointments?"

"I do," she said. "But it's Thanksgiving in a couple of days. I've never spent one Thanksgiving without my family."

"Can you miss it this year?"

"I don't see why not," she said, but wasn't so sure how her family would feel about her absence at the dinner table. And suddenly, she didn't care.

"Okay, then. We're going to Miami," said Samson.

Alyson didn't respond, just turned her head away from Samson and smiled at the thought.

She watched the sun as it began to set, but her thoughts were a million miles away. She couldn't stop thinking about how Samson made her feel. Whatever it was they were doing, she didn't want it to end anytime soon.

Miami was a beautiful seventy-five degrees in November. Coconut Grove's CocoWalk was bustling with shoppers. Samson and Alyson strolled hand in hand along the beautiful brick patio lined with tall palm trees, high-end boutiques and bistro cafés.

"This is where you do your Christmas shopping?" Samson asked.

"Some of it. I like to pick up nice perfume and scarves for my mother and sisters. Things they can't get on the island," Alyson explained. "And I need to find a nice wedding gift for Jasmine and Jackson."

Samson wrapped his arm around Alyson's shoulder. "I don't care where we go. I just want to be near you."

She rested her head on his chest for a moment.

They stopped to listen as a live jazz band serenaded the crowd. Samson wrapped his strong arms around Alyson's shoulders as the two swayed to the music. She relaxed in his embrace, and Samson leaned down and planted a sensual kiss against her neck.

On the way back to Alyson's condo, they stopped for a café con leche at a little café tucked away on the nontouristy side of South Beach. At Las Olas Café they stepped up to the outside take-out window and ordered cups of predawn café cubanos. They took a seat on the shaded patio, and Samson was grateful for the reprieve. Christmas shopping with Alyson had been exhausting.

"So how long do you think you'll be on the island before you head back to Chicago?" Alyson asked out of the blue.

"Actually, I've been in touch with some old business contacts, and I'm strongly considering politics again."

"Seriously?" she asked. "I thought you'd never consider that again. I thought that's why you were on the island in the first place…because it had been such a horrible experience."

"It was a horrible experience. But someone very dear to me told me that I shouldn't run from my fears. I should face them."

Alyson smiled and took a sip of her café con leche. "Glad you listened."

"I guess you could say I've been inspired to not give up on the things that I really want."

"If you let a little opposition stop you from achieving your dreams, you'll never achieve anything."

"You're right. I watch you, and how dedicated you are to Alyson Talbot and Associates, and I admire your work ethic, your tenacity," he said. "I have to start building my team and planning for the next campaign. I can run for city council in two years, but I have to start now."

"Sounds like you have a plan."

"I have a little something. So after the holidays, I'm going back."

She changed the subject. "Let's go out tonight. Catch some nightlife."

"Are you serious? After you dragged me all over the state of Florida shopping for Christmas gifts?"

"The state of Florida? That's a bit of an exaggeration."

"Okay, the city of Miami, then."

"I say we get dressed up and catch a party on South Beach."

"I'm in."

Alyson wore a tight black bodycon dress, one with artfully placed lace panels. It flattered every last curve on her body. With Samson in a pair of designer skinny jeans, a white T-shirt and a charcoal-colored blazer with the sleeves rolled up, they were a handsome pair. And Samson found it difficult to peel his eyes from Alyson's curves as she sashayed around the kitchen, pretending to tidy things up before they left for their night on the town.

"Are we ready?" she asked.

"Damn, you look good." He completely ignored her question.

She blushed, and then shut the miniblinds over the sink. "Thanks."

"You're making it really hard to go out. I can think of a million things we can do right here." He grabbed her by the waist as she attempted to walk past him.

"Those are things we can do when we return. But for now, let's go have fun."

He smiled and released her. Followed her to the door. He grabbed the keys from her hand and locked the door behind them. He grabbed her hand as they entered the dimly lit parking garage. He knew she'd been to the garage by herself a million times before, but he still felt the need to protect her. He opened her car door and allowed her to step inside.

He found a nice jazz station on her stereo and then maneuvered the car toward the interstate.

"You sure you don't want me to drive?" she asked.

"I can drive. You just lead the way."

The music was loud as they stepped into the South Beach nightclub. Women were dressed in tighter dresses than the one that Alyson wore, but he thought she was by far the most beautiful.

He grabbed her hand and led the way to the bar. Wrapped his arms tightly around her as if they were the only two people in the room.

"I'll have a Heineken, and a cosmopolitan for the lady," he told the bartender, but then asked, "Are you in the mood for a cosmopolitan tonight, or did you want something else?"

"Cosmopolitan's fine."

They turned to look at the crowd. People crowded the dance floor, and all the tables were filled. There was standing room only. One seat opened at the bar, and Samson ushered Alyson there and pulled the bar stool out for her. She took a seat, while he stood close behind. The bartender placed their drinks in front of them, and she swiveled around so that she was facing Samson. He grabbed his beer, took the lime from it, sucked on it and then gave Alyson a lime-filled kiss on the lips.

"You are the most beautiful woman in here," he said in her ear, trying to speak over the loud music.

She crossed her legs and sipped on her drink, "I hope that at some point we're going to dance."

"We will. As soon as I get back from the men's room," said Samson. "Will you be okay until I get back?"

"I'll be fine."

"I'll be quick," Samson said, and then walked away.

* * *

After Samson left, the man at the bar next to Alyson gave her a smile and then leaned toward her. "What a beautiful accent you have," he said.

"Thank you." She barely looked his way. It was a compliment that she received often.

"Where are you from?"

She caught a whiff of his alcohol-filled breath. "Bahamas."

"I knew it was one of them… Jamaica, Bahamas or something," he said. "Is that your man with you?"

It was a question she hadn't pondered, but knew that she needed to provide an answer, even if it meant lying to keep Drunk Man at bay.

"Yes," she said emphatically.

"Corny ass dude. You need a real man. A man that knows what to do with all that damn junk in your trunk." He smiled and touched her rear end.

"Hey!" she yelled over the music, appalled. "Don't touch my ass again."

"You mean like this." He touched her again, and she slid from the bar stool.

He grabbed her arm. "I was just teasing. Where are you going so soon?"

She tried pulling away from his grasp.

"Let her go," Samson said as he approached the bar.

"Or what?" Drunk Man asked.

Samson grabbed him by the collar. "Or I'll take your ass outside."

Samson hadn't had to *take anyone outside* in some time, but being from Chi-Town, he wasn't afraid to do just that. The man released Alyson's hand and gave Samson a hard shove.

"Don't even waste your time," Alyson said as she stood between the two and pulled Samson away. "You have too much to lose."

Bystanders began to look their way.

Drunk man said, "I was only complimenting your woman's accent. And with a beautiful mouth like that, I bet she could suck—"

Before he finished his sentence, Samson had landed a right hook to his face. Alyson let out a loud shriek, and Drunk Man wiped blood from the corner of his mouth with a grin followed by laughter. Within a moment, a large man had grabbed Samson by his armpits and began to escort him toward the door.

"Let's go, buddy!" the bouncer said.

"I'm going." Samson pulled away, straightening his clothes. He grabbed Alyson by the hand, and the two left the club in a hurry.

He handed the valet his ticket and then turned to Alyson.

"I'm sorry." He'd blown it. He'd let his anger get the best of him, something that he rarely did. He was always in control, but he'd lost it in front of the woman who was slowly capturing his heart.

"It's okay." She gave him a warm smile and tried to make light of the situation. "Hopefully no one recognized you and Tweeted it."

"Hopefully," he said drily.

He was disappointed in himself. Spent the entire drive home rethinking things—wondering how he could've handled the situation better, wishing he had the opportunity again. He would do things differently. He was an upstanding man, a man of honor, and had never been thrown from a nightclub before.

When they got back to the condo, Samson lay down on

the leather sofa in the living room and turned the television to ESPN, while Alyson disappeared into the master bedroom, and returned shortly with a wet washcloth. She grabbed his hand and wiped dried blood away from his knuckles with the wet cloth, then gently kissed his knuckles. She got up and walked over to the stereo, turned on some music and finally grabbed the remote control from Samson, muting the television.

"You owe me a dance," she said.

His head bounced against the leather sofa, a half grin on his face.

"Come on," she demanded, and pulled him up from the sofa.

He stood and grabbed her waist. She wrapped her arms around his neck. They moved to the music.

"So you're not mad at me for making a fool of myself?" he asked.

"No," she said simply. "I can't remember a man ever making a fool of himself for me."

"I lost it. It made me crazy hearing someone disrespect you like that," he said. "I'm sorry I ruined your night."

"The night is still young." She stood on her tippy toes and kissed his lips. "And not at all ruined."

He held her tighter and plunged his tongue into her mouth. Grabbed the roundness of her behind. He'd wanted to do that since he first saw her in that dress. He was falling for her, and she him. And neither of them knew what to do about it.

Chapter 15

She opened the white envelope with the red-and-gold monogrammed seal. It was a formal invitation with raised lettering, and a personal note inside.

Alyson,
I hope you can make it.
This is a great opportunity for you to meet my dad.
Pick his brain.
And bring that handsome man you've been seen gallivanting about town with. The sexy one...
Best wishes,
Jennifer Madison

She quickly slipped the note back into the envelope and placed the invitation on the table.

"What's that?" asked Jasmine.

"Invitation to a fundraiser hosted by a client. It's next weekend on Abaco."

"You're not going," said Jasmine. "You can't."

"I am going. I have to. This is about my career."

"We're down to the wire with these wedding plans. Have to make sure everything is right. The caterers, the band, the men getting fitted for their tuxedoes. Christmas is less than a month away. And have you even gone to the final fitting for your dress?"

"Of course…" Alyson lied, but then dropped her head. "No. But I will. This week, I promise."

"Alyson! What is going on?"

"Nothing."

"There was a problem with Whitney's dress, and the seamstress wasn't sure if she could have it altered in time." Jasmine placed her hand over her face and sighed. "I've been looking for you all this week! Where were you?"

"I had to fly back home to Miami. Had business there. I told you I have to split my time between the islands and Florida. My business doesn't stop because you're getting married, Jazzy. My work is priority."

"I know that, but can you let us know when you're going away? The people who love you also worry about you."

"I'm sorry. I should've said something."

"Yes, you should have. Instead, I have to see it on Twitter."

"What?"

Jasmine handed Alyson her phone. There was a photo of Samson punching Drunk Man in the face. The caption read Washed up Illinois mayoral candidate takes his frustrations out on an innocent bystander. #SamsonSteel #MiamiHeat

"What the hell?"

"My sentiments exactly. Imagine my shock when I saw

your face in the background," said Jasmine. "Now again I ask, what is going on?"

"Oh, my God. Samson is going to freak. It was just one big misunderstanding. He was defending me against that creep, and the story got twisted."

"As if he needs any more trouble," said Jasmine.

"It wasn't his fault," Alyson defended him.

"I was just surprised to see you and Samson...in South Beach...together..."

"I know it seems strange, but..."

"Are you sleeping with him, Alyson?"

"Well..."

"You are!" Jasmine exclaimed. "When did this relationship go from dinner at the Rock House to a weekend rendezvous in Miami? Did he stay at your condo?"

"Eat your breakfast, Jazzy," Alyson said, hoping to avoid any further conversation about her love life.

"I want to know every single little nasty detail. And don't leave anything out," Jasmine said.

Their sister Whitney walked up, saving the day.

"Well, if it isn't my elusive big sister," she said.

Alyson stood and gave Whitney a tight squeeze. "Good to see you. Missed you!"

"I can't really tell, honey, because I've been on this island all week, and this is my first time seeing you." Whitney took a seat at the table. "Did you completely forget about Thanksgiving dinner?"

"I'm sorry. I've had business in Miami." Alyson glanced at Jasmine, who raised her eyebrows.

"I understand you have a little business here, too." Whitney grinned. "I've heard rumors about a certain tall glass of water."

Alyson peered at Jasmine, who gave her a look of guilt.

"It's not like you're hiding it," Jasmine defended herself. "And besides, social media tells all your business."

"I'm happy for you," said Whitney. "Glad to see you've finally moved past that Jimmy Franklin thing."

An uncomfortable silence filled their space. Jimmy Franklin had been a sore spot for Alyson and her family.

"Sorry, I didn't mean to open old wounds," Whitney said. "It's just that you and Jazzy lost so much time over that whole thing."

"But we're over it now. After Jazzy told me what really happened."

Jimmy Franklin had been Alyson's high school sweetheart, until he was sent away to Philadelphia. For years, Alyson didn't know why he'd been sent away—only that Jasmine was responsible. Only recently had she learned that all those years ago, Jimmy Franklin had tried to rape Jasmine. The revelation had been the beginning of healing old wounds for the sisters.

"I'm just glad to have both of my sisters back," said Whitney. "And I'm excited about Jazzy's Christmas wedding! Give me all the details of what to expect."

"The rehearsal dinner is scheduled for Christmas Eve. We'll have a Bahamian spread, of course. Raquel is putting a menu together as we speak. The fellas are planning a bachelor party for Jackson, and of course we have some wicked things planned for Jazzy later that night."

"No strippers!" warned Jasmine. "And I mean it. I don't want some strange man shaking his stuff in front of me. I'm perfectly happy with the stuff I have at home."

The sisters laughed.

"You know that the guys are going to have a stripper."

"Jackson promised they wouldn't."

Alyson and Whitney looked at each other, and then laughed hard.

"Anyway," Alyson continued, "early Christmas morning we're having a masseuse and a hairstylist come to the Grove and pamper us and make us pretty."

"Why did you both laugh about the stripper?"

Alyson disregarded Jasmine's question and continued with her wedding itinerary. "The wedding starts promptly at noon. We will be on time. And I mean it, Jazzy. Make sure that everyone knows that this wedding will start with or without them. Groom included."

"Now, how in the world will you have a wedding without the groom?" Whitney asked.

"We'll manage it. We'll put him on speakerphone." Alyson laughed. "Immediately following the ceremony, the guests will migrate to the cabana on the back on the Clydesdale. They'll mingle and buy drinks at the cash bar while the crew rearranges the seating for the reception."

"Sounds wonderful! I'm leaving tomorrow, but will be back for Christmas break. I'll get here a few days early in case you guys need my assistance," Whitney said, her hands propped beneath her chin and a dreamy look on her face. "I'm so happy for you, Jazzy...you found your knight in shining armor. I hope to be so lucky someday."

"First you have to lose these nerdy glasses," Alyson said as she removed her sister's glasses from her face, "and you need to let your beautiful hair down. You look like a schoolteacher."

"I am a schoolteacher. And this from a woman who doesn't even understand what it means to dress down," said Whitney.

"She's been letting her hair down lately." Jasmine smiled. "Now that a certain man has her attention. Or should I say, she has his?"

"About this guy..." said Whitney thoughtfully.

"We're not having this discussion." Alyson stood. "I

have to go. I have a lot of work to do today. Breakfast was nice. I'll see you both at the house later."

Alyson kissed each of her sisters on the cheek, left the Talbot house and walked next door to Samson Place. She rushed up the stairs to Samson's room and knocked on the door. He answered, a plush white towel wrapped around his waist and a toothbrush in his mouth.

"Good morning, love," he said.

"Good morning," she said, feeling as if she'd interrupted him too early. "I'm sorry, I didn't realize you were just now moving around."

"Don't worry about it. Come on in." He opened the door wider. "What's on your mind?"

She held her phone in the air, showed him the Twitter post. "Have you seen this?"

He nodded. "My brother sent it to me last night. Damn shame how they twist details."

"You're not concerned at all?"

"No. People take things to social media all the time, and always out of context. I'm used to it."

She was relieved that the Twitter post wasn't a problem for him. She needed him calm for her next order of business.

"I wanted to ask you something."

"I'm all ears."

"I have this invitation from one of my clients. She's the owner of the magnificent home on Abaco—the one we visited not long ago."

"The mansion," he concluded with a grin, and then sarcastically said, "the one I can't afford."

"Anyway—" she ignored his quip "—the owner, Jennifer Madison, is having a fund-raiser dinner there this weekend. It's a black-tie affair…five hundred dollars a plate—"

"Five hundred dollars a plate!" he repeated.

"Don't tell me you haven't been to functions like this. You're a politician. At any rate, there will be lots of big, important people there. Namely, her father, Jonathan Madison, with whom I'm hoping to do business. He owns several commercial properties, and I think it would be prosperous for Alyson Talbot and Associates to dabble in the commercial industry."

"You mentioned that," he said, and went into the bathroom. Spit in the sink, rinsed his mouth.

"I need a date for the fund-raiser. Well, maybe not a date…an escort," she said thoughtfully. "I just need someone to accompany me."

"So you need me?" he asked, coming back into the bedroom.

"If you don't want to go…or have other plans…"

"I'd love to go."

"Really?"

"Of course," he said.

"It's black tie."

"Okay."

"They have a tuxedo rental shop on the island…" Alyson began to suggest. "I can show you where it is."

"I have a tux, for your information, Miss Presumptuous," Samson said as he grabbed a pair of boxer shorts from the chest of drawers.

Alyson grinned. "It's Saturday night at seven. I'll have Stephen drive us over in his boat."

"I look forward to it." Samson dropped his towel and slowly stepped into the boxers. "Did you need anything else?"

Alyson inhaled deeply. Took in every inch of him, from his chiseled chest to the bulge in his briefs. She needed to feel him between her thighs again, is what she needed. He was quickly becoming her addiction, making her weak. He had her out of character.

"No, I'm good," she said and headed for the door.

Samson stood in front of the door, blocking her from leaving. "You're sure?"

She needed to exercise control, preserve her dignity. She was a strong woman and wouldn't fall prey to the advances of any man. And he needed to know that just because he planted little sensual kisses up and down her neck, she wouldn't give in. And just because his mouth engulfed hers with a passionate kiss, he couldn't break her. Even as he began to gently squeeze her breasts, she was still in control.

Or so she thought.

Chapter 16

Christmas lights adorned the magnificent property. Stately palm trees stood glamorously about the grounds, while huge wreaths and garland played peekaboo in every window. The mansion smelled of cinnamon and cranberry. Red and gold candles burned in every corner of every room. Soft Christmas jazz played faintly as trays filled with flutes of champagne traveled about.

Samson looked dazzling in his navy tuxedo. Alyson wore a matching embellished navy gown that flattered her figure. The two were a handsome couple as they arrived at the Madison property. Alyson slipped her hand into the crease of Samson's arm as he escorted her inside. They quickly began to mingle, and Samson grabbed a flute of champagne for each of them. He handed Alyson hers.

"This place has transformed since we were last here," Samson whispered.

"It's so beautiful here."

"Did I tell you how beautiful you look tonight?" he asked.

"Not once." She smiled.

"Well, you are, Miss Talbot."

"And you are very handsome, Mr. Steel."

Samson leaned into her ear. "If all these people weren't around gawking at us, I swear I would kiss you."

"Good thing you know the importance of public appearances."

"I'm only exercising self-control because of you. If it were up to me, I would pretend we were the only two people in the room."

Alyson took a sip of her champagne.

"Alyson Talbot," she heard a familiar voice say.

"Jennifer." Alyson smiled and gave her a hug. "So good to see you."

"And you, as well," said Jennifer. "And you must be Samson the Great. I've heard so much about you."

"Really?" asked Samson.

"Not really." Jennifer laughed. "Actually, my friend here has been pretty tight-lipped about you. But I'm glad she brought you tonight."

"Samson, this is Jennifer. Jennifer, Samson," said Alyson.

"It's so good to meet you." Jennifer smiled.

"Likewise," said Samson.

"I hate to steal her away so soon, but I have some important introductions to make. You understand, don't you, Samson?"

"I do, indeed," said Samson.

"Good, then. Please feel free to mingle, and do make yourself at home."

Alyson offered Samson a look of apology, as she was whisked away to talk business with Jennifer's father. A tall, handsome man with graying sideburns, Jonathan Madison had a welcoming face and appeared more approachable than she had presumed he would.

"Dad, I'd like for you to meet Alyson Talbot." Jennifer grabbed her father by the hand. "She's the one I've been telling you about. She's the listing agent for Madison House and a few of my other properties on Fisher Island."

"Ahh, Alyson." Jonathan took Alyson's hand in his and kissed the back of it. "I've heard great things about you. I understand that you secured a contract on one of my daughter's properties in a matter of days."

"I did."

"So good to finally meet you."

"You, too, sir. It's an honor."

"Police Chief Taylor just walked in. I'm going over to say hello," Jennifer said before she excused herself.

"My daughter speaks quite highly of you, Miss Talbot," said Jonathan. "I understand that you used to work for Bell, Armstrong and Glenn. One of the best commercial real estate firms I know."

"Yes, sir. However, I've recently stepped out on my own. Started my own company."

"So I'm told," Jonathan said. "How's that working for you?"

"It's a slow grind, but I'm optimistic."

"I remember when I took that leap of faith and started my own development company. I was a youngster back then, fresh out of college. Long blond hair and an attitude as big as the world. I was invincible back then—a smart-ass with audacity." He laughed. "It takes a great deal of courage in this industry."

"Precisely."

"I understand you have plenty of ideas for the company, and I'd like to talk with you further." He pulled a business card out of the inside pocket of his jacket and handed it to her. "Call my office on Monday and schedule a lunch meeting with me. I'd love to hear your ideas for taking Madison Development to the next level."

"I will, sir." Alyson smiled. "I look forward to it."

Alyson shook Jonathan Madison's hand and then worked her way back over toward Samson, who was making small talk with a brunette. Alyson took note of her sexy red Antonio Berardi cocktail dress with the exposed back.

"Hey, babe," Alyson said, placing a hand on the center of Samson's back. She wanted to make the brunette aware that Samson had come with her, and he'd also be leaving with her. "What's going on?" she asked sweetly.

"Alyson, this is Miranda. Miranda, Alyson." Samson made the introductions right away.

"Good to meet you, Alyson. Sam and I were talking politics." She smiled.

Sam? Alyson faked a smile. "Really, Sam?"

"Yes!" Miranda went on to explain. "Turns out we have a common enemy. Conrad Phelps."

"Conrad Phelps was the crooked mayor that I told you about—the one I helped to put behind bars when I was in the DA's office," Samson explained to Alyson. "The one who was accepting bribes and misusing his power as a public official."

"Amongst other things," Miranda added. "That entire Blue Island ring should've met its demise long ago. Kudos to you for bringing Phelps to justice, Sam." She grinned and moved closer into Samson's personal space. "Too bad those Blue Island scumbags got off scot-free."

"Many of them are behind bars, as well," Samson said.

"Take a look around. Many of them are here tonight," said Miranda.

"What do you mean?"

"Many of the scumbags from Blue Island are at this party. Blue Island and Madison Development are one and the same."

"I don't understand," said Samson.

"It's all one big corrupt piece of work. William Blue and Jonathan Madison are old friends," said Miranda. "They're all crooks if you ask me, and should all be behind bars."

"They should be behind bars because they're old friends?" asked Alyson. "Since when did it become criminal to be affiliated with someone?"

"When the principals from one crooked company are the same as the principals of another crooked company, and are all engaged in criminal behavior. It raises an eyebrow," Miranda explained.

"I agree," said Samson.

"Half the folks in this room should be in jail if you ask me," said Miranda. "Everyone from Devin Curry, the company's CFO over there, to Jonathan Madison himself."

A tall man dressed in a charcoal-colored tuxedo worked his way over to Miranda. "Are we having a good time?" he asked casually.

"A blast!" Miranda replied.

The man grabbed Miranda by the waist, taking the champagne flute from her hand. "I think you've had a bit too much to drink."

"Honey, I'm just getting started."

"Champagne really doesn't agree with you, sweetheart. You know that," he insisted, and offered Samson and Alyson an apologetic smile.

"I haven't had that much, and I'm fine!" Miranda said.

"Let's mingle," said the tall man as he pulled her away. "Excuse us."

* * *

Samson gave a nod as Miranda and the other man walked away. He was unsettled. His stomach churned.

"You know there's no merit to anything that drunk woman said," Alyson countered.

"I don't know that," said Samson.

"The Madisons are upstanding people," she whispered. "I know them."

"I know you want this business deal badly, Alyson. But I caution you to proceed carefully. A scandal would ruin you before you even got started."

"I'm not worried." She grabbed a champagne flute from a moving tray, took a drink. "Let's step outside for a bit. You look like you could use some fresh air."

They stepped out onto the veranda, and into the moon-lit night. Samson's mind raced as he looked around at the guests now, trying to put names with faces. He wondered how many of them had been affiliated with Blue Island. Alyson touched his chest with the palm of her hand.

"Relax, baby. You're too preoccupied." She snuggled up to him.

"We should go," he said. "Can't we have Stephen come back for us?"

"We haven't even had dinner, silly. And need I remind you that we paid a pretty penny for these plates?" She giggled. "And besides, we decided to stay on Abaco for the night. Remember? Stephen is halfway back to Harbour Island by now. He won't be back until tomorrow. And we have a room booked at a wonderful resort just a few miles from here."

"You're right." Samson caressed her face with his fingertips and then planted a kiss on her lips.

"Don't forget our plans. We're going to stay up all night, doing God only knows what…" He was shocked at how brazen she was. "And then we're going to sleep late in the morning. Have breakfast in bed. And then do those same things all over again."

Samson conceded. He'd never seen her like this, with her guard down. He wanted to take her to that room before she came to her senses, or sobered up. It was clear that, like Miranda, she'd had way too much champagne. His mind raced a mile a minute, and as much as he wanted to spend a romantic night with the woman who'd hijacked his heart, the truth was, he couldn't wait to get to a computer to research everything that Miranda had said.

He survived dinner, even while speculating that he was breaking bread with criminals—and not just any criminals, but ones that had cost him his career. They were dressed in tuxedos and after-five dresses and pretending to be concerned about a worthy cause. They hid behind their checkbooks and hefty bank accounts. But he knew that as soon as Monday morning arrived, they'd go back to engaging in their shady business deals.

He cut into his juicy fillet, and the steak melted in his mouth. He smiled as he took a glance at the small portion of food on his plate—his five-hundred-dollar plate of food. He knew that before the night was over, he'd be ransacking the kitchen at the resort where they were staying and taking them for every morsel of Caribbean food they could muster. He hoped the property had as good a cook as the Grove did. Sometimes in the middle of the night, he'd sneak to the kitchen for a hearty helping of Raquel's johnnycakes and conch fritters. He hoped he could make it through the night without them.

When Samson looked up from his plate, his eyes met with a pair of familiar blue ones. The wicked smile caused an unsettling feeling in the pit of his stomach. William Blue gave Samson a wink and a wide grin. He stared at the slender blond man. Couldn't peel his eyes from him. William Blue was engaged in conversation with Jonathan Madison. The two of them laughed and toasted with glasses of brown liquor. Samson wondered how long it had been since Blue's release from prison.

"We really must go now." He stood and placed his cloth napkin on the table.

"What are you doing?" she asked. "Sit back down. I haven't even heard Jennifer's speech yet."

"I'm leaving, love. If you're with me, you have to come now."

"What is the matter with you?"

"Just trust me," he pleaded.

Alyson did just that, and it was something she hadn't done in a long time—trust a man. She followed Samson outside. She'd hoped to get Jennifer's attention, to at least say goodbye and to thank her for the invitation, but Samson's urgency prevailed.

Once in the backseat of the taxi, Samson explained his actions to Alyson. "The gentleman who was talking to Jonathan Madison...that was William Blue."

"The William Blue you put behind bars?"

"That would be him."

"Wow!" She sank into her seat. "That had to be uncomfortable for you."

"Yes, extremely."

"I'm sorry you had to endure that."

"I believe Miranda's claims are true. He and Jonathan are old friends," he said.

"Are you saying that Jonathan Madison is engaged in shady business deals?" she asked.

"I'm not saying that the Madisons are shady, but they're in bed with some pretty shady characters. And when William Blue was in prison, someone on the outside set me up. Tarnished my campaign."

"Are you suggesting that it was Jonathan Madison who set you up?"

"I'm only suggesting that they are friends. They looked pretty chummy in there to me. And it's possible that Madison is involved in some bad business practices," he stated. "And if that's the case, they are the last people I want you doing business with."

Samson's discoveries were nothing more than speculation, in Alyson's opinion. She'd already been invited to meet with some of the other principals in the coming week, and the last thing she needed was his speculations to get in the way of her closing the deal. She hated that his career was in shambles, but she refused to believe that the Madison family was somehow involved in unethical behavior.

"I have to do what's right for me," said Alyson. "I can't base my business decisions on what has occurred in your life."

As the taxi pulled up at the beachfront resort, Samson stepped out and held the door for Alyson. He grabbed her small hand and helped her climb out of the backseat.

After checking in to their lavish suite, Samson grabbed bedding from the hall closet and tossed it onto the sofa sleeper. "I'm crashing in here. You can take the bedroom."

"Are you serious right now?" she asked. "What about our romantic evening?"

"I'm kind of tired."

"Are you mad about the whole Blue Madison thing because I won't go on this witch hunt with you?"

Samson shrugged and plopped down onto the sofa. Grabbed the remote control and flipped the television on. "I have legitimate concerns."

"Okay, okay." Alyson held her hands in the air as if to surrender, then stumbled backward.

"You've had too much to drink, love. Why don't you lie down?"

He escorted her to the bedroom, lifted her in his arms and then placed her onto the bed. He removed the heels from her feet. She struggled with the zipper on her dress, and he helped her.

She wrapped her arms around his neck and pulled him onto the bed. "I want you."

"I don't want to take advantage of you."

She laughed. "Please take advantage of me!"

Samson stood, removed his jacket and loosened his bow tie. He slipped the perfectly shined Calvin Klein tuxedo oxfords from his feet and removed his pants. Tight briefs hugged his strong thighs. Alyson watched intently as he loosened every button on his shirt and tossed it onto the chair next to the bed. He slipped into the bed next to her and wrapped his strong arms around her.

Alyson fell asleep quickly. Light snores crept from her lips. Samson got up, tiptoed through the suite and turned off the television and the lights. He went into the bathroom and hopped into the shower. Tried washing his negative thoughts away, but to no avail. He replayed her words in his head: *I can't base my business decisions on what has occurred in your life.* They felt like a punch to his stomach. She wasn't grasping the scope of the situation. He was convinced that the Madisons were bad news, and he worried about Alyson's future with them. He knew he had to get through to her, but tonight he'd allow her to sleep.

He opened the bedroom's French patio doors and breathed in the sweet ocean air. He could hear the waves crashing against the shore just a few feet away. Sheer white curtains danced in the wind. Samson found some relaxing Caribbean music on his phone and settled back in bed. After meeting Alyson, he'd taken the time to download music by artists that she claimed were her favorites, and he was slowly becoming a fan of Caribbean music. He allowed Jah Cure to serenade them for the remainder of the night.

His eyes grew heavy, and sleep crept up on him. He grabbed Alyson a bit tighter and then closed his eyes. When he opened them again, his eyes met those blue ones again. William Blue stood over the bed, a wide grin on his face. He looked down at Samson and puffed on a Cuban cigar. Samson glanced at the French doors. They were closed, and one of the white curtains had been ripped from the curtain rod.

Samson's heart pounded rapidly. "What the hell are you doing here?"

"You thought I'd be gone forever, Steel?"

"You're a criminal, and criminals belong behind bars." Samson was cool and calm, and hoped that Alyson would remain asleep.

"Luckily I have friends in high places."

"You mean friends like Jonathan Madison?"

William Blue laughed. Heartily. He reached into the inside pocket of his tuxedo jacket, swiftly pulled out a silver-and-black .22 handgun and pointed it at Samson. He laughed, and his blue eyes turned bloodshot red. Then they were blue again.

Samson opened his eyes. Sat straight up. His breathing was rapid and heavy, and he wiped sweat from his face. He glanced over at the French doors. The white curtains blew in the wind, still intact—just as they were before he'd fallen asleep. When he glanced over at Alyson, she was still soundly sleeping. He relaxed, controlled his breathing.

As he slipped beneath the sheets next to Alyson, he gently kissed her forehead. He grabbed her in his arms again. Held her through the night.

Chapter 17

The sunshine was invasive, not shy at all about shining brightly through the room. Alyson squinted as she opened her eyes.

"Good morning, sleepyhead," Samson said.

"What time is it?" she asked.

"Just past nine."

"Oh, my! I never sleep this late," Alyson said as she tried to lift her head. A sharp pain shot across her temples, and she winced. "Ooh."

"I went down and got you some coffee," he said. "How do you take it?"

"Black with two sugars." She attempted a smile. "Why didn't you wake me?"

Samson sweetened her coffee and handed the ceramic cup to her. "You needed the rest."

She sat up and took a long sip. "We should enjoy the island today. Let's grab a quick breakfast and do a little shopping."

* * *

Alyson took Samson to a hidden jewel along the beach, an authentic Caribbean restaurant with Bahamian cooks. They chatted casually while enjoying hearty plates of grits, corned beef, jack mackerel, bowls of fish stew and johnny-cakes that tasted remarkably like her mother's.

"This is definitely a different type of breakfast," Samson noted.

"This is as normal as eating eggs and bacon in North America," Alyson explained. "We always start with grits for breakfast, and add fish as our protein. And you can't have any Bahamian meal without a johnnycake."

"I've definitely had my share of johnnycakes since being in the Bahamas." Samson smiled. "However, these can't hold a candle to your mother's."

"She would kiss your face if she heard you say that. I think my parents like you. But I can't think of many people they don't like. They're a congenial bunch of people… that family of mine."

"I feel as if I've known them forever," he said. "You have a wonderful family."

"I like them most times," Alyson teased, though there was some truth to her statement.

"I get the impression that you and Jasmine haven't always been on the same page."

"When we were younger, there was a boy who lived in the next town over. I was hopelessly in love with him. His name was Jimmy Franklin." Alyson cut her mackerel croquet into fours. "Jasmine talked my father into having him sent away. And I never knew why."

"And you blamed her," he concluded.

"I hated her! For years, I hated her." The pain of the memory caused her to drop her fork. She placed her hands over her face.

"We don't have to talk about it, love."

She gave him a warm smile, and tears filled her eyes. He was so gentle with her, so accommodating. She hadn't met a man like that before.

"I don't mind talking about it. We're past it now," she explained. "One day after school, Jimmy Franklin followed her home, and…and he tried to rape her. She fought him, kicked him where it hurts and ran all the way home. She told my father what happened, and the next thing I knew, Jimmy was on a one-way flight to Philadelphia. I never saw him again after that. I blamed Jasmine for years. It was just last year that she told me what happened. The tragedy is, we lost so much time…so many years because I was stubborn."

"But things are better now, right?"

"Things are wonderful now! I have my sister back, and I've been lucky enough to be an integral part of her wedding and her life."

Samson grabbed Alyson's hands in his. He kissed her fingertips and smiled.

"So where are we going after this?" he asked.

"We aren't going anywhere until you finish all of your food." She stuffed fish and grits into her mouth.

"Yes, ma'am." He took a hearty spoonful of fish stew.

After brunch, they headed over to Marsh Harbour, which was the heart of the Abacos. Alyson explained the history of it. "It's where the majority of the island's services are located, including the post office, grocery stores and laundries. Marsh Harbour is the 'bright lights, big city' of all the Out Islands, with one traffic light."

"Plenty of boat docks and marinas," he observed.

"Yep, it's the main gateway to the other Out Islands."

Samson swung his legs as they hung over the boat dock. "The waterways are busy."

"American R & B singer Aaliyah was leaving Marsh Harbour Airport when her plane crashed," Alyson said.

"I remember that. She was filming a music video somewhere in the Bahamas. That was here, huh?"

"Right here. Such a sad time."

"Yes, it was. She was so young."

"Only proves how short life is," said Alyson. "We should enjoy every moment."

"I intend to." Samson grabbed her hand and held it tightly.

When they jetted across the turquoise waters, Alyson held on to his waist as tightly as she could. Her chin pressed against the center of his back as water splashed in her face. She loved being close to him. The Jet Ski bounced against the water, and she laughed like she'd never laughed before. She would never have been caught dead on anyone's Jet Ski before, yet suddenly Samson Steel had her doing things outside of her comfort zone.

As they reached the shore, she hopped off the Jet Ski. Wearing her one-piece bathing suit, she went for a swim while Samson returned their rented equipment. Soon he joined her in the water. She did several flips, turns, breaststrokes and backstrokes. Samson watched with a grin.

"Stop showing off," he said.

"What are you talking about?"

"Turning flips and doing backstrokes. Being a show-off."

"I'm not being a show-off. I'm a swimmer. Been one all my life." She laughed. "I grew up in the Bahamas. And I took swimming lessons."

"You're a show-off." He jumped into the water and grabbed her by the waist. His cold, wet lips gently touched hers.

"Would you like me to teach you some techniques?" she flirted.

"No! I can swim rings around you."

"Well, let's see what you got," she said.

He began to swim a backstroke and attempted to do a flip turn. She looked away as she laughed at his flip.

"So you think I'm funny?" he asked.

"No." She couldn't help but laugh.

"You think I'm funny."

He swam toward her and lifted her in his arms. She screamed as he picked her up and dunked her into the water. She wiped her face as she popped up out of the water. She splashed water at him. He, in turn, splashed her, and before long the two were engaged in a water-splashing war. Finally Samson called a truce, held his hands in the air in surrender. He invited her to jump onto his back, and he carried her to shore.

They made the short walk back to the resort. With wet, bare feet, they rushed across the hardwood floor in their suite. Samson flipped on the shower and warmed the bathroom. He stepped into the shower and beckoned for Alyson to join him.

"We don't have time to mess around. Stephen will be here to pick us up soon."

"We have to shower. Get the sand out of our cracks and crevices," Samson reasoned. "Come on. It'll only save time if we shower together."

Alyson removed her bathing suit and stepped into the shower. The warm water cascaded over her body. Samson washed her back and caressed her breasts with warm, soapy water. She closed her eyes and relished his touch. She leaned her back against his strong chest as he explored her naked body, touched her in places that had lacked attention for so long. His fingertips danced between her thighs and found her warm spot—explored it. She moaned. Her breathing increased, and she lost control.

"Just relax," he whispered and nibbled on her earlobe.

She turned to face him, began to wash his chest. She reached for his groin, caressed it as gently as she knew how. He kissed her lips with vigor.

He carried her to their bed and hovered over her. His lips kissed wet breasts and nibbled on hardened nipples. A trail of kisses was planted along her stomach, lingered at her navel. He kissed her inner thighs, and she held her breath. His tongue explored the place where his fingers had just abandoned. She curled her toes and dredged her heels into the mattress. Samson moved from her thighs and back up to her breasts. He relaxed his muscular body against hers. Pressed her legs apart, pushed himself into her. Made sweet love to her.

When her phone rang, she wished it would stop. Tried to ignore it as she moaned and buried her face in Samson's neck.

"It's probably Stephen," she finally whispered.

"I can't let you go."

"I should get it."

"Tell him to go back to Harbour Island. Let's stay another night."

"I have work this week. I need to get back to Miami," she said. "I have to schedule a meeting with Jonathan Madison."

He pressed into her one last time, collapsed on top of her and then rolled to the other side of the bed. She could tell the mention of Jonathan Madison's name annoyed him. Killed the mood for him. He stood and grabbed Alyson's phone from the nightstand, handed it to her.

"You should call Stephen back," he said.

"What's wrong?" she asked the obvious.

"Nothing," he lied.

"Oh, you thought that I wouldn't do business with Jonathan Madison because you saw him talking to your archenemy?"

"It's not just that I saw them talking, Alyson. Don't you get it? It's that there's probably more to that relationship than you know. And you shouldn't pursue this venture."

"In business we have to take risks."

"Indeed we do, love. Indeed we do." He grabbed a pair of trousers and went into the bathroom, shutting the door behind him.

On the boat ride back to Harbour Island, the atmosphere was just as cold as it had been on their first return trip from Abaco. Samson sat in the bow of the boat and never turned around to look at Alyson, who sat in the port and stared into the ocean. Stephen made small talk with Samson.

"We're expecting rain this week, and it looks like we might be getting quite a bit over the next few weeks," said Stephen. "I hope the weather is cooperative for Jazzy's wedding."

"I hope so, too," Samson said drily. The last thing he wanted to discuss was Jackson and Jasmine's impending wedding. He wanted to get through to Alyson. Shake some sense into her.

Once they reached Harbour Island, Samson and Stephen guided the boat to the deck and secured it with a rope. Samson helped Alyson climb out of the boat.

He held his hand out to Stephen. "Thanks again, man," he said.

Stephen grabbed Samson's hand in a strong shake. "Don't mention it."

"Are you bringing a date to Jasmine's wedding?" Alyson asked Stephen.

"I haven't decided yet," said Stephen.

"You should probably let us know sooner rather than later so that we can plan accordingly," Alyson said. "We haven't received your RSVP."

"I'll probably just come alone."

"What about that girl from Spanish Wells?" she asked. "The one you were all cozy with at the Grove's grand opening."

"We were just friends. And besides, she moved to Nassau," Stephen explained.

"Well, I know a nice young lady you might be interested in."

"I don't need any help in that area, Alyson. But thank you."

"She's young, beautiful…a musician," insisted Alyson. "She's in the band that we've hired for the wedding reception. Her name is Bijou."

Samson glanced at Alyson and shook his head. He couldn't believe she was actually trying to pawn Bijou off on her cousin. Anything to remove her from Samson's reach—if, in fact, he had any intentions of reaching.

"I don't need you playing matchmaker," said Stephen. "Just put me down for one."

"Are you sure you don't want to meet her?" Alyson asked.

"Positive." Stephen shook his head. "You're something else."

"I'm just trying to help."

"Handle your own affairs," said Stephen, who leaned in for a kiss to his cousin's cheek. "It seems you're not doing a very good job at it."

"I'm doing just fine, for your information," Alyson insisted.

"Really?" asked Stephen. He patted Samson on the back. "Well, let's just hope you don't run this guy away. He has an enormous amount of tolerance."

"Goodbye, Stephen." Alyson walked away from the men, pulling her cell phone out. "Thanks for the ride."

"You're quite welcome," said Stephen with a smirk. "Love you."

"Love you, too." Alyson held the phone to her ear.

Stephen turned to Samson and whispered, "She doesn't like to be challenged. Have to keep her on her toes."

"I'll remember that."

The men shook hands once more before parting ways.

Pictures were scattered about on the coffee table. Scissors and scrapbooks were on the floor. A near-empty bottle of wine was in the center of the table. Jasmine sat on the floor, her head resting against the leather chair, and Whitney laughed at something until she cried.

"What is going on?" Alyson asked her sisters.

"Well, well, well... I see we made it back from Abaco," said Whitney as she looked past Alyson and smiled at Samson. She stood and held her hand out to him. "Hello, I'm Whitney. Alyson's sister."

"A pleasure to meet you, Whitney. I'm Samson Steel."

"Yes, you are," Whitney said as she gave him a long examination.

"What is all this mess?" Alyson asked.

"We're scrapbooking. And looking for photos for the video presentation we have planned for the reception," Jasmine explained.

"We have photos of Jackson, too. His mama sent them." Whitney held a photo in the air. "Wasn't he just the cutest?"

"Adorable." Alyson was unimpressed. "And how much wine have you two had while walking down memory lane?"

"We are not drunk, if that's what you're asking," said Jasmine. "We're tipsy."

Both women giggled.

"This doesn't look good, ladies," explained Alyson. "We have guests staying here, and this just isn't a good look for the Grove."

"We're fine, Alyson. Really." Whitney changed the subject. "How was your trip?"

"It was wonderful," said Alyson.

"I'm going on up to my room," Samson whispered to Alyson. "I'll catch you later."

"You want to have dinner on the terrace tonight? I can have Raquel whip something up for us."

"Nah, I'll probably just grab a burger from Ma Ruby's later." Samson kissed Alyson's cheek.

"Okay, then. I'll chat with you later." She tried to remain upbeat in front of her sisters, but knew that something was different between them.

She watched as he climbed the stairs. Her sisters witnessed the entire exchange in silence.

"Trouble in paradise?" Whitney asked.

"No!" said Alyson. "We had a great time. He's just tired."

Jasmine and Whitney gave each other a look. Alyson took a seat in the leather chair and began to sift through the photos. She hated that the weekend hadn't ended on the best note, but she figured Samson would let things go soon. He would see that he was wrong about Jonathan Madison. He would understand that she needed to do what was best for her company.

Her business was all she had.

Chapter 18

The Brazilian restaurant was crowded during the lunch period. With an extensive wine list and one of the best porterhouse steaks in Florida, the Capital Grille was where important business meetings were held. Alyson had chosen her best business attire—a black Ralph Lauren suit with a gray silk blouse underneath. She wanted her appearance to prove that she was capable of handling most anything—particularly Jonathan Madison's collection of commercial properties.

A young, dark-haired gentleman sat across from Jonathan at the table. Both men stood when she approached the table.

"Alyson, good to see you again. You left so abruptly the other night, I didn't get to say goodbye," said Jonathan.

"My apologies. I had an urgent matter to attend to."

"I'm glad to know that everything is all right. I'd like for you to meet Dustin Rose. He's head of finance at Madison.

He works diligently to get our buyers qualified for financing. And he has a pretty good track record."

Dustin took Alyson's hand in his. "Pleased to meet you, Miss Talbot."

"Likewise," said Alyson.

"Alyson, should we hire your company to handle our leasing and sales, you'd be working very closely with Dustin. So I thought it fitting that he join us tonight."

Alyson picked up her menu and gave it a quick glance. Her nerves had the best of her, and her appetite was barely there.

"I explained to Dustin that you've come highly recommended."

"Your credentials are impressive." Dustin smiled.

His facial expression seemed obscure, and Alyson couldn't quite read him.

"I'd like to hear your plans for our inventory in Miami, Coral Gables, Fort Lauderdale and West Palm Beach," said Jonathan. "They're close to being completely developed, and we'd like to get them on the market as soon as possible."

"I've already done a market analysis of your properties in those areas. And I've developed a marketing plan for each of them." Alyson opened her briefcase and handed Jonathan and Dustin copies of her plans. She was grateful that she'd printed an extra copy. "If you'd turn to page one, I'd like to walk you through what I have in mind."

Alyson had worked hard on her proposal. She'd done her homework and presented a well-developed plan. It was aggressive, yet realistic, and Jonathan seemed impressed with her. He knew that because her business was new, she was hungry and would put forth more effort than someone who was a veteran. She couldn't quite read Dustin's thoughts about her plan. But she didn't care. As long as she'd impressed Jonathan, it was all that mattered.

"I know that I'm being somewhat optimistic here, and this is a great deal of responsibility for a small agency such as yours..." Jonathan began.

"We're small, but capable."

"This will require your intentness. You don't have anything pressing that would distract you from this, do you?"

You mean besides my sister's impending wedding that's scheduled to take place soon?

"No, of course not," she said.

"I like your marketing strategy. Let's get these properties listed right away," he said. "Can we do that?"

"Absolutely," said Alyson.

"Then congratulations are in order." Jonathan smiled and reached across the table to shake Alyson's hand. "Welcome to the team."

Dustin took a long drink of his Cognac and then shook Alyson's hand. He cleared his throat. "The holidays are upon us. Christmas is right around the corner. But at Madison...we don't really have time for celebrations. Time is money, and we can't afford to waste either one," he explained. "On December 24 we have a huge company meeting at our resort in Daytona Beach."

"You mean Christmas Eve?" Alyson asked.

"Yes, Christmas Eve. While the rest of the world is drinking eggnog and Christmas caroling, we'll be talking about strategies for the upcoming year. It's how we stay ahead of our competitors," he said. "If you're a part of the Madison team, we'll expect you to be there. Right, Jonathan?"

"Well, I'm a big fan of spending the holidays with family. But I suppose if sacrifices must be made, then they just do," said Jonathan in an apologetic manner. "We'd like for you to be available during the holidays, Alyson."

"It's just that my sister is getting married on Christmas Day in the Bahamas."

"Congratulations to her," said Jonathan.

"What does that have to do with Christmas Eve, and with you?" Dustin asked.

Besides the fact that the rehearsal dinner is on Christmas Eve, and I'm the maid of honor?

"Nothing. I'll be there."

"The Bahamas is a short enough trip from Florida. Fly out on Christmas morning, and you'll make it just in time for the nuptials," said Jonathan.

"Absolutely."

"Jennifer told me that you're a single woman, no husband, no children. Is that correct?"

"That is correct."

Dustin smiled. "Family is a wonderful thing. But without it, you can devote more time to Madison."

Jonathan smiled. "You bring those bright ideas that you just shared, and that energy that you've shown me tonight, and we'll all make a bundle of money."

"Looking forward to it." Alyson took a sip of her wine.

Her priorities had quickly changed, and she wasn't sure how she was going to handle them.

When she returned to her condo, she opened all the blinds, unleashed the beautiful sunshine and ushered it into her space. She hit the power button on her stereo. The upbeat Caribbean rhythm bounced against the walls, and she danced. With hands raised in the air, she rotated her hips to the music. She opened a celebratory bottle of champagne, one she'd found buried in the pantry. It was a bottle that she had stashed from last New Year's Eve.

Last New Year's Eve she'd spent the holiday flipping between Carson Daly and *Dick Clark's New Year's Rockin' Eve with Ryan Seacrest* on her television set. She'd fallen asleep before midnight and never got around to popping the cork, and thankfully so. She needed the champagne now to celebrate her new partnership with Jonathan Madison.

"You should come over and have a toast with me!" she told Jules over the phone.

"I wish I could, but I'm babysitting the kiddos this afternoon," Jules said. "My sister had to work."

"Well, I'm raising my glass in a virtual toast to you," said Alyson. "Here's to us doing great things in the coming year."

"Cheers! I'm looking forward to it," said Jules. "And I want to hear all the details. But right now, I have to go before these rug rats destroy my house."

"Go!" said Alyson as she placed her glass of champagne onto the coffee table and lit a few candles. "We'll talk later."

"Let's do breakfast or lunch tomorrow and catch up."

"I'll meet you in Little Havana for breakfast."

"Oh, how I desire a café cubano!" Jules exclaimed. "Meet at Café Versailles?"

"Eight o'clock."

"I'll be there!"

"Don't be late, Jules. You know how I hate when people aren't on time."

"I'll be there," Jules assured.

"Okay, I've got to go. Someone's knocking at my door," Alyson said.

The knocker was relentless, and she was hesitant to answer. Very few people knew that she was at home in Miami. She was gone so frequently, and she did not appreciate visits that weren't prearranged. And she would let the person on the other side of her door know just how displeased she was.

After a quick peek through the peephole, she swung the door open.

"And to what do I owe this visit?" she asked.

Edward was dressed in an oxford-gray tailored suit. He always looked dapper. A precise haircut and a clean shave was his signature look. He stepped inside. "I'm really shocked that you're here. You spend so much time on the islands these days. What's that about?"

"I'm helping Jazzy with the wedding."

"And spending lots of time with that fellow, I hear. What's his name?"

"I don't know who you're talking about."

"You know who I'm talking about. Jackson's friend, the politician."

"Oh, you mean Samson." She pretended to be enlightened.

"Yes," he said. "I'm hurt that you didn't share your little love affair with me."

"Don't pout."

"Every man who has ever been interested in you, you've run away from."

"Well, there's no future here, either. He lives in Illinois, and as soon as he's done gallivanting about the Bahamas, he's going back there."

"So where does that leave you?"

"I don't know! In Miami thinking about him, I guess. Wondering what could've been. And before you say it, long-distance relationships never work. Everyone knows that. And I'm perfectly fine without the stress of a commitment."

"Sure you are." Edward smiled.

"I am!" she said, and then changed the subject. "And what are you doing here, anyway?"

"I was in the neighborhood." He picked up the bottle of champagne, held it in the air to see how much she'd drunk.

She snatched the bottle from her brother. "Palm Beach is hardly my neighborhood. What's really going on?"

Edward collapsed onto the couch and sighed. "Savannah's getting married."

"Really?" Alyson asked. "The one you don't want around Chloe because he hasn't been preapproved? And the one who's been spending too much time at the house that you're still paying a mortgage on?"

"You think I'm overreacting, don't you?"

"I think you haven't quite let go of your ex-wife."

"Things were just fine the way they were. We have such a great friendship, and we've gotten this coparenting thing down to a science. Now is not the time to switch things up for Chloe. She's finally getting it together. The divorce really messed her up."

"Kids are way more resilient than we think. They bounce back," said Alyson. "It's the grown folks who have problems coping."

"I'm over her," he tried convincing her.

"Then why is this so hard for you?"

He walked into the kitchen and rummaged through the cupboards until he found a champagne glass. He returned to the living room and filled his glass.

"I'm concerned about Chloe. I don't know anything about this guy. What if he's a sexual predator? What if he mistreats my daughter or Savannah, for that matter?"

"I don't believe that Savannah would allow anyone to mistreat Chloe," said Alyson. "But if you're so concerned, why don't you just go meet the guy?"

"I'm supposed to. This evening, actually. I'm meeting the two of them at Pascal's on Ponce for dinner."

"Ooh, Pascal's. Fancy."

"I need you to come."

"No!"

"Yes," Edward exclaimed. "I can't do this alone."

"I have tons of work to finish before I head back to the islands."

"Please, sis," Edward begged. "We won't stay for the entire meal. Just long enough for me to read his ass some rights, and share my dos and don'ts when it comes to my daughter. Now, are you coming or not?"

"Not," Alyson said emphatically. "This is none of my business, and already very awkward for *you*. Why should I suffer, too?"

"Because you love me."

"I do love you," she said.

"And because you love Chloe."

"Both very true statements," said Alyson. "But what's love got to do with anything?"

"I'll wait while you go get dressed."

"I can't go, Edward. I have a ton of work to do this afternoon, and I have an early morning with Jules. I'm hoping to be back in the Bahamas by tomorrow afternoon. You should do this alone. Get it over with."

"Yeah, you're right." He finished the glass of champagne with one gulp and set the glass on the table. Stood. Adjusted his tie.

"You can do this, big brother. And it won't be as bad as you're anticipating."

He kissed Alyson's forehead before heading for the door. "I'll call you later."

She was relieved when Edward left. The last thing she needed was to engage in someone else's drama. She had drama of her own. She knew that doing business with Jonathan Madison was a risk, particularly if Samson's intuition was right. The business arrangement was bittersweet for her—she was overjoyed to be taking her company to the next level, but the stakes were high. Besides possibly doing business with criminals, she risked losing Samson.

She couldn't wait to see his face when she returned to the Bahamas. In just a short time, he'd managed to rearrange her life and her emotions. He'd penetrated her hard exterior and made his way into her heart. She loved the way he made her feel—mentally, emotionally, physically. To imagine her life without him was painful.

She didn't know what their future held, and she didn't care. She just wanted to enjoy each breathtaking moment while it lasted.

Chapter 19

It was important that Alyson return to the Bahamas as soon as possible. There were many loose ends that needed to be tied up before the wedding. She needed to ensure that all the bridesmaids' dresses had been altered, the grooms-men had been fitted for tuxedoes and the menu had been finalized. She needed to speak with the caterers, the cake decorators and the florist. And just as she'd promised, she needed to take her mother shopping for a dress. So many things needed to be done in such a short time. And since she'd be handling the Madison portfolio soon, she needed to help Jasmine finalize as many wedding plans as she possibly could.

Alyson's head bounced against the leather seat in first class. No need getting accustomed to flying coach, she thought, because she had a feeling she'd be flying first class from now on. With the money she was going to make soon, she wouldn't be doing anything low budget. She could continue to support her lavish lifestyle without worry. She decided to indulge in a celebratory drink. She'd gotten exactly what she wanted, and she was proud of her accomplishments.

It was midafternoon when she landed and made her way to the Grove, which was still and quiet. Most of the guests were out and about, enjoying an afternoon swim at the beach or a tour of the island. Alyson found Jasmine wandering about the Clydesdale with a notepad in her hand, her hair tousled and a permanent wrinkle in the center of her forehead. The wedding was taking its toll on the bride-to-be.

"We have a situation," said Jasmine frantically. "Daddy's tux didn't ship with the others, and it won't get here in time."

"That's an easy fix. I'm sure Daddy has a suit in his closet that he can wear."

"A silver tuxedo with a red bow tie?" Jasmine asked.

"He doesn't have to wear the same tux as the rest of the bridal party, sweetie. He's the father of the bride, not a groomsman. He can wear a regular old suit to give you away in."

"And what about Carina's dress?"

"What about Carina's dress?"

"It doesn't fit! It's too tight, and the seamstress says there's nothing more she can do about it."

Alyson shrugged. "Bottom line, Carina's got to lose weight. She has a few days to lose a few pounds, and I would suggest she get started right away. She needs to miss a few meals between now and the wedding."

"We're talking a few weeks, Alyson. I don't see her losing a few pounds before Christmas." Jasmine was near tears.

"It's doable. Bread and water diet." Alyson laughed in

an attempt to lighten her sister's mood. "Now calm down and don't be a bridezilla."

"I'm serious, Alyson. I'm stressed beyond words. I'll feel better once we get past rehearsal dinner," said Jasmine. "By the way, can you make sure Jackson's parents get from the airport to the Grove? Their flight gets in right about the time of the rehearsal dinner. Which means neither Jackson nor I can get away."

"I'll send Daddy. He can pick them up and deliver them to the Grove, safe and sound."

"Perfect," Jasmine said with a sigh of relief. "Pastor Johnson will get there at six. What time will you arrive for the dinner?"

Alyson was speechless for a moment. "Um…what time would you like for me to arrive?"

"Early," Jasmine said matter-of-factly. "We have to decorate, remember?"

"About Christmas Eve… Jazzy…" Alyson began to explain that she had a conflict.

Raquel rushed over in a panic, interrupting them. "Jasmine I really need to talk to you about the food for the rehearsal dinner. We're getting close, and I know you've been busy, but we really need to get this menu finalized."

"I know, I know." Jasmine threw her arms into the air. "What were you saying, Alyson?"

"Nothing that can't wait. Go handle the menu." Alyson shooed them along. "We'll talk later, after I get unpacked and settled in."

She was grateful for the reprieve, but knew she'd have to break the news to Jasmine at some point. She took the stairway up to her room, just long enough to drop her luggage off and take a glance in the mirror. She checked her hair and refreshed her lipstick before closing the door behind her. She almost skipped as she went next door to

Samson Place. She rushed up the stairs to Samson's room and knocked on the door. No answer.

"Where are you?" she whispered to herself.

"He's on the cabana," said Bijou as if she'd heard her. "We just had a drink together."

"Thanks." There was something about that woman that she couldn't stand, but she'd vowed to never let her know it. Instead, she killed her with a kind smile and a cool demeanor.

She found Samson on the cabana at the bar, just as Bijou had said. He was nursing a bottle of Kalik beer. His eyes were glued to the television as he watched a soccer match. She crept up behind him and wrapped her arms tightly around his waist.

"Don't you have anything better to do with your time?" she asked.

"No, nothing." He turned around, faced her with a smile and then pulled her close to him. Kissed her lips. "When did you get back?"

"Less than an hour ago."

"Good to see you," he said. "Have a seat. What would you like to drink?"

"The usual. So I understand you just had a drink with Bijou."

"Well, she was just down here at the bar. I had a drink, and she had one. If you consider that having a drink together, then I guess we did." He laughed.

"What is with her?" Alyson asked.

"She's young and infatuated with your man."

"My man?" Alyson leaned her head back to get a good look at him. "Is that what you are?"

"I'd like to be." He caressed her face with his fingertip and then grabbed her chin, pulled her in for a kiss.

"Deuce, give the lady a cosmopolitan," Samson said to the bartender.

"Are you new?" Alyson asked the Rastafarian with long locks that spanned the center of his back.

"Yes, ma'am," he said. "Today's my first day."

"Who hired you?" Alyson asked. "And what happened to Vick?"

"I believe your sister Jasmine hired him," Samson interjected.

"I guess I've missed some things." She sighed and climbed onto a bar stool next to Samson.

"All this back and forth between the islands and the States. It has to be exhausting," said Samson. "You miss so much."

"I won't have to go back to Miami until the week of Christmas," she said. "I have a meeting on the twenty-fourth."

"Must be an important meeting. That's Christmas Eve, in case you didn't know."

"I know."

"And isn't the rehearsal dinner on that day, as well?"

"I'll be back in time."

"Will you, Alyson?" Samson asked. "This is an important day for your sister."

"I'm going to try my best."

"Aren't you the maid of honor?"

Alyson was quiet. He already knew what her position was in the wedding. And he wasn't making this any easier. The thought of not being on the island on Christmas Eve had already caused her angst. She couldn't remember a single Christmas Eve that she hadn't spent with her family. All the Talbot children would arrive home a few days before Christmas. They'd spend time cooking, singing and dancing to Caribbean rhythms while wrapping gifts.

They drank wine and told stories until the wee hours of the morning on Christmas. It was an important time for the Talbots, even when there wasn't an impending wedding.

"Have you told Jasmine that you're going to miss her rehearsal dinner?"

"She's got so much going on... I don't know how to tell her."

"What kind of meeting is scheduled on Christmas Eve anyway? Can't it wait until after the holidays?"

"I wish it could." She took a sip of the drink that Deuce set in front of her. "But the Madisons—"

"The Madisons?" Samson interrupted. "That's who you're meeting with?"

"Yes," she said solemnly.

"So you're still planning to do business with them, despite my warnings," said Samson. He laughed sarcastically and took a long drink of his beer.

"Yes."

"You know, I did my homework. Discovered some pretty alarming things about that company."

"Really?"

"Just as I suspected, many of Blue Island's principals are the same as Madison's. And guess what else I discovered?" He didn't await her response. "Madison is up to some of the same old business practices that his buddy William Blue was. Bribing building inspectors and city officials, tampering with public records. The city's chief of development got a new SUV this year...and I can only guess whose name is on the bill of sale. I bet if I were to dig deeper, I'd find Caribbean cruises and payments of mortgages, too."

"It's all hearsay. I don't think Jonathan Madison would knowingly engage in such behavior."

"Don't be naive, Alyson. If I were the DA in that town, I'd throw the book at them!"

"Well, you're not the DA. Isn't that why you're here in the first place?" she asked and instantly regretted her words. The last thing she wanted to do was say something hurtful to Samson.

"It's only a matter of time before they're brought to justice. And when it happens, you'll be caught up in it, too," said Samson. He stood, placed two bills on the table to cover their drinks. "Consider yourself forewarned."

"So what does that mean for us?"

"There is no *us* if you're planning to do business with criminals."

"Are you asking me to choose between you and my career?"

He thought for a moment, and then brought his lips to her ear. "I guess I am."

He awaited her response.

Finally, her silence was response enough. He walked away.

She was stunned. Couldn't move. Her heart raced a million miles per minute. She wondered if there was any truth to Samson's findings, or if he was simply being paranoid. William Blue showing up at the party had him shaken, and seeing things that perhaps didn't exist. She wasn't an unethical person, but she needed more than the accusations of a former assistant DA and a washed-up politician to make her squander such an important business partnership.

Her career was dependent upon it, and no one came between her and her career. Not even Samson Steel.

Chapter 20

It had been a few days since he'd spoken to her, and Samson was beginning to rethink everything he thought that Alyson Talbot was—beautiful, intelligent, brilliant, strong. At the end of that list, he thought he should add *unethical, immoral* and *calculating*. Her choice to continue to work with Madison Development would drive a wedge between them, and he knew it. He questioned whether or not he could trust her, and decided that it was better to cut ties with her sooner rather than later—before his feelings were all caught up in a woman who couldn't care less about him. She had her own agenda, and she was willing to carry it out despite the costs.

He'd come to the Bahamas to get away from his troubles in Illinois. Now it seemed that trouble had followed him there. Perhaps it was time to return home and face his fears. Jackson would understand if he missed the wedding. He lifted the suitcase onto the bed and opened it, began to fill it with his clothing. There was a struggle going on between his heart and his mind. His heart wanted to believe that he could get through this with Alyson. He'd already begun to feel things for her. But his mind had always been the more dominant force. It kept him out of predicaments.

His afternoon flight was on schedule, and he made it to the airport just in the nick of time. Dressed in a pair of khaki-colored cargo pants, a blue T-shirt and a white blazer, he stepped out of the taxicab. His pageboy hat blew from his head, and he quickly grabbed it before it took flight. He handed the driver two Bahamian bills, both with Queen Elizabeth II's face plastered across the front of it. The portrait of Hope Town, Abaco, depicted on the back of the bills reminded him of time spent with Alyson on the Abaco Islands. He enjoyed those moments with her. He would miss her gorgeous smile and her incredible body. Despite their differences, he would feel her absence.

"Keep the change," he told the driver.

The flight from the Eleuthera Islands to Chicago was long and exhausting. But he was grateful when the aircraft's wheels hit the pavement at Chicago's Midway. The brisk winters in Illinois were a far cry from winter in the Bahamas. He was grateful that he'd packed his insulated parka with the hood. He slipped his snow boots onto his feet before stepping out to the curb to hail a taxi. Large snowflakes brushed against his unshaven face. He slid into the backseat of a yellow cab.

Twenty minutes later, he stepped inside his loft on Printer's Row. The 1960s warehouse had been transformed into a trendy living space equipped with beautiful hardwoods, high ceilings and brick walls. An abundance of natural light beamed through massive windows. He tossed his keys onto the end table, headed straight for the thermostat and turned on the heat as he shivered from the cold. He plopped down onto the caramel-colored leather sofa, still bundled in his parka. A glimmer of guilt rushed over him as he looked around his contemporary loft. He'd teased Alyson about her downtown condo, while he enjoyed much of the same luxuries that she did. He'd moved from his old neighborhood years before.

After the space began to warm, he took off his coat. His kitchen was modern, with granite counters and stainless-steel appliances. His refrigerator was bare except for a two-liter bottle of flat Coke, a half-dozen eggs and a carton of milk. He frowned as he poured spoiled milk down the drain. He removed his boots from his feet and flipped on the television, tuned it to CNN to catch the latest goings-on.

Once the snow subsided, he headed out to visit his mother. Antionette Steel had short, silver hair and golden-brown skin. She looked smaller than he remembered her being just weeks ago, but then she'd always had a petite frame, even before she became ill. Even as small as she was, she was a feisty ball of fire. He loved her spunk. Chemotherapy had managed to steal her hair, but not her positive energy.

She screamed when she saw him. "What are you doing here?"

"I had to come see what mischief you were up to," he teased her and gave her a strong hug.

She grabbed his face in her hands. "So good to see you, baby. I can't believe you left the gorgeous Bahamas for this terrible weather."

"Some things you just have to do."

"What's really going on?"

"I told you. Had to come check on my favorite girl." He smiled.

"I'm fine." She pulled a pound cake from the oven. "You need to find yourself a nice girl, settle down and have some babies."

"I found a girl, but I don't think she's the right one."

"Really?" she asked. "In the Bahamas?"

"Yep." He pinched a piece of cake between his fingers and quickly stuffed it into his mouth.

Toni slapped his hand. "Are you crazy, boy? Messing up my cake! Now tell me about this girl."

"Nothing to tell. She came. She went."

"Was she pretty?"

"Gorgeous!"

"From a good family? Got good child-bearing hips?" Toni giggled.

"Ambitious, successful…" He moved his face close to her ear. "Sexy."

She waved him away. "Then what's the problem? You have too many rules and expectations, Sammy Steel."

He explained to his mother about the relationship between Alyson and Madison Development, and the man he'd sent to prison, William Blue. He told her how Alyson had refused to heed his warning.

"I don't know if I trust her," he said.

"I understand how you must feel," said Toni. "But you have to understand her position, as well. This is her livelihood, and she can't be expected to put her life on hold for a man she barely knows."

"I don't want her to be cautious for me. I want her to be cautious for her own good."

"You sound so protective." She brushed her hand across her son's face and then said emphatically, "You love her."

"That's beside the point."

"You didn't deny it," she pointed out. "You love her, Sammy?"

"What does love have to do with any of this, Ma?"

"It has everything to do with it. If you love her, you can't walk away from her or give up. You have to make her understand that you fear for her safety. You have to rescue her."

"How do you propose I do that when she's a hardheaded woman who won't listen to me?" he asked. "You can't rescue people who don't want to be rescued."

"If you love her, you'll find a way," she said. "You've allowed your fears to rob you of your candidacy. Don't let fear rob you of love, too, son."

He wanted to lie and tell his mother that he didn't love Alyson. But he couldn't. He did love her, though he hadn't admitted it to her.

"What difference does it make now? I'm here, she's there."

"And there are flights between here and there every day of the week."

"I came home to spend Christmas with you and the rest of the family."

"And your father?" she asked.

"He doesn't care if I'm here."

"He loves you, despite what you think, Sammy. He just has his way about things. He's set in his ways."

"He still blames me for not being a cop," said Samson. "I can't change who I am."

"Give him a chance."

"To hurt me again? I don't think so."

"Carve out some time to spend with him."

Samson gave his mother a sideways glance. Toni knew that he was just as stubborn as his father, and neither of them would give in to the other. Samson's dad was prideful and rigid. But Samson's heart was bigger, and he could be persuaded.

"For me?" she asked with a wink. "Can you do it for me?"

"I'll try." He kissed her cheek. "For you."

Toni Steel knew exactly how to appeal to Samson's heart.

Chapter 21

Alyson had suddenly found herself in a position of choosing between her career and the man she'd become quite fond of. Going to her parents' home was exactly what she needed at the moment. She needed to see her father. Needed his advice—he was the best advice-giver she knew. She had no clue about how to handle the situation she'd found herself in, and her father was great at making sense of things. He'd know what to do.

She found him in his favorite position—on the front porch of their family home in Governor's Harbour, the Eleutheran newspaper in his lap, his reading glasses on his face, eyes closed and light snores escaping from his lips.

"Daddy," Alyson said and took a seat next to him.

"Hey." He smiled when he saw her. "I almost fell asleep out here."

"Almost?"

"Good thing I didn't."

"Yep, good thing." Alyson laughed at her father's antics. Then she sighed, remembering her purpose for the visit.

"What's on your mind?"

"Man troubles."

"Already?"

"What do you mean, 'already?'"

"The fellow... Jackson's friend," he said matter-of-factly. "Are you two already having troubles?"

"Is anything on this island sacred?"

"Very little."

"How do you choose between a man and your career?"

"I think that question would be better answered by your mother. She sacrificed her career for me," he said. "So I guess I'm somewhat biased."

"This is different."

She explained to her father about the Madisons, William Blue and Samson.

He removed his reading glasses, sat straight up in his chair and, with a look of concern, said, "Maybe you should listen to what he has to say. It appears that this could be a potentially dangerous situation."

"He's overreacting. I get that he was a victim, but you can't go around accusing innocent people of wrongdoing."

"Just be cautious is all I'm saying."

"I will, Daddy. But this is an important deal. This could make or break my real estate business," Alyson explained.

"And he must be a pretty important fellow if you're going through the fuss of it all."

"I like him a little," Alyson lied.

Her father was intuitive. "You'll make other business connections, but will you find a man that makes you smile like I've seen you smile lately? You haven't been happy for a long time, but you seem carefree now. You should consider that."

"Working with the Madisons can transform my career."

"No doubt, making a name for yourself in the industry is important," said Paul John Talbot, "but at what cost? Love?"

"Nobody said anything about love." Alyson was in denial.

"Well, you've found something. And you owe it to yourself to find out if that *something* is worth the fight."

"So just forget about everything that I've worked hard for?"

"I'm certainly not saying that. Being an achiever is who you are," he said. "But don't discount your heart."

"I think I've lost him, Daddy," said Alyson. "He caught a flight back to Chicago this afternoon."

"It's only geography, baby," said Paul John. "There are flights between here and there every day of the week."

Alyson looked at her phone when it buzzed. She opened the text message: Can you meet me this afternoon for a site visit?—Dustin.

She typed, I'm in the Caribbean.

Can you be in Miami by tomorrow afternoon? Say 2 pm?

Of course. She typed.

I'll arrange for an early morning flight and we can charge it to your new expense account. I'll be in touch soon with the details.

Thank you was all she could think to type.

When she looked up, she noticed her father observing her closely.

"Chicago fellow?" he asked.

"No. Business," she said. "I'm headed back to Miami in the morning."

"Then you should get a good night's sleep. Why don't you stay here, and I'll drive you to the airport in the morning."

She stood and kissed his cheek. "Anything good to eat in the kitchen?"

"Your mother always has something prepared. Go check things out." He gave her a wink.

"Thanks, Daddy, for listening to me."

"That's what I'm here for."

She rushed into the kitchen and found her mother's Bahamian spread. After finishing off a huge plate of grouper fish and pigeon peas with rice, she curled up on the sofa in the den. Surfed through the channels on the television and finally settled on a local news station. Thoughts of Samson filled her head. She missed him more than she was willing to admit. She longed for his kiss and touch. She missed his smile. Life with him had been glorious, though short-lived. Life without him was unbearable, uncomfortable. She was listless.

She dialed his number, and dared herself to press the send key. She couldn't. She wouldn't know what to say if he answered. And if he dismissed her, she'd be embarrassed. She was prideful.

She tossed the phone aside. Samson Steel would not get the opportunity to snub her twice in one lifetime. She would will herself not to think about him. Focus on business and forget he even existed. It was better that way.

Chapter 22

Cecil Steel was the last person Samson wanted to see, but he'd promised his mother. His father was set in his ways. A man of average height, brown skin and graying hair, he was an older version of Samson. His father had been a thorn in his side since adolescence, since the first time Samson played an organized sport. He knew early on that he wouldn't be much of an athlete. He had no desire to play football or basketball. While his brothers excelled in both, Samson found greater pleasure in gaining knowledge. Learning became his sport.

"I thought I'd bring you out tonight, have a drink… spend some quality time with you, Pop."

"We could've had quality time at the house," said Cecil as he relaxed in the booth. "You don't need to take me to fancy restaurants to spend quality time with me, son. If you would just come by the house more often…"

"I didn't bring you here to argue."

His father placed reading glasses on his face and

grabbed the menu. Gave it a glance. "Have you seen these prices?"

"I eat here all the time, Pop. It's one of my favorite places," said Samson.

"A waste of good money," he mumbled, and continued to sift through the items on the menu.

"I recommend the shrimp and grits," Samson said. "Delicious!"

"Who eats shrimp with grits, and in the middle of the afternoon?" his father asked, peering at Samson over the top of his reading glasses.

"It's not all that unusual, Pop. I know lots of people who enjoy grits in the middle of the afternoon, as well as folks who eat fish for breakfast."

His thoughts drifted to the Bahamas and Alyson. She'd taught him to eat many things he hadn't experienced before. As much as he hated to admit it, he missed her. Couldn't get her out of his head.

"I've never heard of anyone eating fish for breakfast," said Cecil.

"It's because you live in a box, and you never step outside of it."

"It's not necessary to do all of these things that aren't going to make a bit of difference when you die," he said. "You love your family, and do the best you can in your career, and that's it."

"You love your family, huh? Does that mean all of your family, or just some?"

"Are you implying that I don't love you, Sammy?"

"I'm saying you don't respect me and my choices."

"Because your choices are absurd." He shut his menu and removed the glasses from his face. "For instance, you just got back from the Bahamas. The time you spent over there could've been time spent looking for another job. Did you forget that you're unemployed?"

"I needed a vacation," said Samson. "And besides, it's not like I'm broke. I can afford to take some time off. I need that."

"What you need is a career you can be proud of."

"I am proud of my career. At least the one I had," said Samson. "And I'm proud of my life, despite what you think."

"You don't seem proud at all. You seem confused," Cecil said.

"I'm not confused. I was a little distraught over what took place on the campaign trail, but I'm clear about what I want now."

"And what is it that you want?"

"I want to run again. In fact, I'm putting my campaign together for the next election."

"I never understood why you just didn't go into law enforcement, a meaningful career, like the rest of us."

"It's the same reason I didn't play football or basketball in high school, Pop. I have to do what makes me happy."

The server walked up, pad in hand, interrupting whatever Cecil was about to say.

"Are you gentlemen ready to order?" she asked.

Samson hadn't even taken a look at the menu. He didn't need to. Big Jones had always been one of his favorite restaurants, with its southern New Orleans cooking. He knew the menu like the back of his hand.

"I'll start with the crab cakes and a bowl of gumbo," Samson said. "And for my entrée I'll have the Carolina shrimp burger."

His father peered at him. "Hungry?"

"Famished," said Samson. He turned to the server. "Whatever the old man is having, put it on my tab."

"No. No. Young lady, I'll have my own tab, thank you," Cecil insisted.

Samson found pleasure in getting his father worked up. "And bring him a big fat order of the *boudin rouge*."

Samson laughed. He knew that his father would never order something that sounded so wicked. Although it was only Cajun sausage, Cecil Steel never veered outside his comfort zone. He'd either order the fried chicken or the fried catfish. Nothing that he couldn't pronounce.

"I don't even know what the hell that is, but I'm going to pass. I'll just have the fried chicken."

"Yes, sir." She smiled and grabbed both menus.

Samson snickered.

"Oh, you find that amusing, do you?" Cecil asked. "I don't know why we couldn't just go on over to the soul food place in our neighborhood. Why we have to go to this overpriced fancy-ass spot is beyond me."

"Because I want you to understand who I am."

"I know who you are! I raised you." His father took a sip of his iced water. "I gave your ass life."

"My mother gave me life," Samson said. "And you didn't quite raise me. You were never there. You were working all the time."

"A cop's job is never done. And I had to work to take care of my family," said Cecil. "You're not going to blame me for that, are you?"

"I blame you for not loving me unconditionally."

Cecil was unsettled in his seat. He adjusted his posture. "I love you in spite of your bad decisions. I'm hopeful that you'll figure things out one day. Before it's too late. You're getting too old for these shenanigans, Sammy."

Samson ignored his father's last comments. Getting through to him was a lost cause. And he knew that dinner had been a bad decision. His father would never respect anything he attempted in life, simply because he wasn't a cop. He could become the president of the United States, and Cecil Steel would find fault with it. It was just his way, and Samson had already made peace with that. His goal was to get through dinner with his father, and return to his loft. He wanted to be alone while brooding over missing Alyson.

Chapter 23

Alyson met Dustin at an unfinished condominium development in Coral Gables. It was one that she was quite familiar with. She'd done market research in the area and already had a potential buyer in mind.

"There's quite a bit of buzz about this property," she told him.

"It's beautiful, with lots of amenities," he agreed. "Of course there's buzz!"

"Perfectly located," she said. "But the price is a little on the high side for the area."

"Madison properties are highly desirable, and they're priced accordingly."

"They are indeed, but we want to make sure our pricing is competitive, don't we?"

"If you check the comparables, we're not that far off," he said, and then changed the subject. "Sorry to pull you from your visit in the Caribbean, but Jonathan insisted that I show you around, bring you up to speed on our inventory."

"So you're more than just the finance guy," she said thoughtfully. "You show the properties, too?"

"I wear many hats," he said as he moved closer to her, and his hand slid to the small of her back. "Today, I'm your tour guide."

"As soon as I come on board, you won't have to show clients the inventory. I'll do that." She eased away from his touch. "Maybe we should move on to the next property."

She spent an uncomfortable remainder of the afternoon perusing Madison properties with Dustin. Some she'd already visited on her own, and most she'd researched online. A private tour wasn't necessary, in her opinion, but she obliged anyway. Particularly since Jonathan felt it was necessary. As the sun began to set, she could think of nothing more than retiring to her condo. She would order Chinese takeout and open a bottle of Riesling, try to drown the pain of missing Samson.

"Can I buy you dinner?" asked Dustin as he drove her to pick up her car at the office.

"Actually, I'm not hungry and I have plans. But thank you," she said.

"You have plans? With a boyfriend?" he asked.

"I think that's an inappropriate question, and I'm going to pretend that you didn't ask it," she said.

"I'm sorry," he said. "I'm just trying to figure you out. See if you're a good fit for the team."

She was grateful when he pulled into the parking lot next to her car.

She opened the passenger's door. "You have a good evening, Mr. Rose."

"I intend to," he said.

The moment she stepped into her car, she dialed Jonathan Madison.

"Hello, Mr. Madison. I'm sorry to bother you."

"No bother, Alyson. It's good to hear from you. I was going to ask you to drop by my office sometime this week so we can take a look at some properties. When will you be returning to Miami from the Caribbean?"

"I'm here now," she said. "I just met with Dustin at your request."

"At my request?"

"Yes. He flew me back here this afternoon. He said that you asked him to take me to a few sites," she said.

"That's strange. I haven't spoken with Dustin since the three of us had lunch together. But I'll give him a call and see what's going on. I'd like to have a sit-down with you and go over our inventory, whenever you have a moment."

"I can stop by in the morning."

"That sounds great. I'll meet you at my office at eight."

Her heart pounded rapidly. Her head began to spin. Dustin had lured her to Miami and had used Jonathan as an excuse. The thought of it gave her the creeps.

She tried to rid her thoughts of him as she entered her condo, flipped on the lights and removed her pumps. She collapsed onto the leather sofa and rested her head against the back of it. She couldn't quite put her finger on the source of the uneasiness she felt in her gut. She didn't know if it was her new relationship with Madison Development that was causing her the most angst, or Dustin Rose himself.

She pulled her cell phone from her purse, dialed the number for her favorite Asian spot and ordered dinner. She opened a bottle of Riesling and poured herself a glass. After changing into a pair of sweats and a T-shirt, she pulled her laptop out of its bag and spread paperwork all over the sofa, then got lost in her work.

Phones were constantly ringing, and conversations permeated the office of Madison Development Company.

She'd dressed carefully in one of her most conservative pantsuits. If she bumped into Dustin, she didn't want him to misunderstand their interaction again. Not like the last time they'd met. He'd thought it fitting to say inappropriate things to her in their last meeting, and to touch the small of her back without her permission.

"I'm here to see Jonathan Madison," she told the receptionist.

"He was expecting you, Miss Talbot, but he got called to one of our sites. He asked me to apologize profusely and to reschedule with you."

"It's okay, Carol. I'll take over for Jonathan," said Dustin, who appeared out of nowhere. "You can step into my office, Miss Talbot."

She reluctantly followed Dustin down the hallway and into his office. He motioned for her to have a seat. She slid into the leather seat across from his desk.

"I think Jonathan just wanted to bring you up to speed on the inventory. He wanted us to go ahead and sign a listing agreement—document your relationship with us as our agent." He pulled a contract from his file cabinet.

"I spoke with Jonathan yesterday about our little housing tour. He didn't ask you to fly me back here and take me on a tour yesterday. In fact, he didn't even know anything about it."

"Of course he did." Dustin laughed nervously.

"No, he didn't. He thought I was still in the Bahamas."

"The old man is starting to forget things," said Dustin. "Which is why I've suggested that he seriously think about retiring. He's been doing this for a long time, and he's starting to slip. I think he should go enjoy his family and his wealth and leave the hard work to us young folk."

"So you're telling me that he asked you to fly me back here to Miami to visit properties, and then he forgot about it?"

"That's exactly what I'm telling you," Dustin said. "Jonathan is a great man, but he's forgetful. Just like he forgot that he had another commitment before scheduling a meeting with you this morning."

She had thought that odd. Had something really come up, or had Jonathan Madison forgotten about their conversation?

"I don't know what games you're playing, Mr. Rose, but I'm not the one to play with," she warned.

"I don't have time for games, Alyson," he said. "Can I call you Alyson?"

"Call me Miss Talbot."

"I'm a busy man, Miss Talbot. And this is a busy office. Jonathan Madison doesn't have time to worry about the little details of running this company. Which is why I'm here. I free him to handle other things."

"You can just give me the listing contract. I'll take a look at it and bring it back over later." Alyson stood.

"It's just your standard listing agreement, Miss Talbot."

"As I said, I'll take a look and bring it back when I meet with Jonathan."

"That's fine," said Dustin. "No worries."

"And by the way, I have a potential buyer for the Coral Gables property. I'd like to see if we could get him prequalified through your preferred lender as soon as possible."

"We'll take a look at it, just as soon as we get a signed copy of that listing agreement." He came around and sat on the edge of his desk right in front of her.

"Fine." She walked toward the door.

"Welcome to the team, Alyson." He failed to use her professional name.

She left without another word.

She slipped into her car and relaxed into the seat. Alyson was a strong person. She didn't back down to anyone, and she didn't allow people to get under her skin. But Dustin Rose was under her skin. She didn't like him, and she was uneasy about working with him. She thought that she'd be happy about Madison Development, but so far she'd been everything but. She carefully backed the car out of the parking space and simultaneously answered her ringing phone with the push of a button.

"Jules, what's up?"

"I did some research on that Dustin Rose fellow like you asked," she said. "He has quite the history."

"Does he now?"

"He's connected to a laundry list of scandals, from unethical real estate deals to bribery."

"Are you kidding?"

"Not in the least," said Jules. "It pays to have private detectives as friends. Especially friends who owe you favors. This guy Dustin is a piece of work, to say the least. He went before a judge in Illinois and somehow managed to get probation for the bribery charge. Left the company that he worked for in Chicago and moved here. Turns out, he knew some people. He was able to land a job at Madison Development without so much as a background check. He's been here for less than a year now."

"What was the name of the company he worked for in Chicago?" She already knew the answer, but needed to hear it anyway.

"Let me see," Jules said as she riffled through some pages. "Blue Island Properties."

An unsettling feeling rested in the pit of Alyson's stomach. At that moment, she knew that Samson's suspicions were correct.

"That's not all," said Jules.

"There's more?" She was afraid to hear the rest.

"They're using straw buyers to get these deals pushed

through the lender," she said. "You're not under a listing agreement with them, are you?"

"I haven't signed one yet."

"Don't sign anything with them. My advice is to cut all ties."

"Samson was right."

"Who's Samson?" Jules asked. "The mystery man you haven't told me anything about?"

"Yes. He probably hates me now. I've messed up everything," said Alyson. "And now he's gone back to Chicago, and I'll probably never see him again."

"Do you need me to find him, too?"

"No. I just need to put on my big girl panties and call him."

"Go get your man, girl!" Jules said.

Alyson was beginning to rethink everything she thought Madison Development was or wasn't. She'd come from a good Bahamian family with strong values, and she knew that a company built on unethical behavior would never last. Good companies were built on strong foundations, and Alyson Talbot and Associates wouldn't be the exception. As much as she needed the hefty commissions and the exposure, she knew what she had to do. Besides that, she needed her man. However, she'd already dismissed him. To win him back meant admitting that she was wrong, which was something that wasn't easy for her. But she was willing to do it. She wasn't sure if he'd welcome her with open arms, but she needed to try. She needed to make amends with the man she loved.

Yes, *loved*.

Before it was too late.

Chapter 24

Nat King Cole crooned about chestnuts roasting on an open fire. The house smelled of gingerbread. Garland and scented candles rested upon the mantel. Samson opened the door as wide as he could get it and held on to the trunk of the tree, while his father pushed the branches inside from the other end.

"Oh, my, what a beautiful tree! Y'all picked a good one," his mother raved. She pointed toward the corner of the room, near the fireplace, where Christmas trees had always been set up for most of Samson's life. "Set it up right over here, baby. You know the spot."

Samson steadied the tree on its stand, while his father tightened the screws. The smell of pine filled his nose. Needles from the tree bounced against the polished hardwoods. He let go of the tree and then stood back, marveling at how beautiful it was. He and his father *had* picked a good one. It was the one thing they'd agreed on that day, that the eastern white pine was the perfect tree.

"Cecil, come with me to the basement to grab the skirt and decorations," Toni said.

Cecil groaned but followed his wife.

"I'll come, too, Grandmother!" Samson's ten-year-old niece, Natalie, followed her grandparents.

"Good to see you, Sammy." Samson's older brother, Jessie, reached for a handshake. "I was wondering if you'd be home for Christmas."

"Are you growing a beard, or you just too lazy to shave?" Samson asked Jessie.

Jessie grinned widely and rubbed the hair on his face. "You like it?"

"Makes you look old."

"Makes me look distinguished," Jessie said. "What about your beard?"

"Mine isn't nearly as rustic."

"My wife likes it. Right, babe?" Jessie asked Patricia as she entered the room from the kitchen.

"The beard has got to go! Please talk to your brother, Samson. Please tell him to cut it. Yours is perfect. But this right here, a hot mess," said Patricia. She gave Samson a strong embrace. "Good to see you."

Samson's younger brother burst through the front door, his daughter in tow. Calvin stomped the snow from his boots on the rug, and Olivia followed suit. She removed her wool hat and rushed toward Samson.

"Uncle Sammy!" the six-year-old exclaimed before jumping into his arms.

He held his niece tightly in his arms and kissed her plump cheek. "Who's your favorite uncle in the world?" he asked.

"You are!" she shouted.

"What?" Jessie asked Olivia. "Then what am I?"

"You're my favorite, too, Uncle Jessie," said Olivia, who rested her head on Samson's shoulder.

"Well, if it isn't Sammy Steel!" Calvin embraced his brother. "Nice tree, chump. Glad she didn't ask me to go with the old man to pick it out. I bet it was a horrible experience."

"I went last year," said Jessie. "It was a painful process. He's anal."

"Actually, it wasn't all that bad," said Samson. "But you're right, he's anal about everything. I took him to dinner, and all he did was complain."

"Here we go!" Toni placed a box filled with decorations in the center of the floor. "Let's get to decorating. You know this is my favorite Christmas tradition, decorating the tree with you guys."

Cecil plopped down in his easy chair in the corner of the room. He never helped decorate, only watched. He'd done his due diligence by picking out the tree and bringing it home. It was his philosophy for everything. *I'll bring it home—you deal with it from there.*

Toni began to decorate with bulbs, lights and garland. The children placed their handmade ornaments onto the branches. Samson and his brothers drank beers and tried talking louder than the music, until it was time to place the star at the top of the tree. It was a tradition for the youngest member of the Steel clan to do the honors of situating the star in its rightful place.

"Higher, Uncle Sammy!" Olivia squealed . Her legs dangled against Samson's chest as he lifted her in the air. "Lift me higher."

"Yeah, higher, Uncle Sammy!" Calvin teased.

"You should be over here lifting your own daughter," Samson said to Calvin. "Why do I have to be the designated person to lift these little rug rats on my shoulders every year?"

"I'm not a rug rat, Uncle Sammy!"

"No, you're not. And I'm sorry for calling you that." Samson kissed his niece's ashy knee apologetically.

"You're the designated child-lifter because you're tall," Calvin said. "You're the tall one, and I'm the smart, handsome one. Everybody knows that."

"The smart, handsome one." Samson laughed.

"And when you're done with your Christmas tree duties, I'm sure Ma has some other duties she'd like for you to perform," Calvin said.

"That's fine. And while I'm performing my Christmas tree duties, you can run on down to Albertson's Supermarket and pick up the canned milk and sweet potatoes so that Ma can make her famous sweet potato pie," Samson said.

"I believe she asked you to go to the store," Calvin asserted. "If I remember correctly, sweet potato pie is your favorite, not mine."

"I would go, but I'm busy right now." Samson shrugged. "Christmas tree duties."

"We could live without sweet potato pie," Toni interjected. "We have plenty of other sweets in there—pecan pie, a chocolate cake, banana pudding…"

"Besides, the streets are getting pretty slick out there," added their father.

"The streets aren't that bad yet, Pop," said Samson. "And, Ma, what is Christmas tree decorating without sweet potato pie?"

"It is his favorite," said Toni.

"My car is blocked in the driveway anyway. I would need to shovel my way out, and I'm hardly in the mood for shoveling," Calvin countered, and then plopped down on the sofa next to their mother, gave her a light kiss on the cheek. He was more of a mama's boy than Samson was.

Samson dug into the pocket of his jeans and retrieved his keys, then tossed them to Calvin. With a wicked grin on his face he said, "Take mine, I'm parked on the street."

"Not this time, big bro." Calvin tossed the keys back.

Samson gave in. He put on his wool coat, bundling it as tightly as he could. He placed a toboggan hat on his head and secured a woven scarf around his neck. "Ma, is there anything else you need besides canned milk and sweet potatoes?"

"A chocolate bar!" exclaimed Olivia.

"Okay, canned milk, sweet potatoes and a chocolate bar," Samson said as he headed for the door. "Even though chocolate bars will rot your teeth, I'll bring you one."

Samson loved his niece and thought that she was Calvin's greatest achievement. He'd been a screwup most of his life, but Olivia had changed all of that. She was the one thing that kept Calvin focused. He'd become a master at single parenting after the child's mother had abandoned her.

Samson's boots slid against the concrete on the front porch. Whatever was falling had already turned to ice. He made it to the two-door sedan, got inside and slammed the door. He drove slowly down their parents' block, the same block that he'd grown up on, played kickball in the middle of the street and tossed a football to his brothers more times than he could remember.

His phone buzzed, and he struggled to pull it from the pocket of his jeans. He looked at the screen and was surprised to see Alyson's number. He'd wanted to call her a million times, but hadn't built up the nerve. They hadn't ended on a good note, and he didn't know how to make things right between them. He missed the call, but vowed that he'd call her back at a better time.

In the middle of the block he picked up speed, misjudging the roads. When he made it to the end of the street, he lost control and drove right through the stop sign, not even hesitating. Samson was in a state of shock as he dropped the phone and slammed head-on into a truck moving in the opposite direction.

Chapter 25

The yellow cab eased down Congress Parkway, and then pulled up in front of the historical brick building. Alyson reached into her purse for cash, but then realized she only had Bahamian bills.

"Shit," she whispered under her breath. "You take credit cards?"

"Yes, ma'am," the Ethiopian driver said.

She hated using her plastic in cities that were unfamiliar, and for a cab ride no less. But she didn't have a choice in the matter. She paid the driver and then stepped out of the car, wearing her Pedro Garcia boots with the peep toe. She'd underestimated the weather in Chicago and wished she'd worn a much heavier coat. The designer leather trench coat was neither practical nor warm. She shivered as the driver placed her Gucci luggage on wheels at the curb.

She stepped inside the brick building and pulled her

notes from her purse to double-check the unit number. She was surprised to learn that the elevator was broken in such a nice building, and that she'd be taking the stairs in her leather boots. She stood in front of the unit with her fist raised. She was about to knock, when the door swung opened and a man with a strong resemblance to Samson appeared in the doorway.

"May I help you?" he asked.

"I'm looking for Samson Steel," she said.

"He's not here at the moment," said the tall, handsome man. "Who can I say is looking for him?"

"I'm Alyson Talbot. A dear friend of his—"

"Alyson." He smiled. "You're much prettier than he described."

"And you are?"

"I'm Calvin. His brother." He opened the door wider. "Why don't you step inside?"

"When do you expect him to return?" She glanced around at the meticulous space. It was quintessential Samson.

"The doctors are saying a few days, but you know Sammy's impatient ass! He's ready to come home now."

"Excuse me." She had no idea what Calvin was rambling on about. "What is this about doctors?"

"He's in the hospital," Calvin said matter-of-factly. "Still recovering from the accident."

"Oh, my God! What accident?"

"You didn't know?" he asked. "There was some trauma to his head, and a broken collarbone…"

"Where can I find him?"

"He's at Mercy Hospital," said Calvin. "I dropped by his place to pick him up some fresh clothes. I can give you a ride over there if you give me a minute."

"That would be great. Thank you."

* * *

She was disconcerted when she saw him. A bandage was on his shoulder, and his eyes were lightly closed. She stood in the corner for a moment and observed him sleeping. Her heart ached for him.

It was her fault that he was there. Had he remained in the Bahamas, the accident would never have taken place. She felt tears welling up. He opened his eyes.

"Hey, love," he said softly and smiled. "What are you doing here?"

"I'm so sorry."

"For what?"

"You were right all along. About Madison."

"I didn't want to be right."

"I'm sorry I didn't listen to you. I was being stubborn, only thinking of myself."

"I was only thinking of you, sweetheart, and your well-being. I hoped for the best, but had a bad feeling in my gut."

"I wish I'd listened. Maybe you wouldn't have left the islands, and you wouldn't be in this predicament." The tears crept down her face. "You're here because of me."

"I'm here because I underestimated the ice storm." He held his hand out. "Come here."

She walked over to him. She leaned in and kissed his lips. "I've missed you."

"Not as much as I've missed you." He held her tightly in his arms.

She felt safe there, didn't want to let him go. She composed herself, and then walked over to the window and opened the blinds to let some daylight into the room.

When Samson observed her clothing and boots, he chuckled. "You wore that here?"

"Don't judge me. I've never been to Chicago." She laughed, too.

"Obviously. You look gorgeous, and those boots are nice, but not very practical." He laughed, and it hurt. "We'll have to go to Walmart when I get out of here and get you some warmer clothing."

"Fine." She smiled through her tears, then went back to his arms. "I can't wait for you to get out of here."

His parents walked into the room, and stopped in their tracks when they saw the embrace.

"Well, hello," said Toni. "I didn't know you had company, Sammy."

Alyson stood. Straightened her clothing.

"Ma, this is Alyson. Alyson, my parents—Toni and Cecil Steel."

"So nice to meet you, sweetheart." She shook Alyson's hand, and then behind her back gave Samson an exaggerated wink.

"Pleased to you meet you, Alyson. We've heard absolutely nothing about you," said Cecil.

"I heard about her," Toni countered.

"So great to meet you both."

"You live here in Chicago?" Cecil asked.

"No, sir, I live in Miami."

"You came all the way here from Miami?" he asked, a puzzled expression on his face.

"She's from the Bahamas, Cecil," Toni boasted. "This is the young lady Sammy met while he was over there."

"Oh, when he was over there wasting time doing nothing," said Cecil.

"Don't start, Cecil," Toni warned.

"So you're from the Bahamas, but you live in Miami." Cecil was attempting to piece the details together.

"Hello." Samson interrupted the interaction between

his parents. They were talking about him as if he wasn't in the room. "So glad to see you both."

"I brought you some fried catfish, baby." Toni handed Samson a brown paper bag. "I know the food here can't be that great."

Cecil took a seat in the corner of the room. "I thought Calvin was bringing you clean clothes," he said.

"He went downstairs to the cafeteria for a cup of coffee," Alyson offered.

"You met Calvin?" Samson asked her.

"He brought me over here. I went to your loft first. Had no idea that you were in the hospital. Calvin was there."

"Whatever he said about me, don't believe a word of it," Samson said.

Calvin walked in on the tail end of the conversation. "I only speak the truth."

"He's been jealous of me his whole life," Samson teased.

"Is that Mama's catfish I'm smelling?" He reached for the brown paper bag.

"Get your paws back, bro," said Samson. "Reach for my catfish and draw back a nub."

"He's always been so selfish," Calvin told Alyson. "I don't know what you see in him."

Alyson giggled. She loved the banter between Samson and his brother.

"How long will you be staying, honey?" Toni asked Alyson.

"I don't know. Until he's better." She smiled at Samson.

"You're welcome to stay at the house with us. I'll fix up Sammy's old room for you," said Toni.

"She can stay at my loft, Ma. She'd probably be more comfortable there."

"I'm going to stay right here with Samson until he leaves. I don't want to leave his side."

"That's so sweet." Toni grabbed Alyson's hand.

"I love that accent," said Calvin. "You have any sisters or cousins who talk like that?"

"She's an only child," Samson lied with a grin.

"She's not an only child," said Calvin. "You just told me that her sister was getting married on Christmas Day."

"Damn! I did, didn't I?" said Samson.

"Oh, how romantic. A Christmas wedding in the Bahamas," said Toni. "If your sister looks anything like you, she's going to be a beautiful bride."

"Thank you." Alyson smiled at Toni.

"Well, let's get going, Cecil," Toni said. "Give these lovebirds some privacy. I'm sure they've got some catching up to do. And I need to finish my Christmas shopping."

Cecil stood and grabbed Calvin's foam cup filled with coffee.

"Pop, that's my coffee."

"Mine now," said Cecil as he headed for the door. "Pleasure to meet you, Alyson."

"Likewise, sir," said Alyson.

"Lovely meeting you, sweetheart." Toni gave Alyson a warm smile. "Make sure you bring her by the house, Sammy. And take her to Walmart and buy her some warm clothing."

"'Bye, Ma," said Samson.

Toni grabbed the sleeve of Calvin's coat. "Let's go, Calvin."

"I'm coming."

"Love you, baby," Toni said to Samson as she walked out of the room.

"Love you, too, Ma."

Alyson crawled up into the bed with Samson. She told him everything that had occurred in her world since he was gone. And how she wished she'd taken heed of his warning. She needed him to fix what had been broken. His heart ached because he hadn't been there when she needed him the most, to protect her—to make things right.

"When you didn't answer my call the other day and didn't return it, I thought I'd lost you," she explained.

"It was the day I had the accident. I saw the call just before I slid into an 18-wheeler."

She pressed her hand against his face. "I was miserable without you. Can you forgive me for being so hard-headed?"

"Forgiven."

He kissed her lips. He'd come back home with intentions of staying and organizing his campaign. He didn't know where he would go from here, but he knew that wherever it was, he wanted Alyson Talbot right by his side.

Chapter 26

Alyson streamed Christmas lights around the leaves of the ficus tree. Samson rested his back against the leather sofa, an afghan thrown across his legs. The loft smelled of Bahamian spices. Alyson was overjoyed that she finally had an opportunity to cook for her man and his family. She stirred the cabbage and pulled the Bahamian macaroni and cheese from the oven. The fried chicken was perfectly golden brown, and the grouper fish was seasoned to perfection while it baked in the oven.

She sipped on a glass of sky juice and handed Samson one.

"I don't think my home has ever smelled this good," said Samson.

"Dinner's almost done," she said. "And your family will be here shortly."

"We can call them and cancel if you want. They're a dysfunctional bunch of folks, and I would understand if you changed your mind."

"After I cooked all of this food? Don't be silly!" She laughed. "They can't be any more dysfunctional than my family."

"Believe me, they are," he told her. "My brothers certainly have their issues. Calvin's divorced and raising his daughter alone. Jessie is married but threatening to leave every other week. Why get married if you're planning to walk away every time you turn around?"

"I agree."

"That's not happening to me. When I get married, it's forever."

"Me, too."

It was as if they were talking about each other, but not directly. Testing the waters. Marriage had never been a subject that he and Alyson had discussed.

Samson changed the subject. "Besides everyone else, my father is the most ornery person on the face of the earth."

"I didn't get that vibe from him. He seemed so sweet."

"He was on his best behavior in front of you," said Samson. "He has a low opinion of me, and makes it a point to let me know it every chance he gets. He wanted me to be a cop and, because I didn't, he thinks that I'm worthless."

"He doesn't think you're worthless."

"He does," Samson insisted. "All my life, I've had to work for his approval. And I've never gotten it. Finally I stopped looking for it."

"I'm sorry, baby."

"It's cool. I don't try so hard now," said Samson. "My mother tries to place us in these situations where we have to bond or spend quality time. I try to make her happy, but I've come to terms with the inevitable. He's never going to be proud of anything I do."

"He's proud," she said. "Maybe he just has a hard time expressing it."

"Maybe," Samson said. "I don't care anymore. Remind me to never treat my son that way."

"So you're planning to have a son someday?"

"If you're asking me if I want children, of course I do," he said. "At least a dozen."

"A dozen kids?"

"Okay, maybe five," he said. "All boys."

"Five?"

"Okay, maybe not quite that many. But all boys for sure," he reiterated.

"No girls?"

"Girls are too high maintenance for my taste. Too emotional and too much baggage." He smirked. "Look how much trouble you are."

"I'm not that bad."

"Your father's hair is completely gray. And I'm willing to bet it's because of you and your sisters."

"I beg your pardon." Alyson tossed a pillow at Samson. "I didn't give my parents any trouble at all. I did everything by the book."

"A Goody Two-shoes," he said matter-of-factly.

"Pretty much."

Samson pulled her down onto the sofa, held her tightly. She stretched her body on top of him. Her lips kissed his, and his tongue danced inside of hers. His fingertips began to gently caress her breasts. He started to unbutton her blouse, and she grabbed his hand.

"Your family will be here in a minute," she whispered as the doorbell chimed.

"Damn," he said. "We'll pick up where we left off later."

Alyson adjusted her clothing before heading to the door. She opened it.

Toni kissed her on the cheek and handed her a pie. "I brought sweet potato pie for Sammy, seeing as how I didn't get to make him one," she said. "Oh, my, it smells so good in here!"

"Hello, Alyson." Cecil reached for her hand. "Good seeing you again."

"You, too, Mr. Steel." She bypassed his handshake and gave him a hug.

Just as she was about to shut the door, Calvin pushed it open. "I brought Cognac!" He held a bottle of Hennessy into the air and kissed Alyson's cheek.

Olivia rushed past her father and jumped onto the sofa with Samson. "Uncle Sammy!"

"Careful, now. Your uncle Sammy's shoulder is hurt," Toni told her granddaughter.

Alyson reached for Calvin's bottle to take it to the kitchen, but he tightened his grip.

"I'll hold on to it for now." He smiled.

Samson kissed his niece's forehead. "Alyson, this pretty lady is Olivia."

Alyson reached for the little girl's hand. "Pleased to meet you, Olivia."

"Are you going to marry my uncle Sammy?" Olivia asked.

All eyes were on Alyson. Everyone seemed to want an answer to that very question.

"Well, I don't know." Alyson glanced at Samson, who gave her an inquisitive look. "You'll have to ask him."

"Maybe one day," said Samson.

The doorbell interrupted an uneasy moment, and Alyson started toward the door.

"I'll get it," said Calvin. "It's just Jessie and his family. I saw them pull up after I did, but they were arguing so I didn't stick around."

Jessie walked in with his daughter, Natalie, and greeted everyone. His wife, Patricia, came in a few seconds afterward. Her eyes were red.

"Is this guy still faking an injury?" Jessie asked, motioning toward Samson. "And you must be Alyson."

"Yes, hello." Alyson shook Jessie's hand.

"I'm Jessie, Samson's older, better-looking brother," he said. "And this is my daughter, Natalie."

"Pleased to meet you both."

Patricia rolled her eyes at her husband for not introducing her. "I'm Patricia, Alyson. So glad to meet you."

"And you." Alyson shook the woman's hand and gave her a gentle smile.

"We need music," Calvin announced, and reached for the remote to Samson's stereo. He muted the television.

"You don't even care that the Chicago Bears are playing right now?" asked Cecil.

"Pop, they're down by thirty points, and it's the fourth quarter." Calvin started his hip-hop playlist despite his father's protests.

"I'm going to check on dinner," Alyson said, heading for the kitchen.

"I'll give you a hand, sweetheart." Toni followed. "You've got it smelling so good in here."

"Thank you," said Alyson as she pulled the fish from the oven.

"Everything looks so good!" Toni exclaimed. "Where'd you learn to cook?"

"My mother. She made sure we all learned how to cook when we were growing up."

"So many young girls these days don't have a clue about cooking, cleaning or raising children."

Patricia walked into the kitchen. "Can I help you do anything, Alyson?"

"If we could just get the table set," Alyson said. "Samson only has table settings for four, so we'll have to use paper products."

"He's been a bachelor for so long," Toni said. "He needs a woman who knows her way around a kitchen."

"I haven't seen Sammy smile so much," Patricia added. "I used to make Jessie smile like that, but lately things haven't been so good."

"Marriage is tough, baby." Toni rested her hand against Patricia's face. "And Jessie isn't the easiest person to get along with."

"I try so hard, Mom."

"I know, baby," said Toni. She grabbed the stack of plates from Alyson and went to set the dining room table.

"Samson is a sweetheart," Patricia whispered to Alyson. "I've been around a long time. Jessie and I were high school sweethearts. And I've seen women come and go in Sammy's life, but none have ever made him smile like he has since meeting you."

Alyson's heart danced, but she kept a straight face. She and Patricia carried dishes filled with food to the table. Cecil had managed to steal the stereo's remote control from Calvin, and the music had changed from hip-hop to old school. Marvin Gaye's "What's Going On" began to amplify through the speakers.

"Come on, Cecil, dance with me," said Toni.

"I don't feel like dancing, Antionette," Cecil protested.

"Oh, come on! Let's show these young people how it's done," she insisted, and pulled her husband up from the chair.

Cecil rolled his eyes, but joined his wife in the middle of the floor. Alyson watched with admiration as the two of them slow danced. They reminded her of her own parents, and she smiled. She glanced over at Samson, who was also watching his parents with the same admiration. She caught his eye, and he gave her a smile and a wink.

Her heart was so full of joy at that moment. There was nothing more satisfying than good music, a good meal, family, and the man that she was quickly falling head over heels in love with.

Chapter 27

Toni washed pots, pans and glasses by hand. Soapy suds covered her arms, and a dish towel was draped over her shoulder.

"You know, we could've just loaded those dishes into this overpriced, state-of-the-art dishwasher," Alyson told Toni.

"I hate dishwashers. I always wash by hand," Toni said with a smile.

"I could've done this," said Alyson.

"You did enough, young lady. Dinner was fabulous. You're a great cook, and such a beautiful young woman," she said. "I've certainly enjoyed meeting you."

"And I've enjoyed meeting you."

"I don't know you very well, but I have good intuition about people. You're good and wholesome," said Toni. "What are your plans? Are you staying around here for a while?"

"I have to get back to the Bahamas soon. My sister's

wedding is fast approaching," Alyson explained. "And I've got some loose ends to tie up with my business in Miami."

"You're a busy woman. Where does that leave you and Sammy?"

Alyson shrugged. "I don't know. I guess we'll take things a day at a time."

Toni handed Alyson the last glass to dry. She dried her hands on the towel. "I hope to see you again real soon," she said.

Alyson followed Toni into the living room, where Samson and his father were enjoying the last few minutes of a football game together.

"Let's go, Cecil!"

"It's three minutes left on the clock," Cecil protested.

"We have to go. It's late, and these kids want some privacy." Toni grabbed Cecil's wool topcoat and handed it to him.

Cecil groaned, but stood. Toni secured the buttons on her coat and wrapped a knit scarf around her neck. She placed a matching knit hat onto her head. Samson stood and walked with his mother to the door.

"I like her," Toni whispered when she and Samson were alone.

"Love you, Ma." Samson kissed his mother's cheek. He was overjoyed by his mother's comment. He'd hoped that Alyson and his mother would get along.

"Dinner was wonderful, Alyson," said Cecil.

"Thank you," said Alyson as she gave Cecil a hug.

"Safe travels when you return home, sweetheart," Toni told Alyson.

"Thank you and good night," Alyson said.

She found her place next to Samson as he wrapped his arm around her shoulder.

"Tonight was good. The dysfunctional people approved of you," said Samson. "You know what that means, right?"

"No, what?"

"You're just as dysfunctional as they are."

"Your family is sweet. And very normal."

"There's nothing normal about them." Samson found his way to Alyson's lips and kissed them gently. He balanced himself against the wall and pulled her into him. "Let's finish what we started before they got here."

Alyson followed Samson into the bedroom. He gently lay on the king-size bed. Alyson carefully pulled his T-shirt over his head and began to plant soft kisses along his muscular chest. She loosened his sweatpants from around his waist and pulled them down. Samson assisted as much as he could until he was wearing only boxer shorts. She undid the buttons on her silk blouse and unbuttoned her jeans. She slid the jeans over her hips and let her blouse slide from her shoulders. She loosened the clasp on her front-hook red bra and freed her breasts.

Samson became aroused while watching her. He reached for her breasts and squeezed each one tenderly. He lifted himself up and placed one into his mouth, and she moaned as he nibbled on it. Alyson kissed his neck and chest and worked her way down to his navel. She reached for him, began to caress him through his boxer shorts. She removed his shorts, and her lips found his.

When Alyson felt Samson inside of her, she knew that life without him would be unacceptable.

She watched as the snow fell outside. As daylight crept through the window, she pulled the thick comforter close to her chin. She'd completely underestimated Chicago weather. Even with Samson's thick socks hugging her feet, and his light blue, tailored dress shirt buttoned all the way up to her neck, she was still cold. She wished she'd taken him up on that trip to Walmart for some insulated sleep pants, as she struggled to keep her legs warm.

Samson grabbed her from behind. "What are you thinking, love?"

"That I've never seen snow before."

"Never?"

"Well, on television and in movies. But never in real life."

"And what do you think about it?"

"I can live without being out there in it. I love looking at it from this window, though."

"You ready to go back to the Bahamas?"

She turned to face him. Placed her hand against his face. "I need to wrap things up with Jazzy's wedding. Christmas is in a few weeks."

"Will you come back?" he asked.

"To this weather? I can't live in Chicago, and my work is still in Miami. Even after I cut ties with Madison Development, I'm still in the process of building my business."

"Where does that leave us, then? Because I can't live without you in my life."

"It puts us in a difficult situation," she said.

"It certainly does."

"I'm sorry I didn't have your back before. I should've trusted you," she told him.

"Yes, you should've."

"I need you," she found herself saying. She couldn't believe she'd actually said those words to another human being.

"What about your career? What about Alyson Talbot and Associates?"

"You were right about the Madisons," she admitted.

"Besides it wouldn't make any sense to gain all the wealth in the world, but lose the man I love in the end."

"Did you say love?"

"Okay, yes. I love you," she admitted, "but let's not dwell on it."

"You've never said that to a man before, have you?"

"Only once. And it was a very long time ago."

He pulled her closer, and his lips met hers. His kiss sealed the deal, and the return was far better than any commission she'd made on any deal.

Her return flight home was long and emotional. She left Chicago not knowing where her relationship with Samson stood. She knew that she could never relocate, and his political career was calling him back to Illinois. He had already begun to arrange his campaign. Her home was in Florida, his was in Illinois and neither of them was willing to change that fact.

She leaned her head against the seat. Earbuds were plugged into her ears, and a magazine lay facedown in her lap. She tried reading, but kept becoming distracted. Thoughts of Samson rushed through her mind, and she wondered if she'd left too soon. She wanted to spend Christmas with the man she loved, but she had other priorities in the Bahamas. Jasmine was depending on her, and she wouldn't let her down.

Chapter 28

The altar was decorated with Christmas orchids and beautiful red poinsettias. The baby grand piano was garnished with fragrant red and white candles. Little bouquets of fresh red roses and calla lilies were sprinkled with Christmas greens and hypericum berries and strategically placed around the room, while sweet Bahamian music played softly.

Alyson stood at the altar, as her heart was filled with joy. She watched as Jackson stood on the other side of the altar and awaited his bride. She gave him a comforting smile. He needed it because he was nervous. Sweat beaded on his forehead, and he fidgeted with his hands.

Jasmine was a beautiful bride, dressed in the gown that she'd chosen in Miami. It was perfect. As she glided down the aisle, Alyson couldn't help but feel a great deal of happiness for her sister—and pride. Jasmine had found love. Alyson dabbed the tears from her eyes with a handkerchief as she watched her father deliver her sister to her knight in shining armor. Before Samson waltzed into her life, she'd never even considered marriage for herself, but she had to admit, it wasn't completely out of the question. She could see herself in a similar perfect gown—not necessarily a Vera Wang one, but a perfect one. A gown that would speak to her like her mother said it would.

Suddenly she understood her mother's sacrifices. She knew that love changed things, and she wouldn't judge her mother ever again. Samson had transformed her mind and heart. She'd been married to her career for years, but now she could finally see herself married to a man. She would make the sacrifice, even if it meant uprooting her business and relocating to a new city.

Alyson glanced over at her mother, who was also dabbing tears from her eyes. Her father gave her mother a quick kiss on the cheek, and Alyson couldn't help but smile. Her parents had found love at a young age. And her mother had sacrificed her career for the man of her dreams. She quickly realized that love sometimes went hand in hand with sacrifice.

While Jackson and Jasmine exchanged vows, Alyson smiled with pride. Her heart was filled with joy for them. Jasmine handed her the bouquet of white roses to hold while she kissed her groom. Everyone applauded when Pastor Johnson introduced the new husband and wife to the congregation.

"I now present to you Mr. and Mrs. Jackson Conner."

The couple faced their guests and took their long stride back down the aisle—this time together.

Alyson watched the dance floor fill up as couples danced to the sound of the Caribbean band Onyx.

"Do you need me to dance with you?" asked Edward. He was dressed in a handsome tuxedo, the jacket draped over his shoulder.

"Of course not."

"Well, you're sitting here looking all sad and desolate."

"I'm fine."

"She's missing her boo," said Whitney.

"Who is her boo?" Alyson's younger brother, Nate, asked.

Alyson's brother Nate had flown in from Atlanta the night before. The family hadn't seen him since the Grove's grand opening, and probably wouldn't see him again for another year. Nate was determined never to return to the islands long-term, and he wouldn't stay for visits very long. The Bahamas held too many bad memories for him. Memories of being jilted by his high school sweetheart still haunted him. The Bahamas, his home, was a constant reminder of that. But he would never miss Jasmine's wedding. Jasmine and Nate had been comrades their entire lives.

"Her boo is Samson Steel, Jackson's handsome friend," Whitney explained.

"And why isn't he here?" Nate asked.

"He went back to Chicago," said Whitney.

"Can we please stop discussing my business as if I'm not standing here?"

"I'll go grab you a glass of wine," said Edward. "You want white or red?"

"White's fine," said Alyson.

"I'm going to check on Mother," said Whitney. "She was hoping that Denny would make it home for the wedding. It's sad he's not here."

"I was hoping Denny would make it home, too. Maybe next time."

"You did a fabulous job helping Jasmine to plan this wedding," said Whitney as she gave her a hug. "Everything is so beautiful."

Alyson rested her head against her sister's for a moment. "Thanks."

"I'll be back in a minute. Before the father-daughter dance," Whitney said before disappearing into the crowd.

"Look up," a familiar voice whispered into her ear.

She didn't bother to look around. She already recognized the strong arms that wrapped themselves lightly around her, careful not to squeeze too tight as he healed from his injuries. She looked up at the mistletoe that hung over her head, and Samson kissed her lips. Not a peck, like before. He kissed her deeply, and she kissed him back.

"What a nice surprise," she said.

Alyson and Samson swayed to the music. Her heart was filled with joy.

While Jasmine danced with their father, Alyson spotted Jennifer Madison across the room. Jennifer gave her an apologetic smile. Alyson had invited her weeks before, but after discontinuing her relationship with Madison, she expected that Jennifer would cut all ties with her—including removing her from the property on Abaco.

After the two made eye contact, Jennifer made a beeline for Alyson.

"Do you have a moment?" she asked. "I know this isn't the best time, but I really need to talk to you."

"You're right, it's not the best time," Alyson said.

"I owe you an apology," said Jennifer. "An apology for such grave behavior and corruption. My father had no idea that these things were going on in his company. He has been so far removed for a long time, and I've finally convinced him to let me help run Madison. My first order of business has been removing about 80 percent of his staff and replacing them."

"Really?" Alyson said.

"You'll be happy to know that Dustin was the first to go." Jennifer smiled. "We've hired all new people. Ethical people."

"That's good to know."

"I'd really like for you to continue to handle my father's commercial developments in Florida. If you're still interested in doing business with us."

Alyson was overjoyed by the proposition, but remained cool. "Okay."

"I'm sure I speak for my father when I say we wouldn't trust those properties to anyone else, Alyson. You're in a class all by yourself," Jennifer said. "What do you say?"

"What about the vacation property on Abaco? Am I still the listing agent?"

"Unfortunately, your services aren't needed for that property anymore. We sold that property yesterday."

"Really?"

"Of course you'll still earn the commission from the sale," said Jennifer.

"Who's the buyer?"

"Should I tell her or will you?" Jennifer asked Samson.

"I bought Madison House," said Samson.

"You got money like that?" Alyson asked.

"You're the one who insisted that I was broke." Samson laughed. "It was the kitchen that sold me. Not for me, but for you."

"Are you serious right now?" asked Alyson.

"Yes, love." He embraced her and waited for her to contain herself.

"So that means you're staying on the islands?"

"At least until I figure out what our future holds."

Jennifer interrupted the lovers. "What do you say about Madison Development?" she asked.

"I'm trying to get myself together. All of this is overwhelming."

"We'll talk next week," Jennifer said. "Drop by my office, and we'll talk about it." Jennifer extended her hand to Alyson. "I look forward to hearing from you soon."

Alyson shook her hand. Life had certainly taken a surprising turn.

Alyson rested in a chair next to Samson. They each sipped on flutes of champagne and watched as Jasmine smashed cake into Jackson's face. They laughed as Whitney nearly broke her neck trying to catch Jasmine's bouquet. As the group of women piled onto the floor in a scuffle for the flowers, it was Bijou who ascended with the coveted bouquet and waved it in the air.

"Looks like she got the bouquet," said Samson.

"But she didn't get the man. Not my man, anyway." Alyson gave Samson a warm smile.

"Not that you ever had anything to worry about."

Later, loud Caribbean music filled the night air. People in wild, outlandish and brightly colored costumes danced along Bay Street. Cheers and whistles drowned out any hopes of conversation among the guests. Drums were beat and horns were blown as every islander and guest enjoyed Junkanoo on Harbour Island. The annual street parade began promptly at one o'clock in the morning the day after Christmas, on Boxing Day. Junkanoo was a nice encore to Jasmine's beautiful wedding celebration.

"Nothing like this ever happens in Chicago," said Samson as he squeezed Alyson's hand.

"Chicago has its own special elements of Christmastime," said Alyson. "The snow is beautiful when you look at it from the inside. I could, however, get used to the frigid cold as long as I've got someone to keep me warm. I did some research. There's a nice real estate market there, and once my man becomes mayor…"

"You would consider relocating to Chicago?"

"If it means I get to spend my life with you, I'll go anywhere."

"That's sweet." He kissed her lips. "But I was thinking I might like to live somewhere warmer—like Miami. Build a career there."

"You would move to Florida?"

"I only want to be where you are, love."

"What about your new vacation home on Abaco?"

"I say we sail there tonight. Fix ourselves a nice Bahamian meal. Take a long walk along the beach, watch the sunset…"

"And after the vacation ends?"

"Who says it has to end?"

"We both have careers."

"You've been commuting between the islands and Miami anyway. So continue."

"What about you? What about your mayoral campaign?"

"I've had my eye on a few investment properties on the island of Abaco. Thought I'd purchase them, have my buddy Jackson renovate them. Then I'd hire a beautiful Realtor to get them on the market for me. You know any beautiful Realtors?"

"I know one, but she doesn't come cheap."

"Does she work on the barter system?"

"Possibly." She grinned. "Depends on what you're bartering."

"Love," he said emphatically.

"Hmm. How much is that worth?"

"More than any commission you'd ever earn."

"Okay, what else?"

"My love's not enough?"

"I make a pretty good commission. You'd have to step up your game."

"How about marriage and a lifetime of happiness?"

Alyson placed a fingertip on her chin, as if she was contemplating his offer.

"I don't come cheap. I'm high maintenance, and I like nice things."

"I know."

"And what about kids? Are you expecting some of those, too?"

"Absolutely! At least two or three. And one of them should be a girl that looks just like you."

"But not too soon. I have a career, and I'm not quite ready for my body to be all disproportioned."

"Sooner rather than later," he stated. "I'm ready to start a family."

"You drive a hard bargain. But I think we might be able to work something out."

"Good. We need a formal agreement."

"Should I have Jules draw something up?"

"No, we won't need Jules for this." He leaned down and kissed her lips. Pulled her close. "We'll sign this agreement later tonight."

"I love the sound of that."

In a short time, Samson had come into her life and re-arranged it. She'd vowed never to return to the Bahamas long-term, but she'd quickly learned that some vows were meant to be broken. She'd been afraid to give too much of her heart to any one man, but Samson was now demanding her trust.

As she stood on Bay Street and leaned her head against his chest, she closed her eyes and knew that when she opened them again, the man of her dreams would still be standing there, holding her and loving her fears away.

* * * * *

HIS BY CHRISTMAS

TERESA SOUTHWICK

To Susan Mallery.

Your amazing creativity is only exceeded by your generosity in sharing it. You've always charged forward with your arms outstretched, urging other writers along with you. I'm grateful to be one of them and even happier to call you my dear friend.

Chapter One

"I've had sex recently." Calhoun Hart hoped there was enough self-righteous indignation in his retort to make the lie believable.

"You are so lying."

"You don't know that."

Sam Hart, his older brother, stared at him for several moments, gave him a pitying look, then laughed. "I'd put money on the fact that I'm right."

"I don't need money." Cal was the president of Hart Energy and had plenty. "What I want is that classic car Granddad left you."

"The Duchess? That's never going to happen. And it wasn't personal. He said it needs tender loving care and that takes time. Which you don't have because you're always working." Sam shrugged. "And I'm the oldest. Get over it."

Cal knew he meant get over second-son syndrome. He would never be first. In the line of succession he was the spare to his older brother's heir. For as long as he could remember, if Sam was going somewhere, doing something, Cal wanted to do it, too.

Although not marriage, which is why family and friends

were gathered in a banquet room at Blackwater Lake's newest hotel—Holden House. Sam had just gotten married and promised to love and honor Faith Connelly, the town florist. The invitation had said Reception Immediately Following and apparently the groom believed it was open season on Cal's sex life since his own was in pretty good shape. And he'd never seen his older brother look happier. For once the thought didn't crank up his acute competitive streak. The truth was, Cal envied him.

"I'm over the whole car thing," he declared. It was another lie, but he was hoping the groom would be distracted and quit ribbing him about his missing-in-action personal life.

"You'll never be over it, little brother."

"You're only nine months older," Cal reminded him.

Sam straightened his black bow tie, the one he wore with his traditional black tuxedo. "And an inch taller."

Cal couldn't do anything about that, either. He blamed the combination of chromosomes, DNA or whatever it was that had resulted in his own light brown hair and blue eyes and being six-feet-one instead of six-feet-two or more. But the reminder was just as annoying now as it had been for his whole life.

"Sam, you're an ass," he said. "Tell me again how you talked Faith into marrying you."

His brother glanced around the crowded room until he found the beautiful bride dressed in a lacy, long-sleeved, floor-length white gown. She met his gaze as if somehow knowing he'd been searching for her and blew him a kiss. "I had a little help from a miniature matchmaker named Phoebe."

The bride's little girl. Cal couldn't deny she was a cute, precocious child. "What did she see in you?"

"Good question. Maybe she knew I needed her and

her mom more than they needed me." Sam was dead serious. "I'm adopting her."

"Even more reason to congratulate you," Cal said just as sincerely. "You really do have it all."

"And you don't," his brother needled him. "In fact, you're not getting any, either."

So much for having a moment. "How can you possibly know that? Are you stalking me?"

"Don't have to. I always know where you are. Working."

"So you're studying surveillance footage?"

"Don't have to do that, either, now that you've set up an office for Hart Energy here in Blackwater Lake." Sam slid his hands into the pockets of his tux trousers. "And, in spite of that, there was still some question at the last minute about you being here for the wedding."

Cal felt a little guilty about that, but negotiations regarding a parcel of land for a wind farm were going south and he needed to be involved. "I made it, didn't I? I should get points for that. I haven't missed a Hart wedding yet. Except the one ten years ago Linc didn't tell anyone about."

"True. And you're the last Hart bachelor. Here alone, I notice. Evidence that you work too much to have a life and a plus-one."

There was more truth in that statement than Cal would admit. "Who retired and promoted you to relationship monitor?"

Just then Katherine Hart, their mother, joined the conversation. "Calhoun, this is your brother's day. Be nice."

And so, Cal thought, just like in football, it was the retaliatory hit the official penalized, not the inciting one. "He started it."

"Sam—" The older woman stood between them, link-ing arms with them. She was ageless and still beautiful, even after raising four children. "What did you do?"

"I simply pointed out that Cal is a workaholic."

"Not exactly how you phrased it." Cal didn't miss the gleam in his brother's eyes, the one that dared him to tell her the disagreement was all about him not having sex in a long time. That would happen when pigs went airborne.

"You do work too hard," Katherine said. "I was seriously thinking about staging a family intervention."

"Isn't that a bit dramatic, Mother?"

"No." Her expression said she wasn't kidding. Not only that, she'd left no room for rebuttal.

That didn't stop him from trying to make an argument. "It takes time and effort to run a successful company."

"No one understands that better than me. But some things are more important."

Not when he was competing with Sam for the best bottom line of all the companies that encompassed Hart Industries. "Look, Mom—"

"No." There was that rebuttal stopper again. "Working too hard is a flaw of the Hart men. It's a trait that nearly destroyed my marriage to your father, as you both well know."

Cal was aware that his parents legally separated when he and Sam were hardly more than babies. Because they were so close in age, she'd always called them twins the hard way. His dad worked all the time and she'd felt isolated and alone. Katherine's one-night stand during the separation had resulted in her getting pregnant and his brother Lincoln was born. Against the odds, Katherine and Hastings Hart had reconciled and their union became even stronger.

"I'm not married," Cal reminded her.

"You were once, but you never will be again if you don't make changes in your life."

Cal had left himself wide-open for that one. "Look, I just wasn't very good at marriage."

"That's no reason to give up. It's like vegetables. One taste doesn't get you a pass from them. Your body needs them and they're good for you."

Kind of like sex, Cal thought.

"You'll wither and die if you don't get any." Sam's remark was a clue that he was thinking along the same lines.

"Seriously," Katherine said, "there are studies that prove married men live longer. I want you around for a very long time, not working yourself into an early grave."

"Come on, Mom. You're exaggerating." When her eyes flashed with maternal intensity, he knew that was the wrong thing to say.

"When was the last time you took a vacation?" she demanded.

He thought for a moment and drew a blank. "I'd have to check my calendar. Can I get back to you on that?"

"I already checked with Shanna and she told me you haven't taken time off since she's been with the company, so that's at least four years."

"You went over my head to my assistant about this?"

"You have a problem with that?" There was a warning expression in his mother's eyes.

"No. Just wondering." He couldn't believe she'd done research on him. "She's probably right. Excellent at her job."

"She's so good you never give her time off, either. She's tired."

"I have an idea," Sam said. "Give her a vacation and you take one, too."

"I don't need a break—"

"Recharging your batteries would be good for you," his mother interrupted. "Your father and I recently took a trip to an all-inclusive island. There were so many activities available, or you could just veg out on the beach, sit in a lounge chair by the pool."

"Doing nothing would drive me nuts." Cal could feel his stubborn streak kicking in. That was never good.

"You can do as much or as little as you want," she insisted.

"I'll check it out." Again, when pigs took flight. Hopefully that response would get her off his back.

But Katherine's eyes narrowed as if she was onto him. "You think I don't know you just threw me a bone and have no intention of doing any research on a vacation?"

"Mom, can we talk about this later? Sam just got married and I'm sure he has stuff to do at this shindig."

"He's right. Faith just threw her bouquet, so it's almost time for me to do the garter thing." Sam's eyes took on a calculating look. "But I think I know how to resolve Cal's vacation issue right now."

"I bet you don't," Cal said.

"It's like you're channeling me." His brother looked way too self-satisfied. "I think you should take a week off for every year of avoided vacation. So, I'll bet you that you can't go to that island and stay for a month."

"Of course I can. If I wanted to."

"Ah," Sam said. "Wiggle room. I knew you couldn't do it."

The tone and the words hit a nerve and started Cal's competitive juices flowing. "Why would I want to?"

"For the Duchess." There was a dare in his brother's voice.

"But you love that car," Cal protested.

"I do. But you're not going to stay on the island for a month, so there's no chance I'll lose the car."

It was like they were kids again, and Cal felt that honor challenge clear to his core. A double dog dare if he'd ever heard one. Plus, he really did love that car. It was a Rolls-Royce Silver Shadow and something that belonged to his grandfather, which made it priceless.

He stuck out his hand. "You're on."

"Excellent," Sam said, shaking on the terms of the wager. "Mom, you're a witness."

"I am." She pointed to the activity on the other side of the room. "Look, all the single men are gathering. Sam, I think you're being paged. And, Cal, go catch the garter."

"No way."

"I've been looking forward to this." Sam rubbed his hands together. "I'll throw it right to you."

"Don't do me any favors."

A few minutes later Sam removed the garter from his bride's leg and threw it over his shoulder into the crowd of single guys. Unfortunately, Cal caught the blasted thing. The satin-and-lace symbol of the next guy to walk down ball-and-chain lane sailed just close enough that he couldn't resist the challenge of snagging it. Damn his competitive streak. And he was pretty sure Sam had done it on purpose, to prove relaxing was too big a challenge for Cal, that he was going to lose the bet.

His brother was wrong, Cal thought.

The problem was going to be finding ways to fill his time for a month on an island. Or die trying. Really, what could go wrong?

Calhoun Hart broke his leg on the first day of vacation, so now he was going to work on the island. Justine Walker believed she'd drawn the short straw in agreeing to fill in for his vacationing secretary. But that was before she stepped off the plane and saw sun, sand, sea. And palm trees swaying in the gentle trade winds. That's when it hit her. Working in a tropical paradise wasn't like being the one who had to stay behind to manually blow a nuclear device and prevent an asteroid from wiping out Earth.

Technically she hadn't drawn the short straw anyway. No one else in the clerical pool at Hart Energy wanted to work with Cal Hart. In desperation, Human Resources made her an offer she couldn't refuse. Putting up with the infamous workaholic who signed her paycheck meant she was that much closer to being her own boss.

Pulling a carry-on bag behind her, she limped up the flower- and shrub-lined path to Mr. Hart's private villa at the resort. Her leg was as good as it would ever be, but long stretches of sitting still made it ache. In spite of the discomfort, she was grateful the doctors had saved it after the accident. She'd come a long way from wishing she'd died, too.

In front of the impressive double-door entry, she stopped and took several deep, cleansing breaths, counting each one to slow down her racing pulse and heart rate. It took more effort than usual, but she didn't usually go to work in a villa with a three-hundred-sixty-degree view of the ocean. The crystal clear varying shades of turquoise water defied words. It was one of those sights one simply had to see. The stunning beauty almost made her forget about the discomfort in her leg.

She inhaled one last deep breath, counted, slowly released it, then knocked on the door. While there was no expectation of a speedy response since her boss was an invalid, the wait dragged on long enough that she debated going for help. But finally it opened and the man standing there, propped up on crutches, looked the picture of masculinity, in spite of the white, no-nonsense cast on his lower left leg. For the second time since his private plane had landed, she found herself without words. He was very sexy and that was more than a little distracting.

She'd heard about him, none of it flattering, but had only actually seen him from a distance at work. He was very good-looking with his light brown hair and deeply intense blue eyes. The white cotton shirt he wore framed his shoulders and probably made them look broader. Only a hands-on examination would confirm, but the odds of that happening were lower than zero.

"Good. You're finally here." He backed up awkwardly and negotiated a turn. "Would you mind getting the door... um—"

She realized he was hesitating because he either couldn't remember or didn't know her name. "Justine Walker. And I don't mind at all, Mr. Hart."

"Cal."

"Excuse me?"

"My name is Cal. Short for Calhoun, and it will save time if you use it."

"Of course."

She shut the door and limped after him into a spacious living area. The plush white sofas had throw pillows in tropical ocean shades, and a light-colored wood floor seemed to stretch on forever to the sand and sea beyond, merging inside and outside. Overhead was a high-pitched wooden ceiling and several fans with blades that resembled palm fronds circulated the refreshing breeze coming through the open French doors. Beneath her low-heeled pumps was the thickest, cushiest area rug she'd ever felt.

"Something wrong?"

Justine dragged her gaze from the floor and looked

up at her boss. She might as well be honest. "I think I'm on luxury overload."

"Oh?" He looked amused.

"I've never been on a private plane before or anyplace like this." She glanced around, not bothering to pretend she wasn't in awe. "And a villa with that ocean view— the sand and palm trees. It's amazing."

With a sigh he lowered himself to the sofa that looked big enough to hold an extended family reunion and elevated his injured leg. "Feel free to look around. Your room is over there." He lifted one of his crutches and used it to point to a recessed doorway on the other side of the enormous area. "The valet has instructions to bring the rest of your luggage, and he'll use the patio door so you won't see him."

The Human Resources director at Hart Energy had explained the accommodations—the fact that this villa was over five thousand square feet and contained two very large, very private suites. Mr. Hart's injury limited his mobility and he preferred his assistant nearby to facilitate the work environment.

The subtext was that she didn't need to worry about any hanky-panky. After meeting him that was oddly disappointing. But the compensation for this assignment was so generous, she would have slept on a lounge chair under a tree if he wanted. Before she could check out her room, there was a knock at the door.

"That should be room service," Cal said. "Would you mind letting them in?"

"Of course." She walked to the door and felt Cal watching her. When she was tired, like she was now, the limp was more pronounced, but she tried very hard to minimize it. Because she didn't want to show any weakness in front of this man.

She opened the door to several hotel employees who waited with wheeled carts containing covered dishes. Stepping back, she let them move past her and set everything up on the coffee table, where it was easily accessible to Cal. He signed for it and the servers discreetly left.

"Can I get a plate for you?" she asked.

"Yes. Thank you."

She lifted silver domes from the serving dishes and saw there were multiple entrées to choose from, as well as potatoes, rice, pasta, green salad and fruit. And a sampling of chocolate desserts made her mouth water.

She filled a plate and brought it to him, then arranged eating utensils where he could reach them. "You ordered a lot of food."

"I didn't know what you like and thought you might be hungry."

"I am." How considerate was that? He worked hard and expected his employees to match his pace, but no one had ever said he didn't treat the people around him well. Still, she'd pictured a heartless beast, and this unexpected thoughtfulness was a nice surprise. After fixing herself a plate, she sat on the plush chair to his right. "How did you break your leg?"

"Skydiving." He met her gaze. "What happened to yours?"

"You noticed the limp." She'd heard about his attention to detail and the demand for it from anyone he worked with. So he wouldn't miss much. Still, she hadn't anticipated his blunt question. She should have. There was no reason not to tell him, but he didn't need to know she'd lost more than her runway-model strut. "Car accident."

"Ah."

She took a bite of fish and nearly groaned out loud, it was so good. They ate in silence for several moments, long enough that the need to fill it became necessary. "So, skydiving. You're one of those sanity-challenged, adrenaline junkie thrill seekers who jump out of perfectly good airplanes on purpose."

"Yes."

Thank goodness she wasn't drinking anything when he smiled, because it rocked her like a 9.5 earthquake. He was a handsome man even with a serious expression on his face. But the smile made a girl want to raise her hand and shout, *Over here.* Fortunately she didn't choke, spit or utter a sound to embarrass herself, but it took several moments to gain solid mental footing again.

"Apparently the parachute opened," she observed. "Or the damage would have been much worse."

"I landed wrong." He shrugged. "It was a clean break and the doctor assured me it will heal quickly."

"Good. Are you in pain now?"

"It's been several days, so not much."

Justine knew a thing or two about pain, but didn't push him. Everyone handled it in their own way, and she was curious about something else. This assignment was supposed to last for a month so it begged the question, "Did you have any other activities planned besides skydiving?"

"Scuba diving. Parasailing. Rock climbing. For starters," he said.

"Bummer. So why not just cancel the vacay? You've obviously changed your plans and are going to work. Wouldn't it be easier to go home and schedule more time here when you're healed?"

Something that looked a lot like stubborn determination hardened his eyes and tightened his jaw. "The view is a lot better here."

"I can't argue with that." She looked through the patio doors to the luxurious, private, crystal clear pool, the pristine white sand and the ocean that stretched as far as the eye could see. "It's something special. But so is the scenery at home. The lake and mountains take my breath away."

He stared at her for several moments, then seemed to realize he was doing it. "So, you're part of the advance team from Dallas setting up the new office in Blackwater Lake."

"Yes."

She'd found the charming, rapidly growing town a good place to open her business. She'd been saving and moved to Montana with the idea of working there until she had enough start-up money. It never occurred to her that an opportunity like this would come along to speed up her timetable. Now that she thought about it, the offer had escalated because Cal Hart had a reputation for being difficult and demanding, and no one else who was clerically qualified had wanted it. So far he had not lived up to his advance billing.

Justine finished eating and set her plate on the table. "That was delicious. Thanks."

"Is there anything else I can get you?" he asked.

"No." She toyed with the cloth napkin still in her lap. "It was nice of you to think of this. Honestly, I wasn't expecting it."

"What were you expecting?" He didn't sound defensive, just curious.

"Everyone said you're a difficult boss who works twelve-to fourteen-hour days and requires your employees to do the same."

"You've been talking to Shanna."

"She's a friend. And having a lovely cruise, by the way." At his quizzical look she added, "Ships have internet. She emails. There was even one warning me not to take this job with you."

"Oh?"

"Yes."

"So why did you?" he asked.

"Do you have any idea what you're paying me?"

"A lot, apparently." He shrugged. "I can afford it."

She had no doubt about that. The question was, could she? He had her for a month. It hadn't occurred to her that four weeks in paradise with a man who wasn't a bastard and looked like a movie star could be a very long time.

Chapter Two

"So do you want the good news first? Or the bad?" Justine asked.

It was late afternoon on their first full day of working together, and Cal was stretched out on the corner group with his broken leg propped on a pillow. He glanced up from his laptop, focusing on his new assistant, who was sitting at the desk. Her red hair was parted on the side and pulled back into a messy side bun. She was wearing black, square-framed glasses that made her look smart and sexy, a one-two punch that had his gut tightening, not for the first time.

"I'm sorry," he said. "What was the question?"

"I've got good news and bad. Are you a get-the-bad-over-with-first kind of guy? Or a put-it-off-as-long-as-possible sort of person?"

"There's something to be said for both. So...surprise me." He'd been surprised by many things since she arrived yesterday. What was one more?

"I just received a preliminary environmental report on the wind farm property in upstate New York, and so far there's no negative impact on the animals, fish or ecosystem in the area affected by the project."

"Just a guess, but I'd say that's the good news."

"It is."

"And the bad?"

"The people aren't as open-minded as the wildlife. They're circulating a petition to squash the project." She slipped off her glasses. "The land is flat and the turbines are tall, visible for miles."

"They have to be tall. The higher they are, the more wind is harnessed." Even he heard the frustration in his voice.

"Protests are in the beginning stages. There may be some things you can do to sway public opinion and get everyone on board with this. Or at least the majority." She shrugged. "Can't please all the people all the time."

What could I do to please her?

Cal couldn't believe he'd just thought that. He was uncomfortable and it had nothing to do with his broken leg. Working with Justine was disconcerting. She was smart, efficient and seemed to know what he needed before he did. It had gone really well if you didn't count the part where he wanted to turn the lie about his active sex life into the truth. With her.

Redheads weren't even his type, but that didn't seem to make a difference. Maybe it was her eyes—brown with flecks of gold and green. They were different. Exotic. Mesmerizing and calm at the same time.

Beside him on the coffee table, papers were scattered around along with file folders and his cell phone. A half-empty coffee mug was right in the middle of the chaos, like a circus ringmaster. Her desk, on the other hand, was tidy to the point of making his teeth hurt. And it was time to get his head back in the game. There was a lot to accomplish, and one of her responsibilities was to clean up after him. Normally he wasn't quite this disorganized, but his mobility was limited with the cast on his leg. Work was why she was here in the first place.

"I'll talk to public relations about the protests and strategies to win over the people," he said. "Right now, I need you to pull together some alternative energy research. Statistics on the output of wind turbines at different heights. And reports on solar. There's a parcel of land I'm looking at in Nevada, and that's the place to go for sun."

Instead of going along with the directive, his assistant closed her laptop and calmly met his gaze. "I'm happy to take care of that for you in the morning."

Did he hear her right? Maybe the hard landing from his skydiving misadventure had broken more than his leg. "I'd like you to start compiling it now."

"If I hadn't already put in a full day—"

"We stopped for lunch."

"Yes, and it was incredibly delicious." Her look was sympathetic. "But I'm officially off the clock now."

Cal needed to get up and move. The urge to prowl was strong in him, but the plaster on his leg made it problematic, along with reducing the power of the pace as a means to show he was the boss and in charge. That was pompous, but having only one good leg threw him off his game.

He grabbed the crutches and hauled himself to a standing position, then hobbled over to the desk and rested his hip on the corner, letting it take his weight. This wasn't as effective as looming, but he could still stare her down.

"The fact is," he said evenly, "I'm always on the clock. There are pros and cons to being the president of a successful company and that's one of the downsides."

"So, you're saying that by extension your assistant needs to always be available?"

"Exactly. I knew you were smart." And not just another pretty face. But he kept that part to himself.

"Let me ask you this." She folded her hands and rested them on the unnaturally tidy desktop as she met his gaze. "Is it a matter of life and death for you to have that information this evening?"

"Hart Energy didn't get to be number one by not being prepared."

"That's not what I asked. It was a yes-or-no question."

Cal was hoping she hadn't noticed his evasive answer. Buying time, he studied her and couldn't detect a single sign that she was unnerved. Not a flicker of an eyelash, twitch of her mouth or jump in her pulse. This reaction was as unusual as the shade of her eyes shifting from brown, to gold, to green.

It *was* a yes-or-no question, but that was irrelevant since he ran the show. "It should be enough that I want what I want when I want it."

"First of all, that statement comes very close to temper tantrum territory." The corners of her mouth curved up.

The movement distracted him, drawing his attention to the delicate sensuality of her lips. It was several moments before he realized that she'd called him on his crap.

With an effort he pulled his thoughts together and kept his voice even when he asked, "And second of all?"

"Hmm?" She blinked.

Maybe he wasn't the only one distracted. "You said 'first of all.' That implies there's a second thing that you wanted to say."

"Right." She nodded. "If the reason you're asking me to work late comes under the heading of life and death, I'm happy to be flexible and accommodate the situation. Otherwise it's overtime and not part of my contract for this assignment."

"You have a special contract?"

"Yes. One that has very specific limitations on overtime. It was Shanna's suggestion after she advised me not to take the job. I could show you the agreement if you'd like."

Another yes-or-no thing that he was going to side-step. "So, it's not enough that there's more work to do?"

"There always is," she said serenely.

"I guess it's pointless to say that since you work for me you're finished when I am?"

"You're certainly free to continue working, but I'm off the clock. In the morning I will be at my desk and ready to give my all for Hart Energy. But to be at my best, I need to recharge my batteries."

Cal had a feeling she was laughing at him, and that tweaked him back into temper tantrum territory. Or maybe it was her calm, unruffled demeanor that made him want to ruffle her. Either way, something had him determined to get in the last word and maintain control.

"I would appreciate it if you would stay and complete the tasks that I've requested."

She stood and met his gaze, drawing in a deep breath and holding it for several moments. "I'm happy to work on it bright and early tomorrow morning. If that's not acceptable to you, feel free to fire me."

This was not a good time to find out the problem with temper tantrum territory was that it bordered on cutting-off-your-nose-to-spite-your-face land.

"Don't think I—"

She held up her hand. "Before finishing that sentence, you should know that no one else who is qualified for the position as your assistant is willing to come here and work one-on-one with you."

He would deny it if anyone claimed her words stunned him, but that was the truth. Did he really have a reputation for being a difficult boss? A workaholic? Apparently his family thought so or he wouldn't be in this predicament right now. Were they right?

Before he could come up with a response to the line she'd drawn in the sand, she said good-night and coolly turned away from him, heading for her suite. Staring at her trim back and shapely butt, he was again speechless, but for a different reason. It could have something to do with nearly swallowing his tongue. The woman had a body that would make a man follow her anywhere. Any man but him.

He couldn't decide whether to be angry at her audacity in challenging him, or in awe of her nerve and composure while doing it. She'd surprised him again and not in a good way. And another thing. Why had he pushed back so hard for her to stay tonight? She was right about the fact that the work could wait until tomorrow.

He refused to believe that it had anything to do with keeping her there so he wouldn't be alone. Lonely. He was either tired or just being stupid and didn't know which. Or maybe it was both. That wasn't a riddle that had to be solved right now and he resolved to focus on what he could handle.

He absolutely could get someone to replace her.

The next morning, Justine got ready for work. Cal hadn't fired her, although that was a technicality since she walked away before he could say much of anything. It was certainly possible that he'd fumed all night and was going to can her this morning—face-to-face. But she hoped not. She wanted to open her own yoga studio, and the dream was so close she could practically touch it.

She'd certainly thought it over all night and had no regrets about putting her foot down to keep him from walking all over her. If anyone knew how short life could be, it was her, and no way she was going to burn the candle at both ends for a paycheck. If he sent her packing she'd simply find another way to put together the rest of the money she needed.

And he was supposed to be on vacation, for Pete's sake!

She looked at herself in the suite's freestanding, full-length mirror. Her long hair fell past her shoulders, shiny and straight. For work she normally put it up for convenience, but she might not be working much longer. If a small part of her was using every female asset in her arsenal to get on the good side of her boss, well, so be it. That was, of course, presupposing Calhoun Hart even *had* a good side.

Her silky blouse was off-white, sleeveless and tucked into linen slacks that were long enough to graze the floor even in heels. No chance of showing any bare leg. Plus lightweight enough for this tropical island climate. And professional.

"I am woman. Hear me roar," she said to her reflection. "Meow."

With nerves jumping in her stomach, she exited her room and walked, head held high, as confidently as possible into the villa's main living area. It was early, but Cal was already up. In his khaki shorts and flowered shirt he looked like a tourist. The white cast on his left leg had her heart twisting with sympathy, proof it had not stayed strong and in solidarity with last night's rebellion.

"Good morning," he said. "I ordered breakfast."

Her gaze drifted to the covered dishes on the coffee table. There was an impressive number of them. "I should get to work."

"You should eat something first. It's the most important meal of the day." He poured coffee from an insulated pitcher into a second mug in front of him. "It's breakfast. Break fast. Fuel your body to maximize performance."

It seemed as if he was pretending their difference of opinion had never happened, and that was just fine with her.

"I'd love some coffee. Thanks." She sat in the club chair to his right.

"Cream? Sugar?" He met her gaze.

"No and no. Black is great." She took the cup and saucer he held out.

"I wasn't sure what you liked to eat and ordered a little of everything."

"That's getting to be a habit with you." She was teasing. Sort of.

But this showing his nice side was turning into a disconcerting pattern. She'd prepared herself to deal with the driven workaholic from last night, not this softie who was hard-selling a well-balanced, nutritious meal. This guy made her feel feelings she wasn't at all comfortable with.

"As habits go," she said, "it's not a bad one."

"Full disclosure. It's not entirely selfless, either." He grinned suddenly. "A well-fed employee is a productive one."

A smiling Cal looked younger, more carefree and less tense. And so handsome she could only stare at him. It was several moments before his words registered and the message was received. *Employee.* As in he was not going to terminate her. The weight of uncertainty lifted and she smiled back.

"I will be so productive that you won't be able to keep up with me."

"Is that a challenge, Miss Walker?" There was a gleam in his eyes now, a spark of competition.

"Absolutely."

"Then you're on. Eat up."

Since he'd ordered a little of everything, she sampled it all. Omelet, eggs Benedict, oatmeal and all the trimmings. But the fruit…mango, papaya and pineapple— yum. They ate in silence.

"So you like Blackwater Lake?" Cal finished the last bite of food and set his empty plate on the coffee table.

"Very much. It's beautiful." She met his gaze. "But I already mentioned that. There's a serenity about it. That sounds mystical and spiritual and I don't mean to be woo-woo weird, but peacefulness is in the air."

"That's because you don't have family there," he said drily.

"I wish I did. My parents, brothers and sister all live in Texas. They were not happy when I broke the news about the company headquarters moving."

"Would it help if I apologized to them and did a Power-Point presentation to lay out my reasons for relocating?"

"So it wasn't about being closer to your brothers and sister?"

"My parents are still in Dallas, too. So it wasn't an easy decision." Absently he kneaded his left knee, as if the muscles hurt. "There's still a large dependence on fossil fuels, but renewable energy is the future. It's my gut feeling that overseeing it from Blackwater Lake is the best way to go."

She wouldn't be with Hart Energy much longer and his commitment to its future made her a little sad about that. But that was his dream and she had one of her own.

"I can't eat another bite." She set her not quite empty plate on the table beside his. "And it's time for me to get to work."

"I left a list of what I need on your desk." His mouth

twitched, the only sign that he was thinking about their disagreement.

She stood and nodded. "I'll get right on it."

Moving away from the power of her boss's aura was a relief, and Justine buried herself in the familiarity of work. Reports, spreadsheets, phone calls and research meant she didn't have to think about the way a smile transformed his face, or how his teasing made her laugh. In the last few years laughter had been a stranger in her world. Changing that started with being her own boss, not bonding with her current one.

Four hours later, Justine was paying a price for burying herself in work. Her whole body was stiff and every muscle ached. Last night's mutiny hadn't been only about principle. Working long hours taxed her physically, and her leg needed regular stretching out to keep it from painful cramping.

She straightened in her chair and carefully stood, but couldn't suppress a wince of discomfort.

"Are you in pain?" Cal's voice was sharp, but that didn't hide a note of concern.

She'd thought he was engrossed in work and it surprised her that he'd noticed. That didn't mean she was comfortable with the fact that he had.

"I'm fine," she said.

"Don't do that." He looked and sounded even more annoyed, if possible. "You don't have to be superwoman."

To atone for pushing back against a fourteen-hour day. He didn't say the words, but they still hovered in the air.

"I'm not pretending to be anything. I really am fine. It's just that if I sit for long periods of time, my leg gets stiff and a little uncomfortable."

"I assumed you were kidding about competing work output."

"Yeah, but I also said I work hard while on the clock," she said.

"I appreciate the effort, but you should have said something." Now he sounded ticked off at himself.

"I just did. A fifteen-minute break to stretch it out will do the trick. In physical therapy after the accident, I learned techniques to take care of it. I'll be back shortly—more alert and productive than ever. And most important, it's relaxing. I'm used to this happening and know exactly what to do." She half turned, intending to disappear into her room to do what she needed to in order to loosen up the muscles.

"Don't leave on my account," he said. "In fact, I might need some of those techniques myself after this cast comes off."

Justine knew better than most that he had a point about life after his broken bone healed. Learning yoga during her physical rehabilitation literally got her back on her feet. The experience came really close to saving her life and the lesson was so profound, it changed her life. Or rather, her career goals. The dream to open her own yoga studio was conceived through her intense need to pay it forward and help others the way she'd been helped. How could she say no to this injured man?

"Okay," she finally said. "Just remember you asked for it."

She moved to a large area not far from the open French doors leading to the patio. She breathed deeply of the humid, tropical air, then released it. Turning, she saw that Cal was watching her closely, and her heart jumped. It was prudent to pretend that hadn't happened.

She kicked off her shoes and stood barefoot, facing him. "Normally for a session I wear stretchy yoga pants, so I'll have to wing it in this outfit."

"Do you want to change?"

"I only have a fifteen-minute break," she said to the man who'd gone to battle for more work hours. "It won't be a problem."

"Okay."

"I'm going to show you the tree pose."

"A tree doesn't immediately make one think of stretching," he mused. "Sounds a little like an oxymoron to me."

"Movements don't have to be sweeping and dramatic to make a big difference," she pointed out. "Just stand straight, shifting your weight to your legs and feet. Then bring your right foot up to your left inner thigh. In the beginning it can be challenging to find balance so it's all right to place your foot on the calf instead."

"And then?"

"Hold the pose and breathe."

"And this does what, exactly?"

"Strengthens your legs and back. Standing straight improves posture and works out the kinks from sitting at a desk for long periods of time."

"That sounded remarkably like a dig. Is it supposed to make me feel guilty?"

"Not unless it's working." She switched legs and grinned at him.

"Does that tree pose also turn a person sassy and sarcastic?"

"Just a happy side effect," she said serenely.

"Hmm. And you were preaching it as a relaxation technique."

"Indulging sass and sarcasm can be very relaxing." She finished the pose and had both feet on the floor. "Next we have the triangle pose."

"Sounds intriguing."

She ignored that and continued her running commentary. "This opens your chest and improves balance. Widen your stance and turn your right foot to the side, keeping your heel in line with the center of the left foot. Reach one arm out to the side, bend and touch the other to your extended foot. Again, hold and breathe. Repeat on the other side."

"And is that one relaxing?" There was a slight edge to his voice.

"Are you asking whether or not I feel a zinger coming on?"

"Not really." He shrugged. "I sort of figured that was a given. I'm actually getting used to it."

"Bracing yourself is not a relaxed way to be. For your own well-being, pay attention."

"Right."

"You're a skeptic now, but let's see how you feel when that cast comes off and one calf is half the size of the other because the muscles are atrophied from not being used."

"Have you got a move for that?"

"As a matter of fact...warrior one."

"Battle?" One of his eyebrows rose. "Seriously? I am actually more than a little skeptical of that being relaxing. Or helpful."

"Watch and learn, little grasshopper." She gave him a smirk. "This is for power and strength in the body. Stand straight, then move your left leg backward. Bend your right knee and turn your left foot slightly inward. Then raise your arms above you, stretching as high as you can, feeling that stretch into your fingertips. Hold and breathe. Again, repeat on the other side."

Justine lost herself in the pose, concentrating on her breathing and stretching. When she was finished, she felt refreshed and ready to resume working. The technique never failed to relax her. But one look at Cal told her the yoga lesson had the opposite effect on him.

His mouth was pulled tight and there was tension in the line of his jaw. But the expression in his eyes threw her completely off balance. Since her husband had died in the car accident, no man had looked at her the way Cal was now. As if he wanted her more than his next breath.

Chapter Three

There wasn't enough yoga in the whole world to make Cal relax after watching Justine stretch like that. Reaching up lengthened the lines of her body, showed off the toned muscles and put her spectacular curves on mouthwatering display. The lady had a limp and, in spite of that, she was lithe, limber and luscious. And he felt as if his whole body hurt from trying to pretend he hadn't noticed any of that.

The worst part was that he had no one to blame but himself. She'd warned him. He did ask for it. "Don't leave on my account," he muttered under his breath, thoroughly disgusted with himself. " I might need some of those techniques myself after this cast comes off."

The thoughts he'd been having ever since were inappropriate. He might be a workaholic, but he wasn't a pig.

Thank goodness she was done for the day. He didn't push the overtime issue again. No one could say he wasn't capable of learning. She'd been dismissed at quitting time but he continued to work. At least, he was trying. But after starting to read a technical report for the fourth time, he was about to throw in the towel. His mind kept wandering to the vision of that silky blouse outlining her breasts. The only thing sexier would be seeing her naked.

"Damn it." He rubbed his thigh and mentally smacked himself for more inappropriate thoughts.

What was it about her that was turning him into a hormone-overdosed teenager? Whether she was in the room with him or not, the place just felt different.

He glanced out the open French doors and saw her sitting by the pool in a patio chair, her back to him. Come to think of it, she'd been out there for a while. And as far as he could tell, she hadn't moved.

"None of my business. She's off the clock." He started at the beginning of the report. Again.

Almost immediately his attention wandered back outside to Justine's trim, straight back. She'd changed from work clothes into cotton pants and a tank top for her foray into doing absolutely nothing. Although he recognized the fact that it was a beautiful setting—the crystal clear pool, wicker furniture with brightly colored cushions and the pristine white sand in front of the sea. The sun was setting and turning the underside of the wispy clouds orange, gold and purple. But she continued to do absolutely nothing, and that had him acutely curious.

He grabbed the crutches resting beside him and pulled himself up, then propped them beneath his arms and hobbled outside. There was an empty chair beside her and he lowered himself into it.

"What are you doing?" he asked.

"Not working." She looked at him. "And neither are you, apparently."

"I'm taking a break." Ha. "So, seriously, what are you doing?"

"I'm looking at the sand, the ocean and that spectacular sunset."

"I don't mean this in a bad way—"

"Have you ever noticed that when someone says that, whatever comes next will not be positive reinforcement? It will be disapproving."

Guilty, he thought, then barreled ahead anyway. "You've been looking at the view for a really long time."

"It's worth spending a lot of time on taking it all in."

"Why?"

"Because it's stunning. The beauty of nature fills up my soul."

"Considering the length of your examination, can one assume your soul was that empty?"

The corners of her mouth curved up. "I'm filling the reserve tank. For tomorrow. You should try it."

"So you think my soul is a quart low?"

"Judging by the defensiveness of your tone, I'd say that's a very good possibility."

"Are you always this mystical?" he asked.

"Are you always this nosy?" she countered.

"Maybe."

"That's a lot of negative energy. Why don't you take in that magnificent view and think peaceful, healing thoughts?"

"What if I don't—"

"Just give it a try," she suggested.

"Okay." He set the crutches on the cement patio beside him and rested his injured leg on the chair's matching ottoman.

There was a refreshing breeze blowing off the ocean that gently rustled the nearby palm trees. The sun was an orange-yellow ball that seemed to be disappearing into the sea, and twilight crept closer, kept at bay by the villa's outside lights. Cal let out a sigh as some of the tension left him. It really was a pretty place. But…

"Aren't you getting bored?" he asked.

"No."

"How can you just sit there?" He studied her delicate profile and the beautiful fiery-colored hair blowing off her face. "I know you said you're filling up your soul, but how can you tell when it's sufficiently topped off?"

She met his gaze and there was amusement in hers. "It takes longer when there are interruptions."

"Do you set a timer?" he asked, warming to his cross-examination.

She ignored the question and stated the obvious. "You're restless."

"Because I'm not doing anything."

"Letting your body rest and rejuvenate is actually doing something."

"Doesn't feel that way," he grumbled.

"I have an idea. Why don't you try counting your breaths? That will give you something to focus on."

Besides her? When he could smell the scent of her skin in spite of the strong fragrance of tropical flowers and the sea all around? "Why would I want to focus on counting my breaths?"

"Inhale deeply," she instructed without answering. "And let it out slowly. Then concentrate on the rising and falling of your chest. Up and down is one breath. Give it a try."

"This is silly."

"There you go," she said. "I knew you would have an open mind."

"You're trying to spirit-shame me."

"Is it working?" There was laughter in her voice.

"Yeah, kind of."

"Good. Go with it."

"Okay." He did as instructed and drew in a deep

breath, then released it and noted the rise and fall of his chest. "One… Two… Three…"

"Silent counting would be better," she advised.

"Am I distracting you?"

"Yes."

Right back at you, he thought. She was the personification of distraction. If being a diversion was part of an employee review, she would get very high marks. Now that he thought about it, she was pretty good at her job, too. She worked very hard and was incredibly efficient. His vacationing assistant should be worried about the competition.

That was a bluff. Shanna was excellent at what she did, and the best part was that when she was in the office, he never once thought about her any way but appropriately. Why was that? She was attractive, single, smart and funny. What combination of attributes made Justine such a challenge to his concentration?

The only thing he could come up with was that karma had a lousy sense of humor.

"You've been very quiet." Justine finally broke the silence.

"I thought that's what you wanted."

"It's what you needed," she said mysteriously.

"That's news to me. And it makes you sound like a Tibetan monk," he added.

"It takes a while to get the hang of the technique in order to free your mind. But you did very well with the breathing."

He laughed. "Breathing is easy. If you can't do that, you've got bigger problems than filling up your soul."

"I'll make a convert of you yet. And I've got a month to do it." Justine got up and used the outside entrance to go into her suite.

Cal watched her go and admired the sexy movement of her hips in spite of the slight limp. His pulse jumped and his mouth went dry. There was breathing and there was heavy breathing. Justine could easily push him in the second direction. He'd teased her and she gave it right back, but he wanted her and it wasn't a joking matter.

This whole bet started when his brother needled him about his lack of a sex life. Right now the truth Cal had denied was painfully clear.

The next morning, Justine showered and got ready for work, still a little in awe of her suite and surroundings. She had as much connection to luxury on this scale as she did to a unicorn. Sand and sea were just steps away, for goodness' sake. The man providing this villa was also just steps away and he presented a whole different scale of excess. She really didn't know what to make of him.

When she'd lost her husband and little girl in the accident, it was the aloneness that nearly crushed her. Family and friends tried to help, but she had to fight through by herself. And she had, but there were reminders in Texas. When Hart Energy announced the move to Blackwater Lake, Justine looked at it as an opportunity for a change of scene and the chance to start a new life.

Physical therapy and yoga had helped heal her body and she'd resigned herself to being alone. Like last night on the patio. Then Cal had joined her and that had an effect. He'd actually attempted to master the conscious breathing technique. It was endearing, really.

Other than wanting everyone around him to work as hard as he did, the man was a good boss and very considerate. Too much of everything if she was being honest. Too handsome, funny, smart and sexy for any breathing technique she was aware of to relax her when he was nearby.

She studied her appearance in the bathroom mirror. "There's only one thing to do. Work hard and forget he's around."

Except they didn't work until after breakfast. Cal had given her the option of room service by herself, but having resort staff deliver two separate meals seemed excessive. When she walked into the villa's main area, breakfast was being set out on the dining room table. He signed for it and the staff wheeled away the cart and left.

Leaning on his crutches, Cal looked everything over, then met her gaze. "Breakfast is served."

"Good morning. It looks wonderful."

"It would be even better if you ordered something besides oats and dried grapes."

"Better known as raisins. And that's granola to you. I happen to really like it."

"You might want to consider expanding your culinary horizons."

"I will," she promised, then spotted the cup and saucer. There was steam wafting from the top. "Coffee. A girl could get used to this."

He sat at the head of the table. "Are you telling me that at home no one has coffee waiting for you in the morning?"

Justine took the chair at a right angle to his, where the bowl of granola waited. "Are you really concerned about my coffee consumption habits? Or is that a not-so-subtle query into my personal life?"

He lifted the metal dome covering his scrambled eggs, potatoes and turkey sausage. "The brilliance of my question is that you can interpret it any way you'd like."

"Hmm."

"Hmm?" he asked. "What does that mean?"

"It was either a noncommittal *hmm*, or a thinly veiled rebuke of your humility."

"You think I'm not humble?"

"When you call yourself brilliant? Duh." She couldn't help laughing at him. "And, just so you know, I'm going to answer what was asked. I take full responsibility for my morning coffee needs. What about you? Does Jeeves grind beans and brew the perfect cup of joe for you?"

"There is no Jeeves," he said. "I have no staff. A cleaning service comes in once a week to make the condo habitable."

"Condo." She poured almond milk into the bowl, then spooned up a bite of granola. After chewing and swallowing, she said, "I'd have figured you for a palatial country home kind of guy."

"There's not a lot of choice in Blackwater Lake. The town is growing and housing is struggling to catch up and stay current."

"I see." She sipped her coffee, studying him over the rim of her cup. "You're a complicated man, Cal Hart."

"Keeps people on their toes."

"People? Or women?" she asked.

"Women are people, too," he pointed out.

"And they no doubt fall at your feet. From all that brilliance, whether you're complicated or not," she teased. "In fact, I bet most of them prefer not."

"What do you prefer?" There was a deep, husky quality to his voice that could be called seductive. His eyes widened slightly and he said, "Don't tell me. Simple hard work is your preference. It gets the job done. Speaking of which...what happened to the contract my lawyer emailed? There are pages missing."

Apparently he was keeping this purely professional.

Hence the pivot back to work. That was for the best, even though she was enjoying their verbal sparring. "I know. It's on my to-do list. The internet was really slow, and then it just shut down."

"Damn it."

"I'm sorry. I checked with resort management late yesterday and they said the system can often be over-loaded with data."

"Then the system should be upgraded. If I was run-ning this place..." He was buttering a slice of rye toast and stopped.

"What?" she prompted.

"Technology would be more efficient, for one thing." The frustration in his expression grew more intense as the muscle in his jaw jerked.

"Think about this place," she advised.

"I am. If someone is expecting some important docu-ments or business negotiations requiring paperwork, their expectations will not be met."

"Unless this location is intended to cater to expecta-tions other than business. Outside are sea and sand, nei-ther of which is particularly user-friendly to computer circuits or memory chips."

"Of course not. No one's going to use a fax machine on a paddleboard."

"Exactly. People actually come here to get away from the rat race. To decompress outside in the water while soaking up the sun. Maybe upping their absorption of vitamin D while they're at it."

Cal glanced across the room, where the French doors were open to the patio. Outside, dark clouds had obscured the blue sky and were very swiftly rolling over the ocean toward them. Lightning flickered within the billowing black mass and a bolt zigzagged into the ocean.

"Great, just great," he mumbled.

Justine thought the approaching storm closely mirrored the expression on her boss's face. From the looks of it, he could use a refresher course in care and feeding of peace and relaxation. Something had him on edge. She hadn't missed the way he'd abruptly changed the course of breakfast chitchat from personal back to business. If she hadn't walked into this room prepared to work hard enough to forget he was there, she might not have noticed. But that was her plan of action and he'd gotten there first.

There was just one flaw in the all-work-to-avoid-play plan. And it was hard to ignore. "Cal, this is paradise. People come here to unplug. Technology doesn't have to be business-fast. It's not designed to do that. Probably so someone who's even tempted to choose work over relaxation will just give in and let it go."

"Try explaining that to my high-priced attorney who is waiting for me to look over that contract and get back to him. Strike while the iron is hot and all that. And there are other time-sensitive interests that are affected…"

A roaring sound outside made them both look out the doors. The storm had moved in really fast. Huge drops of torrential rain suddenly started bouncing on the patio, and the steady pounding was like the white noise on a sound machine. Then there was a crack of lightning and almost simultaneously the boom of thunder.

"It's right over us." The lights flickered and his expression grew even darker. "Paradise isn't perfect, after all."

"And yet, what most people wouldn't give to ride out an electrical storm on a tropical island as opposed to being at home."

"I'm not most people."

"Maybe you should give it a try," she snapped back. "Ordinary isn't so bad…"

There was another flash and the booming sound of thunder. Then the lights went out.

"Isn't that just swell?" Cal leaned back in his chair. "People, ordinary or otherwise, can't do much of anything now. Including work."

Justine glanced from the downpour outside to the irritated, angry look on Cal's face. "Wow. Bummer. Since the business machines are out of commission, you might have to sit here and talk to me."

"This would not happen in Blackwater Lake. And before you remind me the power can go out anywhere, I have a generator there."

"Then why don't you go back there?" That was a very good question, one she'd asked the first day and hadn't received an answer to. Call it the weird vibe of electrical energy in the air, but now she wanted to know. "Now that I think about it, carrying on business at the level you seem obsessed with is a challenge here. So, why didn't you go home after breaking your leg? What's going on, Cal? And don't tell me 'nothing.'"

Chapter Four

"But nothing is going on."

Pushing back against a statement of fact had put Cal in this predicament in the first place. You'd think he would know better than to keep doing it. Maybe he wasn't capable of learning, after all.

"Calhoun Hart, you're a big, fat fibber." Justine put her spoon down in her empty bowl. Her eyes narrowed on him and made him want to squirm, but he resisted the urge.

"I have no idea what you mean." He'd been about to say again that there was nothing going on, but decided it was protesting too much. He had to play this just right. "And 'big, fat fibber'? Really? Is this junior high?"

"And there it is," she said triumphantly.

"There what is?" He looked around the shadowy interior of the villa. "And how can you see it without the lights?"

"You're so glib."

Her tone didn't make the comment sound like a compliment, but that didn't stop him from running with it. "That just might be the nicest thing you've ever said to me."

"You tap dance pretty well for a man with a broken

leg." The words were spoken in a pleasant voice, but her eyes were still narrowed on him. "Your behavior is classic."

"How?"

"It tells me that you're hiding something." She held up her hand and started ticking things off on her fingers. "You turned the conversation back on me being 'junior high.' Then deflected to electricity. And tap-danced to twisting my words into a compliment. You better start talking, mister."

"Or what?"

"Now who's acting all junior high?" she accused him.

He grinned. "Then I'm going for it all the way. You're not the boss of me." Since when was being on the hot seat so much fun? The only variable was Justine. "There's nothing you can do to make me talk."

"Oh, you're so wrong about that. There are many, many ways I could bring you to your knees."

"One comes to mind. Using my crutches for a bonfire on the beach." He met her gaze and shrugged.

"There's no reason I have to be that cruel. Or literal." She tapped her lip. "I can think of a much quicker, much simpler way."

"What could be easier than commandeering a man's crutches?"

"I could call your mother." She smiled slowly and with more than a little wickedness.

"That's low, Justine."

"A girl has to do what a girl has to do." She pulled her phone out of her pocket. "I wonder if there's cell service during an electrical storm."

For several moments Cal wasn't sure that the pounding he heard wasn't in his ears. His sneaky assistant frowned at her phone and he guessed Mother Nature was giving him a reprieve.

"You can't call my mom. You don't have her phone number."

"Want to bet?"

He was beginning to wish he'd never heard the word *bet*. Little Miss Serene had a fairly ruthless expression on her face. Not unlike the stubborn set of her mouth when she refused to work overtime. She obviously wasn't going to let this go.

"All right. You win. There is something."

"Aha." She pointed at him. "So you are a big, fat fibber."

"Prevaricator. My vocabulary has improved since middle school."

"Then start using your words and tell me what you're up to. Pronto."

"Would you mind if I sat on the couch and propped my leg up for this?"

Her eyebrows rose. "Is it a long story?"

"There are some things I need to explain. All to give you context," he said.

"Well, we can't go to work until the lights come back on anyway..."

"Good." That would give him time to figure out how to say this so he wouldn't drain all the reserves her soul had so recently stored up.

Cal pushed to a standing position and balanced on his right foot while he grabbed the crutches and propped them under his arms. He swung himself over to the huge couch and sank into it, then put the injured leg up and stretched it out.

"Do you want me to bring your plate over?" There

was a spark of amusement in her eyes. "Keep up your strength for this?"

"Funny girl." He'd lost his appetite halfway through. "No. I've had enough."

"How about coffee?"

"Yes. Please," he added.

She ferried cups, saucers and the insulated pot of coffee to the table then poured refills for both of them. Taking hers, she sat in the club chair beside him and looked expectant. "I'm listening."

"Okay." He met her gaze and had the absurd thought that she looked pure and innocent even when threatening to tattle to his mother. Hopefully his confession wouldn't crush that out of her. "I'm a very competitive guy. Could just be my nature or where I fall in the family birth order."

"You're the second son."

Cal remembered his brother telling him to get over second-son syndrome. "So it's common knowledge."

"Hart Energy is a subsidiary of Hart Industries. If one works there, it would be hard not to know."

"I guess. The thing is, that's just a fact. It doesn't convey any of the reality of growing up in Sam Hart's shadow. We were born nine months apart."

"Twins the hard way," she interjected.

"That's what my mom always says. Anyway, I had the distinction of trying to keep up with him, pretty much right out of the womb. I wanted to do everything he did, including getting my parents' attention."

"This is where you own up to acting out."

He shook his head. "I did my best to be bigger, faster, stronger."

"Going for bionic?" Her mouth twitched, as if she was holding back a laugh.

"No, only first."

"Ah." She nodded her understanding. "And that could never be."

"I could never be firstborn, but in every other way I needed to win. School. Sports. Girls. We competed for the same ones."

A shrink would have a field day with the fact that he married a woman who had loved another man first. That man happened to be his brother Sam. Cal shouldn't have been so surprised and hurt when it didn't work out, but they said love was blind.

"So, your whole life has been like the second-place car rental company that has to try harder?"

"Yes. We run different companies under the Hart Industries umbrella, and I want him to be successful. I just want my bottom line to be better than his."

"That's why you work so hard."

"Exactly."

She nodded thoughtfully. "But that still doesn't explain why you didn't go home after breaking your leg. In fact, it just makes me more curious."

"I was getting to that part." As slowly as possible. He was dreading the expression of disappointment that he knew she would wear. The why of that was a mystery he didn't have time right now to think about. He took a sip of his lukewarm coffee, then set the cup back on the saucer. "It happened at Sam's wedding."

"It?"

"Apparently my family was concerned about the fact that I hadn't taken a vacation in a while."

"How long is 'a while'?"

"Four years."

"Wow. Long time." Her eyes widened.

"Then Sam made a crack about my social life."

"He thinks you're burning the candle at both ends?" she guessed. "He doesn't like your girlfriend?"

"I don't have one. And he—"

"Said something about you not having sex, which got your macho all in a twist. Am I right?" she asked.

"Not about the macho part, but the rest is pretty accurate. How did you know?" And why did she say it straight out without any awkwardness? Maybe because the lights were still out and clouds filled the sky. There was no way he could see whether or not she was blushing. It was one step shy of making love in the dark.

"I know because I have brothers. Two." She shrugged.

"Okay." He let out a breath. "His comment touched a nerve and then there's the classic car—"

"Just a hot minute. If this is you digressing to distract me, you should be warned that it won't work."

"That never crossed my mind." Because he'd already tried that and found out she was too smart to be side-tracked by his charming repartee. "It's important."

"Okay, then. Carry on."

"Our grandfather left Sam his classic Rolls-Royce Silver Shadow, even though I always told him I wanted it. He said it was about Sam being the oldest." Cal sighed. "I really love that car. But apparently Granddad told Sam that I worked too much to care for the Duchess the way she needed to be cared for. To make a long story short—"

"Too late for that," she teased.

He laughed. "Sam bet me that I couldn't stay on this island for a month."

"By 'stay' I assume he meant vacation?"

"That's not what he said," Cal stressed. "There was no stipulation about not working."

"But it was implied. That's the very definition of vacation," she insisted. "And yet you brought me here to help you work."

"I can't deny that."

There was the dreaded judgment in her eyes and it was definitely going against him. "That violates the very spirit of the wager. You're supposed to be here taking a break. Resting and relaxing."

Very little of either was going on, Cal thought. And it had only gotten worse since Justine showed up. "I honestly had planned to do that. I had a schedule of activities every day. A spreadsheet—"

"I'm sorry, what?"

"I had something on the calendar for every day. Parasailing, hang gliding, wave riding, rock climbing—"

Her mouth opened, hinting that she was appalled. "Those aren't gentle, peaceful or restful. They're life-threatening."

"I prefer to think of them as aggressive leisure interests." She was really putting him on the defensive. "The point is that I broke my leg on the first day and had to cancel everything. And I couldn't leave the island and lose the bet. Sitting around and doing nothing would have pushed me over the edge." He shrugged. "I figured that I might as well work."

"Wow. You would rather work when there's a beautiful, exciting island just outside the door to this luxury villa and it's yours to explore?"

"Not when you're on crutches," he retorted. "Believe me, I checked. No wave riding or parasailing when you've got a cast on your leg."

"You've never heard of plan B?"

"Of course I have. But, like I said, I'm complicated. And nothing fun is cast-friendly."

There was a gleam in her eyes when she said, "I bet

there's a lot of fun things you can do with that plaster on your leg."

"I challenge you to come up with a list of activities for a guy in my situation. Until then, don't judge."

It wasn't long before the lights came back on, the clouds disappeared and paradise was restored. Outside. Inside, Justine went to work, and when not busy doing something for her boss, she researched available activities on this tropical island. At lunchtime they took a break and she was ready with a list. After finishing a delicious meal of grilled fish, delicate rice, salad and the yummiest sugar cookies ever, she figured it was as good a time as any to bring it up.

She was sitting in the club chair beside the cushy sofa where Cal was stretched out. "I'm ready for your challenge," she said.

"Which one would that be?"

"I think asking the question is a stall technique, but we'll play this your way." She opened a file folder containing information she'd printed out. "There are many things to do on this island. Even for a man with limited mobility."

"Don't even mention the *W*-word."

She was drawing a blank. "I'm sorry. The what now?"

"Wheelchair."

"Ah." She nodded her understanding. "You're thinking limitations. My focus is broader. That's the difference between us."

"No. The difference is that my leg is broken. Yours are just fine." He stopped and that declaration settled in the air between them. "I'm sorry. By 'fine' I meant you're not on crutches."

"I know what you meant."

Her leg was fine if you were just talking mobility. It had taken surgeries, time and hard work to regain function, albeit with a slight limp, but the extensive scars would always be a visual reminder of what she'd lost.

"Moving on, then. No wheelchair. Got it." She scanned her paperwork. "You were right."

"I'm surprised to hear you admit that." But he looked puzzled. "What exactly is it that I'm right about?"

"Activities at an island resort heavily favor guests who are not in a cast."

"Like I said, there's nothing for me to do and I couldn't just sit around and do nothing. Hence the work. Given my circumstances, that's not a violation of the spirit of the wager with my brother. It comes under the heading of Circumstances Beyond My Control."

"Not completely true," she told him. "I said it favors noninjured people, but there's plenty to keep the physically challenged occupied."

"Such as?"

"Massage." She let that sink in for a moment. "The resort has a lovely menu of them. For example—the Swedish massage using long, fluid strokes to relieve muscle tension and improve circulation. Optimum blood flow will facilitate healing in your leg. And the technique will ease you into relaxation and relieve stress throughout your entire body. That's not just the spirit of vacation. It's proactive participation in it."

She looked up from her notes to gauge his reaction. There was a tight, tense expression on his face that wasn't exactly disapproval, but something that made her heart skip a beat. It was as if he could think of something *else* to relieve his body's tension, and that thought made her blush.

Looking back at her notes, she started talking, anything to fill the silence. "Here's one you might like. Vi-brational massage using specially blended oils that vibrate with the frequency of the seven energy centers of the body to open and revitalize the chakras. This synergis-tic experience of breathing in each of the powerful aro-matic oils, along with light massage, leaves you feeling balanced."

"Seriously?"

"Balance is good. That's why one takes a vacation. There's nothing wrong with working hard, but you need to offset it with play." She glanced up and saw amuse-ment on his face. "What?"

"You know what they say. Your chakras can't be opened enough."

"Okay. Moving on." She flipped through the research. "Oh, here's something. Artistic palm arrangement."

"Basket weaving."

"Well…yes, but it would be helpful if you weren't an activity snob. The pictures of what people have done are quite impressive. And you can do it sitting down. All you need are two good hands and a yearning for artis-tic adventure."

"I bet thrill seekers from all over the world are just flocking to that one," he said wryly.

She nodded. "Good to know your chakras might be closed but your mind is completely open to possibilities."

"I'm glad you noticed." His voice dripped with sar-casm.

What she noticed was the way his smile and the gleam in his eyes warmed a path straight inside her and made her heart beat a little faster. Talk about possibilities. And no scenario in which she indulged them would end well. *Look away*, she told herself.

"I'll put you down as a maybe for artistic palm arrangement." She turned a page. "Now, this sounded like fun."

"Don't keep me in suspense."

She ignored him. "A cooking class specializing in cuisine from the island. As the description says, 'Extend your vacation by bringing home the palate-pleasing recipes for the foods that enhanced your leisure experience.'"

"Three strikes and you're out."

"You're determined not to be receptive to anything. I still won the challenge. There is stuff to do."

"It was a nice try, but work makes time go faster." He shrugged. "I just want it to pass so I can win the bet and go home to collect on it."

"That's just wrong, Cal. Do you have any idea how many people would give almost anything to be in your shoes right now?"

"You mean the broken leg, right?"

"That's just being deliberately obtuse." She stood and glared down at him. "You have the opportunity to be in this gorgeous place and the means to enjoy it—even with your leg in a cast. You're just feeling sorry for yourself, and it has to be said that it's not a good look."

"Oh?"

"No. You're determined to be miserable and bring everyone around you down, too. If you're going to win that bet, you have a responsibility to at least make an attempt to live up to the terms of it. Cheaters never prosper," she added. For all the good it would do.

"Are you going to rat me out?"

"As tempting as that is—no. You have to live with your dishonesty. Guilty conscience and all that." She shrugged and let the words sink in.

Anger, annoyance and amusement had all drifted over his face, but now he just looked thoughtful. "If you were here on vacation instead of work, with or without a broken leg, what would you do to occupy yourself?"

"I would sit on the beach in a lounge chair under a palm tree and read a book," she said without hesitation. "Parasailing or hang gliding would not be my first choice, in case you were wondering."

"I wasn't. And just so we're clear, if I tried to get to the sand, I'd get stuck." He nodded toward the crutches beside him. "And then there's the whole issue of getting sand inside the cast."

"That's the thing," she said. "Just steps from this villa's patio, there happens to be a lounge under a tree. You can make it that far and I'll help you get the rest of the way. Your bum foot will never touch the sand." It wouldn't take much effort, and Justine didn't know why she hadn't thought of it sooner. "What do you say?"

"I don't have a book."

"I can loan you one," she offered.

"Is it about breathing techniques and chakras?" he asked suspiciously.

"Actually, I can give you a choice. I have a romance novel or the action-adventure *High Value Target* written by Blackwater Lake's very own bestselling author, Jack Garner."

"I don't know—"

"Come on, Cal. Based on the schedule you had to scrap, you're not a man who shies away from a challenge. I can't believe you're afraid. What's the worst that could happen?"

"Famous last words—" But he swung his legs to the floor and grabbed the crutches, then stood and positioned them under his arms. "Well played, Miss Walker."

"That's the spirit. Your vitamin D is doing the dance of joy at the prospect of replenishment."

"That's something. It's the only part of me capable of dancing at the moment."

"Okay, then. Let me think this through. A good general plans out a mission. So, wait on the patio."

She hadn't considered the sand inside the cast and decided to put a fluffy beach towel on the lounge. Then she retrieved his sunglasses and handed them over before putting the book on the umbrella table anchored in the sand.

Moving back beside him, she said, "I'm going to set your crutches against the palm tree there. You can balance for a moment, right?"

"Yup."

"Okay. I'll be a human crutch. I'll put my arm around your waist and you lean on me."

"Yeah. I figured that part out."

She put the plan in motion, then moved beside him and slid her arm around him. "You're not in pain, are you?"

"I'm fine." His voice sounded deeper than usual, and it was usually pretty deep.

She wasn't sure whether or not he was just being tough but decided to take his word for it. "Can you hop?"

"Yes."

"Okay. Let's do this."

He was big, Justine realized. And solid. Not to mention warm and so very *male*. The thought put a hitch in her breathing. She hadn't been this close to a man since losing her husband and for the first time realized how very much she'd been missing it. She missed being touched, and a whole bunch of other feelings broke free and nearly overwhelmed her. But she couldn't think about that now. *Concentrate and don't let him fall.*

Fortunately Cal was athletic and his balance was good. He could have done this alone but she wouldn't let him. Because it had been her idea. They were standing in the sand by the lounge, and with his hand on her shoulder for balance, he maneuvered himself down onto it.

"Easy peasy," she said.

"Not from my perspective," he grumbled.

Justine was breathing a little too fast and chalked it up to physical exertion. Admittedly the sparks she'd experienced from touching him were a bit disconcerting. Other than that the strategy was successful.

"You're going to love this." She infused her voice with enthusiasm. "The sun. Wind in your hair. Looking at the ocean. When you're not reading, of course."

"Yeah." No enthusiasm.

"The best part is relaxing. No work. No talking about work." She sighed. "Heavenly."

"If you say so," he said.

"I do. Don't worry. I'll check on you. Just give me a wave when you want to come back in and I'll be back out to give you a hand."

"Excuse me?" There was disapproval in his voice, but the aviator sunglasses hid his expression.

"I have work to do."

"Not so fast. You're not going anywhere."

Chapter Five

"I'm not sitting out here all alone." Cal didn't care if there were dancing girls and acrobats. Justine had pushed him into this and now she was abandoning him? Uh-uh. Not going to happen.

"But you're paying me to do a job."

"I'm paying you to be my assistant. And I need assistance with this. Sit." He pointed at the lounge beside his. "Stay. Talk."

"But—"

"That's an order."

She didn't sit. "Seriously, Cal. There are things that I really need to get done. Be reasonable."

"I am."

"You definitely are not." She settled her hands on her hips.

Very shapely hips, he noticed. He sure would like to see her in a pair of shorts, or something besides loose linen slacks or long, flowing dresses.

"I think it's perfectly reasonable to request your company here on the beach." He looked up at her and realized he was enjoying this quite a bit. He might even go so far as to say it was relaxing.

"You said you were going to read a book," she reminded him.

"I don't believe I actually ever said those words. I said I didn't have one and you challenged my manhood by implying that I was afraid." He folded his arms over his chest. "Now, here we are. I think you're afraid to be alone with me."

"That's ridiculous." She huffed out an indignant breath. "We're alone all the time."

"Ah," he held up his index finger. "But there's always the structure of work to our aloneness. This will be different and I think that scares you."

"There are things I'm afraid of but this isn't one of them." She pointed her finger right back at him. "You're just being crabby and dictatorial. You realize that, right? A little while ago you were complaining about how slow technology on the island is and the pace was messing with work. Now you want me to sacrifice productive work hours to keep you company out here?"

"I've earned the right to be as crabby as I want. My leg aches. My scheduled activity plan is in the Dumpster. And the only assistant who will work with me seems to have a problem following orders." Her issues didn't appear to be with work so much as with him. "So, let me spell this out."

"Please do. I'm listening."

The words were consenting but that didn't fool him. Her tone was pure pushback. "There is no way you're marooning me under this stupid umbrella by myself. You pushed me into not working and there's a price to pay. Keep me company. You can put on a bikini if you want. I'll wait."

He knew she had a bathing suit because every night before bed she swam laps in the pool without the patio

lights on. The dark was probably some yoga trick to elim-
inate nuisance and distraction so she could concentrate
and push that beautiful body to peak performance. But the
fact was, he didn't know what she looked like with fewer
clothes on and would give almost anything to find out.

Cal watched emotions flicker across her face, rang-
ing from stubborn to shy. And possibly scared. And darn
if the freckles on her nose weren't as cute as could be.

"Really. You should put on your suit. One of us should
take advantage of that beautiful, warm ocean. Or at the
very least not get weird tan lines."

She sat on the other lounge, probably to shut him up.
"I'm fine."

There's no way she was fine and he wondered about
that. They stared at each other for several moments without saying anything. If she would start talking, maybe he
could find out what wasn't fine. One thing he realized—it
was far more interesting to wonder about her than think
about the boneheaded choices that had landed him in this
mess in the first place.

"So," he started. One of them had to go first and she
showed no sign of cracking. "Say something."

"Is conversation with you in my job description?" She
sat straight as a poker with her hands folded in her lap.
Prim and proper, some might say.

For some reason that got his pulse pumping. Probably
because he would very much like to find out the parameters of her prim and proper. "Talking isn't spelled out,
but it's kind of implied."

"For work. Not this."

"I think the line between the two blurred when you
bullied me into telling you about the bet." Cal was pretty
sure that would get her to at least defend herself. He
wasn't disappointed.

"I didn't bully you."

"Yeah, you kind of did."

"It would be impossible for me to push you into anything. You're bigger than me." Indignation looked good on her.

"Yes, but I'm fragile," he said.

"Oh, please. About as delicate as a charging rhinoceros."

"I think you're pouting and, quite frankly, I'm a little shocked by it. Didn't take you for a pouter." Cal continued to deliberately bait her, just to see how she would react. He wasn't proud of it, but since hang gliding wasn't going to happen, what was a guy to do? And maybe there was a little payback thrown in for good measure because she'd pushed him outside.

"Pouting? Me? Really?" Her chin lifted slightly. "I'm not going to bite. I'm made of sterner stuff."

And for some reason, that reminded him about her limp. "Tell me about the accident."

Again, her face was a kaleidoscope of emotions, which she quickly shut down. "That's not very interesting. Ancient history."

A swing and a miss, he thought. The lady didn't want to elaborate. "Then you come up with a topic for discussion. It was your rule not to talk about work."

"That was when I was going back inside to earn my paycheck," she said.

"I think we should take the rule out for a spin and see where we go." Because that left personal stuff up for grabs and he was very curious about her personally.

"Well, I've got nothing." Now her arms were crossed over her chest—classic defensive pose.

"Okay. How about this? We do questions. Back and forth."

She thought about that, then nodded. "I'll go first."

"I wouldn't have it any other way." He smiled and put as much charm as possible into it. "A gentleman always lets a lady go first. Hit me."

"Are you married?" she asked without hesitation.

The way she fired that one off, he would bet that had been on her mind, especially after he'd hinted at his pathetic social life. "No. Now me. What's your favorite food?"

The query was designed to throw her off balance because she would be prepared for him to ask the same thing. Judging by the expression on her face, the ploy worked.

Finally she answered, "Cookies-and-cream ice cream."

"That's not food."

"It might not be nutritionally well-balanced, but it is edible. Hence, food." Her mouth curved up at the corners. "It's an honest answer. I shouldn't have to defend it."

"You're right. My bad. There's no right or wrong here. How often do you eat it?"

"No you don't." She wagged a finger at him. "It's my turn." She seemed to be warming to the game. After thinking for a moment, she said, "So you're not married now. Have you ever been?"

"Yes." He could tell she wasn't pouting anymore and was glad about that. "I bet you want to know what happened, don't you?"

"Aha. That's your question. And my answer is yes. What happened?"

The stigma of failure didn't twist as painfully as it once had. "We got a divorce because I wasn't very good at being married, and I don't do things I'm not very good at."

She looked at the cast on his leg, then met his gaze. "So, no more skydiving?"

"An odd term for jumping out of an airplane when you analyze it. The words imply a soft, free-floating experience."

"And it is," she agreed. "Right up until you hit solid ground."

He winced. "Don't think I didn't notice you trying to sneak in a turn with that question. I believe the next question is mine." He was trying to think of something to ask that would get her to open up and give him more than a yes-or-no response. "How does your family feel about you moving away from Texas?"

"They're conflicted. We're close, so it's hard not having them nearby. But everyone also encouraged me to branch out and try a change of scene."

That was interesting, and Cal wanted to know why she'd needed encouragement to relocate. "So, you're making friends in Blackwater Lake?"

"Don't think I didn't notice you just took cuts," she scolded him. "But yes. I like the small-town feel and everyone is superfriendly. Why did you decide to move Hart Energy there?"

"Besides the fact that my brothers and sister are there, it's conveniently located with a lot of land for research and development. When the new airport opened, that sealed the deal for me."

"Why?"

"I travel a lot, and the closest one was nearly a hundred miles away. Now I have a place to park the private plane."

She frowned slightly. "Still, it seems a little surprising that you'd move to the same small town with the older brother you're still competing with. Aren't you trying to get out from his shadow?"

"Since our companies don't overlap, it's not him so much as leaving my ex behind." He'd been such a moron.

"Marrying her was a big mistake, but the stupidest thing was dating her at all."

"Why?"

"She went out with Sam first."

"Oh, my—" Her eyes went wide.

"Yeah. She loved my brother first, but he didn't feel the same and was honest with her, let her down as easily as possible. She turned to me for comfort and I thought I could come first with her. I was wrong, probably because she never stopped loving Sam."

"And you don't blame him for what happened?"

"No. I love my brother." Cal knew it was his own fault. Work helped him get through that difficult time and somehow it became a habit he couldn't seem to break. "The mistake was mine alone and one I'll never make again."

"That seems wise," she agreed.

Cal must have needed to get that off his chest, because she was extracting a lot more information than he'd intended. Turnabout was fair play.

"Okay, it's my turn. And I think you owe me about six questions."

"In your dreams." But she laughed. "Okay, shoot."

He'd run off at the mouth about his very personal life and stopped short of all the reasons he'd moved to Blackwater Lake. A major objective was to be close to his niece, and his sister, Ellie, was pregnant with her second child. He envied Ellie, her husband, Alex, and the beautiful life and family they were creating. The thought made him curious about Justine.

"Do you like kids?" he asked.

For a moment she looked as if all the air had been sucked out of her lungs. Then she took a deep breath and seemed to be counting. Then she said, "Yes."

"Care to elaborate?"

"No." The breeze blew strands of her red hair free, and she tucked them behind her ears. "Do you like kids?"

Maybe if he shared more information with her she would do the same. "I like them very much. I'm especially fond of my sister's little girl, Leah. Ellie is going to have another niece or nephew."

"Ah, because it's all about you." Justine smiled but it faded almost immediately. "Do you want children?"

"Hmm…"

She stared at him while he mulled it over and finally said, "That's a yes-or-no question, Cal."

"Not for me." He wouldn't take the step without being married, and his competitive streak had seriously messed with his better judgment. That made him reluctant to trust himself, so kids seemed unlikely. "It's a question mark. How about you?"

"Question mark." She'd kicked off her sandals and now wiggled her toes in the coarse white sand. When her gaze met his there was soul-deep sadness in her eyes. She shivered even though the tropical air was warm and humid.

He was getting a vibe and couldn't not ask. "Are you married?"

She looked back at him for several moments, and he doubted he'd get an answer. Finally she grabbed her shoes and stood. "Was. I'm starting to get sunburned. A redhead's skin and all that. Do you need help getting back to the villa?"

"I can manage."

"Okay." Without another word she walked away.

It took Cal several moments to realize that she knew a hell of a lot more about him now. But he knew very little more about her than he had before playing Twenty Questions. Something had made her sad and he felt bad about reminding her of it. Possibly it was the fact that she'd been married. Past tense. He also knew her skin was sensitive to the sun, but he was pretty sure that wasn't the only reason she'd called a halt to the game. She was running away from something.

Most women wanted to talk feelings until a man's head was ready to explode. Not Justine. Cal found himself in the unfamiliar position of wanting to know more. He was acutely curious about what she *didn't* say.

Later that night, Justine stroked and kicked her way from one side of the pool to the other. In the dark. She moved smoothly through the warm water, turning her face to the side to breathe. The same way she'd done since her first night here. She'd had no idea that Cal was aware of her evening ritual. And she wore a one-piece tank suit to do it, not a bikini, thank you very much. The exercise normally soothed her, but not this time.

Playing Twenty Questions on the beach had brought up memories and feelings of a life that seemed surreal now. Two years ago she'd been married to a wonderful man and had a beautiful little girl, but they died in the accident that nearly took Justine's life, too. The doctors saved her leg. If given the choice, she would have gladly sacrificed it to keep her family, but one didn't get to bargain or negotiate. Life and death didn't work that way.

Now she did yoga and swam laps to stay strong because nothing else made sense. And she was swimming those laps on a tropical island to earn money for her own yoga studio, to help someone else find the will to live like she had. For some reason she was still alive and clung to the belief that there was a reason. Something she was meant to do.

The thing about laps was that muscle memory took

over, freeing your mind to go wherever it wanted. Hers apparently wanted to go to Cal because that's where it kept ending up. Why hadn't he mentioned that he was aware she swam every night? And insisting that she stay on the beach today and keep him company. What was that about?

It wasn't spelled out in her work contract that she couldn't enjoy talking to her boss, and that was a good thing because she'd enjoyed it very much. He was handsome, yes. The sight of him was enough to make a girl weak in the knees. But he was also very smart. He really listened and remembered, so a person had better be careful what she said.

Justine was so caught up in her own thoughts that it startled her when the patio area suddenly lit up like a big-league ballpark. She swam to the end of the pool and grabbed on to the side. Cal was hobbling out of the villa and saw her watching.

"Hi." He moved closer and looked down at her, leaning on the crutches. "I'm sorry about the light. Just wanted some air and figured it probably wouldn't do my leg any good if I tripped over something in the dark."

"Of course."

"Hope I didn't mess up your yoga, breathing, Vulcan mind-meld meditation technique."

"What?"

"Swimming in the dark. No nuisance light or distractions to interfere with your concentration."

"Right. But seriously, the *Star Trek* reference?"

"You got that." He smiled. "Are you a fan?"

"Big time. The actor who plays Captain James T. Kirk in the new movies is perfect. You actually remind me of him a little."

"I'll take that as a compliment," he said.

"Just a fact."

"And it's a fact that you're swimming in the dark. Why do you do it?"

"It's beneficial after a long day of work." He started to say something but she interrupted. "This isn't about you working me too hard. I swim at home, too. At least, I used to in Dallas. It calms me and strengthens the muscles in my legs. And it's relaxing."

Although her nerves were anything but calm at this particular moment. She swam in the dark here mostly because she was self-conscious about the disfiguring scars on her right leg. This man had dated actresses and supermodels with perfect bodies. That was probably an unrealistic standard and didn't allow for photoshopping or body makeup. But that was her perception and that made it true for her.

She shouldn't compare herself or care what he thought but she did. That was obvious because she didn't get out of the pool. And even with all her physical therapy and yoga breathing techniques, she couldn't count high enough to breathe herself into serenity.

What was she going to do? If she got out there's no way he wouldn't see.

The answer was simple. She wouldn't get out. She'd keep swimming. A metaphor for her life.

"I'm going to finish my laps," she told him.

"Will it bother you if I sit here on the patio?"

"Not a bit," she lied. She pushed off from the side of the pool and started gliding through the water again. Back and forth.

His presence actually bothered her a lot. Not because he might critique her freestyle form, but her female one. If she was being honest, it was more than that. Just being around him had all her senses on red alert. There was something about him that made her want to say the right thing, be perfect. If she made him laugh, that made her feel so good.

Except vanity wasn't the only reason she hid her leg. If he saw the hideous marks and gouges out of the flesh from accident trauma and evidence of multiple surgeries to save it, he'd feel sorry for her, and his reactions would reflect that. He'd treat her differently, cut her slack when he otherwise might not have. All she wanted was to stand on her own two feet. Sink or swim on her own merit and not pity points.

So she kept swimming for as long as she could, but simply didn't have the stamina to outlast his apparent need for fresh air. If ever there was a time for strategic planning, this was it. When she touched the side of the pool farthest from where he was sitting, she pushed her shoulders out of the water and rested her arm on the side. There was a chair two feet away where she'd left a sarong and her towel.

She decided to hang here for a sign that he was going inside or was somehow distracted. Her hair was pulled into a knot on top of her head to keep it out of her face and she blinked the water from her eyes. Smiling brightly she said, "That was so refreshing."

"I can imagine." There was envy in his tone.

"Swimming will be good exercise for you when that cast comes off. It will build up the atrophied muscles in your calf."

"Wow, that sounds so attractive."

"Don't worry. It won't take long before you'll be back to impressing the ladies with your manly legs."

He laughed. "That will be an improvement since I never impressed anyone with them before."

Although she wasn't going to correct him, that wasn't

completely true. He wore shorts every day—to accommodate the cast on his lower leg, but also for the tropical climate. Along with the cotton flowered shirts, the look suited him. Justine liked his legs, muscular with a masculine dusting of hair. Even what she could see of the injured one looked good. Strong thighs. Unlike her, no one would stare at him because he was different, unattractive.

"It won't take long to get back in shape. The cast will be gone and you'll be off and running again before you know it."

"Time flies when you're having fun."

A breeze blew over her wet shoulders and made her shiver. Time was not flying nearly fast enough for her. There was no sign that he was going inside, so she needed a distraction and went with the best one she could think of.

"Is that your cell phone?"

"What?"

"I thought I heard your ringtone," she said.

He felt his shirt pocket. "Damn, I left it inside. Stupid since I've been waiting for a call from my attorney. His timing stinks."

The lie wasn't without consequences. Justine felt guilty and would have to live with it. She watched him stand, gracefully prop the crutches under his arms, then propel himself to the doorway. He was getting really good on them, a sign of his athleticism. As soon as he was inside she hauled herself out of the pool, grabbed the towel and quickly dried off. She was just tying the sarong around her waist when he came back outside.

"No one called."

"Sorry. Must have been water in my ears. Or the wind rustling the palm trees." She walked closer. Now that her leg was covered by the floor-length, flowered material, her confidence was properly back in place. "It's a pretty night, don't you think?"

"Yeah." He looked up.

"Without the nuisance light, the moon and stars are spectacular. And that's not a yoga thing. Just a fact."

"I'm aware."

Justine had been staring up at the sky, but the hoarse, slightly ragged edge to his voice drew her gaze back to his. There was a tense and hungry expression on his face, exactly the way he'd looked at her when she'd demonstrated her stretching technique.

Instantly her heart started racing as if she'd set an Olympic record in the one-hundred-meter freestyle. Her body had been so cold a few minutes ago and she'd been desperate enough to lie in order to get out of the pool. Now she was hot all over and the last thing she wanted was to move away from him.

Cal cleared his throat. "I'm going to try to get my attorney on the phone. It's still business hours in the States."

"Right."

A muscle in his jaw jerked as if he was clenching his teeth, and the tension in his eyes looked very near the snapping point. "I'll say good-night."

"Okay. See you in the morning."

Without another word he turned and went back into his suite, shutting the door behind him.

Justine stood there, thought about what just happened and waited for the wave of shame to pull her down because she'd felt something for another man. Recognizing survivor's guilt for being alive when her husband and child weren't didn't mean it would magically go away. She'd struggled with it for a while, even when everyone told her she had to go on living. That if she could change what happened she would. That her husband and child would want her to move forward and not live in the past.

Tonight, with Cal, she had her *aha* moment. She knew what they meant. It had been a long time since she'd thought about sex, but the way Cal looked at her changed that. He made her realize she had physical needs. So, why now? Why him?

He was her boss. Which just proved that fate had a warped sense of humor.

Chapter Six

So now he'd seen Justine Walker in a bathing suit. The problem was, what he *hadn't* seen kept him awake last night.

Cal was sitting on the large sofa with his leg propped up and his computer in his lap. From here he could watch her at the desk—reading email, going over cost projections and reports. There was the cutest expression on her face, the one he knew meant she was concentrating. So was he, but it had nothing to do with work.

A time or two she'd caught him watching her, and color rose in her cheeks. Did that mean she could read his mind? Because the fact was, he would really like to see her in a bathing suit. Technically he had but she'd been in the water and that blurred everything. And he wouldn't turn down the opportunity to get a look at her without that thing she put on as soon as she got out of the pool. That's not to say what he had seen wasn't top-notch. She had toned arms and a trim waist, but maybe he was an all-or-nothing kind of guy.

He wanted to see all of her and couldn't get the thought out of his mind. So he couldn't focus on much of anything except sliding those loose, gauzy pants off to find out if her body was as spectacular as he suspected. Just like that he was the sultan of slime and he wasn't proud of it. Enough. Time to get his mind back on work, and talking about it would be better than looking at a computer screen. That made it too easy for his mind to wander.

"What are you reading?" he asked.

Justine glanced up and met his gaze over her laptop. "A report on renewable energy from Las Vegas."

"And?"

"The city government is drawing one hundred percent of its power from renewable energy sources to run everything from city hall to parks, community centers and even streetlights."

"Impressive."

"Solar generates the energy to power on-site facilities with tree-shaped solar panels, solar shade canopies at city parks and solar arrays on rooftops."

"I'm guessing that because of its size the city can't get all the necessary power from on-site sources."

"You'd be correct." She removed her glasses and set them on the desk. "But the shift to renewable resulted in significant savings."

"Hmm." He nodded thoughtfully. "I'm going to talk to Mayor McKnight about doing that in Blackwater Lake."

"I haven't met the mayor. What do you think the chances are that she'll be receptive?" Justine asked.

"She's open-minded, so I think there's a fair shot. But she's a formidable woman." Not unlike the one in front of him. "There was a fire this summer that caused widespread evacuations. It was just before I moved into my condo, so I wasn't there yet. But my brother Sam said that in addition to coordinating state and local firefighting resources, Madam Mayor made sure everyone was housed with a family in a home and not in the high school gym."

"Wow."

"In fact, she's responsible for Sam getting together with Faith Connelly."

"Oh?"

"Sam has a big house. Faith and her daughter, Phoebe, needed someplace to go. Mayor Loretta gave him a little push, and while living under the same roof, the two of them fell victim to their tender emotions."

"Be still my heart. So what's the moral of the story?" she asked.

"What makes you think there is one?"

"You're so relationship-averse that you can't even say the word *love*. So there must be a cautionary tale in there somewhere."

"Did you just call me the love Grinch?" He closed his laptop. "And did you notice how I just said the word there?"

"No one will ever accuse you of being Cupid." She smiled. "And yes, I noticed."

"Okay. Fair enough."

"But, if you think about it—" she tapped her lip "—it's not an evacuation, but you and I are living under the same roof."

"For three more weeks," he pointed out. There was a time limit and that made it different somehow.

"How long did it take for Sam and Faith to fall for each other?"

"I have no idea."

"So, it could have been an hour? A day? A week?" She met his gaze. "Or a month?"

When had this conversation gone from him relating a pleasant anecdote to an inquisition? "What's your point?"

"I don't actually have one. It's just fun to watch when you start to sweat. And for the record, it's remarkably easy to push your buttons and make that happen." She also closed her laptop, then stood and started to do her stretching.

Cal forced his gaze away from the seductive sight and held in a groan. Just like that he did, in fact, start to sweat, proving that Miss Prim and Proper was right about him being easy. But no way was she right about close proximity turning a man and woman into a couple. The only couple he recognized was him and work.

And Justine worked for him. No matter how beautiful and intriguing she happened to be, he was her boss. Sure, he'd been preoccupied with her. But he broke his leg—there was nothing wrong with his eyesight. Noticing that a woman was pretty, shapely and sexy was hardwired into him. But he knew where the line was drawn. His R-rated thoughts would be an issue only if he crossed it. He'd had a chance to fire her and wasn't sure whether or not he was sorry he hadn't.

"We haven't finished discussing the list of activities I came up with for you." Her statement came out of the blue.

"What?"

"Yesterday you challenged me to come up with a list of things someone in a cast could participate in. Without a wheelchair. Remember?"

"Vividly. Especially the part where you tried to abandon me on the beach."

"You're so dramatic."

"And you want to discuss it in more detail," he guessed.

"Actually, no. Because that would be your cue to push back and find something wrong with each and every one of them."

"You're implying that I don't have an open mind?" he accused her.

"Implying is too vague. I'm flat-out saying that you refuse to even consider any leisure interest in which your safety wouldn't be jeopardized. And no one who has a lick of sense would let a man with a cast on his leg go wave riding. Which leaves the matter of alternatives."

He smiled because she had him dead to rights. "You must have me mixed up with the vacation Grinch."

"My mistake." There was a knock on the door and she said, "That must be lunch."

Sometime in the week that she'd been here, Cal had let her take over deciding on the menu, and so far her choices had been perfect. Also, sometime since her splashdown in his life, annoyance at the work interruption had turned into anticipation at the prospect of sharing the meal with her and wondering what she would say next.

The room service waiters set up everything at the dining room table and Justine signed the check. With the ever-popular let-us-know-if-you-need-further-assistance, they quietly left the villa. Cal crutched himself over and sat down.

"Smells good," he said, realizing he was hungry.

"I hope you like it. I was assured that this is a signature dish for the chef."

He lifted the silver dome over his plate and the smells got even better. "Sea bass."

"Yup. Along with risotto, salad and vegetables sautéed in olive oil."

"One of my favorites."

"Mine, too." She sat in her usual place at a right angle to him.

They ate in silence for a few moments, savoring the delicate flavors, the way they all complemented each other. Watching her enjoy her food was about the sexiest thing he'd ever seen. He had to say something before he swallowed his tongue.

He glanced at the other things on the table and wondered if she'd missed something. "What, no dessert?"

"About that—" She met his gaze. "You're going to have it later."

"Am I?"

"Absolutely, because I know how important it is to you. I've been asking around, and—"

He had an uneasy feeling. "Where am I going?"

"It's a surprise." She was looking very mysterious, which was the opposite of comforting.

"Does it have anything to do with that list of things for a mobility-challenged person to do without a wheelchair?"

"As a matter of fact—" she chewed the last bite of sea bass and swallowed "—the list is now a spreadsheet. Your idea."

He wished he'd never confessed about the bet and his strategy for dealing with it. "You didn't."

"It's morphed into a schedule. Something different every day. Not unlike what you had planned before your unfortunate accident."

"What if I don't want to be that scheduled?"

"Let's ignore the fact that you sound like a disgruntled eleven-year-old. Look at it as an opportunity to silence your guilty conscience, stay true to the spirit of the bet and learn how to do down time. In the process you'll feel really good about yourself."

"Okay. None of that is going to happen. And before you accuse me of pushing back and finding something wrong for no reason, this is for the sake of argument. What are we doing this afternoon?"

"I'm not—"

"Yes, you are. I'm not going alone. So, give it to me straight."

"It's a surprise." She wiped her mouth with the cloth napkin, then set it by her plate.

The only surprise he was in favor of was her walking into the room naked. Zero chance of that happening, so he said, "If you won't reveal the secret activity, it means I'm not going to like the surprise."

Her look challenged him. "Let's go and find out."

"I thought participating in activities was supposed to relax a person."

Justine ignored the death-by-stare look Cal gave her and threaded another reed into the beginner basket she was weaving. "Are you whining? Because that sounded an awful lot like a whine to me."

"Is that any way to talk to your boss?"

"It's the same way I've talked to you since I arrived. Seems a little late to start complaining about it now." She looked up at him sitting beside her on the bench at the picnic table. They were in a group craft lesson where she was trying to ignore the heat that consumed her every time Cal's shoulder or any other part of him touched her.

"There are limits to what I'll endure," he grumbled.

"Probably. But so far I haven't seen it. Makes me feel powerful."

"Good for you." He glared down at the mess of split, torn and discarded reeds in front of him. "For the record, I was right."

"Of course you'd think that." She pushed her threaded fronds closer together to make the weave tighter. "But because I'm a good assistant and kindhearted, too, I'll humor you. What is it you think you're right about?"

"That statement, Miss Walker, is the very definition

of patronizing, and if I'm not mistaken, there was a good deal of condescension thrown in, too."

"Excellent that you noticed." She smiled up at him. "I was afraid you'd missed it."

His lips twitched, canceling out his bad-tempered remarks. "What I'm right about is that you surprised me with a basket weaving class precisely because you knew I would hate it."

"Your open-mindedness is truly inspiring."

"Don't think that sunny attitude will distract me." There was a twinkle in his eyes. "Everyone knows basket weaving is a joke. It's what you tell your parents your college major is in order to watch their hair turn white."

She laughed. "On the contrary. It's big business. There are classes all over the States and supply stores. Serious stuff. These baskets can be decorative or practical."

He looked ruefully at his attempt. "Not from where I'm sitting."

"Cheer up, Cal. Don't forget I promised you ice cream afterward if you're a good boy. That's why I didn't order dessert at lunch. It's part of the surprise."

He ripped another reed trying to get it into place and swore under his breath. "Tell me again how this is supposed to be relaxing."

"Because you're not being graded."

"Ha." He gestured to the eight or ten people working at other tables. "They're all judging and not in a happy way. I can feel it."

She looked around and in spite of his complaints, this class delivered on its promise—beginning basket weaving in paradise. She'd found it online, offered at a nearby resort, signed them up and arranged transportation. The tables were in an open-sided structure and shaded by a thatched roof. There was a spectacular view of the ocean, and flowered shrubs, palm trees and grass surrounded them. A sea breeze made the air temperature practically perfect.

"Let me explain the concept of vacation to you." She picked up another reed and easily worked it through while teaching her boss the intricacies of Vacation 101. "Most of your time is spent doing things that are important for one reason or another. Making money, sustaining jobs, providing a service or product. The prospect of not being able to fulfill one of those commitments produces stress."

"I'm painfully aware of all that—"

"And I'm aware that you're aware." She held up a hand to stop him when he opened his mouth to argue. "It's vacation you're woefully inadequate with. The stress will burn you out if you don't take a break and figure out how to power down. It's a time when you can do nothing at all." She held up her basket. "Or do something that doesn't matter whether or not you succeed."

"It matters to me."

"You're a perfectionist." She nodded her understanding. "That's a completely different motivational speech and I don't have the notes with me."

He looked unhappily at the mess of destroyed foliage in front of him. "I don't like wasting anything—resources or time. Since I have nothing to show for this hour, it must be classified as wasteful."

Justine watched his determined attempt to weave another reed into his creation. His big hands were not delicate, making the task harder. On top of that he was all thumbs. Athleticism didn't automatically translate to an activity requiring fine motor skills. And yet she thought he was completely adorable. A fish out of water who made her insides tap dance. Words that she would never say out loud.

"Okay, tell me this. In the last hour have you thought about work even once?"

His big hands stilled as he considered the question. "No."

She grinned at him. "Mission accomplished."

"Not really." He glanced at the people who were standing up now, showing off their beginner baskets before drifting off to their next recreational pursuit.

"Did you see that?" Cal met her gaze. "Everyone else made a functional item. A receptacle capable of holding something. Post-its. Paper clips or staples."

"Vacation means you have to stop looking at the world through a prism of work. What those people made could be used to hold individual eye shadows, seasoning packets or hair accessories."

"Exactly. They made something useful." He held up his sad attempt. "This is a flat nothing."

"Well, you really are Danny Downer today." She tapped her lip, mulling over the misshapen thing. "Maybe it could be a place mat."

"For a rodent." He shifted, moving his injured leg to a more comfortable position.

"Oh, please…" She took a breath and counted, taking control of the shivers skipping through her when his arm brushed hers. Studying the irregular square, she said, "I see the beginning of an area rug."

"Seriously?" He gave her an incredulous look.

"Why not? The journey of a thousand miles starts with a single step."

"It must be exhausting," he said.

"What?"

"Being a glass-half-full person all the time." He shook his head.

There was a time when she wasn't. Her heart caught

as memories kaleidoscoped through her mind—a man's strong arm draped casually across her shoulders, a laughing, red-haired toddler. But when a person suddenly lost their spouse, child and reason for living, the line between despair and optimism was razor-thin. She'd walked it a long, painful time, more than once nearly slipping into the emptiness.

Then she made a choice, a conscious decision to focus on the positive. At first it was impossible to find anything hopeful. But she found if you worked on something long enough it became a habit. Still, she could never forget that the habit had grown out of the glass-half-empty time of her life.

Working those optimism muscles now, she managed to smile at him. "How about that ice cream?"

"If it means I don't have to work with these weeds anymore, I'll race you," he said.

She laughed. "I wouldn't want to take advantage of a man on crutches."

"My odds are improving." He stood, balancing on his uninjured leg while he reached for the crutches leaning against the end of the table beside him. "I'm getting pretty fast on these things."

"No argument there." She got to her feet and picked up the woven basket she'd made. He, on the other hand, was walking away without his. "Aren't you going to take yours?"

"My what?" He pivoted and met her gaze. "It isn't anything."

"Sure it is."

"What?" There was still faux bitterness in his voice.

"Maybe a coaster?"

He rolled his eyes. "If you leave it I'll buy the ice cream."

"No way. This is my treat."

The little shop was located down a path right near the hotel's lobby. It was a charming place with circular tables and metal chairs that had padded red seats and heart-shaped backs. Behind the glass display case, the different flavors of ice cream were displayed.

The young woman behind the counter was wearing a white apron and a big smile. "What can I get you?"

"I'd like a scoop of cookies-and-cream. In a dish, please," Justine said.

"A decisive woman," Cal observed. "Remarkable."

"And for you, sir?"

"Make mine two scoops of salted caramel vanilla with chocolate sauce." He looked down. "The second one is my reward for persevering today."

"I'm not judging," she assured him.

"Both good choices," the ice-cream lady said. "I'll have it ready in a jiffy."

Cal insisted on buying, and Justine was both pleased and uncomfortable. Even though he expensed her presence here for work-related items on the island, his buying even a simple thing like ice cream had a more intimate vibe. It seemed personal and she didn't know what to do with that. She carried their cups to a corner table because he had his hands full of crutches. When they were settled, both of them started eating. Did he feel awkward or was it just her? Not a question she was going to ask.

After a few moments of silence, Cal said, "This is really good. Almost worth the humiliation of that class."

"I think you secretly enjoyed it. Or maybe the part you liked best was picking on me and complaining. Of course you'd never admit it if I'm right."

"About that…"

"So I am right," she said triumphantly.

"No. I really hated it." He met her gaze and his expression turned serious. "But I was taking it out on you. Did I say something wrong?"

"No." That answer was automatic because she had no idea what he was talking about. Then curiosity kicked in. "When? What? I'm not sure what you mean."

"When I asked if it makes you tired being upbeat all the time. You had a funny look on your face. And by funny, I mean sad."

Bam. There was her reminder that he didn't miss a detail. And didn't forget. After his question, she'd been thinking about pulling herself out of the dark pit of depression she'd fallen into following an unimaginable loss. It was quite extraordinary that after their stroll for ice cream and ordering it, he would remember her reaction to his offhand remark.

"I hope you know I was teasing," he said sincerely.

"Yes."

"What were you thinking about?" he asked.

"Stuff." Not an ice-cream sundae conversation. "And it's only fair to warn you that I have a dark side."

As she'd hoped, he interpreted her remark as more teasing. "You have layers. That just makes you more interesting."

"I'm a lot like basket weaving." The look on his face made her laugh. "What you saw on my face was empathy for the poor palm fronds who were sad. Many reeds were sacrificed in the artistic yet noble pursuit of your trivet."

"There it is." He pointed his spoon at her. "The snarky streak is strong in you."

"May it live long and prosper," she joked.

"Unlike my weaving skills."

"The only way to improve is by doing. Practice and repetition."

"Please don't make me."

The serious mood scattered, replaced by teasing and banter. Just the way she liked it. Because thinking about Cal made her head hurt. He had so many wonderful qualities and today she'd discovered another one. Two, actually. He was perceptive and sensitive. If she had known how much she would like this man, all the money in the world wouldn't have made her take this job.

Chapter Seven

Cal was more than happy to shoot his mouth off when he was right but not so much when Justine was. Especially since he'd given her such a hard time about non-work activities. The truth was, he'd had a great time on the outing this afternoon. Oh, he did in fact loathe basket weaving, but it was fun finding out that he shouldn't quit his day job for it.

On top of that, the break from work had been rejuvenating. Considering all of that, a different setting for dinner seemed like an excellent idea. With Justine, of course.

He saw her pick up the phone at her desk and knew what was coming. "Are you planning to order room service?"

"Yes." She set the receiver down again. "Was there something in particular you wanted?"

"There is, actually. I'd like to try the five-star restaurant here at the resort."

"Oh?" She smiled and there was a little smugness in it. "Someone had a good time today and is looking to broaden his horizons again."

So much for thinking she might not notice there was a connection. "Okay. The field trip didn't bite. You've got thirty seconds for a victory lap and then we're moving on."

"Only thirty seconds?"

He looked at his watch. "And...go."

"Am I allowed to say I told you so?"

"At your own peril," he warned her.

"Okay. I told you so." She grinned, a look full of satisfaction, and damned if it didn't look good on her. "Whatever peril you have planned is worth it."

"Good, because you're going with me to try that five-star restaurant."

"Oh—" The smile disappeared. "I'm not sure—"

"No you don't. You're not wiggling out of this. I want to go to the restaurant, and better than anyone you know how resistant I've been to outings. That suggests I'm going a little stir-crazy. You must be, too, eating here all the time. There's just one condition."

"What's that?" she asked suspiciously.

"When you're back to work in Blackwater Lake, tell everyone what a sweetheart of a boss I am."

Justine laughed, a lovely, happy sound. "So the next time you break your leg on vacation, everyone will volunteer for drudge duty on a tropical island paradise?"

"And I thought I was being so subtle." He got up from the sofa and propped himself on the crutches, then moved over to the desk. "Don't make me eat alone."

"Well...it would be nice to get out of the villa." She glanced around the elegantly appointed deluxe surroundings and laughed. "Now, there's something I never expected to say."

"Excellent."

"I'll make a reservation."

An hour later the resort's golf cart shuttle dropped them off in front of a stand-alone building adjacent to the hotel's main five-story tower. Out front there was lush landscaping, including flowers in yellow, red and pink. Tiki torches lighted the path to the heavy front doors with vertical handles.

Cal was going to be a gentleman if it killed him. He hobbled over and balanced himself on his one good leg, then opened the door. "After you."

"I could have done that," she scolded him. "You don't have to show off for the hired help."

It hit him that he *was* showing off and didn't think of her as only an employee. His perception had changed and he wasn't exactly sure when that happened. When she'd demonstrated her stretching moves? Or the day she'd half carried him to that lounge on the beach and he got just a taste of her appealing curves? Maybe it happened today when the basket weaving and ice cream had turned into a flirt fest. At least, he thought she'd been flirting and knew for a fact he had been.

No one would accuse him of understanding how a woman's mind worked, but he wasn't entirely clueless, either. A little rusty, but not oblivious. They'd had fun together today. Not that work couldn't be fun, too, but it was different outside the office, even if his office was in a luxury villa. He decided to let the showing off remark pass without a comment. Anything he said would just complicate an already complicated thing.

"Chivalry is not dead." Holding the door open with his shoulder, he breathed in the floral scent of her skin as she walked past him.

There was a high desk, and an attractive woman who must be the hostess stood behind it, waiting. She gave them a friendly smile to go along with the greeting. "Good evening, Mr. Hart. I do hope your leg is mending nicely."

"Feeling much better, thanks. I'll be in a walking cast soon."

"That's good to hear. I have a lovely, secluded table for two. The most romantic we have, in my opinion."

His assistant opened her mouth, probably to clarify that this wasn't a romantic dinner. Before she could get the words out he said, "Lead the way. I'll follow you, Justine."

She hesitated a moment and there was a confused expression on her face. Then she shrugged and said, "Okay."

Several couples dined at nearby tables and watched curiously as they passed. A few minutes later they were sitting at a booth in the corner. There was a pristine white tablecloth and a lighted candle along with fresh flowers in the center of it. And silver salt and pepper shakers.

"Lorenzo will be your waiter," the hostess informed them. "You're in good hands with him."

"Thanks," Cal said.

Justine looked around and said, "This is nice."

"Yeah."

There was elegant dark wood trim on the walls and paintings of the ocean and local landscape. It was quiet except for the low hum of voices. Moments after they settled, their waiter appeared.

"My name is Lorenzo and it's my pleasure to take care of such a beautiful young couple."

Justine lifted a finger, signaling her intention of setting him straight. "You should know—"

"When did you arrive on our beautiful island?" the middle-aged man asked.

"About a week ago," she answered. "And I have to tell you that—"

"You're going to tell me that you're honeymooners. I suspected since this is your first visit to Castaways Restaurant. I would remember if you had been here before. But you've been keeping to yourselves. Being alone is the goal of a honeymoon, but sooner or later a change of scenery is good—to keep the romance alive. Yes?"

"It's a challenge." Justine's tone was wry. Apparently she'd decided not to burst the guy's bubble. "Especially with a broken leg."

Lorenzo made a sympathetic *tsk*ing sound. "A story from your honeymoon trip to share and laugh about one day."

"Right." Cal noticed empathetic looks from other male diners around them.

"It is my job to make sure you keep up your strength. For healing." He winked as he handed over the menus. "Can I get you something from the bar?"

"Wine?" Cal looked at his assistant, who shrugged as if to say, *Why not?*

"I'd like a list, please."

"Of course, sir." The waiter left and moments later returned to hand it over.

Cal studied the choices and saw one of his favorite labels, an expensive and very nice pinot noir. Justine confirmed that red was fine with her and he ordered a bottle. Lorenzo disappeared and they were alone again.

"So," she said, "that guy is full of local color."

"And observant," Cal joked. "Pegging us as being on our honeymoon."

"I know, right?" She laughed.

"Congratulations." The middle-aged man sitting at the table closest to them raised a wineglass. His companion had just left, presumably to visit the ladies' room. "I couldn't help overhearing."

Cal wasn't sure how to respond. She was his assistant and they were working together, but that explanation would get a wink and a *Yeah, right, that's what they all say.* Whether or not they ever saw this guy again, Cal wouldn't take a chance that Justine might be embarrassed. So he shrugged and let the man believe what he wanted.

"Tough break," their table neighbor said, glancing at the cast up to the knee. "The leg, I mean. Don't let it hold you back, if you know what I mean."

"I'm pretty sure we do," Justine said wryly. "Thanks for the advice."

"My wife and I are celebrating ten years together. This is our anniversary trip. The kids are with my folks."

"Congratulations," Cal said. "What's the secret to marital longevity?"

"Listening," he answered promptly.

"Excuse me?"

"It's a component of communication. We took a marriage seminar because I interrupted all the time and it was driving Carol nuts." He shrugged. "Turns out if you're thinking about what you're going to say next, you're not really listening to what she's saying."

"Makes sense," Cal told him.

"Seems simple, right?" The guy laughed. "It takes a lot of practice but it's worth the effort. And the other thing I would say is to make the most of alone time. Before you know it, kids come along and it's not just the two of you anymore. I'm not knocking it. I love my kids, and having a family is the best thing that ever happened to me. It's just that you have to work a little harder on the couple thing. Don't take it for granted."

Cal was looking at Justine and noticed a wistful expression on her face. That seemed to happen when the subject of couples and kids came up. "I can see how that happens."

"So," the stranger said, "this is worth what you paid

for it, but look at that cast not as an obstacle but as an opportunity."

His wife returned to the table and gave him a look. "Alan?"

"What? Just chatting up the honeymoon couple and sharing what's worked for us, sweetie." He did seem sincere. "It's been the best ten years of my life."

"Congratulations on your anniversary," Justine said.

"Thank you." Carol sat down. "I hope the two of you will be as happy as we've been."

Lorenzo returned with a bottle and two glasses, and they went through the ritual of checking the label, tasting and pouring. Cal stole looks at Justine and saw her stealing looks at the other couple. There was such longing on her face mixed with a generous dose of envy.

The more time he spent with her, the more intrigued he became. She'd obviously wanted to correct the erroneous impression of them as honeymooners, then had gone along with it. That took Cal to a place where he wondered what it would be like if they were a couple. The thoughts seemed to throw kerosene on the sparks of his fascination with her body and all that he hadn't seen.

He wanted to know more about her. Was she flirting earlier today? Could she be as attracted to him as he was to her? Unless he was way off the mark, that was very possible, and he didn't think he was so rusty that he was seeing things that weren't there.

That decided, he planned to test his theory.

Justine and Cal stood outside the restaurant, waiting for the shuttle to pick them up for the return trip to the villa. It was a night so beautiful, she had no words to describe the spectacular dusting of stars glittering in the sky. A nearly full moon bathed them in silver light and a gentle breeze brushed strands of hair back from her face. Sharing a bottle of wine meant she'd had two glasses and that was a lot for her, but this happy haze was really nice.

"You're very quiet," Cal observed. "Did the whole mistaken honeymooner thing upset you?"

"No. It obviously made Lorenzo and Mr. and Mrs. Ten-Year Anniversary happy to think that we were. I finally decided that setting everyone straight would somehow let them down. No harm done." She sighed. "It was perfect. In fact, this whole day has been absolutely perfect."

"Even the work part?"

"It's necessary and made me appreciate the rest of the day. Balance. Don't you agree?"

"It was great, with the exception of the basket weaving class, where I was a standout underachiever."

"That should have made you appreciate having ice cream afterward, a wonderful dinner and the excellence of this moment right now." She breathed deeply. "Smell the flowers mixed with the sea air. It's simply…paradise."

The golf cart shuttle pulled up in front of them just then, cutting off his answer, but she dared him to disagree. Justine climbed in and slid over to make room for Cal. He handled the maneuver so gracefully she almost forgot he was on crutches. When they were safely in, Cal instructed the driver where to drop them, and the guy took off.

The movement was so sudden that she lurched forward. Automatically Cal put his arm around her shoulders, settling her securely against him. He was strong and solid, the kind of man a woman could depend on. She prepared herself for him to let her go when the ride smoothed out, but he didn't. And she wasn't sure what to make of that.

Feeling their bodies pressed together was more intoxicating than the lush, lovely night. The inclination to lean her head on his shoulder was strong, and if the ride had lasted any longer she almost certainly would have succumbed to temptation. But before she was ready for it to end, the driver pulled to a stop in front of the path lined with bushes and trees that protected the villa's privacy.

Cal tipped the driver, and it must have been generous because the man thanked him profusely. They slid out and stepped safely back from the vehicle before watching it dart forward. Then solitude surrounded them along with the moonlight. She had had such a good time and felt oddly like Cinderella at the ball when it was five minutes until the clock struck midnight. Five minutes to soak up the magic before the world turned back into ordinary.

"I think you should have moved the Hart Energy corporate offices to this island," she said.

"An interesting thought." There was a smile in his voice. "I wonder if anyone would move here and work for me."

"When I get back to Blackwater Lake and sing your praises, that won't be an issue for you ever again," she vowed.

"Okay. That makes me feel obligated to reveal that the secret to keeping me in line is setting parameters."

"Better known as laying down the law," she said.

"Yes." He was studying her closely. "So, you're not sorry you came?"

"Absolutely not."

He angled his head toward the villa's front door. "Then can I interest you in a nightcap?"

"I'd like that very much." It's what Cinderella would have done if her fairy godmother had given her even the slightest bit of wiggle room on that deadline. "On one condition."

"Which is?"

"We can sit on the patio and enjoy this night. When we go home, winter and the holidays will be staring us in the face. Let's take advantage of this setting while we can."

"I don't know. You drive a pretty hard bargain. Let me think about it." A moment later he said, "I thought about it and you're on."

They went inside and Cal leaned on the crutches while he poured brandy into two snifters. "Will you do me a favor and carry—"

"Happy to take them outside." She'd thought ahead, knowing he'd have his hands full with the crutches.

With glasses in hand, Justine followed him through the French doors onto the patio. Pool and patio lights were on, illuminating the area with two chairs and a small table between them. When Cal was settled, she set down his drink, then sat on his right, a couple of feet away.

Not quite near enough to feel the heat from his body. Her heart skipped and she missed the closeness they'd shared in the golf cart shuttle. Since he was her boss, that probably should have been a red flag, warning of trouble. But, since she was identifying with female characters from books tonight, she was going to channel Scarlett O'Hara and worry about it tomorrow.

"That was the best dinner I've ever had in my life," she gushed.

"It was good," he agreed.

She noticed the tone and glanced at him. There was something in his expression that made her ask, "You've had better?"

"My meal tonight was excellent. And the companionship was exceptional." There was a gleam in his eyes.

"No you don't." She wagged a finger at him. "It's not going to work. I refuse to be distracted. Where have you ever had a better dining experience than we had tonight at the five-star restaurant on this island?"

"It's a very close call, but I'd have to go with Paris."

"Oh. Well. Paris." She shrugged. "I guess that's to be expected. Do you remember the name of the restaurant?"

The corners of his mouth curved up. "No, but I'm pretty sure it was French."

She laughed. "Only in Paris would they give a restaurant a French name."

"Go figure." He sipped his brandy.

"In the City of Light, do the waiters automatically assume a couple dining alone together are honeymooners?"

"I couldn't say about all of them. But in my case, I was on my honeymoon."

"Oh?"

"Yes, I took Daria—Tate, of the Dallas Tates—to Europe for our honeymoon. I combined the trip with business to research alternative energy sources. They're doing some remarkable work with algae."

"Oh, be still my heart. You got a tax deduction for taking your bride to Paris after your wedding? Oh, Cal—" She groaned, then couldn't help laughing. "And everyone wondered why the marriage didn't work out."

"I couldn't be objective then, but now it's clear to me what the problem was."

"That there was no romance?" She found herself deeply curious about his relationship. More than she should be, given that they were boss and assistant.

"If she hadn't fallen in love with my brother first, then made me her rebound guy, a trip to energy-rich land in the middle of nowhere would have been fun." He looked at her, intensity crackling in his eyes. "With the right woman, anywhere would have been romantic."

"You're right."

"I am?"

The shocked expression on his face was so darn cute it made her laugh. "Did you want me to disagree?"

"Of course not. But I expected some pushback."

"Sorry to disappoint."

"You are surprising and many other things, but disappointing is not one of them."

Justine didn't know whether to be flattered or ask for a raise. Since he was already paying her very generously, asking for more seemed wrong. "I agree with you because it makes sense. It's practical. The feelings come from within and you take them wherever you go. The place doesn't have to be special if you're with the right person."

"Well said. And it begs the question—did you have a honeymoon?"

Although she didn't want to talk about this, it wasn't fair to grill him like raw hamburger, then refuse to answer his question. If anything, she was unsure why he hadn't brought this up before now. She took a sip of her brandy and let it burn all the way to her belly.

"Sort of."

He waited a few moments, probably giving her a chance to elaborate. When she didn't, he asked, "What does that mean?"

She took a deep breath and counted to five, willing herself to relax. "We had no money and were too poor to go anywhere."

"That doesn't explain the 'sort of.'"

"No, it doesn't. And I heard the pity in your voice in case you were wondering. There's no reason for it. Our 'honeymoon' was the best."

"What did you do?" He cleared his throat. "I mean, I know *what* you did. But something made it the best. Tell me about that."

"My husband was planning to paint our apartment anyway, so he drew a picture of a fireplace on one wall." She smiled, remembering how young they'd been and how wonderful it was. "It was August in Dallas and there was a heat wave. The humidity was awful. But we made a bed on the floor in front of that fireplace art and pretended we were snowed in at a cabin. It was sweet and romantic and just right. We didn't have two pennies to rub together but felt like we had everything a person could ever want."

"You're lucky. I was in Paris and we were barely speaking to each other."

"I'm sorry, Cal."

He shrugged. "It's in the past. Putting a positive spin on the whole thing, it was a learning experience."

"Now who's being a glass-half-full person? And yet, it's kind of sad."

"Not anymore." He met her gaze, and his turned thoughtful. "But I can't help wondering—"

"About?"

"What happened?"

"We turned up the air-conditioning and snuggled together for the whole weekend. Both of us had to go back to work on Monday."

"No." He shook his head. "That's not what I was asking. When you asked if I was married, I said no, and the next question was whether or not there was a divorce."

"I remember." She tensed, knowing what was coming.

"When I said there had been a divorce, you wanted to know what broke us up." He took a breath. "When I asked if you were married, you answered in the past tense but never talked about a divorce. What happened to your husband, Justine?"

Chapter Eight

Cal forgot about the moon, stars, perfect night and romance. He was mesmerized by her body language. It went from lush and loose to tight and tense in a heartbeat. Part of him wished he could take back the question, but another part wanted to know everything about this woman. She was special and whatever she'd gone through had contributed to the person who sat to his right. She was close enough for him to feel the warmth of her skin and hear the slight increase in her breathing.

What she'd already told him was that a car accident had left her with a limp that mostly she was able to hide. But he had a bad feeling her husband was tragically connected to the accident.

Justine was quiet for a long moment, staring at her empty brandy snifter. He wanted to pull her into his arms so badly that it hurt, but all he could do was wait and hope she would share whatever was making her look like that.

In the end he couldn't stand the silence and gently nudged her to answer. "Justine? What is it?"

She looked up at him then. "My husband, Wes, died in a car accident along with our little girl, Betsy. It wasn't his fault and she wasn't even two yet."

Cal felt as if she'd just slugged him in the stomach with a two-by-four. He'd put the pieces together with her husband but didn't know she'd had a child. He thought of his niece, who was just a little older than Betsy was when she'd died, and what losing Leah would do to his sister, Ellie. Devastating didn't even describe it. He couldn't think of words adequate to express such a loss.

"My, God—I—" He'd been about to say how sorry he was, but that sounded so stupid.

"It's all right. You don't have to say anything."

"I do. But anything I can think of sounds trite and inconsequential."

"Don't worry about it, Cal."

What was wrong with this picture? Her comforting him? "No, just give me a minute. I'll come up with something besides 'I'm sorry.'"

"Believe it or not, that happened a lot. People want to make you feel better and that's the accepted phrasing, with slight variations." She smiled sadly. "It made me so furious at first, because no one could possibly be sorrier than me."

"It's a helpless feeling," he admitted, "not having something to say besides 'That really sucks.' Not a comfortable place to be."

"In hindsight I appreciated that friends and family were there for me. But at the time, the anger inside me was so big, so consuming. I was looking for someone to blame, a target for my rage. But there wasn't one."

"What about the other driver? The one who caused the accident?"

She set her glass on the table between them, then folded her hands in her lap. "He was an older man who'd had a medical episode—heart attack or stroke. He lost control at the wheel and plowed his big, heavy car into ours. The impact was on the driver's side and Betsy was strapped into her seat behind her daddy. So I could see her from the front passenger seat."

Cal swore he heard a break in her voice, but she looked composed. There was no sheen of tears in her eyes. This time he had to say something—even if it was clichéd and stupid. "You know, playing 'what if' or 'if only' will make you crazy, right?"

"You mean what if she'd been behind my seat? Or if only she wasn't in the car at all?" She met his gaze. "Yeah, I know. For a long time I lived in 'if only'-ville. While there I met my three BFFs—'what if,' 'you should have,' and 'why didn't you.'"

"Sounds like an inhospitable place," he commented.

"It is. I don't recommend visiting."

"Not high on my list."

"The problem was that I had a lot of time on my hands in the hospital."

"The accident. That's how you got the limp." Duh. She'd told him that very first day when she arrived on the island to work. It seemed more pronounced after her long flight, and in the days since, he'd noticed that when she was tired or needed to stretch it was the most obvious.

"What caused the limp?"

"My leg was shattered from the knee down." Her voice was calm and controlled, as if talking about a glass she'd dropped on the floor. "For a while, the doctors thought I might lose it. They fought for me because there was a time when I really didn't care one way or the other. I was damaged in places the doctors couldn't fix, parts of me hurt so much more than my leg."

"Survivor's guilt," he commented.

"Yes." Absently she brushed a hand over her thigh. "For the longest time I tried to understand. Why didn't

I die, too? What made me so special that my life was spared? Was I saved for some divine purpose?" Her expression was wry. "I didn't get any answers to those questions and it was very frustrating, I can tell you."

"I can't even imagine." Cal could see that she'd loved her family very much, and he had no frame of reference. Except… "The idea of suddenly losing my parents, my brothers or sister, my niece… It's unthinkable. How does a person get through that? How did you move from such a dark place?" To the strong, sassy, serene woman he knew now. And he had to ask, "What's your secret?"

"To what?" She met his gaze.

"You obviously pulled yourself out of the pit of hell. You're tough, smart, efficient and a really good assistant. Shanna is better, but that's because we've worked together for a number of years. Still, you're a close second. No matter how much no one wanted to work with me, the fact is that Human Resources wouldn't have sent someone incompetent." So he looked into her eyes and tried not to drown in the beauty, warmth and sadness. "How did you come back from the edge?"

"Yoga."

"There has to be more." He'd seen her stretching and breathing and she'd instructed him on the technique for relaxation. But it just couldn't be that easy.

She shrugged. "I was in the hospital a long time and had multiple surgeries to save my leg. When the docs gave me the green light for exercise, I had rehabilitation and physical therapy. That's where I found yoga's healing for mind, body and spirit. It changed my life."

And watching her yoga poses had changed his, Cal thought. Although that carnal reflection didn't make him proud. And for a moment he was afraid he'd actually said it out loud, but when the placid expression on her face didn't change, he figured he was in the clear.

"You are a remarkable woman, Justine Walker."

That was the truth and he hadn't meant it in an intimate way, just a statement of fact. But when the words were out of his mouth, they felt very personal. He felt personal. His gaze wandered to the pool and its lights under the crystal clear water. He remembered Justine swimming in the dark, staying in the water while talking to him, then pretending to hear his cell phone ring so she could get out and put on a cover-up. Clearly she didn't want him to see her from the waist down, and it dawned on him that her self-consciousness was also tied to the accident. It was why she always wore long pants and dresses that fell to the floor.

"Your leg is scarred, isn't it?"

"Yes," she said without hesitation. "Surgery is an invasive technique to fix the body, but you have to inflict trauma on the outside in order to repair what's wrong underneath. A catch-22 for doctors who have taken an oath to do no harm."

She looked at him for a moment, conflict raging in her eyes, then seemed to make a decision. Slowly she slid the hem of her dress to just above her knee. Thick, purplish-red marks marred the skin and crisscrossed her shin and calf.

"There were a lot of surgeries," she said simply.

He nodded. "I can't believe how much I whined about something as insignificant as a broken leg. I'm officially a candy ass."

She laughed. "If anyone knows how much a broken leg hurts, it's me."

"Still, the least I could have done is bite down on a stick and set it myself."

There was amusement in her eyes when she said, "Have I ever told you you're very dramatic?"

"Probably. But I'm cured now."

"Hardly. It's in your nature, I think." She let her skirt fall and cover the scarring that clearly made her ill at ease.

Cal had a nature, all right, but he wouldn't call it dramatic. Dishonorable, distasteful, detestable and sleazy would certainly describe his nature. The disfigurement she'd revealed to him was both deep and shocking, but the sight of it did not take the edge off his wanting her. And that was damned inconvenient.

It was tangible proof of the profound loss she'd experienced with the death of her husband and child. Continuing to want her was bad enough, but hitting on her in spite of it would make him the slimiest life form on the planet. He was a guy and couldn't help the attraction that wouldn't go away, but there were lines a decent man wouldn't cross. Cal considered himself a decent man, and this was one of those uncrossable lines.

"I just got this report faxed from the corporate office." Justine sat on the couch beside her boss. She was ready to take notes as he looked it over. It was the way he liked to work. "Ready when you are."

"I'll look it over later and make notations in the margin." He put the papers on the coffee table, topping a stack that would eventually end up on her desk to deal with.

"Good. Because lunch will be here soon. You must be starving."

"Not really."

That was odd since he'd picked at his food that morning. He was a big man with a healthy appetite and missing a meal was out of character for him. "Are you feeling all right?"

"Fine. I guess my physical restrictions have pared down my need to eat."

Justine had been here almost two weeks and in that time saw no evidence of that until the last couple of days. It was official. Cal was acting weird, and not just in his eating habits. He was avoiding her—some with the work stuff, but mostly everything else. No field trips to weave reeds into something functional—or not.

The only difference was that she'd told him about losing her family. Maybe that cured him of wanting to talk to her. Or seeing her hideous scars had turned him off. Or worse. He pitied her. And that just made her insane. But since the night they'd gone to the restaurant and were mistaken for honeymooners, he'd been distant.

Justine didn't like it. "You're sure you don't want to scan that report? I can respond if you have any questions or need clarifications."

"No, I'll get to it later. Why don't you work on email?" he suggested.

That would put her at the desk and far away from him. She could do that. Without a word she stood and moved across the room, then sat down in front of her laptop. There wasn't much to look at and nothing pressing. The way he'd acted, you'd have thought lasting world peace depended on her taking care of this.

In the process of trying to read his mind, she stole peeks at her boss and had been all morning. If she was being honest, she'd been doing that since the first day she came to work for him. Nine times out of ten she caught him looking back at her and the expression in his eyes made her pulse jump and her heart race. Not today. For all the notice he took of her, she could be a mixed green salad.

Mercifully there was a knock on the door, breaking the tension in the room.

"I'll get it." The words were automatic since she always took care of this.

Justine jumped up and hurried to let in the room service waiters. She'd gotten to know them pretty well and smiled at the two men. They were wearing their resort uniforms of dark slacks and beige cotton island-print shirts.

"Hi, William." She looked at the other man. "George, how is your little boy's cold? Is he feeling better?"

"Yes, ma'am." The dark-skinned, brown-eyed young man smiled. "He is getting into everything again."

"That's a good sign." She glanced at the other server. "William, did you patch things up with your girlfriend?"

"I took your advice, Miss Justine, and was honest with her about my feelings." His voice was heavily accented, like those of most of the staff who worked and lived on the island.

She walked with them to the dining table as they wheeled the cart over and set everything out. "And? How did it go?"

"She was very happy that I opened up and explained that talking about such things is not easy for me."

"A lot of men feel that way," she said sympathetically. "But we can't read your minds."

"So she told me. I asked for her patience and she was very understanding."

"I'm glad to hear that." At least she'd been useful to someone. She glanced over her shoulder at Cal, who was uncharacteristically engrossed in his laptop. "So, is the fish good today?"

George smiled. "It is perfection, Miss Justine."

"Great. You guys haven't steered me wrong yet." She

signed the room service check and the two waiters left with the wheeled cart. "Lunch is served."

Cal moved at the words, almost a flinch. Then his shoulders tensed. He stood and, without looking at her, said, "You go ahead. I'm not hungry."

"Really? You barely touched your breakfast." Then she wondered if he'd had a setback in his recovery. "Is your leg bothering you? Maybe we should call the doctor and—"

"I'm fine. Some air and sunshine are all I need."

"Then I'll help you get to the lounge. You can lean on me and—"

"No." The single word was almost as shocking as the loud crack of a bullet ricocheting around the room. He sighed, then turned toward her and said in a quiet, controlled voice, "I can make it by myself. You eat before the food gets cold."

And with that, he pivoted toward the exit and disappeared through the French doors. Justine crossed the room to watch and make sure he didn't fall. On the contrary, he made it easily, hopping on his good leg the two steps to where he stretched out in the shade of the palm trees. She could see only his legs, one muscular and tan, the other encased in white plaster.

Her feelings weren't hurt, exactly, that he hadn't insisted she keep him company. But she liked his wanting her around a lot better than shutting her out. And it wasn't so long ago that she'd tried very hard to avoid spending more time with her boss than was absolutely necessary.

Basket weaving and masquerading as honeymooners had certainly changed her attitude. This sudden cold shoulder was puzzling, to say the least.

"Be a jerk. See if I care," she said to herself. "You're not going to spoil my lunch."

She went back and plopped herself into one of the chairs at the dining table that suddenly seemed much too big. And a little bit lonely. A personality as big as Cal Hart's left a very large space to fill and Justine missed him. No one liked to eat alone but she'd been forced to get used to it. Until she took this job with Cal. This reaction was unexpected and, if she was being honest, a little disconcerting.

She lifted the silver dome from the plate and the perfect fish did look delicious, which was too bad. "Now I'm not hungry."

Her cell phone rang and she checked the display. She didn't recognize the number but answered anyway. Apparently it hadn't taken long for her to crave the sound of another human voice.

"Hello?"

"Miss Walker, this is Rudy from Island Tours. I'm double-checking your reservation for this afternoon, as you requested."

"Right." In case something work-related had unexpectedly come up, she wanted the company to be aware that a cancellation could happen. "Yes. We're still on." At least, she thought they were.

"Excellent. Then I'll see you and Mr. Hart at two o'clock."

"We'll be there." She crossed her fingers, hoping that wasn't a lie. It also meant she had to remind Cal. After basket weaving she ran all activities past him. No more surprises. He'd seemed enthusiastic about touring the island, but that was before.

Justine left the table and went outside. She walked past the patio table and pristine pool, then stopped to slip off her shoes before stepping into the sand. Uninvited and without a direct order, she sat in the lounge beside Cal's.

"It's good to see you relaxing." If this time-out in the sun had worked its magic and his normal attitude was restored, he would respond with something like *Do I look relaxed?* or *Relaxation is for sissies.*

"Yup. I am so calm."

Justine had seen tranquil and stress-free, and this wasn't it. He looked tense, tight and ready to snap any second. But she would play his little game. "Great. And there's more where this came from. We have a tour of the island this afternoon. An open-air jeep and knowledgeable driver will show us the high points and explain the history of this ocean paradise."

"Yeah, about that—"

"We discussed this and it's on your schedule," she reminded him.

His mouth pulled tight. "Something came up. I had to reschedule the conference call for this afternoon."

"I thought that was all arranged for tomorrow."

"The timing is delicate. It's about arranging financing for a project and everyone's available today."

As far as she'd known, everyone was on board for tomorrow, but she was nothing if not flexible. Even though she'd been looking forward to an afternoon drive along the ocean. But it would keep for another day.

"Okay," she said. "I'll call the tour company back and cancel."

"That's not necessary. You go."

By herself? "There's work. I'll need to be here to take notes during the call."

"I'll manage."

Was it her imagination or did he seem awfully eager to get rid of her?

"Take the afternoon off."

"Why?"

"Why what?" he asked.

"Why do you want me to take the afternoon off?"

"So you can go on the tour," he said. "It seems like canceling now is kind of abrupt."

"This is out of character for a man who thinks a fourteen-hour day is normal." She met his gaze. "And I made the reservation with the stipulation that there could be a sudden cancellation. Just in case something work-related came up. And it did."

"I'll be fine. You should go."

She studied the too eager, too sincere expression he was using to sell this idea. "Correct me if I'm wrong, but for the last conference call you insisted I be present, even though there was overtime involved." It was the only time since her first night, and it had been important.

"And I shouldn't have. So take this afternoon off. It's my way of making things up to you."

"What's really going on, Cal?"

He didn't answer right away, obviously thinking carefully about his response. "This is hard for me to admit, but it bothered me when you said no one wanted to work with me. I'm making a determined effort to change. So, take the time. I'm rehabilitating my image and I'd appreciate it if you'd help me out here, then spread the word back at the office about your excellent afternoon off."

Justine didn't buy this phony-baloney for a second. She'd scheduled the conference call with all parties involved and there was no conflict. The fact that Cal had been vague about details was a big clue that he was grasping at straws to get her out of here. And, presumably, to get out of spending the afternoon with her. If that's the way he wanted it…

"Okay." She stood. "It's a beautiful day for a drive. A real shame you have to miss it."

"Enjoy."

"I absolutely will," she said firmly.

And she wouldn't think about him.

Without another word she walked back to the villa. Her vow to put him out of her mind lasted less than a minute. The acute disappointment coursing through her meant something. Something big.

She was falling for Cal Hart. She refused to think the word *love*, but she was falling pretty deeply in like with the man. And wasn't that just her luck. She was finally ready to dip a toe back into the pool of life, only to be rejected by the man who had made her want to do it in the first place.

She had two more weeks with him and it was going to be hard. Trying to act as if she didn't notice his distant manner toward her that was in direct contrast to his attitude in the beginning was going to take everything she had.

Grit. That's what she needed. Fortunately she had a lot, earned the hard way. She'd never expected to use it on a man.

Chapter Nine

Vacation sucked.

Cal had experienced more stress since Justine Walker showed up than he had in four years of not taking time off. The guided tour of the island must have been good because she hadn't shown up for dinner, and he'd been surprised when it arrived since he hadn't thought to deal with food. Turned out her efficiency had no bounds, she'd ordered room service for one and everything was his favorite.

He wanted to be mad at her for abandoning him, but he'd given her the afternoon off and all but ordered her to take it. Selfishly it was to get a break from resisting the yearning to carry her to his bed and explore every inch of her bare skin. Although the carrying was a tad ambitious considering he was still on crutches, but when she was in the room some version of that fantasy never failed to roll through his mind.

Movement on the patio caught his attention, and he left the chair in his room where he was reading reports to hobble over to the open door. Justine stood there, straight and strong, the sole of one bare foot balanced against the other leg. She was wearing stretchy black pants that

fit her like a second skin and a snug racerback top that
sweetly outlined her breasts. She faced away from him
and didn't know he was watching each successive gracefully executed pose.

Cal knew he was going to hell for not turning away
but…there really was no excuse except that he couldn't
not look at her. The sight of her was better than a sunset
to fill up his soul. That's when he realized the fantasy of
carrying her off didn't just happen when they were in the
same room. He'd been alone all afternoon and thoughts
of her wouldn't go away. Worse, he'd missed her.

She was a lethal combination of smart, beautiful, sexy
and serene. The need to touch her bordered on painful.
But seeing her scarred leg had hit him like a bucket of
ice water. Life had kicked her in the teeth and he was her
boss. Doing what his body was urging him to do would
be wrong for those two reasons alone, and he could think
of a dozen more. He would not compromise her.

Finally, she finished and rolled up her yoga mat before heading inside. Cal needed fresh air and a drink, not
necessarily in that order. Somehow he managed to pour
a Scotch and get outside without spilling it. He had just
settled in one of the chairs and taken a sip of his drink
when Justine came back outside.

"Cal? Your cell rang and I answered." Looking apologetic, she walked over and held out the device. "It's your
mother."

He barely held in a groan and hesitated as if she was
giving him a snake that would take a painful bite. No
guts, no glory, he thought before taking the device. "Hi,
Mom."

"Hello, Cal. How are you?"

"Good." If *good* was defined by lusting after his executive assistant. "How are you? Everything okay?"

"Excellent."

"Is Dad all right?"

"Fine. And so are your brothers and sister and your niece. And now that the pleasantries are out of the way, I have to ask about the young woman who answered your phone."

"That's Justine, my—" He'd almost said *employee* but remembered just in time about the bet. He wasn't supposed to be working. If Katherine Hart found out he was, that sweet classic car would never be his. Worse, the family would never let him live this down.

"Your what, dear?"

"Friend. We met here at the resort." That was true.

"She sounded so professional." There was a note of suspicion in his mother's voice.

"She works as an executive assistant and that requires phone skills, so it's probably just her habit to be that way when she's on the phone."

"Even on vacation?"

"I know, right?" Cal neither confirmed nor denied.

"She has a lovely phone voice," Katherine observed.

Everything about her was lovely, but he wasn't telling his mom that. Especially since Justine's door was open and she could overhear. Cal knew this was Katherine's way of trying to get information out of him. He figured it was a mom thing but that didn't make it any less irritating.

"Justine has many fine qualities," he finally said in an attempt to pacify her.

"How did you two meet?"

It was like this woman could read his mind and knew he was lying, if not outright then in spirit. How was he going to respond without an actual falsehood?

"Believe it or not, Mom, I opened the door to the villa

where I'm staying and there she was. Turns out that some-one at registration sent her here."

"It's a sign," said his mother, the romantic, the match-maker, the woman who believed that love truly did con-quer all. It was probable that she also believed unicorns were real. "Maybe you two are meant to be."

Not likely. The attraction was probably him being pun-ished for some horrible crime against karma. "She's a very special woman," he said sincerely.

"I'm so glad you met someone to spend time with on your vacation. What have you been up to?"

"Well, I went skydiving." That was before Justine and seemed like a lifetime ago.

There was a groan from the other end of the line. "I can't believe you jumped out of a perfectly good airplane on purpose."

Hmm. Justine had said something similar. Although she'd called him a sanity-challenged, adrenaline junkie thrill seeker. "Believe it."

"Obviously you lived to tell about it," she said wryly. "But that is not my idea of a good time."

As it turned out, she was right. A broken leg wasn't much fun. But he wasn't going to mention that part. Not only had it resulted in him violating the spirit of the wager with his brother, the information would worry his mother needlessly.

"It was actually exhilarating." Until the hard landing.

"Please tell me that Justine's interests run to safer, less adventurous activities."

Justine had actually called his pursuits life-threatening but that was irrelevant to this conversation. "She has sched-uled things to do that don't require one's feet to leave the ground."

"I'm liking her more and more," Katherine said enthusiastically. "Tell me all about it."

This wasn't new for her. Some of his earliest memories involved this woman encouraging him to talk about things. But for some reason, this time bugged him more than it usually did. This was more of an inquisition. He imagined a hostile witness felt this way when an attorney was trying to trip him up and reveal more than intended.

"Are you spying on me for Sam?"

"No." There was a long pause. "Yes. Well, spying, maybe, but Sam didn't put me up to it. I'm concerned and want to know that you're relaxing, recharging your batteries."

He wasn't, but that was his own fault. "I'm fine, Mom."

"If you say so." There was a moment of silence before she said, "So tell me what you've been up to."

"Well…Justine convinced me to sit on the beach with a book."

"No," she said, sounding shocked. "You actually sat still long enough to read?"

Not exactly. He'd actually made her sit still long enough to talk. "It was a beautiful day. Sun, sand, sea."

"That sounds lovely. What else?"

"Justine signed me up for a basket weaving class."

"I did that to your father when we were there." Katherine's laugh was full of delight. "I'm pretty sure he's never forgiven me. His finished product looked like a funky coaster."

"I feel his pain." Cal shook his head ruefully but the revelation made him smile. And the memory of that afternoon washed over him, warm and bittersweet. "Justine tried to put an optimistic spin on it—the beginning of an area rug. A place mat for a very small plate."

"She sounds charming."

And so much more, he thought. She had a way of getting him to do things he didn't want to, then wonder why he ever thought it would be so bad. Or maybe just doing them with her made all the difference in the world. He wasn't willing to find out which.

"She's very pleasant company," he finally said.

"Oh, Cal—" Katherine sounded disappointed in him. "You're still doing it."

"What?"

"Keeping women at a distance."

Just this one, he thought. When he looked at his marriage, he could trace the reason for failure back to his decision to move forward with the woman who'd loved his brother first. He was in that place now with Justine, at a crossroads. The path that brought them together was riddled with land mines and the one that they traveled separately kept everyone safe. That's the one he planned to take, for her sake. And maybe a little for his.

"Let it go, Mom. I'm on vacation."

"You're right. And it sounds like you're having a wonderful time. I'm so glad."

"So you're going to stop worrying about me?"

"Fat chance." She laughed. "I'll just keep it to myself."

"Fat chance," he said back. But he wouldn't have it any other way.

Cal chatted with her a couple more minutes before ending the call. He set the phone on the table and finished his Scotch, thinking about how his assistant had been a big part of the conversation. He wasn't sure what that meant.

And speaking of her, she poked her head out the door and asked, "Is everything okay?"

No, he wanted to say. He'd missed her today and dinner was lonely. None of that came out of his mouth. "You are in so much trouble."

She moved outside and sat in the chair beside his. "I wasn't sure whether or not to answer. The caller ID came up as private and I didn't know who it was. I thought it might be important, so—"

"My mom wanted to know all about the professional-sounding woman who answered my phone."

"Oh, Cal—" She looked upset. "I hope I didn't ruin anything for you."

"The wager is secure." He stretched his bad leg out in front of him. "And I really need to thank you."

"Why?"

"If you hadn't bullied me into leisure activities I would have had to lie outright instead of tweaking the truth. So I'm grateful to you." But much less thankful for how hot she looked in the yoga clothes she still wore.

"I'm glad. So in addition to relaxing you, the excursion gave you cover." She met his gaze. "You missed a good one today. The island is beautiful. The guide took me up to the highest point and you could see everything. It was absolutely spectacular."

And you're an idiot, he filled in silently. That was probably true and wouldn't be the first time. The real question was how he moved forward. He had two options. Send her back to Blackwater Lake and soldier on alone or tough it out for the next two weeks.

Both had a downside. He'd undertaken projects that were time-sensitive, and bringing in another assistant—assuming anyone would accept the job—would be challenging. It would be time-consuming to get them up to speed. And the fewer people who knew he was violating the spirit of the wager, the better.

If he changed nothing, he would have to continue to keep Justine at a distance, and every day his willpower was tested in new and different ways.

But with two weeks left until he won the bet, the smart move was to put on his big boy pants and stay the course. Even if it killed him.

Vacation really sucked.

Two days after the phone call, Justine was done feeling guilty about answering Cal's cell and forcing him to explain her to his mother. Ever since then he'd been crabby and monosyllabic. If he'd been that way when she first arrived to work for him, it would be easier to deal with now, but that wasn't the case. In the beginning he'd treated her to his charm and sense of humor. The boss he'd turned into since seeing her scarred leg was like Mr. Hyde to Dr. Jekyll. She'd nearly used up all of her grit trying to pretend things were normal, but maybe she could manage to dredge up just a little more.

"I think this chicken might just be the best I ever had." She was sitting at the villa's dining table to Cal's right.

"It's like shoe leather."

"Maybe it's just the piece you got," she said, putting as much cheer as possible into her voice. "I'll switch with you."

"No. It will do." Without looking at her he took another bite.

She, on the other hand, had to bite her tongue to keep from calling him a martyr. "I was thinking about ordering dessert tonight. George was telling me about a cobbler the chef does with fruit grown here on the island. In fact, I saw the fields on the tour the other day."

His scowl turned a little darker at the mention of her solo excursion. "No dessert for me. With this damn cast on I can't work out."

"You told me the cast is coming off in a week. How much weight can you really put on?"

"Easy for you to say, being in such good shape." He looked at her then and his gaze dropped lower to the region of her chest. That didn't make him happy because it appeared he gritted his teeth before saying, "Order it for yourself if you'd like."

"I wouldn't eat it in front of you."

"Then I'll leave. Maybe go out on the patio to count my breaths and fill up my soul with sunset. There are no calories in that. No harm, no foul."

That did it. Justine put her fork down. "Cal, what's going on with you?"

"I have no idea what you're talking about."

Even though he looked her in the eye, she knew he was lying, that he was painfully aware of the situation. There was a subtle note in his voice. It had been there when he was on the phone with his mother and playing fast and loose with the truth. Part of her wondered when she'd gotten to know him so well, and the other part wished he was a complete stranger and easy to ignore. But the truth was, she liked him. A lot. Not this petulant, self-centered man as much, but she knew another side to him. One that was generous, kind and understanding. What had happened to send that man into hiding?

"I am many things," she said, "but a stupid fool isn't one of them. You've disappeared into your man cave."

"On the contrary, I'm sitting right here. And I have always been visible."

"The cave thing was a metaphor and you know it. You've been different for the last couple of days."

"I disagree. Maybe you're the one who's different."

That was probably true, but not the way he meant it. She had changed since meeting him. For the first time since losing everything, she was ready—no, eager—to live again. The difference in her attitude was Cal.

"No. I'm right about this," she insisted. "You haven't badgered me into keeping you company on the beach. Or tried to talk me into going to dinner. I have no illusions about another basket weaving class, but you didn't look this peeved when I was sure you were going to fire me. Even that would be better than pacing around mumbling that vacation sucks."

"You heard that?"

"Yes. The richness of life is about the effort you put into living it. If anyone knows that, it's me."

"Next you'll be preaching that when life gives you lemons make lemonade." He tapped his lip. "Or the ever-popular 'It's always darkest before the dawn.'"

"I was trying to avoid clichés." She could tell he was fighting a smile. At least that was a somewhat positive reaction, but why did he feel the need to suppress his amusement? Could be because sharing humor was a form of intimacy and that's what he was resisting. "What are you thinking?"

"That answering your question crosses a boss/employee line."

"Kind of late to draw that distinction now, don't you think?" They'd already shared a lot of personal details about their lives.

He pushed his plate away, the food barely touched. "It's a distinction that should have been drawn in the beginning. My bad."

"So you expect me to forget all that?" Disregard the way he looked at her with a hungry intensity that took her breath away?

"Pretend it never happened."

That was impossible. "That would be like trying to put glitter back in a bottle."

"Try." His voice had an edge and there was an expression in his eyes that hovered somewhere between anger and frustration. And warning.

"This doesn't make sense. Did I do something? You never had a problem before telling me if you were irritated by whatever I did. The second day I was here you were deeply annoyed because I refused to work overtime. Since when did you start holding back?"

He opened his mouth to say something, then shook his head and stood. "I'm going to sit outside on the patio and silently count my breaths. If my soul gets a refill in the process, well, that's okay, too. For sure it will be quiet."

"I think you just told me to mind my own business."

"However you interpret that is your call." Almost as an afterthought he grabbed the crutches, only to keep weight off the injured leg for the prescribed length of time, she guessed. His balance was excellent and he probably didn't need them now, so close to the cast coming off. He went to the French doors, then moved through the opening to sit beside the pool.

Left alone, Justine was angry and hurt. She stood and started pacing. There were so many thoughts and feelings swirling inside her that she couldn't sit still. And there was an *aha* moment while she was at it. When she was in such a dark place after the accident, well-meaning family and friends told her to keep putting one foot in front of the other. Live life to the fullest. She could be happy again and going through the motions would put her back on the road to normal.

All she heard was *blah, blah, blah*. Platitudes she disregarded. How frustrating it must have been for the people who cared about her and were only trying to help. Right now, this moment, she knew how it felt to try to get through to someone who refused to listen. It was damned annoying and she made a mental note to apologize to friends and family for her behavior.

And speaking of advice, she remembered giving the room service waiter relationship advice, telling him to be honest and open about his feelings. If Justine did less than that, she'd be a do-as-I-say, not-as-I-do kind of person. Your basic hypocrite.

She stopped walking and looked out the French doors to the patio bathed in twilight. Perimeter lights showed Cal sitting with his back to her, broad shoulders tensed as he presumably counted his breaths. If she told him exactly what she was thinking he might just fire her for real. The second day of work, when she defied his order, she'd ignored his irritation and was still here, but if she was honest now and he went with the nuclear option, she might very well be packing her bags. Still, saying nothing would drain her soul to the point it might never be filled up again.

Before she could change her mind, she marched outside and stopped beside his chair. "I have something very important to say to you."

"Damn it."

"What?" The knot in her stomach expanded painfully.

"I lost count of my breaths."

Under different circumstances that would have made her laugh. "I have to say what's on my mind or my head just might explode."

"Okay, then, but—"

"No *buts*. There's something going on between us. And don't tell me it's business because I know better. It's personal and—"

"Could it be you're imagining things?" Might be wishful thinking, but that sounded like desperation in his voice. He was trying to dodge the issue.

"Look, Cal, I'll be the first to admit that I'm out of practice with this sort of thing." She thought about that for a moment. "I guess, technically, I was never in practice since I got married pretty young, but..." She took a big breath and pushed on. Couldn't stop now. "I think you're attracted to me."

"And why do you think that?" The words were meant to mock, but there was a ragged edge that stripped away the sarcasm. It almost sounded as if he was running out of places to hide.

"I haven't forgotten how a man looks at a woman when he wants her. And I'm almost positive you've been looking at me that way."

"Justine, it would be best if you stop—"

"No. This has to be said. I've *seen* you look at me that way, until you wouldn't look at me at all. But you're my boss, and a good one in spite of what the clerical staff thinks." She was trying to cut the tension with humor, but judging by his strained expression, it wasn't working. *In for a penny, in for a pound*, she thought. "I know you walk a fine line and might think it's inappropriate to cross it. That would be the case if I didn't want you to cross it, too."

"Justine, please—"

She barreled on before the warning in the way he said her name could take hold. "But then I realized that you changed after I told you about what happened to my family. If you're worried about offending me because of that, don't be. It took a while, but I've realized something and you should know this."

"What's that?" He was looking down, then met her gaze.

"They'll always be in my heart, but they're gone and never coming back. No matter how much I wish I could change it. But I know they would want me to move forward and be happy." She sighed. "If the situation was reversed, that's what I would want."

He hadn't fired her yet. But then, he hadn't exactly commented, either. Trying to stop her didn't count. Suddenly her legs felt as if they wouldn't hold her up, so she sat on the chair beside him.

"You told me once that you didn't do things that you're not good at. Rumor has it that you've had sex with a lot of women, so one could assume that you're good at it." She twisted her fingers together nervously, then linked her hands, settled them in her lap and stared there instead of at him. "Here's the thing, Cal. I'm pretty sure I've been looking at you the same way you've been looking at me."

"Justine," he nearly groaned, and that couldn't be a good thing.

"In case that wasn't clear enough—I want you, Cal. That's a very big line to cross, but I'd be willing to bet you've been crabby because you feel the same way but you're afraid of hurting me somehow. Either because of my past or the fact that I work for you." She looked at him then. The jerk of a muscle in his jaw hinted at a conflict raging inside him. "I really wish you would say something. Preferably not about firing me."

He met her gaze, and the darkness in his was a little frightening. "Please go back inside, Justine."

"But—"

"Please. Now," he begged.

She heard, *Pack your bags and go.* Something broke inside her and she couldn't stop the words. "Why don't you want me?"

Chapter Ten

Justine was horrified and humiliated by what she'd said. She had to get away. Now. "I'm sorry. That was—"

A sob choked off her words and she stood, blindly turning away with tears stinging her eyes. Then she felt Cal's big hand curve around hers before he gently tugged her into his lap.

"Justine—what am I going to do with you?"

She blinked furiously, trying not to cry and make this worse than it already was. "You could start by not pitying me."

"Is that what you think?"

"Among other things." Their faces were inches apart but she couldn't look at him. She wouldn't be able to stand it if she broke down. That would take this horrifying, humiliating scene to a whole new level of awful.

Cal cupped her face in his hands and forced her to meet his gaze before tenderly touching his mouth to hers. His lips were soft and warm, gentle and sweet. It both shocked and charmed her. If this moment never ended that would be all right with her. As soon as that thought flashed through her mind, he stopped kissing her, but instead of pulling away, he rested his forehead against hers.

"I don't pity you. In fact, I'm a little annoyed that you didn't recognize me being noble."

"What I got was you being a gigantic jerk." She stared at him and decided it didn't really matter what she said. After this she was probably getting booted out of here anyway. "You were distant and kind of jackass-y."

Amazingly, he grinned. "Don't hold back. Tell me how you really feel."

His smile seeped inside and warmed her in places that had begun to freeze and shrivel. "I feel as if Cal Hart disappeared right after I showed off the scars on my leg and told you about losing my family. There was no explanation from you. Just radio silence."

"Jackass-y?" he asked.

"Exactly. Obviously you were repulsed by how my leg looks. How is that noble?"

"You've got it all wrong." He slid both arms around her waist and snuggled her a little closer. "I think you're beautiful—inside and out. And I wanted you. When you showed me the scars and told me how you got them, I still wanted you. That was a problem. Because seeing the signs of trauma to your leg made what happened to you real for me. It seemed wrong to make a move, and I didn't want you to feel awkward what with working together or anything else."

"So you disappeared?"

"I was protecting you," he protested.

"From yourself," she clarified.

"Yes. If I hadn't pulled back, there's no way I could resist touching you, and that would make it impossible not to have you." Sincerity and longing darkened his eyes.

"You wanted me?" She couldn't quite believe what she was hearing even though she'd suspected. Now she was almost afraid to believe it was true.

He kissed her and whispered against her lips, "I've wanted you from the moment I first saw you."

"That's hard to believe. I've read about your dalliances. Every last woman was beautiful and perfect."

"No one is perfect," he said.

"The women you dated came pretty close."

He studied her. "Sounds like you're having second thoughts."

"Not really. I'm just giving you an exit plan."

"What if I don't want one?" He took her hand and lifted it to his lips. "In case you're still not convinced, I'll make this as clear as I know how. I want you more than I've wanted any woman. Ever."

"Oh, Cal—" She could hardly breathe. It felt as if he'd just plucked the brightest star from the sky and handed it to her. Shyly, she met his gaze. "There was a time when I didn't believe I'd ever be happy again. Even for a moment. But I am right now."

"Good."

"But—" She hesitated, then figured she might as well get it all out there. "I'll be honest. I haven't done this for a long time. There's been no one since my husband. I'm a little nervous."

"If it makes you feel any better, now I'm nervous."

"I'm not worried. You don't do anything you're not good at." He'd said that about marriage, but she was pretty sure he'd made no such vow about sex. "I hope I'm not a disappointment."

"You never could be. And, just so you know, this is my first time with a cast on my leg. There will be logistics."

The heat of his gaze warmed her skin and started tingles dancing inside her. "I think I can handle logistics."

"That's my girl."

Cal kissed her with a little more intensity. More focus.

As if now that they'd made their intentions and expectations clear, he was making his move. Finally. He kissed her mouth, her nose and cheek, then nuzzled her hair aside and went to work on her neck. She was pretty happy about that when she shuddered in the most delicious way, just before he caught her earlobe between his teeth.

She gasped with pleasure. "Oh, boy—"

"You like that?" he whispered.

"That is a big two thumbs-up."

So he did it again, then blew softly on the moistness he left behind. The sensation drove her crazy and made her shiver. His hand at her waist, he moved his thumb and brushed it back and forth on the underside of her breast. Even through the material of her dress and bra, the touch had excitement blasting to every part of her body.

He was kissing her neck and smiled against her skin. "I feel your pulse racing."

"It definitely is."

She felt him touch her back. Then the zipper on her dress slowly lowered. When it was at her waist, she shrugged her arms out of the bodice and let it pool in her lap. A balmy, light breeze caressed her naked shoulders as Cal cupped her almost bare breast. Rubbing his thumb lightly across the peak made it tighten in response. With a desperation that was heady and new, she wanted to feel his hand on her bare skin. Then a cloud drifted over the nearly full moon, throwing them into shadow for a moment.

It was enough to remind her they were outside, not so far from the sand, where anyone might walk by. "How private is the beach?"

"Very private." He met her gaze, his eyes searching hers. "But you're uncomfortable."

"Yes."

"Can't have that. Stand up," he ordered.

She did, and he reached out to slide her dress down to a puddle of material at her feet, leaving her in just her bra and panties. "I can't believe you just did that. What if someone walks by?"

"First, that was logistics in action. Second, no one will see us. But if they did, you could be wearing a bikini." His eyes grew hot as he stared at her. "I lost track of how many times I thought about you swimming out here and wondering how you looked in a bathing suit."

"In case there's any question, I'm not a *Sports Illustrated* swimsuit model. That's got to be a disappointment—"

"Oh, sweetheart—believe me, I'm the exact opposite of disappointed."

The words and husky, heartfelt tone made her heart soar. She stepped out of the dress and picked it up. "Your room or mine?"

He retrieved his crutches from the ground beside the chair and stood. "Surprise me."

"Logistics will be easier in yours, since you're used to it."

"The condoms are there, too."

Justine felt her cheeks flush with embarrassment. "I forgot about that."

"I didn't." He pointed with a crutch to the French doors opening to his suite in the villa. "Ladies first."

Her heart was beating so fast she could hardly catch her breath. "Okay. I'll turn down the bed."

"And I'll enjoy the view."

There was a sexy male satisfaction in his voice that somehow nudged her confidence further into positive territory. As she moved in front of him, she barely gave a thought to the limp she normally struggled to hide.

He'd seen her flaws—the uneven gait, the disfiguring scars—and wanted her in spite of that. It was a precious gift. Walking in front of him, she smiled.

The room was dark, so she flipped a switch just inside the door and a standing lamp in the corner bathed everything in soft light. Even though her confidence was up, dim lighting was definitely her friend. The layout was a mirror image of her suite—king-size bed, matching nightstands on either side, dresser and armoire. She hurried to fold the thick comforter down along with the blanket and sheet.

Cal moved to her where she stood by the bed. He rested his crutches on the bench at the foot, then sat down on the mattress.

"Come here," he said, his voice deep and edgy.

"Okay."

When she did, he took her hand and pulled her between his legs, then reached behind her back and unhooked her bra. He peeled it off, and before her modesty to cover herself kicked in, he cupped her breasts in his hands. Modesty was highly overrated, she thought, given how good the touch felt.

"Beautiful," he breathed. "And that doesn't do you justice."

She couldn't have responded even if she wanted to, what with the erotic things he was doing to her. He brushed his thumbs over her nipples, then took one into his mouth. Electricity crackled through her and settled low in her belly. She moaned and her breaths came in little gasps. Feeling light-headed, she put her hands on his broad shoulders to steady herself. But the width was a solid reminder of how powerful his body was, so at odds with the gentle way he stroked her.

He lavished attention on her other breast until she was

quivering with need. And then he dropped his hands lower, fingers toying with the waistband of her panties. She held her breath as he hooked his thumbs and drew them down, over her thighs, knees and ankles. He curved his fingers at her hips and urged her closer, then kissed the underside of each breast, her midriff and belly, slowly moving lower.

She didn't think she could take much more and was about to tell him so when he grabbed her playfully and pulled her down onto the bed beside him.

"I've got you now," he said, laughing.

"Right where I want me." She dragged her index finger over the T-shirt covering his chest, then frowned. "You still have all your clothes on."

"So I do."

He took care of that faster than she would have expected, what with the bum leg and all. He also retrieved a condom from the nightstand drawer and put it on. Then he lay back and pulled her on top of him.

"This is logistics," he said and shrugged.

Justine smiled, and it felt extraordinarily tender. He was so adorable she thought her heart might explode. "I'll show you logistics."

She straddled him, then slowly lowered her hips, positioning herself over his thickness. Slowly she took him inside her and sighed with satisfaction at the joining of their bodies. It had been so very long and she hadn't realized how much she'd missed this intimacy. The gratification of being held by a man and making love with him.

She stayed still for several moments, letting their bodies grow accustomed. Then Cal slid his hand up the inside of her leg and brushed his thumb over the bundle of nerve endings at the juncture of her thighs, the most sensitive of places. The touch was like lightning and she gasped at the sizzle of sensation that made her toes curl. He arched into her and lifted her hips up and down, slowly at first, then faster. Before she was ready, pleasure built to the breaking point and exploded through her.

When she collapsed on his chest, he held her as the delightful tremors rocked her world. When she pulled herself together, she started to move again. For him. In moments he went still and groaned, hands reaching for her, pulling her to him while he found his release. The sound of their panting breaths filled the room as they held each other.

Justine had no idea how long they lay there, arms around each other, moonlight spilling inside, the distant sound of waves lapping against the shore. She just knew this couldn't be more perfect.

Playfully she dragged a finger over the dusting of hair on his chest. "I'm glad you didn't fire me tonight."

He rubbed a strand of her hair between his fingers. "Never crossed my mind."

"I thought it might happen."

"Then why did you push the issue?" he asked.

"Because you were acting weird. Walking around like you wanted to put your fist through the wall and mumbling about how much vacation sucked."

He grinned and settled his palms on her thighs, still straddling him. "All things considered, it doesn't suck anymore."

"That's a relief."

"However, I am starving."

She nodded. "Because you were pouting earlier, just before you threw a tantrum and walked out before eating dinner."

"I'm not comfortable with the pouting and tantrum parts of that, but the rest is essentially true." Without warning, he tumbled her to the bed and leaned over to kiss her, and they were a little breathless when he pulled back. "That was for making fun of me."

"Ooh, I'll have to think of more insults."

"I'll help. But first I think we should call room service."

"Excellent idea," she said.

Technically she was working and not on vacation, but her situation definitely didn't suck. It felt balanced. And as close to heaven as one could get on earth. Paradise, indeed.

Cal felt movement in the bed beside him and opened one eye. Sunshine streamed into the room and Justine was curled up next to him. Memories of making love to her flashed through his mind and he smiled. He was pretty sure the look on his face would give sunshine a run for its money in the brightness department.

Not wanting to wake her, he stayed very still and simply looked at her—the full mouth, delicate nose splashed with freckles, strands of beautiful red hair tickling his chest. A feeling of satisfaction and contentment stole over him, a sensation he'd never experienced before. Maybe it was because he'd been so sure he would never have her and something about that felt so wrong. And yet, after carbo-loading on a late dinner last night, he'd had her several more times—each more mind-blowing than the last.

He'd always thought it a romantic cliché that you could never get enough of another person, but that thought crossed his mind now as he stared at her. Silly. This was an interlude, nothing more.

"Are you going to ogle me all morning? Or are you going to order room service?" Her voice was raspy from sleep and incredibly sexy. She opened one eye. "I'm starving."

"For me?"

"Someone's ego got a shot of adrenaline last night." She smiled tenderly and moved closer, touching her lips to his collarbone. After that she gave him a mysterious look. "I'm starving for many things. You might make the list. If you buy me food."

"Breakfast in bed with a beautiful woman. Vacation is getting better and better."

After she gave him the extension for room service, he picked up the phone on the nightstand, then called and ordered. Since they'd shared meals for the last couple of weeks, he knew her favorites and ordered all of them.

He hung up the phone, then reached for her. "Your wish is fulfilled, my lady."

She sat up suddenly, then remembered she was naked and pulled the sheet up to cover her breasts. The gesture was adorable, if unnecessary, since he'd seen and kissed every part of her all night long.

"Cal, there's a problem."

He met her troubled gaze. "Not from where I'm sitting."

"Be serious. I have to let the waiters in. That's what I always do."

"George and William can handle it," he assured her.

"But we don't have clothes on. We can't just let them in here—" She waved a hand to indicate the large bedroom. "They'll know what happened."

"They probably already suspect."

"No, they don't." There was feminine denial in her tone. Also adorable. "Why would they?"

"They're guys. Men know the way another man looks at a woman he wants."

"And you looked at me like that?" Her face took on a pleased expression.

"Yes." He tugged on the sheet, pulling it away. "They noticed."

"But unless they come in here, there's no way for them to confirm. I'm getting dressed to answer the door."

He liked looking at her just the way she was. "Is there any way to talk you out of that?"

She thought for a moment. "I could answer the door without getting dressed."

"That's a big negative." He sighed. "All right. If you must. No one can say I'm not self-sacrificing."

"A prince of a guy." She rolled out of bed, grabbed his shirt off the floor and slipped it on. "I'll be back."

"Promise?"

"Yes." She smiled at him, then was gone.

And the sun seemed not as bright. Wow, that was sappy. But true.

And then other thoughts crept in. Such as—maybe Justine wasn't comfortable having breakfast in bed. It might be too soon for that. As her boss, he'd crossed a line and couldn't go back even if he wanted to. But he wouldn't do anything to make her ill at ease, either. She was putting on clothes, so he would, too. After a quick shower.

About thirty minutes later she wheeled a fully loaded food cart into his suite, where he was dressed and scrolling through messages on his cell phone.

She stood beside the bed with a hand on her hip, looking pretty and casual in a long flowered dress and sandals. "Seriously, omelets? Crepes? Eggs over easy, medium, hard and scrambled? Bacon, sausage *and* ham? Eggs Benedict?"

"You were right here when I called."

"I know—" She sighed. "Apparently I'm a visual person and seeing the volume is—wow."

"And you're responsible for eating half of this," he said seriously.

"You are incorrigible."

"That's what the principal always said when I got sent to the office." He patted the bed beside him. "I just didn't want to miss any of your favorites. And there are so many."

"Someone is feeling his oats this morning." She set out plates on the quilt he'd pulled up. "There should be something on the menu for an occasion like this."

"Breakfast for honeymooners?"

"That's not what we are. I was thinking more a tryst tasting. A sampling of different items instead of the full order to be enjoyed the morning after the night before."

"An excellent marketing idea. We should suggest it to someone."

When the food was all set out, she climbed into the bed beside him. "Without telling that someone how the idea happened."

"Why? It's not an illicit affair. Neither of us is married—" He kicked himself when her smile slipped a little. "I'm sorry. I didn't mean to bring up…anything." He shrugged, not quite sure what to say.

"You didn't. Like I said last night, I've reconciled my past and I'm moving on." She looked at the array of food that filled nearly every square inch of the king-size bed, leaving only enough room for them to sit. "Let's eat before it gets cold."

"Excellent idea."

They each picked up a dish and sampled it, then fed bites to each other. This was their method of working through the array of entrées, fruit and side dishes of potatoes. When neither of them could eat another bite, they leaned back against the pillows and groaned.

"That was too good, but I'm stuffed," Justine said.

"The idea of a sampler is very appealing right about now. Or—" he glanced sideways at her "—someone could have used some self-control with the menu."

"Don't look at me, hotshot. That was all you." She pointed at him. "And it was very sweet of you."

"Glad you think so. Tomorrow morning we'll approach breakfast after the night before a little differently."

A lovely shade of pink colored her cheeks at the suggestion that he would be sleeping with her again later. It wasn't a suggestion, actually, but more of a fact. Resisting her was impossible. He could hardly wait to wake up with her beside him again.

"And by approaching breakfast differently, what you really mean is that I'll be ordering, right?"

He grinned. "It's like you can read my mind."

Her eyes were shining with humor that brought out the gold and green flecks. Beautiful. "You say that as if it's a challenge."

"Them's fightin' words." He started to reach for her.

"No." She shrieked and slid away. "There are plates of food everywhere."

His cell phone sounded and he automatically looked at caller ID, though he was prepared to ignore it and kiss her, letting the chips fall where they might. Except he couldn't.

"It's Sam on Skype," he said, then put his finger to his lips, a sign for her not to make a sound. She nodded her understanding.

He hit the talk button and saw Sam's image. "Hey. What's up?"

"Hi. I'm calling to see if you're surviving vacation."

"Uh-huh." Cal didn't believe that for a second. "You're checking up on me."

"Are you accusing me of not trusting you?"

"Yes."

"Okay. You caught me. I want to see that you're really on the island and living up to the bargain you made."

"I am. And that sweet car is mine."

"You expect me to take your word for it?" Sam asked skeptically.

"Okay. Hold on." Cal slid off the bed and retrieved one crutch, then hopped over to the suite's French doors. He aimed the phone away from him and outside, scanning the patio and pool, then the sand and ocean. "Just another day in paradise."

"Nice. Definitely not Blackwater Lake, Montana," Sam said drily.

"No." He loved the charming, picturesque town and friendly people, but on the island he didn't feel alone—lonely—like he did there. Not since Justine showed up anyway. "It's a great getaway spot."

"I still can't believe you took Mom's suggestion of where to go."

"It saved time not to look and I didn't much care. It's a bet." Speaking of his mother… "Have you talked to Mom?"

"No. I've been busy with work."

"And your new wife and daughter. How are Faith and Phoebe? Everyone healthy and happy?"

"Doing great." Sam smiled. "Best thing that ever happened to me. You should give marriage a try—"

"I already did."

"Again, I meant."

No, Cal thought, he shouldn't give it another try. He wasn't very good at it the first time, so it wasn't something he wanted to do again. "I'm glad things are good with you."

"Speaking of healthy, I saw the crutch. Is there something you want to tell me?"

"Skydiving isn't as easy as it looks. The landing is tricky. I broke my leg. Simple fracture."

"Bummer."

"The cast is coming off in a week."

"Good." Sam hesitated a moment. "Knowing you, there were other activities on your agenda equally life-threatening. That bum leg must have put a wrinkle in your plans."

"I'm managing."

"How? By working?" Sam asked suspiciously.

Cal glanced at Justine, who was quietly removing plates from the bed. He felt his pulse jump, not unlike when he'd stepped out of that plane and plummeted toward the ground. Instead of a yes-or-no answer to his brother's question, he said, "I have sat on the beach with a book and taken a basket weaving class. There are guided tours around the island and cooking classes. Massage. Many activities to keep busy."

"Wow. I'm really impressed that you're fulfilling the bargain."

"I'm an honorable man." Cal saw Justine give him a thumbs-down on that declaration. He shrugged. "And I won't hold it against you for checking up on me. If the situation were reversed, I'd have done the same to you."

"That's the way brothers roll," Sam agreed. "I have to run. It's good talking to you, Cal. Take care of the leg."

"Will do. Thanks for calling. See you soon."

He hit the off button and hopped over to Justine, just clearing the last plates and stacking them on the cart. She looked at him and *tsk*ed.

"What did I do?"

"You are morally bankrupt."

"Me?" He pointed to himself.

"Not only are you violating the spirit of the wager, but you deliberately showed your brother the suite, the patio and the ocean, everything except me. That's a lie of omission."

"I can live with that." He curved his hands on her hips and tugged her close, then started sliding the material up with every intention of pulling the dress over her head and dropping it on the floor. "You know, it's not so bad that you got dressed to let in room service."

"Why is that?"

"Because I get to take your clothes off all over again." He kissed her and she kissed him back.

He just couldn't wait until tonight to have her.

Chapter Eleven

Justine was sitting at her desk, trying to be an efficient assistant and failing miserably. It was logical to assume that her concentration at work would improve after sleeping with Cal, because of the whole tension-relieving aspect of it. That seemed to work for him but was definitely not the case for her.

She kept looking at him and marveled that he seemed to have no problem focusing on the work. He wasn't stealing looks at her, and she would know since she couldn't seem to lose the habit of glancing at him all the time. Apparently the ability to concentrate had become his post-sex superpower.

It had been a week. Seven days since she'd bared her soul to him and her body, too. Every one of those nights had been spent in his bed. Maid service was no doubt happy there was only one suite to clean. And Justine was more than content to be in his arms, especially because Cal seemed eager to have her there. On paper she didn't have a care in the world, but deep inside she had a great many cares.

"Do you have the cost projections for the wind farm

project in Maine?" Cal was sitting on the couch as usual and looked up from his laptop when he asked the question.

"They're here on my desk somewhere." Her work space was uncharacteristically cluttered and might just reflect her inner turmoil. She started to go through a stack of papers. "I'll find it."

"No rush. When you can." He looked down at his computer screen again. Displaying his superpower in all its glory.

And Justine studied her own monitor—for the fourth time. The environmental impact study just wasn't especially compelling today for some reason.

"I'm going to take a break," she told him. "Is that all right with you?"

"Of course." He glanced up and smiled, then turned back to work.

It felt like a lifetime ago that he'd pushed back on her taking regular breaks. At the time, making her point seemed a very big undertaking, but it now paled in comparison to what was going on with her boss.

She picked up her cell phone and went into her old suite to stretch and try to clear her mind. That always seemed to help restore her balance and serenity. Both had been sorely tested in the three weeks she'd spent with Calhoun Hart. She'd tried meditation-heavy yoga but her mind kept straying back to him, vacillating between elation and unease.

She decided to do hatha yoga, combining deep breathing with poses to promote flexibility, balance and relaxation. All of those qualities were lacking in her right now.

She was positioning herself when the phone rang. After checking caller ID, she smiled and hit the talk button. It was her good friend and Cal's vacationing assistant. "Hi, Shanna."

"Justine, is this a bad time?"

"No. I'm taking a break."

"I hoped you would be. How are you?"

"Good." The answer was polite but not enthusiastic. When you went to bed with the boss, life tended to get complicated. "How was your cruise?"

"Oh, my God—" There was a pause where her friend was no doubt putting a hand to her chest and wearing a rapturous expression on her face. "It was fantastic. Better. The most awesome trip ever."

"You met someone, didn't you?" Justine guessed.

"How did you know? You're psychic. I always suspected but that's proof."

"I didn't read your mind, but I know you pretty well. That's your I-met-a-man voice."

"I didn't realize I had one. And it's a little scary that you can read me so accurately," Shanna said.

"So, I'm right." It wasn't a question.

"Yes. I did meet the most wonderful man on the entire planet."

Justine could argue that point given the turn in her status with Cal but decided not to go there. "Wonderful, huh? Do you expect me to believe you didn't fall for a cad?"

"Since my pattern is hooking up with bozos, I can see why you'd be skeptical. God knows I've kissed a lot of frogs…but this man is really something special."

Justine sat on the bed. She was hearing something new in her friend's voice. "I know it was a relatively long cruise, but it was short enough to hide flaws if one wanted to."

"I know what you're saying, Justine, and I can't really explain why I'm so sure." She took a deep breath. "His name is Mark Shelton and he's a big-time movie producer from California. He brought his whole family on the trip and it's a big, close family—parents, brothers, sisters, their spouses and children."

"Wow. Very generous."

"I know, right?" There was an ecstatic squeal from the other end of the line. "You can really get a sense of a man seeing him with the people who know him best. He's a good guy and they love him. He's great with the kids. I watched him in the pool with them and the nieces and nephews just adore him. He even took care of his sister's infant. That was a seriously take-no-prisoners moment when I saw him holding a baby. Be still my heart."

"Shannie, I have to ask. How can you be sure it wasn't an act for your benefit? He's Hollywood, after all."

"I get it," Shanna said. "I was skeptical, too, and watching carefully, waiting to catch him. But you can't fake the baby thing and the kids weren't coached. We both know children do not suffer fools or filter comments when something pops into their mind. His nieces and nephews just blurted things out like, 'Remember when you took us to the snow?' or, 'I loved when you dug a hole in the sand and buried me.'"

"So you're convinced he's the real deal?"

"Not a doubt. His parents and siblings are genuine, too. He's very close to them."

"Is he the one, Shan?"

"Yes."

"And you're his Ms. Right?"

"Yes. When you know, you just know." Shanna sighed happily. "You know?"

"Yes."

It seemed like another lifetime, but Justine remembered falling in love, that uncomplicated feeling of pure joy at finding the one man she wanted to be with forever. She'd been so young and it was all so easy because she never thought that anything bad could touch them. Until it did.

"I've never been so happy," Shanna gushed.

Justine had been that happy once. When it was so cruelly and suddenly snatched away she'd believed loneliness was all she would have for the rest of her life. She'd never expected someone like Cal.

"But he lives in California, right?"

"Yes."

"And you...don't," Justine pointed out rationally. "I hate being the voice of reason, but just how are you going to work this out?"

"You sure know how to let the air out of the excitement balloon and throw water on the fire of romance, don't you?"

"What are friends for?" she teased. "But seriously, you and Mark must have talked about the geographic consequences of a long-distance relationship."

"More than talked," Shanna confirmed. "We made a decision that it wouldn't work. He proposed and I accepted. I'm moving to California."

"Wow." Even though Justine had suspected that this was where her friend was headed, she was still shocked. "Congratulations."

"Thanks."

"That means you'll have to give Cal your notice."

"I know, and I'm not looking forward to that." For the first time her friend's enthusiasm slipped. "He's driven, but still a great guy and a good boss. I'll miss him."

"But you just moved to Blackwater Lake," Justine protested.

"Yes, I did. On the bright side, half of my stuff is still packed and in storage. And my moving mojo is still going strong." There was another silence on the other end of the line and her friend was probably chewing nervously on her lip. "Be happy for me, J."

"Of course I am," she said quickly. She was also envious. First love was simple, easy and wonderful. "I'm sure you'll be very happy, and I hope I get to meet the man responsible for it."

"You will. Count on it." Shanna blew out a long breath. "I just wanted a break from work. It never occurred to me that I'd find my destiny on vacation."

"Isn't that always the way?" Justine said.

"Speaking of getting away…listen to me going on about myself. How are you?"

"I'm fine."

There was a pause, as if Shanna was waiting for more. "Is that it?"

"What else should there be?"

"For one thing, how is it working with Cal? Worth the big bucks you're getting to put up with him?"

"Since it took you four years to get a vacation, you know better than anyone what he's like."

"That's exactly why I'm asking. Is he driving you crazy?"

Yes, but not the way her friend meant. Their time in bed was sweet, sexy, hot, satisfying. All the more vivid because she'd missed being physically close with a man. But at work, he seemed able to compartmentalize, which should have been reassuring. And it was, in a way. So why wasn't she completely reassured? Probably she needed therapy.

"Justine?"

"Hmm?"

"What's really going on with you and Cal? Is he working you too hard? I warned you not to take this assignment—"

"No. We settled that early on when I threatened to quit. So there's no overtime and I get regular breaks to stretch out my leg." She remembered the intensity in Cal's eyes the first time she'd demonstrated her poses. The thought made her shiver now as it had then and she knew he'd wanted her as badly as she wanted him. And the explosion of desire between them was way better than okay.

"I'm glad you didn't let him walk all over you. But—" An uneasy silence followed that word. "I'm not psychic, either, but I know you and I can hear in your voice that everything's not right. What's going on? A vacation romance for you, too?"

"Why would you say that?"

There was a long silence on the other end of the line. Then Shanna said, "You know the way you know me so well? It works both ways. I nailed it, didn't I? There's something going on between you and Cal, isn't there?"

"Not as dramatic as what's going on with you," she answered.

"No way." Shanna's voice wasn't quite a shriek, but close. "You and Cal? Doing the wild thing?"

Such a fitting way to put it. "Yes, we are mixing business with pleasure," Justine admitted, without detailing the numerous ways he pleasured her every night.

"So, the workaholic has a heart, after all." There was an approving smile in Shanna's voice.

"As you said, he's a good guy when you get to know him. But it's a little soon to talk about heart involvement."

"Hey, I'm engaged to be married and it's been a similar time frame. Is there something I should know?"

"You're asking about love—"

"Duh."

"The answer is that there is no answer. It's still new—"

"What do you want, Justine?"

"That's a good question. We haven't discussed anything, and even if we did—"

"This is me, J. I know you're afraid." Her friend's voice was as gentle and supportive as a hug.

"I prefer to think of it as being unprepared. Even though I made a conscious choice to move on with my life as Wes and Betsy would want, I was thinking in terms of letting myself not be sad anymore. This, with Cal, isn't something I ever expected to face again after losing the people I loved most in the world."

This ambivalence seemed so stupid since she was the one who had opened the door by asking Cal why he didn't want her. Talk about mixed signals.

"You were prepared to be alone but not to face falling in love and the potential pain of it. And I'm not just talking about losing someone the way you did your husband. There are other ways to be hurt. And Cal has baggage."

"I know. He told me about his marriage." The newly reawakened part of her had accepted that living life meant opening herself up to a relationship—the highs, lows and complete mess of it. But now… "You nailed it, Shannie. I think this uneasiness is resistance to potential pain."

"Oh, honey—" Her friend sighed loudly. "I wish I could tell you it will be all right, but there's no way to be sure. So the best strategy I can come up with is this. Just enjoy yourself and don't create problems where there aren't any. Have no expectations and live in the moment."

That made sense. She was making this complicated when it didn't need to be. *Have fun and don't expect more.*

"Excellent advice, Shannie."

Justine truly meant that and planned to take it. She felt as if the weight of the world had lifted from her shoulders.

* * *

"Well, well, well." Cal ended the call with his soon-to-be ex-assistant and looked at Justine working beside him on the sofa. "Shanna said you already know about her engagement and resignation."

"Yes. She called during my break."

It hadn't escaped his notice that she'd come back from that break much lighter of spirit than when she left. He knew that was his fault. Things had changed between them and she would want definition of what was happening. He knew only one way to define it. Simple and straightforward. Being with her was...good.

"She sounded very happy," he said.

"I thought so, too." Justine took off her glasses and tossed them on the coffee table, on the spreadsheet they'd been studying before Shanna called him. "Believe me, I grilled her like raw hamburger. It's a big step to pick up your life and move it to another state. I wanted to make sure she'd given this decision a lot of thought."

"And?"

"She said when you know, you just know."

"Hmm."

Cal knew a lot of things. He liked Justine very much. In fact, he'd go so far as to say he'd never felt this way about a woman, ever. But these circumstances were different. It wasn't the real world, where things had a way of not working out. "For Shanna's sake, I hope what she thinks she knows goes the way she wants it to."

"I agree. On the other hand, I've become a believer in not wasting time."

Because no one knew how much time they had, he thought. That must have been a hard lesson for her. He wanted to scoop her up, pull her against him and make the shadows in her eyes disappear. But this was work time. When he'd crossed the line from professional into personal, he'd promised himself to keep the two separate. It wasn't easy with her looking like temptation in a sleeveless cotton dress. If he was being honest, it wouldn't matter what she wore because he knew every inch of what was underneath. And he couldn't seem to get enough of that.

And that's why he didn't look at her during work hours unless it was absolutely necessary.

"So," Justine said, "you're going to need a replacement for Shanna. Do you want me to start looking through your existing employees? If you don't find anyone, we can open up a wider search."

"That sounds like a good plan." He noticed her giving him a strange look. "What?"

"For a man who barely gave his assistant a day off, you're taking this resignation of your right-hand person remarkably well."

"On the outside," he clarified. "On the inside I'm having a spectacular meltdown."

"No one would ever guess. Maybe your vacation has given you the reserves to keep your inner pouter just where he belongs."

She might have a point about the battery recharge. And in a few days the revitalizing would be over. When he'd arrived, his attitude was resentment, as if he'd been given a time-out even though he'd accepted the bet. He was all about hunkering down and gritting his teeth to get through, to do whatever he had to in order to win. Then he went skydiving. What was that saying? Men plan and God laughs.

He looked his fill at Justine's fresh, pretty, peaceful face and felt his chest grow tight with tenderness. Hurting his leg might just have been the luckiest break he ever got.

"Okay, then," she said. "I'll contact Human Resources in Blackwater Lake and get them going on finding a replacement for Shanna. Then we can finish going over the cost analysis for this project—"

He held up a hand to stop her. "That can wait."

"What?" She blinked at him, obviously surprised.

"Finding another Shanna will work itself out, but we only have a few days left on the island. I think we should take advantage of that and do something fun today."

A slow smile curved up the corners of her mouth before she wiped an imaginary tear from the corner of her eye with a knuckle. "My little boy is all grown up."

"Very funny." He was pretty sure last night in bed he'd shown her exactly how grown up he was, but that's not what she meant. He grinned. "What do you say we go basket weaving again?"

"I say the surprises keep on coming." She was staring at him as if he'd just sprouted another head.

"Let's just say I'm determined to master the skill."

"Your aggressive streak is showing." She thought for a moment. "Competitive basket weaving. Could be an Olympic event."

"You mock me, but never say never. Are you game for it today?"

"Twist my arm." She stood and walked over to the desk to get her purse. "Ready when you are."

After securing transportation, he took her to lunch at the nearby resort. Then they joined a few other guests for the class being held at the picnic table area with a spectacular view of the ocean. The breeze was more than pleasant and the sky an indescribably stunning shade of blue without a cloud in sight. Justine sat beside him, her shoulder brushing his as they laughed and teased. The afternoon was perfect—in spite of basket weaving.

Cal followed directions and carefully wove the reeds together, doing his damnedest to create a functional thing. But his hands felt too big and clumsy. The materials were too unwieldy and delicate.

He stared ruefully at the finished product. "Guess what it is."

"A colander?" Although she tried to look serious, there was laughter in her eyes as she studied the dysfunctional crisscrossing of palm fronds. "There are so many spaces for water to drain."

Frowning, he held up what he'd made—whether for inspection or more ridicule wasn't clear. "There was a time when this being less than perfect would have bothered me. But not anymore."

"Really?"

"Truly. Now I see it as a way to spend an afternoon outside and enjoy the view. Today wasn't about fortunes being made and lost or life and death. Just a pleasant diversion."

"What you're trying to say is that you're relaxed."

"I really am," he agreed.

"So the family intervention was a good thing and made you a vacation convert."

"Yes." He sighed, then looked away from the view and met her gaze. "There's only one downside as far as I can see."

"Oh?"

"I don't want to go back."

Part of that was about wanting to stay in this perfect paradise. But mostly it was about Justine. Leaving would change—this—whatever it was. He couldn't label the feelings and didn't really want to. He just wanted it to *be*. Leaving could and would make everything different, and for reasons he didn't want to examine closely, he wasn't looking forward to that.

"I would say that your time off was a rousing success." She beamed at him as if he was her prize pupil. "Maybe more important—you have learned that work and play are better with balance."

"That's very Zen of you." He studied her. "And you're responsible for making me aware that this is beneficial. You may have noticed that I wasn't very open-minded about this in the beginning."

"No. Really?" She laughed.

"Smart aleck." But he was serious. "I realized that the rest of the world can go on without me for a little while."

"You embraced the message. And it can be life-altering," she agreed.

"There you go being glass-half-full again. You're very good at this whole yoga thing."

"Thanks. Coming from you that's high praise." She looked at the tidy little basket she'd made, then at him. "And it reassures me that my decision to open my own yoga studio was the right one."

"What?" Had she mentioned this before?

"Yes. The whole reason I accepted this assignment with you was the generous salary. That will make it possible for me to open my own business sooner than I'd planned."

"You're abandoning Hart Energy? We just talked about picking up one's life and moving."

"That was about Shanna and getting married. My situation is very different."

"How?"

"For one thing, I've already moved."

And unlike Shanna, she wasn't getting married, he

thought. The *M*-word always put a knot in his stomach. "When did you decide this was what you wanted?"

"I've been planning for this quite a while. It was more than exercise, but a course of therapy that literally got me back on my feet after the accident. I want to pay it forward and help others."

"It's really important to you." That wasn't a question.

She tucked a strand of red hair behind her ear and nodded. "When the announcement was made about the move to Blackwater Lake I started researching the area. There's development happening that will bring in a clientele who will benefit from the lifestyle, service and philosophy I want to provide. Another plus is that there's nothing like it in town. In Dallas there was a yoga studio practically on every corner. And—"

"What?" he asked softly. Her eyes had turned more green than brown, and he had a feeling he knew what she was going to say.

"I needed a scenery change. There were memories everywhere and it seemed like a good idea to move forward in a new place."

"Sounds like you've really thought it through."

"They say you never work a day in your life if you do something you love. For me there's no downside."

For him it felt just the opposite, although Cal couldn't say exactly why that was. He'd been surprisingly okay with Shanna jumping ship, but not so much with Justine doing the same thing. It had nothing to do with work because she hadn't been his assistant in the Blackwater Lake office. Briefly he'd considered offering her Shanna's position but immediately discarded the idea.

Justine was a distraction he couldn't afford on a permanent professional basis. No, his unease was strictly about change. It was the only thing one could count on, but that didn't mean he was okay with it. His instinct was to fix whatever made him uneasy, and he knew from past experience that actions taken under pressure never went well.

Note to self: there is nothing here to fix.

Another note to self: repeat until the first note sinks in.

Chapter Twelve

"I can't believe it. No more plaster leg, no more hobbling around supported by sticks."

It was late afternoon. Justine and Cal had just returned to the villa from the doctor, where he'd had his cast removed. He was ecstatic and grinned from ear to ear.

Justine smiled back. If anyone knew how good it felt to have free use of a limb again, it was her. "At the end you were better than a hobble. Just saying."

Cal spontaneously pulled her into his arms and held her so tight she could hardly breathe. Against her hair he said, "I honestly don't think I could have gotten through this without you, Justine."

"I'm glad I was here."

For so many reasons, but one was completely selfish. Because of him she'd taken a giant step forward in her emotional recovery. She knew now that it was possible for her to be happy again, truly happy and content and not simply pretending for everyone else.

Taking a step back out of his arms, she looked up and met his gaze. "So, it's your last day here. Do you want to tie up loose work ends? Just pack everything up? Or—"

"Are you kidding?" He looked at her as if she'd suddenly turned green. "It's our last day on the island."

"I know. That's what I just said. Where do you want me to focus my time and energy? Organizing paperwork? Making phone calls—"

He touched a finger to her lips to stop the flow of words. "It's our last day on the island. I'm quite sure it's in the vacation convert handbook that on the final day before returning to one's humdrum, mundane life, the inexperienced vacationer must pack as much fun as possible into the remaining hours. Work?" He crossed his fingers, making an X. "Until we're on the plane home tomorrow, whoever says the word *w-o-r-k* will have to pay a forfeit."

"Which is?"

He thought for a moment, then grinned. "A kiss."

"Now there's a deterrent," she scoffed, before standing on tiptoe and touching her mouth to his.

"What was that for?"

"I just banked a forfeit," she said.

"Yeah." He scratched his head. "I'll have to think of something really bad. Like cuddling in the corner."

"Right. A time-out with benefits?"

He shrugged. "We could stand here and debate or go have an adventure."

"Well, you're the one dealing with physical limitations for the last month, so what would you like to do? And before you answer, defining *adventure* would be good. Your last one ended with that leg in a cast."

"Right. No parasailing, hang gliding or rock climbing."

"I knew you weren't just another pretty face. So, what'll it be?"

"I want to walk on the sand, down by the water. Get my feet wet." His blue eyes darkened with focus and it was all directed at her. "With you."

Her pulse jumped once as if to say, *Oh, boy.*

"That sounds like just what the doctor ordered," she said.

"Good. Go put on a swimsuit."

"Why?" she asked suspiciously.

"Because water is wet." It was half statement, half question and all mischief.

"But—" She glanced down at her right leg and realized that covering the scars was always uppermost in her mind.

Cal's expression gentled. "Every single part of you is beautiful. The marks made you who you are, and that's a person I admire and like very much."

"Thank you—"

"I hear a *but* in your voice because you were going to say my good opinion means zilch when a stranger stares at your leg."

Amused now, she folded her arms over her chest. "Was I?"

"Yes. And you know what my response would be?"

"Don't keep me in suspense," she said drily.

"It's late in the afternoon so the beach will be less crowded. And probably someone will see your leg and wonder about it. But you'll never see them again."

She'd expected something along the lines of *You're beautiful inside and out. Let it go. Don't think about that because it doesn't define you.* She'd thought for a moment about pushing back that she might return here for another vacation. Then it hit her that he hadn't meant the statement literally. No one cared about the marks on her body except her. If she didn't give it a thought, neither would anyone else.

"You're absolutely right. Thank you." She stood on tiptoe again and kissed him.

"Are you banking another forfeit?" There was laughter in his eyes.

"No. *Work. Work*," she said. "Now we're back to square one."

They changed into their suits and his look said he clearly approved of her bikini. Then came slathering sunscreen on each other. The touching ignited fires for activities that would keep them indoors, but a sincere need to be in the open air put that on hold.

Justine preferred wearing a sarong, with or without the scars on her leg, unless she was in the water. After putting on her sunglasses, it was time to head out.

Both of them were limping. Cal's injured calf was skinny from lack of exercise and the muscles in Justine's compromised leg protested the exertion of moving through the coarse white sand. They took it slow, and near the water things got easier.

A small wave lapped at their feet and Cal sighed in ecstasy. "I have taken for granted the sheer pleasure of this all my life. Not having something really makes you appreciate what you've been missing."

"And here I thought you were shallow. That was an extremely profound statement, Mr. Hart."

"I have levels," he said proudly.

Justine's comment was deliberately teasing because it was either that or get serious. And she sensed that was the last thing he wanted. Especially during their final hours here in paradise. But he was right about appreciating something you didn't have. She'd missed this closeness with a man, and finding it again truly did make her cherish it. For so long she'd felt that dating was a betrayal of the love she'd had for her husband. Now she knew it validated the relationship she'd lost. That had made her who she was, a woman who was her best self when she gave and received love.

After today she had no idea where this thing with Cal would go. They wouldn't be living under the same roof or possibly even see each other at all. Nothing future had been defined. The unknown was a big, black void, a perversion of this bright, spectacular day with the sun turning the blue water into a carpet of diamonds. So, she was going to do her best not to think about tomorrow.

Strolling slowly, Cal took her hand, a small gesture that seemed as natural as breathing. "I was just thinking—"

"Uh-oh. I thought I smelled smoke," she teased. "I'm not sure I want to hear this."

"Oh, you'll be all over it, Miss Violating the Spirit of the Wager." He smiled down at her.

"I like the sound of that. Continue, please."

"If my brother and my mother hadn't pushed me into this bet, it's quite possible I would never have slowed down long enough to experience a day like this. And I would really have missed that."

"Stop the presses. There's breaking news. Calhoun Hart is waxing poetic and feeling guilty," she added.

"I don't know if I'd go that far. It's just that I feel as if I've gotten so much already. I don't need Sam to pay off the bet." He looked down at her then, but his eyes were hidden by the aviator sunglasses. "This is enough."

Justine's heart pounded and anticipation knotted inside as she hoped he would expand that thought. "Oh?"

But the moment was shattered when a man and woman jogged past and splashed them.

"Oh, God, that felt so good," he said.

Without warning he picked her up and walked deliberately into the ocean. Justine didn't know whether to shriek because she knew what was coming or simply hang on, enjoy the ride and savor this moment being close to him. Before she could make up her mind, he tossed her into the water, then dived in after her.

It was the temperature of bathwater, but salty, clear and beautiful. Cal surfaced, his wide shoulders and broad chest gleaming and gorgeous, wet and wild. What was it about a wet man that made a woman's mouth go dry? But she knew in her heart not just any man would do that to her. Only this one.

She pushed dripping hair off her face. "My sarong is all wet. You're going to pay for that."

"I'm sure it will involve *work*." He moved in close and put his arms around her.

"Forfeit," she cried.

"You got me."

The sun moved lower in the sky and turned the under-side of the clouds pink, purple and gold. People walked by but everything disappeared and a perfect moment be-came the simplicity of their lips touching. It was only the two of them and a balmy breeze caressing their bodies. She could feel Cal's arms tightening around her and his breath coming faster.

Reluctantly he pulled back and drew in a deep breath before releasing it. "Walk on the sand—check. Dip in the ocean—check. Kiss a beautiful woman in the water—check. But I think we should head back to the villa." There was a husky rasp in his voice that said so much more.

"I'll race you," she said. "Last one there is a rotten egg."

He laughed. "Good thing no one is timing us."

They moved from the water to the shore and slowly

walked back, hand in hand. Not many people were out, but an older couple strolled by with their arms around each other's waists. Hellos were exchanged and the silver-haired man and woman smiled indulgently, the way people did at lovers. Justine smiled back, the way people did who envied a man and woman who had grown old together.

That's what she wanted.

The villa came into view and they headed to it, trudging through the sand. Passing the lounges where she'd first convinced him to relax, she thought about how far they'd come since that day she'd helped him to sit.

They moved by the low outside wall, onto the decking where the crystal clear pool was.

Cal stopped and looked down at her. "Lose the sarong. We're going in. After watching you in there night after night, I want to swim with you."

It wasn't easy to untie the wet knot at her waist with shaking hands, but she managed. Then she dived into the water and glided as far as she could go without kicking. Cal did the same and they ended up in the shallow end, just where her feet could touch bottom.

His arms came around her and he smiled in the waning light. "I like swimming with you."

"Technically this isn't swimming, but I can show you some exercises to help rehabilitate the muscle tone in your calf."

"I bet you could." His voice was deep, ragged, seductive.

"However, fair warning," she said, smiling coyly. "It's a lot of *work*."

"I really like forfeit." His smile widened just before his mouth claimed hers.

Wet man, wet kiss. All wow. She was so caught up in

the sensations he was evoking that she hardly felt his fingers unhook her bikini top and strip it away.

"Oh, Cal—"

"Hold that thought."

He pulled himself out of the pool and disappeared inside, then was back faster than one would think a man who'd recently had his cast removed could go. He had a condom and was ready when he walked back into the water and kissed her again. This time her bikini bottom came off and he lifted her. She wrapped her legs around his waist as he entered her.

She was so ready. The walk, dip in the ocean, touching—it all turned her desire into a need so deep it couldn't be denied. Feeling him inside her was all she wanted.

He rocked her against him and kissed her neck, that magical spot beneath her ear. Pleasure exploded inside her and she trembled with the force of it.

Suddenly Cal went still and groaned, holding her tight against him as his release came. They stayed that way for a long time, wrapped in each other's arms.

He cleared his throat. "One more on the list. Making love to you in the pool—check."

She was happy and satisfied, more than she'd been in longer than she could remember. So it was a shock when her eyes filled with tears. Bad things happened in life and you never saw them coming, but tomorrow's departure from here wasn't a surprise. They were going home. That meant things would be different and it made her sad.

The month was over and she wished with all her heart that it didn't have to end.

Late in the afternoon the next day, Cal watched Justine look through every nook and cranny of the villa to make sure she hadn't overlooked anything while packing. He hadn't missed the tears she'd tried to hide after making love in the pool last night. Even though her face was already wet, he'd seen that something was bothering her. He was pretty sure it wasn't something he did, but a guy could never be certain. All he knew was that he didn't like it when she was unhappy.

There was a knock on the villa door and Justine answered it. George and William, their room service waiters, had come to tell her goodbye.

"Thank you so much for everything," she said, hugging each man. "I think I've forgotten how to cook. Maybe you'd like to reconsider my offer to come back to Blackwater Lake with me?"

The taller man laughed. "It is a very tempting offer. But..."

"Yes." She glanced at Cal, then said, "There's always a *but*. Just remember to be honest with the ones you love and communicate."

Cal walked over to shake hands, then gave each of them a generous stack of bills that made their eyes pop. "Your service was exemplary and you will be sorely missed. Thank you for making our stay one that we will never forget."

The shorter man nodded and spoke for both of them. "It has been our pleasure to be of service to you. Please come back and visit with us again soon."

"I would like that very much." Cal watched Justine hug each of them one last time and knew his stay here on the island had been remarkable because of her. She was the light to his darkness. And yesterday she'd cried. Why?

He had a long plane ride home to find out the answer to that question.

When goodbyes were over and the two resort staffers left, he met her gaze. "Are you all set?"

"Yes." But her eyes said just the opposite, even though everything was in her suitcase.

With his hand at the small of her back, they walked out the front door together. The crutches he'd gladly abandoned yesterday rested against the entryway wall, and he'd instructed the front desk to return them to the medical facility. He never wanted to see those sticks again, in spite of the fact that he'd met Justine because of his accident. The silver lining, he thought. She would be proud of him for that positive mental energy.

The town car driver stood by the open rear passenger door. Cal handed Justine inside first, then followed her. The air-conditioning was blasting and took the humidity out of the air, which would make the short drive to the small island airport more comfortable.

But nothing about the drive was relaxed because his companion was unusually quiet and subdued. Patience wasn't his strong suit, but he reminded himself that in a little while they'd have a chance to talk this through.

They exited the car, and Justine looked for a long time at the three-hundred-sixty-degree ocean view. Her eyes were hidden behind large sunglasses, but judging by body language, she wasn't happily anticipating getting on the plane and leaving this place. Cal shared her reluctance, especially since finding out she was planning to resign from Hart Energy.

Before she'd revealed her business plan, he'd been okay with ending their vacation because he would see her at work. Now that wasn't going to be a possibility for very long, forcing a change in his strategy. But every motivational speech he'd ever heard declared that change was just opportunity.

"So, are you ready to be amazed?" he asked. Did he sound as ridiculously cheerful as he thought?

She turned to him. "What?"

"We're getting on the private jet. Prepare yourself once again for luxury overload." That's what she'd said the first day she'd walked into the villa—the plane, the resort. She'd been awed. Her expression didn't reflect that now. "Hey, I'm trying to lighten the mood. Work with me."

She glanced at the Gulfstream waiting nearby, engines at a low hum, then looked back at him and forced a smile. "Very exciting. An adventure."

"That's the spirit."

"Let's roll." She headed for the portable stairway that had been pushed against the aircraft's doorway. Then she stopped and looked at him. "What about the bags?"

"You really don't have much experience with this luxury thing," he scolded gently.

"I promise not to hold it against you that you do." Her sass was a good sign.

"The driver and plane personnel will put our things on board."

"So we don't need to watch and make sure?"

"You can if you want. But this isn't like flying commercial. I'm pretty certain these guys can handle it. Or we'll know who to hold responsible if our luggage is lost." He held out his hand. "After you."

She nodded and walked ahead of him, climbing the stairs before stepping through the doorway into the plush interior. There was a configuration of soft, leather-covered benches, tables and captain's chairs. The galley was in the back and a bar was set up on the port side. A company flight attendant was there to greet them.

"Hello, Brad," Justine said and gave him a friendly smile.

"Good to see you again, Justine." He held out his hand. "Hi, Cal. Hope it was a good month."

The best, he thought. "I have no complaints."

"The flight crew are doing precheck. The captain wanted me to let you know the weather between here and Blackwater Lake looks good. It should be a smooth ride."

"Excellent news." Cal glanced at his companion and thought time would tell whether or not it would be smooth in every way.

"We expect to have clearance soon to take off, so if you'll buckle up..." Brad indicated the two seats just behind him.

"Okay." Cal looked at her. "Window or aisle?"

"I don't care. You pick. It's your plane."

"It's the company plane and I'd really like you to sit where you want."

She took off her glasses and met his gaze. "Window."

"Done." He moved so she could get by him and sit.

She settled in and sighed. "*Comfortable* doesn't even begin to describe this. It's like being cushioned in bubble wrap."

"Not quite the visual they were going for, probably, but true," he agreed.

Shortly after they buckled in, the captain announced he'd received clearance from air traffic control to take off, and they were ready to go. One advantage of a small airport was no line of planes, so it wasn't long before they'd taken off and reached their normal cruising altitude. The seat belt sign went off and they were free to move about the cabin.

"I think we should have a drink." Cal knew that Brad would be serving dinner soon and Justine was clearly tense. Not good when it was the polar opposite of what she'd preached for the last month. And he expected her to say she was *fine*—the four-letter word men universally hated—depending on a woman's tone and expression when she said it.

"A glass of wine would be lovely," she said.

He'd been thinking a tumbler two fingers full of Scotch, but wine would work. He asked Brad to open a bottle of his favorite red. The other man did as requested, then disappeared after pouring the pinot noir into their crystal glasses.

Cal held his up. "What should we drink to?"

She sighed. "I can't think of a thing."

He remembered last night and the sadness on her face when she valiantly tried to hide her feelings. Screw the toast. He couldn't stand one more second of not knowing what was on her mind. "Why were you crying last night?"

Her gaze snapped to his, clearly understanding what he was referring to and surprised that he'd noticed. "Would you believe happy tears?"

"Maybe if you hadn't looked as if there was a permanent ban on ice cream. This may come as a shock, but you're not very good at hiding your feelings." And he was grateful for that. In his experience, that's what women did.

"Wow, I thought being in the pool and all…" She tried to smile. "You are quite observant."

"I try. So, talk to me about why you're not anxious to get home."

She sighed, then met his gaze. "The island was so wonderful. And everything will change when we get home."

"It doesn't have to."

"Correct me if I'm wrong, but the scenery will be awfully different." Her look was wry. "The lake is beautiful but it's not the ocean. And the pines are awfully pretty, especially against a clear blue sky. But they're not palms."

He knew when she said "different" she meant their relationship, and talking about the scenery was a way to avoid the subject. "We haven't discussed you and me."

"What?"

"Us. We haven't talked about what will happen with us when we get home. And I think it's time to do that."

"You do?"

"Way past time and completely my fault," he allowed.

"I wasn't sure there was an 'us.'" The hint of a sparkle was in her eyes.

"Well, there is." He took a sip of wine. "In case you couldn't tell, being with you was the best time of my life."

Her lips slowly curved up, the first genuine smile in almost twenty-four hours. "It was?"

"Without a doubt. And even though you're deserting me and Hart Energy, we will still see each other when we get back to real life."

"We will?" Suddenly she glowed with happiness.

"Yes."

Cal knew he couldn't *not* see her. He'd spent every day of the last four weeks with her. Every morning he saw her beautiful, serene smile and had breakfast with her. At night she curled up against him and he was filled with the passion of keeping her at his side, safe and happy. Somehow that kept him safe, too.

Tension seemed to flow out of her. "So do you want

to drink to cashing in on the bet with your brother? You did stay on the island for a month."

And she'd been with him during that time—first with work, then with her body. "That isn't my top priority."

"What is?" she asked, smiling.

He'd never brought up the future because he didn't know what to say. He hadn't thought about much of anything beyond wanting her with every fiber of his being. But now the future was staring him in the face and he wanted to do this right, be as honest as he could be. He had to put all his cards on the table.

"Justine—" Her name was a whisper on his lips and he leaned over to kiss her. Her mouth was warm and giving. "I care for you. A lot. And I want us to see each other when we get back to Blackwater Lake. But it's not fair to you not to be straight. I can't make any promises. What we have is fantastic. But I'm not very good at marriage."

"No one said anything about marriage." There was the barest flicker of change in her expression.

"I know. But it's important to be completely open about expectations and feelings."

She didn't make a sound. It was as if the light in her eyes dimmed. "Yes, it is. And I remember very clearly what you said about your feelings regarding marriage."

"Right." This was going better than he'd hoped. He was glad she understood. "I mean, who marries the woman who was in love with his brother, you know?"

"A competitive man," she said almost absently. "You want to come in first. It's what made you take the bet to spend a month on an island."

"Exactly."

"And I also remember you saying that you're not good at love. That you don't do anything that you're not good at."

"You have quite the memory." But Cal studied her closely after detecting something in her voice. "You say that as if it's a bad thing."

"That wasn't my intention. It's good to know one's strengths and weaknesses. Saves a lot of time and trouble. Good talk, Cal." She picked up her wine and took a sip, then stared out the window.

Somehow Cal felt as if he'd just made things worse and wasn't sure how. But clearly her sass had disappeared again. He'd fixed it once and could do it again. He would come up with something by the time they landed in Blackwater Lake.

Chapter Thirteen

The wheels of the plane touched down at Blackwater Lake Regional Airport. It was a smooth landing but Justine felt a jolt all the way to her heart. She'd wished the flight could go on forever. Just Cal and her cruising through the clouds.

That's what she'd been doing for the last couple of weeks, since the night she'd challenged him to take her to bed. Was it so awful to want sun, sand, seduction and sex to go on forever? There'd been no promises or declarations made, not until this plane had taken off and they started the trip home.

Cal had said he cared for her very much. It had been on the tip of her tongue to say that she was in love with him, so his statement made her feel…empty.

The Gulfstream taxied to the small terminal and stopped. Then the engines powered down.

"We're home." Cal smiled and released his seat belt.

"Yes." There was no point in disagreeing with the obvious.

But home? She hadn't lived there long enough to get all warm and fuzzy about it after being gone for a month. And then there was what happened with Cal. Not his fault, not anyone's fault that they were in different places. But she was going to quit her job and open her own business as soon as possible. She'd get it up and running, meet people and be happy in spite of him, damn it.

Tears filled her eyes and she didn't want Cal to see. That would be awkward. He would feel bad and she didn't want him to because she appreciated his honesty. Her life experience had made her who she was today and so did his. It was what it was.

So after freeing herself from the seat belt, she stood and turned away from him to look out the window. It was dark outside. Airport lights illuminated the immediate area where the plane was parked, and she could see into the terminal, which was all but deserted at this hour. There was a ghostlike air about the place, which felt appropriate, given her mood. The termination of hope wasn't a cheerful thing.

All she had to do now was keep it together for the next few minutes while collecting her luggage. Shanna had promised to pick her up. So a quick goodbye to Cal and she could be on her way to her apartment.

The flight attendant opened the rear door and chilly air swept into the cabin.

"It's cold out there," Cal said. "Welcome to Montana in November."

"Yeah." She looked down at her short-sleeved T-shirt and linen slacks. "A month ago the cold wasn't a priority and it never crossed my mind when we left the villa."

She'd been too preoccupied about where their relationship would go after returning to Blackwater Lake. He'd answered the question not long after the plane took off.

"The bags will be unloaded in a couple of minutes," he promised.

"Great." She smiled brightly and realized her jaw hurt.

That's what happened when you sat next to a man for hours and forced yourself to be cheerful when all you wanted was to curl into the fetal position.

"You stay here while I go check on things. Give me a couple of minutes."

"Okay."

When he headed for the open door, she texted Shanna that the plane landed. Her friend replied that she would be there ASAP. Then Justine gathered the personal items she'd kept with her and headed for the exit and climbed down the portable stairway that had been rolled into place. Cal was waiting for her at the bottom. He pulled a fleece-lined jacket around her. It was big and obviously his.

As if reluctant to break contact, he curled his hands into the material and held the coat around her. "You were awfully quiet on the flight. Are you okay?"

"Of course." The muscles in her jaw protested when she smiled.

"I'm not sure I believe you."

She was aware of his attention to detail, but had once again underestimated his powers of perception. "Oh?"

"I feel as if something I said is bothering you. Let me fix it."

She shook her head. It wasn't what he'd said that troubled her, because the truth was always preferable to being strung along. She blamed herself for disregarding the voice in her head that kept warning her not to cross the line from professional to personal with her boss. There were the obvious reasons, but he'd been open and upfront about his own past, the personal baggage he would always carry. She'd thought it was so sweet and sensitive when he'd held back his attraction for her sake. That was irresistible. And a mistake on her part not to resist.

"You didn't say anything wrong," she assured him.

There was enough light to see the questions in his eyes, but he nodded. "Okay, then."

"Good." This was the hard part. "I really enjoyed working with you."

"We do make a good team." His smile turned sexy. "And I'm not only talking about the work. We're very good together, Justine."

"It was a magical couple of weeks." The effort to keep her tone light and carefree took an enormous toll on her emotional reserves. "I'll never forget it."

"Me, either." He dropped his hands from the jacket and glanced over his shoulder. "I have a car waiting. I'll just tell the driver to load up our bags. Then we'll go to my condo and get settled."

Justine didn't know whether to kiss him or slug him. "Why would you assume that was okay with me?"

"You just said we're good together. We had a great time on the island and it doesn't have to end."

So sweet and yet so clueless. "You didn't ask, just assumed that I would be okay with this."

"I knew it." He frowned. "There is something wrong. Don't tell me you're fine when I know you're not."

"I think it would be best if we just—"

"Here's what I think." He took a breath and his lips moved as he silently counted to five. "Come to the condo with me. We'll sit in front of the fireplace and get warm. Have some wine. Hash things out."

There was a disaster scenario if she'd ever heard one. In a setting like he'd just described, their mouths would get busy, but not with talking. One kiss and she would be lost. Then all her clothes would come off, and for a while loving him would make her forget why getting in deeper would hurt so much more in the long run.

"I can't do that. I'm going to grab my bags and go. To my apartment."

"How are you getting home?" he asked, his tone rife with disapproval and irritation.

"Shanna is coming."

"The car is here. We'll drop you at your place. Tomorrow night we'll have dinner together and—"

"No."

He stared at her, apparently shocked into speechlessness at her negative reply. Finally he said, "That's it? No explanation?"

"How about this?" She thought for a moment, trying to figure out how to say this without crying. "The island was fantasy. It's over. Parting ways makes the break quick and clean."

He frowned and his mouth pulled tight. "What if I don't want a break?"

"I think you do," she said.

"And why would you think that?"

Because you're competitive, she thought. He broke his leg and stayed on the island in spite of it because he was determined to always come in first. That would come between them eventually, just like it had with his first wife. Justine had once loved another man but it made her all the more certain about her feelings for Cal.

On the island he'd taught her that she was a woman who needed to give and receive love. She was afraid the love she gave him would never be enough because he would always feel as if he'd come in second place.

"Relationships shouldn't be a competition with preconceived ideas and regulations." She met his gaze. "I think even you would admit that I have the more compelling reason to shy away from anything permanent."

"And I get that, so—"

She held up her hand. She was so close to tears and couldn't last much longer. She needed to get this out while her composure would hold. "Let me finish. I'm not saying I ever want to fall in love and marry again, but I'm not about to shut down the possibility. You're laying down ground rules before the starting gun even goes off."

"I told you I want to see you." He was irritated and oblivious.

"And for someone else that might be enough." She studied him, memorizing every line in his face and the curve of his jaw. How she wanted to touch him, but that couldn't happen. "I know what it feels like when life pulls the rug out from under you. After losing my family all I could think about were the things I didn't do because of being tired, practical or selfish. I could have read to my daughter just a little longer when she was trying to delay going to sleep. I could have gone on that camping trip instead of arguing that it was less work to stay home."

"I'm not going to let you down," he said.

"I know you believe that, but it's not what I heard you say. I came alive again on the island and will be forever grateful to you for that. But you set limits, and I promised myself that I won't live my life with parameters."

"Justine, listen to me."

"No. I have to do what's best for me." She stood on tiptoe and pressed her mouth to his. The hardest thing she ever did was pull away from him. She slid his jacket from around her shoulders and handed it back to him. "Goodbye, Cal."

She took one last look at him, and when her vision began to blur with accumulated tears, she turned and walked away.

* * *

Cal had been back in Blackwater Lake for a week when his brother Sam called and asked to meet at the local pub, Bar None. He was on his way there now. Linc was coming, too, and their cousin Logan Hunt had succumbed to Sam's arm-twisting to meet them. The Harts were planning to kumbaya the guy, convince him that they were family, not jerks like his father.

The problem was that Cal wasn't in a kumbaya kind of mood. When Justine told him they were over before anything really got started, he didn't take her completely seriously. He figured she was tired from the long flight. Her bad leg might have cramped up. His did. There could have been any number of things bugging her, and he would call to smooth over any rough edges of their parting at the airport. So he tried to get in touch but had only been able to leave messages, none of which she'd returned.

That in itself was a message. Over and out. He got it loud and clear. Guys' night at Bar None worked for him because it would involve a beer. Or ten.

He saw the familiar neon sign with crossed cocktail glasses and turned left into the lot next to the rustic building. The parking area was only half-full. Monday was ladies' night and usually standing room only. But this was Tuesday, and as far as he could tell there was nothing promotional going on. Since they were trying to reconnect with Logan, quiet was probably better.

He parked the car and got out, then walked to the heavy front door with a thick vertical handle. He let himself in and was swallowed up by the smell of peanuts, burgers and beer. He spotted Linc and Sam at a bistro table close to the bar. Apparently their cousin hadn't arrived yet.

The muscles in his injured leg were building up again

fast and his stride was strong, stable as he walked over. That was a relief because he didn't want any questions from them leading to things he didn't want to talk about. Plastering a wide smile on his face, he shook hands with his brothers who stood to greet him with bro hugs.

He and Sam were close in height. Linc was an inch or two shorter and his eyes were darker. In spite of the fact that he had a different father, they all shared the bond of growing up Hart. Now that he'd reconciled with his bride, Linc was the picture of a blissfully happy man.

"Hope you haven't been waiting long," Cal said.

"Just got here." Sam grinned. "The first round of drinks is on me. Because I'm the oldest brother."

Cal looked at Linc. "We should let him buy every round."

"Works for me," the other man said.

"Ah, sibling rivalry on display." Sam sighed. "Speaking of that, how was your vacation?"

"Great." Things didn't go sour until he got back to Blackwater Lake, so technically, that was the truth.

"You went to an island resort, right?" Linc studied him. "Is it just the light in here or do you not look very tan?"

"Now that you mention it...not very rested, either," Sam said. "And wasn't that the whole point of getting away? By the way, we'll settle up the bet at a to-be-determined time and place."

"Okay. And just so we're clear, I'm new at the whole vacation thing." Cal remembered Justine's approval that he had finally jumped into the spirit of it. The pain of simply thinking about her sliced through him and he vowed not to do that again. "No one warned me about having to work twice as hard to catch up on the work I didn't get to while I was gone."

That was mostly true. Work here at home had piled up. And now it was time to turn the conversation away from himself. He took one of the empty chairs, and the other two sat down again.

"You two look great." His brothers radiated calm and happiness, Cal noticed. He was pretty sure they wouldn't see that in him.

"Life is good," Linc said.

"How's Rose? Surely your wife has seen the error of her ways and wants that divorce, after all." Cal hoped his tone conveyed that he was joking. His downer mood made it hard to tell if he pulled it off.

"No." His brother didn't rise to the bait. "I would cut off my right arm to make her happy."

"Wow." Cal nodded and met his older brother's gaze. "And Faith? Is she regretting her decision to marry you yet?"

"Well, she leaves me notes all the time, on the little cards that go out with her flower arrangements. This morning I got one that said, 'Roses are red, violets are blue. Sugar is sweet and I can't wait for tonight.'"

"That doesn't rhyme," Cal pointed out.

His brother smiled, the look of a happy and satisfied man. "It doesn't have to. I got the message."

"We are lucky men," Linc said.

"Amen to that." Sam looked toward the bar and raised his hand. "There's Delanie. Let's get this reunion started."

The curvy, auburn-haired bar owner walked over to the table. "Be still my heart. I swear three such good-looking men make my knees go weak."

"Linc and I are already taken. Sorry, Delanie." Sam didn't look sorry at all. "But Cal isn't spoken for yet."

Cal knew Sam was kidding, but it didn't change the frustration and anger coursing through him. A rush of conflicting emotions made him want to pop his brother, but a move like that would generate a lot of questions that he didn't want to answer.

Cal smiled his most charming smile at the bar owner. "I am happily single and wear it with pride."

"Good for you. I expect to see you in here next Monday for ladies' night. My sister will be here."

"Didn't know you had one." Cal suddenly realized he didn't know much about her at all.

"I didn't know about her until a year ago. My dad had a secret." Her mouth pulled tight for a moment. "But I always wanted a sister and she has a little boy. Owen. I'm an aunt."

"Then we'll drink to that. Family," Sam said and looked around the table. "That's why we're all here."

Delanie followed his gaze and noticed the empty chair. "Are you expecting one more?"

"Our cousin, Logan Hunt."

She nodded and looked at Cal. "You'll have a bachelor buddy."

Thank God, he thought. All this marital bliss made him want to put his fist through the wall. The door opened just then and the man in question walked in and looked around.

"And here he is now." Cal waved his cousin over, not that he was anxious for backup or anything.

The man was in his thirties, tall, broad-shouldered and serious. He ran a successful cattle and horse ranch just outside the Blackwater Lake town limits. The only time Cal had seen him in anything other than cowboy boots, jeans, a snap-front shirt and a Stetson was at Linc's wedding, in a suit and tie.

There was wariness, not warmth, in his face as he walked over to them. The cowboy looked as if he'd found a knot in his favorite calf-roping lariat. But he'd shown up. That was something, right?

He stopped at the table and nodded at his cousins, then looked at the bar owner. "How are you, Delanie?"

"Good. Nice to see you, Logan. Your timing is perfect. Saved me a trip back over here to see what you're drinking. I'm taking orders now. What'll you all have?"

"Before you answer that," Cal said to the newcomer, "you should know that Sam is buying the first round."

Logan didn't crack a smile. "In that case, I'll have the lobster."

They all laughed and it broke the tension. Until then Cal had been aware only of his own black mood regarding the situation between him and Justine. Damn, there was that knot in his gut again, followed by a sharp pain in his chest.

"If you want lobster," Delanie said, "I recommend that fancy new restaurant up at Holden House. Here in my place I'm proud to say you'll get a really good burger, fries and beer."

"I'm in," Logan said.

The others agreed, and Delanie brought a pitcher and four chilled glasses before going to the kitchen to order up the food.

Sam poured, and when they all had a beer he held his up and said, "I'm glad you decided to join us, Logan."

The man touched glasses with them but didn't look too happy about it. "To be honest, I'm not sure why I did."

"Look," Sam said, "it's no secret in the family that our uncle, your father, is…"

"A womanizing, treacherous, deceitful jackass is the description you're looking for," Logan said.

"I wouldn't have put it quite that way," Sam said diplomatically.

"Doesn't matter how you say it. That's the truth." Logan looked at each of them, daring anyone to deny what he'd said. "He cheated on my mother and had children with more than one of his mistresses. When my mom had enough of it, she left, even though she had nowhere to go and no money of her own."

"I'm not sure if you're aware, but my father reached out to her. My folks wanted to help her any way they could— money, a place to stay. You're family." Sam's voice was steady but serious.

This was one time Cal was glad not to be the oldest. Glad to hang back and listen while Sam explained how their parents had reached out to the mother of four children, only to be turned down.

Logan nodded. "She was proud and humiliated by what he'd put her through. And frankly, she didn't want anything from Foster's family. She didn't trust anyone with the last name Hart."

"I get the feeling she's not the only one," Linc commented. "And before you get defensive, you should know that Hastings Hart isn't my biological father. He has many faults, but turning his back on family isn't one of them."

Their cousin looked surprised for a moment, then nodded. "We lived in the car for a while before Mom finally went to my grandfather here in Blackwater Lake for help. It's why we ended up here, and the old guy had warned her not to marry Foster Hart in the first place."

"Sounds rough," Cal said. Worse than rough.

There was a whole lot of agreement in Logan's hard expression. "It's why I legally changed my last name to my mother's maiden name. So I'm not particularly willing to claim his family."

"That's the whole point of us being here. To prove

we're not like your father," Cal said. He looked at his brothers, who all nodded their agreement.

"How many times have you heard the saying that the apple doesn't fall far from the tree?"

"And sometimes the tree has one bad one but the rest of the fruit is fine," Sam said. "No offense, but your father is just one bad apple. We want you and your brothers and sister to know that the rest of the family is here for you, man. It's time to get that chip off your shoulder. Give us a chance to screw up before you cut us out of your life."

Logan looked at each of them in turn, taking their measure. Apparently the no-holds-barred words got through to the stubborn man. He nodded and said, "It's something to think about."

Delanie returned with a tray full of food and set identical red plastic baskets containing burgers and fries in front of them. "Ketchup and mustard are on the table. I left onion on the side in case any of you have plans later—if you get my drift."

"Rose appreciates that very much," Linc said. "And we know for a fact that Faith has something in mind. She left Sam a note this morning."

"Okay." The bar owner grinned. "Then I'll just leave and let the four of you have this testosterone zone all to yourselves."

Defiantly, Cal put the onion on his burger with a flourish and took a big bite. *Take that, Justine Walker.* He was a free man and didn't have to think of anyone but himself. But then he felt the emptiness open wider inside him. Taking a deep breath, he counted, then forced thoughts of her out of his mind. As he chewed, he watched Delanie working the room to check on her customers, polishing glasses behind the scarred bar. He thought about her testosterone remark.

"Do you think she's a spy?" he asked, still watching the bar owner.

The other three men looked at him as if he'd sprouted wings and a beak. But it was Sam who asked, "Are we talking Chinese or North Korean?"

"I meant for the women of Blackwater Lake." Cal had thought it was obvious. "Does she eavesdrop on male conversations and pass the information on to the ladies?"

"Now that you mention it..." Logan's eyes narrowed as he looked at the bar owner.

"Whether or not she is passing off secret information," Linc said reasonably, "if you don't say anything you wouldn't want repeated, there's nothing to worry about."

Sam finished chewing a fry. "Exactly. Anyone who wants to can listen in while I talk about being the luckiest man in the world. There's only one woman in my life."

"What about Phoebe?" Logan said.

"Okay," Sam amended. "Two women in my life. And that little girl is something. I'm proud that she chooses to call me Dad."

"You should be." For the first time since walking in the door, Logan smiled. "Phoebe is a tough crowd."

"That's right. Faith told me she went out with you," Sam said.

"Yeah. Just a couple of times. We're just friends. There was never a chance of anything serious between us," their cousin said.

Having so recently been shut down for his aversion to marriage, Cal detected a certain tone in the other man's voice. "Why is that? How did you know for sure?"

"Because I proposed one time, to the mother of my daughter. She laughed in my face. The thing is, I didn't take offense. It was a relief and proof that it would have been a mistake. I don't ever plan to get married." He took a sip of his beer then smiled at their shocked expressions. "It's all good. She understood me and knew we were better off as friends. And now she's engaged to a great guy and I wish them all the happiness in the world."

Cal held up his half-empty beer glass. "I'll drink to that. A woman who understands."

"No female entanglement." Logan touched his glass to his cousin's.

Cal took a drink, sealing the male bonding vow to avoid messy man/woman situations even though he knew his reaction was for nothing but show.

Studying him, Sam had a skeptical expression on his face. "What did you do on vacation?"

"I was away from here." Cal wasn't sure whether or not his tone was defensive.

"Can't argue with that," Sam said. But he didn't look convinced that nothing had happened.

That's because something *had* happened. Cal had a sneaking suspicion that a month on the island had entangled him. He could drink beer, swear up and down that he was happy as a clam alone and put onion on his hamburger until hell wouldn't have it. But none of that changed anything.

When Linc and Sam left here tonight, there were women waiting at home for them. And Sam had something in writing to put a twinkle in his eyes. The truth was that when he and Logan got home they would be alone. It cut him deep and he realized how much he missed Justine.

Looking at his cousin was like looking in a mirror, and Cal didn't particularly like what he saw. A man who put restrictions on the future without giving the present a chance. Justine was right about Cal. He had a feeling he'd blown it with her big time and there was nothing he could do about it.

For a man who was into fixing things, that was a bitter pill to swallow.

Chapter Fourteen

After work, Justine bustled around her cute, cozy apartment, putting last-minute touches on dinner for her friend Shanna. The evening would be bittersweet—catching up and saying goodbye. She decided to think about the sad part later and focus on the excitement of a girls' night and not missing Cal so much it hurt. After being with him 24/7 for the last month, there was a big hole in her life. It had been two weeks since that night at Blackwater Lake Airport, and any day now this acute emptiness would go away. She was sure of it. He'd wondered once if her being so optimistic was draining, and right now she would give him a resounding *yes* to that question.

Just in the nick of time there was a knock on the door, saving her from a pity party. She had one every night, but company coming meant it would have to be postponed.

She opened the door and her friend was there, holding a bottle of red wine. "Hi, you. Come in."

Tall, brunette Shanna bent to give her a hug. "I'm going to miss our girls-only dinners."

Justine wagged her index finger, a warning gesture. "No goodbye-ing until absolutely necessary."

"There are rules now?"

"My bad." Justine figured she'd learned from Cal. He was the one who put up roadblocks before the marathon started. "It's just that I don't want to say goodbye at all and putting it off works for me."

Shanna made a sad face before handing over the wine so she could take off her coat and hang it on the freestanding rack beside the door. "It's not like I'm going to the moon. California isn't so far away. When you're sick of the snow here, hop on a plane. In a couple of hours you can be on the beach."

The word *beach* made Justine think of the villa, helping Cal to hop over to the lounge in the sand, walking hand in hand by the ocean, making love in the pool. As always, a beautiful memory of him was quickly followed by an ugly stab of pain. She forced herself to focus on Shanna. This night was about her.

She took the wine into the kitchen and set it on the granite counter top. There was an electric opener and she used it to get the cork out of the bottle. "How far will you be from the beach?"

"Sand and ocean are Mark's backyard. He showed me pictures. So did his family. They all live nearby, very close-knit."

"It sounds perfect." She put a lot of enthusiasm into her voice, and that wasn't easy when her own life was a train wreck.

"Not perfect," Shanna said. "But really good. I don't want to be one of *those* friends. Someone who makes it sound as if she has it all. I know nothing is perfect."

"Hey, this is me. I'm your friend." Justine took two stemless glasses from the cupboard and poured wine into each, then handed one over. "You're telling me about a very wonderful turn in your life and I'm glad for you."

"I know there will be bumps in the road. Life isn't idyllic all the time. Stuff happens." She tilted her head as a sympathetic expression slid into her brown eyes. "Look who I'm talking to. You know this better than anyone."

"I do." Justine nodded. "Which is why I have a unique perspective that gives a lot of weight to the unsolicited advice I'm about to give you."

"I'm listening." There was an eager, intense look on her friend's face.

"Don't apologize for being happy. Embrace the moment and revel in it. Maybe stuff will happen. Or maybe you've been sprinkled with fairy dust or sneezed on by a unicorn and your life will be magically free of problems."

Shanna made a mocking sound. "Yeah. Right."

"The point is, enjoy this wonderful time and share the details with me. I want to know *everything*."

"Like?"

"Start at the beginning. How did you and Mark meet?"

"At the muster drill, before the ship sailed." She sipped her wine. "All passengers have to attend a meeting about what to do if there's an emergency. Mark and I were seated together. And we got into trouble."

"At a drill to avoid trouble? Sounds like you," Justine teased.

"I know, right? This is going to sound really corny, but when I saw him it was like being struck by lightning. Later he told me he felt the same way. We started talking instantly and didn't notice the announcement coming over the public-address system. We kept chatting and passengers around us gave us the hate stare."

"No surprise. Life and death."

"Yeah. A crew member chewed us out and we had to stay after school for a private tutorial."

"Then what?"

"We got a drink and were inseparable the rest of the cruise."

Justine gave her a look. "And by that you mean…?"

"He was either in my cabin or I was in his suite." She giggled. "Mostly his because—hey—it was the best cabin on the ship."

Justine pictured a villa on the ocean and the luxury that had awed her. She'd be lying if she denied it was nice, but that's not what made her heart hurt. Waking up with Cal was perfect, and not doing that now showed her the difference. This was one of life's crappy times.

"And now that you're home?" she asked her friend. "How do you feel being away from him?"

"Like part of me is missing." In spite of the words, Shanna still glowed. "But he feels that way, too. Three days after the cruise ended, he flew into Blackwater Lake to see me. He said he missed me terribly and he has a private plane, so there was no point in being miserable."

"I see." But the truth was that two people didn't have to be separated by geography to be unhappy. She and Cal lived in the same town, worked in the same building. Apparently he was avoiding her as much as she was him because their paths hadn't crossed. There was no way to know how he felt, but she was in misery up to her neck.

"I know what you're thinking." Shanna caught her bottom lip between her teeth.

Justine sincerely doubted that, but asked anyway, "What would that be?"

"You're thinking that we hardly know each other. That quitting my job and moving to California is a big risk and there's no safety net. That he might talk a good game and break my heart after I've given up everything to be with him."

"Actually, I wasn't thinking any of that."

"No?"

"I don't have to because you already have. You made your decision and you're one of the smartest people I know. So I was thinking that you are courageous for going after what you want. That's to be admired."

"Thanks." Tears sparkled in her friend's eyes.

Justine rounded the bar separating the apartment's kitchen from the living room and hugged the other woman. "Be happy, my friend. No one deserves it more."

"Back at you." Shanna sniffled.

She wanted to add that Shanna would never be alone because Justine would be there for her no matter what. But that would imply doubt about the move she was making and it's not what she meant. Justine would be there in good times or bad. Friends supported each other that way.

The timer over the stove sounded. "Dinner's ready."

"Smells good." Shanna sniffed. "Garlic. Something Italian."

"Good nose. Lasagna."

"Yum. What can I do?"

"Toss the salad while I make the bread," Justine said.

"Aye, aye." She saluted, obviously still in a nautical frame of mind.

A few minutes later they sat across from each other at the small round table in the nook adjacent to the kitchen. Their plates were loaded with food and Justine had refilled the wineglasses. She held hers up. "To a bright future."

Shanna tapped her glass and sipped, then picked up her fork and took a bite of salad. After chewing she said, "I've been going on about my news. Sorry."

"That's okay." Justine would rather hear about her friend's happiness than talk about her own pathetic personal life.

"Apparently I'm not the only one making a move." Shanna cut a bite of lasagna and her fork hovered over the plate. "I heard that you gave your notice, too."

"Yeah, I did." She'd turned it into Human Resources the day before. But it was her impression that they kept things like that confidential. "How did you know?"

"Cal mentioned it."

Justine wanted to fire questions at her friend. Like, how did he take it? Did he seem okay or was he ticked off? Was there anything bothering him? But she held back and simply said, "Oh?"

"Yeah. It seemed as if you two were working well together on the island and…" Shanna's eyes were full of questions.

Justine shrugged. "I always planned to leave and open up the yoga studio. You know that."

"But I didn't think it would be this soon," her friend said.

"The money he paid me to go to the island and be his assistant made it possible for me to speed up my time-table."

"Still, I didn't know you were going to do this quite so fast. I kind of thought you might be my replacement. Not just anyone can deal with Calhoun Hart."

Dealing with him had turned magical after she nearly got fired. He was funny and caring and observant. Being with him never felt like work.

"He just needs someone who will go toe-to-toe with him. Not be intimidated by his intelligence and being all about work."

Shanna picked at her salad, then put her fork down. "The thing is, he's different since he got back."

"Maybe it's you, looking at him through the prism of being deliriously happy," Justine suggested.

"No. It's like he's broken." She held up a hand. "I know about the leg and that it's healed. I'm talking about something that wouldn't show up on an X-ray. A spark has gone out. I don't know how to describe it, but he's changed."

"Because he's losing you."

"He's a big boy, a professional. He knows better than anyone that I can be easily replaced." Shanna met her gaze. "I see the same thing in you."

"Really?" This woman was far too perceptive. Justine was going to miss her terribly. And, bottom line, she didn't want to talk about something that couldn't be fixed. "I don't know what to tell you. Except that I'm very excited about opening the yoga studio. It's been a dream for a while now and finally coming true. A chance to help others. In fact, I have an appointment in a couple of days with a real estate agent to look at space in the retail center near the new hotel and condos at the base of the mountain. Life is really good. So I'm not exactly sure what you're seeing in me."

"I would believe that story if I didn't know you so well. There was just a little too much enthusiasm in your voice. I don't buy it. And I'm not gullible. What happened between you and Cal on that island?"

"It's a blessing and a curse that you know me so well." Justine sighed and put her fork down. "We had a thing—"

"What?"

"I meant to say 'fling.' We agreed that's all it was. He learned to relax and find balance between work and fun. I taught him a breathing technique. And he…"

"What?"

He showed her the part of her that could feel deeply for a man who hadn't died. "I got to experience luxury overload. So I have a pretty good idea how your life will be—private jets, chartered yachts off Greece, houses as big as a small country. It's going to be great."

Shanna stared at her for several moments, then seemed to make a decision. "When you're ready to talk about it, I'm ready to listen."

Justine didn't deny there was a lot on her mind. She appreciated that her friend understood and respected what she was keeping to herself. It's why they'd connected so strongly. Reaching over, she squeezed the other woman's hand. "I know. Thanks. And remember, this night is all about you and your future."

"It's just that I want everyone I care about to be happy, too."

"You're sweet. Which is why I love you. And I hope with all my heart that this move to California and being with Mark will bring you all the happiness you deserve."

For the rest of the evening Justine managed to say all the right things. She truly meant all the good wishes but couldn't help feeling envious because Shanna had her Mark. Cal didn't belong to Justine but she felt as if she'd lost everything. Again. She loved him. She'd been absolutely sure of that when they left the island. Then he was honest with her and it changed everything, convincing her they wouldn't work.

She'd thought when the plane landed and she'd refused his offer to go home with him that breaking things off would take care of everything. It hadn't. She missed him and that wasn't going away. He had changed her and the change hurt.

A few days after the attempted bonding with his cousin Logan at Bar None, Cal drove to his brother's house after work to settle up on the bet. He turned right into an impressive neighborhood of large, stately homes with great views of the lake and mountains. Real estate was all about location and this was probably the best in Blackwater Lake.

Sam had lived in his big, empty house all by himself until the wildfire last summer had forced some local residents to flee their homes. Faith was one of the evacuees and had temporarily moved in with him. They fell in love. Her eight-year-old daughter, Phoebe, approved of the match and, as the story went, had a hand in matchmaking and getting the two adults together. While Cal was on the island, Sam and Faith honeymooned, leaving Phoebe with their sister, Ellie, and her family.

He drove into the curved driveway and parked, then turned off the car's engine. Glancing at the gorgeous, etched glass front doors, he took a deep breath before exiting the SUV. It didn't escape his notice that counting his breaths had become a habit since his month with Justine. Now he had to face Sam and this was Cal's moment of truth.

After walking up a couple of steps, he lifted his hand to ring the bell, but the door opened before he could. His brother must have been watching. Who knew he was so anxious to hand over the keys to the classic car?

"Hi." Sam looked past him to where the SUV was parked. "I thought you were going to get a ride over so you could drive the Duchess home."

"About that…" Cal met his brother's gaze. "We need to talk."

"What is it about those four words?" Sam frowned as he closed the front door. "It occurs to me that I don't like hearing them from you any more than I do from my wife. What's wrong?"

"Nothing. You'll like this, I promise—"

Before he could explain, eight-year-old Phoebe came running into the entryway. "Uncle Cal!"

He got down to her level and grabbed her up when she threw herself into his arms. "Hello, kid."

"Hi." She wrapped her small arms around his neck and squeezed as hard as a little girl could.

It felt pretty good. "How are you?"

"I'm gonna be a Hart." The blond-haired, brown-eyed little cherub looked proud as could be. "Sam's gonna be my dad. For real."

Cal grinned at her. "That means I'll be your uncle for real, too."

"I know." She hugged him again. "I can't wait till Thanksgiving next week to say what I'm grateful for."

"Right." The coming holiday had slipped Cal's mind. His thoughts had been too full of missing Justine to think about much of anything else. And he didn't even want to contemplate how empty Christmas was going to feel. "Is someone hosting the whole family for Thanksgiving dinner?"

"The location keeps changing." Sam's expression hinted at a level of excitement rarely before seen. "Ellie is pregnant."

"I know."

"She's been feeling pretty tired and still has some morning sickness. So, Faith was going to cook, but since—"

"Mommy's going to have a baby," Phoebe blurted out.

Sam didn't seem the least bit upset that the little girl beat him to the announcement. "It's true."

"That's great news." He smiled at Phoebe, her arm trustingly resting on his shoulder. "That means you'll be a big sister. Are you ready?"

"Yes. I hope it's a girl."

"Something tells me you have no preference." Cal

looked at his brother, who nodded. Then he set the little girl on her feet. He straightened and shook the other man's hand. "Congratulations."

"Thanks. But the point is that now Faith is fighting morning sickness. So Ellie swears she can pull herself together and do the cooking. Mom and Dad are here and will help. That's the scoop at the moment. Are you going to be there?"

It was a valid question given his track record of missing family events. In the past if something work-related came up he'd chosen that over family, but not now. Not since Justine showed him what a balanced life should be. And yet he couldn't seem to find his balance without her.

"Phoebe Catherine——" Faith walked into the room looking a little pale, but still beautiful. It was obvious where her daughter got her good looks. "Oh, Cal, I didn't know you were here."

"It's not good when she uses both my names," the little girl informed him.

"I heard about the baby," he said and hugged Faith. "You look beautiful."

"Thank you, but do not tell me I'm glowing. That whole pregnancy glow thing is a myth. I look like something the cat yakked up." She did glow, though, when Sam put his arm protectively around her. "We're excited."

Cal got a double whammy of envy and pain as he looked at the happy family. It was everything he wanted and would never have.

Faith turned a stern look on her little girl. "It's bedtime and you know what that means."

"But you were in the bathroom throwing up."

"Thanks for sharing," Faith said wryly. "That's not humiliating at all. And it still doesn't change the fact that it's time for your bath."

"But Uncle Cal is here." She glanced up at him, a whole bunch of pleading in those big brown eyes.

Cal took her mom's measure and sighed. "I'd like to help you out, kid, but I'm pretty sure your mom could take me. You're on your own."

Sam smiled his approval. "Smart move."

Phoebe thrust out her bottom lip in a pout. "Don't think I'm going to forget this on Uncle Appreciation Day."

"Is there such a thing?" Cal asked, not the least bit bothered by the threat.

"It wouldn't surprise me." Faith shrugged. "There's Short People Appreciation Day on December twenty-first, the shortest day of the year. Grandparents Day—"

"And Grandma and Grandpa Hart will officially be mine when I'm adopted," Phoebe said happily.

"The folks are excited about it. Mom once told me she wants and is expecting all of us to do our part and produce offspring," Sam confided.

Cal figured eventually his mother would notice that he wasn't doing his fair share in the kid department, but that couldn't be helped. Without Justine... He refused to finish that thought.

"Grandma likes to play checkers," the little girl continued. "Maybe she wants to come over and see Uncle Cal and we—"

"Nice try, Phoebs." Sam's voice was firm. "But you've stalled long enough. Your mom said it's time for bed."

"Okay, Dad. 'Night, Uncle Cal." She waved, then headed upstairs.

Bewildered, Faith shook her head at Sam. "I don't know how you get her to cooperate, but keep up the good work."

"That's my plan." He tenderly touched her cheek. "You doing okay?"

"I'll live. Soda crackers and ginger ale are my friends."

She looked at Cal. "Good to see you. I'll be back down after I get her settled."

He nodded and watched her follow her daughter upstairs. Then he met his brother's gaze. "You're a lucky man."

"I know." Sam was grinning like a happy fool. "Want a beer?"

"Yes."

They headed for the big kitchen with its giant island and stainless steel appliances. Sam opened the refrigerator and pulled out two bottles.

He handed one over. "So, we need to talk. You were supposed to get a ride over here. How are you going to get the Duchess back to your place?"

"I'm not." Cal noted that his brother didn't look completely surprised. "I worked while I was on the island and that's a violation of the spirit of our agreement. I can't take the car."

"Well, you're honest. I actually knew all about it," Sam admitted.

"You did? How?"

"You're relatively new to Blackwater Lake so there's something you should know. It's growing, but still a small town. People talk. Your assistant said something to someone about you needing a substitute for her—"

"But she was on a cruise." Even as he said it, Cal remembered what Justine had said about Shanna not being completely out of touch.

"Even on a ship there's internet and there are ports of call. Communication never stops completely."

"My bad. I won't make that mistake again." The mistake he'd made with Justine was so much worse that his lie of omission was hardly a blip on the emotional radar. "But I didn't fulfill the terms of the bet."

"You stayed on the island for a month. You won."

Cal shook his head. "It doesn't feel that way."

"Because of Justine." Sam leaned back against the granite-topped island and met his gaze. "Don't look so surprised. I just told you how fast and efficient news is in this town."

"Still—"

"And you were acting weird at Bar None. Your heart just wasn't in it when you drank with Logan to a woman who understands and no female entanglements. I knew something was up."

"As you probably already know, Justine filled in as my assistant while at the resort."

"Seems like it turned out to be more than work." Sam set his beer on the granite and folded his arms over his chest. "I think you fell in love and somehow you were an ass. Now she won't have anything to do with you. Am I somewhere in the ballpark?"

"How did you know that?" When Cal wasn't feeling miserable and hopeless he was kind of impressed with his brother's intuition. "You went through it, too?"

"I know because Linc did the same thing when he married Rose, then left her. Fortunately, while getting a divorce, they managed to figure out they were in love." Sam looked smug. "I, on the other hand, knew what I wanted and went after it. Even though commitment made me sweat."

"It's not just that. I'm not very good at marriage."

"Baloney. If you find the right woman you don't have to be good at it. It's all about taking a leap of faith." He pointed at Cal. "And that's not a pun because of my wife's name. You're gun-shy because you made one bad choice. It's that damn competitive streak of yours."

Justine had told him almost the same thing, that he wanted to be first. "I'm working on that."

"In the long run it's not even faith as much as knowing in your gut that a certain woman is the only one you will ever love."

"I know what you mean."

"Then do something about it," Sam said.

"It's like you're reading my mind."

Chapter Fifteen

Justine normally enjoyed being with her work friends at Bar None, but not tonight. It was her last day at Hart Energy and she'd hoped to slip away quietly, but her co-workers were having none of that. Especially after losing Shanna the week before. They insisted on having a going-away party for her. Now the four of them were sitting around one of the bistro tables having wine, and the other three didn't notice she wasn't talking much.

At least she hadn't run into Cal on her last day. Since coming back to town she'd been avoiding him and figured he must be doing the same to her since their paths had never crossed after returning from the island. Part of her had hoped to accidentally run into him but that hadn't happened. So obviously coming home had put an end to the fling. If he wanted her, she wasn't that hard to find. The logical conclusion was that he didn't want her.

That thought pulled the knot of pain in her chest a little tighter.

"So, tell me about the yoga studio." Amy Karlik was a blue-eyed blonde who worked in Human Resources.

Justine suddenly realized the table had gone quiet and everyone was looking at her. "Hmm?"

"Your yoga studio?" Mary Davis, a brunette, was young, a local hire and not a transplanted Texan. "How long until you're open for business?"

"I finally found a location in the new retail center at the foot of Black Mountain. It's not far from the new hotel and condo development. I had thought it was out of my price range, but Carla, my real estate agent, did a little digging and found out it's in my budget."

"Cool."

"I want to tap into the tourist population as well as residents of Blackwater Lake. And it's strategically located— a reasonable distance from the heart of town and the resort. Prime location at an amazingly dirt-cheap price."

"Sounds perfect." Sherry Ferguson nodded her approval. "When do you think you'll be able to open?"

"I have to sign a lease first. The owner has been hard to get hold of, according to Carla."

"So you've never met with the person who owns the property?" Mary asked.

"No. Apparently he travels a lot and is difficult to pin down. There's been a lot of phone tag and faxing. But tomorrow I'm going to put my name on the bottom line."

"Let's drink to that." Amy held up her glass and the rest of them tapped theirs against it. "But without a regular paycheck, isn't it a little scary? You'll be on your own."

"No." Justine had been on her own for a while now. Then Cal had infiltrated her heart. Look how that turned out. Alone was better. She'd handled it once and could do it again. Now that she was out of his office there wouldn't be any danger of running into him unexpectedly. That thought should have been a relief, but it was just sad. Then it sank in that her friend had asked a business question, not a personal one. "I've got a financial plan carefully worked out by my accountant."

"That's so exciting," Mary said.

Funny, Justine had anticipated this moment being much more exhilarating than it was turning out to be. But now her life was defined by before the island and after. Since coming home, everything felt dull and drab. It didn't feel as if there was anything to look forward to. Not like at the villa when she couldn't wait to see Cal for coffee in the morning and the day was bright and shiny with promise. The prospect of a whole day with him for work and meals stretched in front of her.

She'd gone to the mat on not working overtime, but she would give almost anything to break that rule now and spend as much time with him as possible. Then she wouldn't have to put on a happy face because genuine joy would fill her and would show on the outside.

"You are excited, right?" Mary asked the question but all three were giving her funny looks.

She put her happy face firmly in place because anything else would require an explanation and she wasn't willing to talk about what was wrong. "This is a dream come true for me. Of course I'm excited."

"Okay. Good. It was hard to tell for a second there," Amy said.

"I just have a lot on my mind."

"Of course." Sherry nodded enthusiastically. "There must be a million things to do."

"Probably more like two million," Justine agreed. "And tomorrow is step one."

The other three fell into a conversation about the upside of having a friend in the fitness business, discounted rates on classes and nutrition counseling. Justine listened and interjected when appropriate. The women laughed when they were supposed to so she was pretty sure the right words came out of her mouth. But her thoughts kept wandering to Cal and his determination to avoid marriage. If only he had an open mind. Without that there was no point in investing time and energy.

Unexpectedly, tears stung her eyes. This was supposed to be a happy send-off for her, and letting her friends see that she wasn't in a celebratory mood couldn't happen.

She dipped her head and told them, "I'm going to the ladies' room."

"Should we order you another chardonnay?"

"That would be great."

She slid to the floor and walked past the long, scarred wooden bar where Delanie Carlson was polishing glasses. The place wasn't very busy.

Justine moved into the short hallway with two doors side by side. One said Gents and the other sign said Ladies. She walked through that one and went into a stall, then locked herself inside. Gathered tears trickled down her cheeks and she tried not to generate any more. Her eyes would get red and puffy; her nose would run. Not only was that an unflattering look, it would be impossible to hide.

"Darn it. Why you, Cal Hart?"

This just wouldn't do. Sooner or later she'd have to come out or her friends would notice.

"Pull it together, Justine." She took a deep breath, then unlocked the door and walked over to one of the four pedestal sinks with the old-fashioned white water handles marked Hot and Cold in solid black letters.

Looking at herself in the oval mirror she thought she'd nipped the meltdown just in time. She washed her hands and put a wet paper towel on her eyes, then checked her appearance one last time and took several cleansing, steadying breaths.

"Good to go," she said.

She walked the short hall and came out into the main

room. Delanie Carlson happened to be standing at that end of the bar. Justine smiled at the woman.

"Hi." The bar owner studied her, then frowned. "You okay?"

So much for being good to go. "Don't I look okay?"

"Honestly?" Delanie's auburn ponytail moved from side to side when she shook her head. "No. You've been crying."

"How did you know? Are you psychic?"

"Hardly." She laughed. "But people are my business. I serve drinks and food and make conversation. You don't work at this as long as I have and not develop an intuition. I've been watching you and I could tell something was off. Then you went to the ladies' room for a cry."

Justine glanced at the bistro table where her going-away party was going on without her. The three women were having a great time. "Do you think they noticed?"

"No."

"Good."

"So you don't want to talk to them," Delanie guessed. "But it won't be so easy to get rid of me because I know something's wrong. And you might feel better if you get it off your chest."

Justine doubted anything would make her feel better but figured she couldn't feel worse. "Okay."

The other woman waited several moments, then said, "Go ahead. I'm listening. Think of me like a lawyer. Anything you tell me is confidential."

She must have needed to talk about her feelings. Or maybe crying in the ladies' room had made her emotionally vulnerable, because it never occurred to her not to talk to this woman. There was no way to ease into this, so she plunged right in. "I spent a month on an island with Cal Hart."

"Oh?" There was surprise in the bar owner's voice.

"It was for work," Justine clarified firmly.

"Yeah, when someone talks tropical island the first thing I think of is work."

Okay, so more clarification was necessary. "He's a workaholic so his brother bet him that he couldn't take four weeks off and stay there. Cal had a schedule of aggressive physical activities planned to keep him busy and pass the time. But on the first day he broke his leg skydiving. He figured he might as well work, but needed an assistant to be effective."

"You?"

Justine nodded. "I was paid a lot. And that allowed me to put together the financing for my business faster than I'd expected."

"But?" Delanie put down the glass that she'd polished and slid her a wry look. "If there wasn't a *but* you wouldn't have been crying."

"Fair enough." Justine sighed. "We got close."

"You slept with him." It wasn't a question.

It was impossible to regret the pleasure-filled hours in his arms, but if she hadn't taken that step, her heart would probably be in better shape now. "Yes."

"Okay. Just wanted to confirm context. Continue."

"I hadn't thought it was possible for me to feel that way again." Justine explained about losing her husband and child and the long hospital stay followed by rehabilitation.

"That's awful. Really rough," Delanie said. Her eyes filled with sympathy.

"I can't even put into words how bad it was." She looked down at her clasped hands resting on the bar. "For a while I didn't want to live and felt guilty that I had. That feeling passed eventually, but I never expected or wanted to get close to a man again. Then I spent time with Cal and something shifted for me. I got what people meant about moving forward after tragedy and that finding personal happiness again wasn't a betrayal of the loved ones I lost."

"But?" Delanie gave her a *seriously?* look. "Again, I should remind you that I saw the crying."

"Yeah." She blew out a breath. "When we flew home, he told me he wanted to keep seeing me, but I should know he never wanted to get married again."

"And that was a deal-breaker for you." Again, it wasn't a question.

"Yes. I realized that it's important to me. It's who I am. And putting limitations on us was not something that worked for me. Doing that at the beginning doomed the relationship to fail."

"That's one way of looking at it."

"Is there another way?" The comment pulled Justine out of her pity party.

"Yes."

"Not for me." She shook her head. "I won't be putting myself out there again."

"The way I see it, that's a little like the pot calling the kettle black." Delanie met her gaze directly. "Now who's into limiting?"

"You think I'm wrong?" It was a little irritating to be judged. "I saw how suddenly life can be taken away. Wasting time doesn't work for me."

"It was only an observation and worth exactly what you paid for it." But Delanie hesitated a moment, then added, "I just wonder if you were looking for a reason not to take a chance on love again."

"I didn't have to look for a reason," she maintained, even as the words resonated.

"I'm just saying that you might be shutting the door on anything with Cal because you're afraid of being hurt again. And who could blame you?"

"Okay, then. And if he says up front he can't give me what I want—"

"Did it occur to you that he might just need time? A chance to wrap his head around what he feels before getting to a place where he wants what you want?"

Justine had every intention of pushing back about that, but there was a ring of truth in what the other woman said. Wow. She'd been so sure she had it all together and an open mind about going for it. She thought about Shanna, who was courageous enough to give up everything for a chance at love.

Justine wasn't even willing to invest a little time because she could be hurt and had shut Cal down flat. No wonder he hadn't bothered to track her down at Hart Energy. Now that she was out of there, no way would their paths cross. She'd preached not wasting time to the exclusion of a judicious investment of time. That philosophy was supposed to prevent heartache, but pain ripped through her. How ironic was that? Not taking a chance had resulted in a broken heart.

Justine drove into the Black Mountain Marketplace, which was directly across the street from Holden House, the new hotel. The recently opened retail center was already 95 percent occupied by high-end boutiques, a jewelry store, an organic food market and a juice bar. The business she wanted to open was the perfect complement to the stores already here.

Eventually she hoped to carry a line of fitness wear, but that was down the line. One step at a time. Hopefully she could come to an agreement with the property's owner on monthly rent and terms. She was getting a little frustrated on the length of time it was taking to finalize this deal.

Her Realtor was supposed to meet with the owner's representative but had gotten hung up, so Justine had wheedled the key from her. The woman was coming here as soon as she was available. Now that she thought about it, that was another perk of this small town. In Dallas no one would trust you with a key to anything unless they were there to supervise.

It would be good to go in alone and quietly study the space one last time, make sure this was what she wanted. More important, that it would work for her vision.

She parked in front of the Space Available sign in the front window, then exited her small, fuel-efficient hybrid sedan. Key in hand, she walked over and unlocked the door. Morning sun flooded the room, giving off a cheerful vibe in spite of the fact that it was empty.

There was wallboard up but no paint. It occurred to her that it was like a blank canvas on which to create her own vision. Now to come to terms with the owner on finishing it to her satisfaction. Apparently he had a contractor who would work with her in making the most flexible use of the area.

"Hello."

Justine whirled around and saw Cal standing in the doorway. "Dear God, you startled me."

"Sorry." He was wearing jeans, boots and a sheepskin jacket.

She'd only ever really seen him in shorts and cotton island shirts. But it was November and cold. The look was a good one, masculine and very Montana. Oh, please, who was she kidding? The man didn't have a bad look. Her pulse was pounding and skipping erratically. She was pretty sure she could concentrate on breathing and count her breaths, but the technique wouldn't calm her down or bring serenity. Not with Cal. She was so incredibly happy to see him.

"How are you?" she asked.

"Okay." He shrugged.

Was it wrong to be the tiniest bit happy that he was just okay? Not fabulous or fantastic, but only satisfactory? She wanted to think he missed her even a fraction of the way she'd missed him.

"How are you?" he asked.

"Okay."

"I guess yesterday was your last day at Hart Energy."

"It was."

His mouth pulled tight. "You won't be easy to replace."

Did he mean at the office or in his life? She'd given up the right to ask that question when she refused to give him time. She wouldn't blame him if he was the tiniest bit happy that she would never forgive herself for that. But if she knew anything about anything it was moving on.

"Leaving wasn't personal. I told you that," she said.

"You did." He looked around. "So this is where you decided to open your yoga studio."

Was that bitterness in his voice? She hoped not but felt compelled to make sure he understood. "It's better for the company to find personnel whose dedication matches your own."

"Funny thing about my dedication." He met her gaze. "Mine got a restructuring. A work/nonwork ratio reset. So when can I sign up for yoga classes?"

Her mouth curved upward, but she knew the smile was sad. "If you weren't ready for the change, you wouldn't have embraced it so enthusiastically."

"Maybe I had a good teacher." There was a breathtaking intensity in his eyes. "I'm sure you're going to be a very successful yoga instructor."

"I hope you're right."

"Of course I am. If you can make a convert out of me, you must be good."

She shook her head. "When you have visual aids like sea, sand and sky, it's easy to get the message across."

"I respectfully disagree." His gaze never left hers. It was as if he couldn't look at her hard enough. "You are the best visual aid."

This conversation was going in a direction that wasn't helpful for her peace of mind or serenity. She was here on business, and speaking of that...

"I have a question. Why are you here? How did you know I would be here?" She didn't know what to think, but one thing was for sure. "It can't be a coincidence that you showed up here at the same time I did to sign a lease on this property. What is going on, Cal?"

"That's three questions and a conclusion." He slid his hands into his coat pockets and moved closer, stopping just in front of her.

One baby step would put her body right up against his, and she wanted that so, so much. *Focus*, she ordered herself. "I'll give you another conclusion. This is very suspicious. And, of course, my real estate agent is conveniently not here. What are you up to?"

"Nothing nefarious, I promise." He sighed. "My brother, Lincoln, is in property development. He owns this retail center."

"Oh, I see. So you're here to break the news that it will be a cold day in hell before he would rent to me."

"Not even close." He smiled but it was tense. "I'm here to tell you that I rented this space from him and am prepared to sublet it to you at a lower cost."

It all became clear to her then. "So that's why the negotiations dragged on and the price went down to a number I would be crazy not to take."

"Yes."

"You would be subsidizing me." So much for everything being clear to her. "I don't understand. Why would you do that?"

"Don't go to the bad place, Justine." He put a hand on her arm as if he expected her to back away and run out of there. "First of all, your dream is a good one. Something to be encouraged."

And it would be realized. Her pride kicked in and her voice was defiant when she said, "I don't need any help, if that's what you're thinking. I can do this on my own."

"I agree. You're the strongest woman I know. And you'll do this with or without me. But you should know that if you decide it's without, I will still sign up for your classes."

"Why?" That was part suspicion talking and part hope, because the pleading look in his eyes was wearing down her pride, her defiance and her resistance.

"As it happens, the muscles in my bum leg aren't the only ones that need attention. Turns out the heart is also a muscle and needs regular exercise or it will waste away. It needs a good workout and you're the only one who can do that."

"I'm not sure I understand what you're saying." That wasn't quite true. She got it but was afraid to believe. "I could do with less muscle metaphors and more straight talk."

"You're right. My bad. So, here goes." He took several deep breaths. "When we got back to Blackwater Lake, my words were clumsy. In an attempt to be honest, I said it badly and should have just gone for the simple truth. I love you." He looked around the big, empty room. "This is your dream. But you're mine. I want to be part of yours in any way possible, but I'm really hoping you'll consider being a part of mine and marry me. If I had another chance, I wouldn't make a mess of it. I'm sorry."

"No, Cal. I am. It took missing you so much my heart hurt in places I never knew were there." She looked down, then back up and met his gaze. "I realized that I was too hasty and judgmental because I was looking for excuses to avoid getting involved. I was afraid of taking a risk and being hurt again."

"'Was'? Does that mean you're not afraid now?"

"I'm a woman who wants to love and be loved in return. You're my dream and I want one minute, hour, day or a hundred years with you. If you're sure—"

He touched a finger to her lips. "I've never been more sure of anything. I want to marry you, spend the rest of my life with you. Have children with you. We'll build our dreams together."

"That works for me. Where do I sign up?"

"Right here," he said, then kissed her for a very long time.

When they came up for air he looked into her eyes. "If it's all right with you, I'd like to marry you on Christmas Eve."

"Although that's very soon, it works for me. I've been

told that when you know you're in love, you just know. But I have to ask why?"

"Because the only present I want to unwrap on Christmas morning is my wife."

"That is so incredibly romantic." Her heart filled with love for this amazing man and there was only one right answer to his question. "Yes, I'll marry you on December 24."

She couldn't think of anything more wonderful than being his by Christmas.

* * * * *

LET'S TALK
Romance

For exclusive extracts, competitions
and special offers, find us online:

 facebook.com/millsandboon

 @MillsandBoon

@MillsandBoonUK

Get in touch on 01413 063232